Mrs Sandra Beeney
6, The Cuttings
Sedlescombe
Herts

Dear Mrs Sandra Beeney,

Has it ever occurred to you that you might be
special? Because that's what we're looking for:
VERY SPECIAL PEOPLE.

If you have a TALENT, no matter how small, the
Department of Paranormal Resources needs YOU.
Now you may think, secure in your home at
6, The Cuttings, Sedlescombe, that there's nothing
you can give to your country.

But paranormal TALENTS are a resource – like
coal, or gas, or water. And if, after testing, you,
Mrs Sandra Beeney, prove to have a TALENT,
YOU TOO CAN BE ONE OF YOUR
COUNTRY'S RESOURCES.

ENTER THE AMAZING WORLD
OF A VERY BRITISH LEAGUE
OF SUPERHEROES

TEMPS
VOLUME 1

———————

DEVISED BY

ALEX STEWART AND NEIL GAIMAN

A ROC BOOK

PENGUIN BOOKS

Published by the Penguin Group
Penguin Books Ltd, 27 Wrights Lane, London W8 5TZ, England
Penguin Books USA Inc., 375 Hudson Street, New York, New York 10014, USA
Penguin Books Australia Ltd, Ringwood, Victoria, Australia
Penguin Books Canada Ltd, 10 Alcorn Avenue, Toronto, Ontario, Canada M4V 3B2
Penguin Books (NZ) Ltd, 182–190 Wairau Road, Auckland 10, New Zealand

Penguin Books Ltd, Registered Offices: Harmondsworth, Middlesex, England

First published by Roc, an imprint of Penguin Books, 1991
1 3 5 7 9 10 8 6 4 2

Printed in England by Clays Ltd, St Ives plc
Set in 10/12 pt Monophoto Melior

CONTENTS

Additional material by Neil Gaiman, Mary Gentle,
Roz Kaveney and Alex Stewart.

From *Lord Orpington Remembers*. Interview and commentary by Garry Hardwick. (Roc Modern History Series, June 2017, £10.95.)

A: ... of course, at this point we found ourselves with two hundred identical female babies. With Cranston dead, the cloning experiment that produced them was impossible to reproduce – turned out the whole thing was scientifically impossible from the word go, anyway.

That was the trouble with Cranston, you see. He could get anything to work, but only from the pseudo-science end of things; his grasp of scientific realities was shaky, to say the least. But what he did worked.

Rarely – very rarely – his results were reproducible by the researchers who came after him. Mostly they'd just throw up their hands in horror and ask for a transfer to another department.

He died in an unfortunate accident – he was trying to split an atom. With a chisel. Terrible mess . . .

Q: *But the Marcia experiment?*

A: Yes, yes. I was getting back to that. Well, Marcia – all two hundred of her – was educated in a small private school in the Cotswolds. We did a number of tests on her – on them – hoping for, I don't know, telepathy or something. No luck. No paranormal talents whatsoever.

However, the Marcias were astounding in many ways. They all developed a crush on George Harrison simultaneously, I remember. Or was it Peter Noone? Or that chap in glasses in Freddie and the Dreamers . . .?

Q: *It really doesn't matter.*

A: No. Probably not. Hmph. It's going to bother me all day, now, that one. Anyway, they all got over it in the same week. Transferred their affections to the gym teacher, poor woman . . .

Well, when they were sixteen, must have been about 1970, they all announced their intention of going into secretarial training when they left school. That was what they all wanted to be. Secretaries.

Having got nowhere much educating them together, we sent them to different secretarial schools across the country, in the way of an experiment. Nature versus Nurture: what would different colleges accomplish with two hundred of them?

The result was perfectly astonishing . . .

Q: *In what way?*

A: At the end of three years of secretarial training, all over the country – including some very select establishments – we found ourselves with two hundred women who were all equally inept at typing, shorthand, or filing; and who were all incapable of making a decent cup of coffee. Two hundred of them. Bottom of the class.

Problem was what to do with them. Her. Them.

Q: *And the solution was yours?*

A: Was it? It was a long time ago, laddie. Could have been my idea. Could have been Loric's – he was an up-and-comer, back then, always having bright ideas.

Anyway, the Department of Paranormal Resources hired them. It was felt she added a certain amount of stability to the lives of our operatives, particularly the temps. Most of our people were temps. Held regular jobs, and we'd pull them in as we needed them. So whichever branch they went to, there she was.

Q: *Did it work?*

A: Haven't the foggiest. To be honest, the other reason we employed her was financial. It was the budget. It really didn't matter which government was in power, it was always the same.

The DPR was starved of cash. Absolutely starved. I said to Loric at the time, I said to him, you really can't blame anyone with a halfway decent talent for going to America. They knew how to treat their paranormals over there.

You have to understand that in Britain the DPR was always treated as something of an embarrassment. Even a bit of a joke . . .

NOTHING SPECIAL

Colin Greenland

It was Monday, but Hussein's giro hadn't arrived. 'Go and see your Mr Cartwright,' said his father. 'Go at once, today,' he said, frowning. 'Do not let them think they can overlook you.'

Hussein's mother said nothing. Hussein knew she disapproved mightily of what her younger son did now that he had left school. She did not understand what it was, she only knew this new job was not a proper one like his brother Jamshyd's. She was deeply suspicious of this 'Department'. It would be no surprise to her that its promises went unhonoured. She opened another tin of condensed milk.

'Go and see Mr Cartwright,' said Hussein's father again, not looking at his son, but at his own reflection in the side of the toaster, checking the trim of his moustache. And because Hussein was a dutiful son, and always obeyed his father, he did.

At least, he tried. He went on the bus to the Regional Office where he had been interviewed, where he had been tested, after a fashion, and accepted on to the register. Mr Cartwright had asked for his personal details and signature on a number of forms, shaken his hand heartily, and given him a shiny leaflet to take away with him. 'See Marcia about your money ... um ... Hussein,' he had said, glancing at the forms before dropping them into a wire tray already overflowing

5

with pieces of paper. 'And don't forget your suit!'

So Hussein went into the Regional Office, which was at the end of Park Street between a video shop and an off-licence, and he stood in front of the woman's desk until she noticed him.

'Can I help you?' she asked, in a voice that implied it was a great condescension on her part to offer, a great insolence on his to be there at all.

'My name is Hussein Azdrubal,' Hussein told her. 'My giro has not arrived.'

'Are you registered?' she asked, looking harder at him. 'You could be anybody, you know. I mean, how am I to know?'

'My name is Hussein Azdrubal,' Hussein repeated. 'I was registered on Thursday, 27 September. You registered me.'

With an effort, she searched a file. Grudgingly, she admitted that his name did indeed appear to be in it.

'We can't remember everyone that comes in here,' she said, airily. It was obviously unreasonable of him to expect anything more. 'You haven't been for your training yet, have you?' she added accusingly, reading his card.

'You put me on the waiting list,' Hussein reminded her.

'Well, then,' she said, in self-exculpation. 'What was it you wanted?'

Marcia had no idea why Hussein's giro had not arrived. She said it might be the post. 'You'll have to talk to Mr Addison,' she said.

Hussein bowed his head slightly towards her. 'I would like to see Mr Cartwright, please,' he told her.

She pursed her lips. 'Mr Cartwright's a busy man,' she said. 'He can't see everyone that comes in here. You'll have to see Mr Addison. Mr Addison's Mr Cartwright's assistant,' she said, pointedly, as though she thought the word might be a hard one for him to understand.

'All right,' said Hussein. He stood upright, expectantly.

The woman glared at him, exasperated now. 'Mr Addison's not here *today*, it's *Monday*, isn't it? You'll have to come back tomorrow.'

Hussein left the Regional Office and went to the railway station. He caught a train to London, and then a bus to Whitehall. Today was the day he had to get his suit, and they did not keep the suits at the Regional Office. After his interview with Mr Cartwright he had had to go to the stores at the Department itself, in Whitehall, to be measured, and today was the day they had told him to come in and collect the suit.

The stores were in the basement of the Department, in the corridor that led one way to the laboratory, the other to the canteen. After being measured, Hussein had gone into the canteen because he had missed his lunch. He had ordered a kebab. It had not been very nice. Today the smell of chips was powerful from one direction, the smell of battery fluid from the other. Hussein stood in the middle, at the door of the stores, and waited.

The storeman was a tall skinhead with HATE tattooed on one hand and KILL on the other. He was talking to a friend, who had enough hair for both of them, tied back with an elastic band. He also had a broom, though he was doing nothing with it. The two men were discussing footballers, or perhaps it was wrestlers. The storeman, grinning, said he had a room full of suits, but no authorization to give a suit to Hussein. There was no record that a suit had been ordered for him. He was sure there wasn't even though Hussein was able to tell him that the order had been placed on Thursday, 27 September, when the storeman had measured him for the suit. The storeman said he would look.

Hussein stood and waited for the storeman to stop talking to his friend and go and look for the order. While he waited, he took off his glasses and wiped them with his handkerchief. He listened to the transistor radio the storeman had behind him on a shelf. 'The gunman, who claims to be holding top-secret government documents, has gone to ground in the five-star Covington Hotel,' said the radio newsreader intensely. 'He is demanding a press agent.'

Hussein smelt the chips and wondered how long he would have to wait here. He started to ask the men if they knew what time it was, but as soon as he spoke the man with the broom said, 'Get some music, Dave, for fuck's sake.' The one called Dave reached for the radio and changed the station, though the newsreader was now telling them reassuringly about what the police were doing. Instead, he produced the voice of a woman who sang yearningly that she wanted him to touch her body, to the rhythmic sound of metal cans being crushed. This pleased him, and he turned it up louder, then continued to talk about wrestling, unless it was football.

Hussein waited a little longer, then realizing he would have to leave at once to catch his train, he went.

Next morning at breakfast, Hussein's father looked round from the television and saw his younger son sitting across from him. 'Hussein, has this girocheque arrived yet?' he asked, and frowned when Hussein admitted it had not. 'Go and see that Mr Cartwright,' his father advised him.

'They said I must see Mr Addison, father,' said Hussein, who had told him so the previous evening. His mother said nothing. She sighed deeply and stared at the television, where a woman with a singing cat was explaining how all its fees went to the rain forests. Hussein knew it had been deeply humiliating to his mother to be told one

8

of her sons was 'Paranormal', even if it was only the younger one. She was sure the neighbours were talking about him. It was useless for Hussein to assure her the neighbours never gave him a thought, being unconcerned which of the young brown men in their street it was that lived next door.

It was raining. The bus was almost full. Several people who arrived after Hussein got on before him, and he had to wait for the next bus. He returned to the Regional Office. He reminded Marcia she had told him to come back today to see Mr Addison, and apologized for being rather late.

'He's not here, is he?' replied Marcia, as though she had mistaken his talent. Perhaps she thought he was the one the papers called X-Ray, or another one, Precogno. 'He's got flu.'

'May I please see Mr Cartwright, then?' asked Hussein, hopefully.

She did not answer his request, but said only, 'Where's your suit?'

'I went to the stores at the Department in Whitehall,' Hussein told her. 'The man there is looking for my order.'

Marcia looked suspicious. 'Are you sure you ordered it?'

'Yes,' said Hussein, patiently. 'I ordered it on Thursday, 27 September. You gave me the form.'

'You'll have to have your suit to talk to Mr Addison,' she said. 'All trainees are supplied with suits. You have to go to the Department, in Whitehall,' she said, slowly and clearly. She lifted her head and looked along her nose at him. 'All right?' she inquired, sounding as if she was challenging him to say that it wasn't.

Hussein bowed slightly. 'I'll go there this afternoon.' And making an appointment to see Mr Addison the following day, he left the office and went to the railway station.

9

Dave the storeman was on duty again. His friend with the broom was nowhere to be seen. Dave was sitting with his chair tilted up on its back legs, reading a newspaper. He had a matchstick in the corner of his mouth.

'Yeh?' he said, when Hussein made his presence known.

Hussein smiled, hoping not to offend the storeman. 'My suit,' he said, as though it was a trifling thing. 'You were going to look for my order. My name is Hussein Azdrubal.'

The man seemed to have forgotten him completely. He went away for a long time, then came back, thumbing with one hand through a stack of crumpled dockets. From the other hand his newspaper was still dangling. 'Jet pack, wasn't it?' he said, not looking at Hussein.

'No,' said Hussein. 'A suit. I'm a trainee Paranorm.'

'Yeah,' said the storeman, unwillingly, 'but you was the one wanted the jet pack, wasn't you?'

'No,' said Hussein. 'I don't know anything about a jet pack.'

The storeman squinted at him with half a smile. He was obviously used to stupid foreigners who said one thing one day and something else the next.

'Have you got the suit?' Hussein asked.

'We've got suits,' the storeman admitted, scratching his HATE hand. 'I'll have to have a look what we've got. What size?' he asked, taking the match out of his mouth and looking Hussein over vaguely.

Hussein gave his measurements.

The man didn't move, or even acknowledge he'd spoken.

'Small, medium or large?' he asked.

'Medium,' said Hussein, supposing it was safest.

The man moved his head slightly, sideways. He put the match back in his mouth.

'Come on, then,' he said, and disappeared deeper into his territory.

Hussein followed, walking curiously after the shuffling man between towering shelves of maps, socks, briefcases, wigs and inflatable dolls. They went down some concrete steps in the glare of a bulb hanging from a white celluloid shade, and into a large room that stank of old wool and mothballs. On either side, stretching away into the shadows, were racks made of dull steel tubing. Hanging from the racks were suits, rows and rows of suits, on plain wooden hangers: more suits than Hussein could count, or even imagine.

Dave the storeman grabbed a jacket at random, gripping a sleeve between his thumb and finger.

'You can 'ave grey,' he said, his voice sounding strangely flat and dead in the clothy aisles, 'or grey ... we got, lessee, I think we got brown ... Wassis?' He snickered. '... grey ...' He slouched away along the rack, tugging suits out at random and shoving them back. 'We got brown somewhere, I know we 'ave. There's grey ...' As he moved further away, hangers clattering right and left, his voice grew fainter and fainter.

Frightened lest the man should go away and not come back again, Hussein called out, 'Grey is fine.'

'What?' called the man.

'Grey will be very nice, thank you,' called Hussein.

'Grey?' The man came back with a suit in his arms. 'What size?' he said.

'Medium,' Hussein said.

The storeman plonked the suit in Hussein's arms. Dust swirled up in the air, making Hussein blink behind his glasses.

'If you don't like it, you can take another one,' said the storeman, chewing his splintering match. 'They're all the same.'

Hussein pulled the suit on. It smelt very old. The trousers were baggy, the turn-ups dragged on the floor. The shoulders were too big and the arms too short. The storeman tugged at them without result, and shrugged. 'They're all naff, ent they,' he said. 'Demob.'

Hussein looked at him blankly, looked down at the suit. It seemed to be much too loose and, at the same time, stifling.

'What they 'ad left after the war,' explained the man. 'Blokes stayed on in the army rather than wear them suits. Sign here,' he said, and handed Hussein an inky ballpoint and a clipboard.

Hussein signed his name, thanking the man for his trouble. He bent down and hitched the turn-ups above the tops of his shoes. When he straightened up they flopped down again.

The storeman was staring vacantly out of the basement window, which gave on to a view of grimy brickwork and an iron downpipe, painted grey. 'You have to sign for it,' he said, searching haphazardly for his clipboard.

'I have,' said Hussein. 'Already.' He picked up the board from where the man had put it down and showed him his signature.

'You'll have to see the lab about the jet pack,' said the storeman. 'Along there.' He gestured down the corridor.

Not liking to contradict the man yet again, Hussein decided it would be best to go to the lab and ask, at least. Perhaps this was some other item of equipment compulsory for trainees that Mr Cartwright had just forgotten to mention.

The lab tech was stooped, Scottish and in a bad mood. He did not like being asked about jet packs by soft-voiced refugees from church jumble sales. 'They're all in for their MOT,' he said angrily. 'I don't know how many times I've told you.' Hussein apologized. He did not mention that he had never been into the lab, never seen the technician before.

On the train home, young girls pointed at Hussein's suit and whispered to each other, holding their noses and giggling. Hussein took no notice. He read another page of his second-hand copy of *Also Sprach Zarathustra*. It was difficult to understand.

Hussein's father wrinkled his nose and frowned vaguely at his son's suit as though wondering whether he had seen it before, and whether he was expected to comment; but he did not, though he greeted him with exaggerated pleasure. He and Hussein's mother had just been arguing about him. 'Tell me, my son,' he said, 'where is the money they said they would send you, this Department of yours?'

'They say it may be stuck in the post, father,' said Hussein.

Hussein's mother said nothing, but stood with her back turned, dusting the photos of Hussein's brother Jamshyd's wedding. Jamshyd was a management consultant now, or perhaps it was a consultancy manager, and he lived in Milton Keynes, the city of the future. Hussein's father glared at her rigid back. He was proud of his younger son for being selected for this scheme of the government's, whatever it was. 'Go and see your Mr Cartwright,' he advised. 'He will sort it out. It is his job.'

Next morning Hussein got up and went to fetch the post. There was a plea for funds from a snail sanctuary, an offer of a collector's edition satellite dish in real Wedgwood, and an advertisement of fantastic free prizes you could win simply by paying your poll tax. There was no giro.

Hussein washed, shaved, cleaned his teeth and looked for his new suit. The trousers had slithered off the hanger in the night and were sprawled under the wardrobe. He tried to brush the fluff off, but it seemed to have bonded with the cloth. Hoping it wouldn't look as bad to everyone else as it now did to him, he put the suit on, hoisted up the turn-ups, and took the bus to the Regional Office, where he asked to see Mr Addison.

Marcia looked distastefully at Hussein's suit as if it was an offence to all right-thinking people, and reached into her desk cupboard. 'Mr Addison's not here today,' she told Hussein, bringing out an aerosol and spraying the air pointedly, her little finger crooked at an angle. 'He's on holiday. You'll have to make an appointment.'

'But I made an appointment yesterday,' said Hussein, hitching the shoulders of his jacket up again. Seeing that she didn't believe him, politely he showed her, written down in the book in front of her, 'H. Azbrul'.

'Is that you?' she asked, banging the aerosol back in the cupboard and peering at the book.

'I think it must be,' said Hussein diplomatically.

Marcia shrugged. 'I wasn't here yesterday,' she said. 'It must have been my replacement. I'll have to call up now,' she said, sounding annoyed, and picked up the phone with a flourish, as if she was going to hit him with it; but just then the door opened and with a rush of air that fluttered the notices about NALGO meetings and AIDS testing, Whizz Kid was standing beside Hussein, leaning on the desk.

'Hello, darling,' he said loudly to Marcia, and grinned. 'I hear you've been trying to get hold of me.'

Marcia's face lit up. She held the phone up in the air, several inches away from her ear, as though unaware she had picked it up. 'Whizz Kid!' she said with pleasure. 'Long time no see! Can I get you a coffee?'

Whizz Kid was over by the noticeboard, picking up all the notices he had blown down, reading them and pinning them back up again. 'Nope,' he said decisively.

'Given up coffee.' He was dusting the leaves of Marcia's sickly Swiss cheese plant, fetching water from the toilet out back and pouring it into the pot. 'Given up smoking, given up –' He popped out to the shops and was back again in an instant, flourishing a packet of chocolate-coated Hob-nobs. '– red meat,' he said. 'But I must admit, I do have a weakness for a choccy biccy.' Smiling winsomely, he offered Marcia the last one, crumpled the empty wrapper and lobbed it over the desk into her bin. 'Hi, you must be new,' he said to Hussein, holding out his hand for him to shake. 'Whizz Kid,' he said, smiling a smile of devastating candour and naturalness.

'Hello,' said Hussein, clutching at the hand as it zoomed by. 'I'm –'

'Like the suit,' said Whizz Kid, wiggling his eyebrows. 'Very retro.' He smirked, and rubbed his nose. 'Is the great man in?' he asked, leaning over Marcia's desk and fiddling with her typewriter.

'Just a minute,' she said. She got up and went and knocked on the door of the inner office.

'Come,' called a voice, and she went inside.

Without ever stopping long enough for him to answer, Whizz Kid asked Hussein what his 'act' was, what projects he was working on at the moment, whether he knew the truth about unsaturated fats and intestinal flora, and whether he had any connections in Japan. 'That's where the future is,' he said. 'Have you ever been to Tokyo? Amazing place, very technical, people living like sardines.' His face was very close to Hussein's suddenly, making him jump. 'Do you know how many acres of rain forest it takes every week to supply the Chinese with chopsticks?' he asked. His conversation seemed to have moved on to Hong Kong, DAT, the Mandelbrot Set, call-forwarding. He flossed his teeth. When he stood still for almost a second, Hussein could see

Whizz Kid's suit was not demob. It was creamy, glossy, with big shoulder pads, sleek all over him like a fresh coat of paint. Curious, Hussein reached out a finger. 'Uh-uh,' said Whizz Kid, halfway across the room. 'Don't touch the suit. Unstable molecules. You like? Still running it in.' He grinned again, self-consciously.

Marcia came back in. 'Mr Cartwright will see you now, Whizz Kid,' she said, smiling sweetly, and Whizz Kid was past her, inside the office, his voice sounding recognizably from beyond the still-reverberating door.

Marcia sat down. She yawned, and covered her mouth and nose. She got out her aerosol and sprayed it all around again.

Hussein sat down. He took off his jacket, but his trousers looked so fluffy he put it back on again.

Before he could button it up, Whizz Kid was back out, hanging on to the doorway of Mr Cartwright's office with both hands, swinging backwards and forwards. Beyond him, Hussein could just see Mr Cartwright himself. He was saying, '. . . Covington Hotel.'

'I don't know, Dennis, it's not really me, is it?' Whizz Kid said with easy good humour. 'Rushing armed desperadoes, rescuing hostages, yes, but government documents –' He pulled a mournful face. 'What's in them anyway? Government documents – I mean, it's not exactly sexy, is it?'

Mr Cartwright seemed to be attempting to reply.

'Tell you what, Den,' said Whizz Kid, 'give me a call. Give me a call . . . say, Friday.' In one smooth motion he produced a sharkskin Filofax, opened it, scanned it, replaced it in his utility belt. 'Call me Friday, we'll have a bit of a natter. Tell you what, if he gets a hostage, call me anyway. A nice hostage, I mean. Photogenic. Children are good. Or a woman. Preferably.' He was at the door, grinning. 'Ciao, everybody. Ciao, Marcia. Take care.'

Then he was gone. All the way up the road Hussein could hear brakes screeching and angry horns honking.

He stood up, hoisting the shoulders of his jacket back into place. 'Mr Cartwright?' he said, cautiously.

Mr Cartwright gazed around the room, and saw Hussein there for the first time. He looked blank.

'You interviewed me on Thursday, 27 September,' Hussein said, going towards him. 'My name is Hussein Azdrubal.'

Mr Cartwright looked disappointedly past him, at the closed door, and then at Marcia. 'Is there anyone else, Marcia?' he asked. His voice sounded very tired and resigned.

'Only this gentleman,' Marcia said, in a voice that suggested Hussein was nothing of the kind and she was corrupting the word by even associating it with him.

'I am Hussein Azdrubal, I have an appointment with your assistant Mr Addison,' said Hussein, not wishing to push himself forward.

Mr Cartwright rubbed his forehead. 'You'd better come in,' he said. Obviously he didn't remember Hussein, from 27 September or any other time. He held the door open for Hussein to step into his office.

Inside, everything was much as it had been, except where papers from the wire tray had now overflowed on to the floor. Hussein wondered if his registration was still among them.

'Sit down, um . . .' said Mr Cartwright, sinking heavily into his own slumped chair. 'What have we found you?'

'This suit, sir,' said Hussein, pulling at the cuffs.

'Remind me – um . . . Hussein, isn't it? – what is it you do?' Mr Cartwright asked him, looking wearily at him as if he was just another item in the mess, something he'd put down earlier and forgotten about. 'I suppose Marcia has all your details, hasn't she? Paperwork,' he said, and smiled lugubriously. 'Never mind that now,' he said, and slapped the desk decisively. 'How do you fancy working with Scotland Yard, um . . .?' He looked among the papers under his hand, as if hoping Hussein's answer might be written down somewhere there already.

Scotland Yard, thought Hussein. The police. He wondered what use he could possibly be to the law of the land. 'I am happy to try, sir,' he said, obediently.

'Good boy,' said Mr Cartwright. He opened a drawer and rummaged in it without result. 'It's this Covington Hotel siege thing.' Giving up the drawer, he turned to his briefcase and rummaged through that instead. He pulled out a folded paper and showed it to Hussein.

It was a copy of the *Evening Standard*. On the front was an Identikit picture of a scowling man. It looked like the Duke of Edinburgh. 'Some bloke who's got his hands on some documents or other. Oh, and a gun. Not bullet-proof, are you, um . . .?'

Hussein swallowed. 'No, sir,' he said.

Still rooting through the drawer, Mr Cartwright waved an airy hand. 'Well, don't worry. They never shoot anyone, these blokes. Haven't got the bottle. And you'll have Scotland Yard there right behind you, don't forget. Finest marksmen in the land. Pop down there, anyway, would you, um . . . and if you get stuck, give me a call here, you've got the number, haven't you? And we'll see who else is available.'

Hussein stood up. He'd got it, his first agency job. Assignment. He didn't like the sound of it, but he would manage. He hoped. 'Marcia will give you the forms,' Mr Cartwright said, shaking his hand vigorously again and clapping him on the shoulder as he ushered him back into the outer office. 'Marcia, would you –?' he said, looking at his hands, then at Hussein's jacket, then diving into his pocket in search of a handkerchief.

Marcia did. There were several forms, all to be filled in in triplicate, because the photocopy budget had run out.

Hussein got the next train, then a bus to Marble Arch. He tried to read his Nietzsche on the way, but was too excited to concentrate. Instead, he looked through the papers Marcia had given him. One of them said fares by public transport would be refunded on receipt of an application countersigned by his section head. There was a leaflet advising him what to do about a pension. Another form was for claims by seconded operatives in the event of loss, damage, theft, injury or demise, which stated that it was not to be returned to the Metropolitan Police, but directly to the DPR.

Hussein folded all the papers and put them in his inside pocket. They felt very bulky there. He looked out of the window of the bus. The streets were nearly dark already. He would be late home for tea. He wondered if he would have a chance to telephone his mother.

There were three police cars parked in front of the Covington Hotel. Several uniformed men were standing around looking bored.

Hussein slipped under the orange tape and went up to an inspector with bushy eyebrows and a flat cap who was leaning on the roof of one of the cars, his foot on the sill of the open door. As Hussein approached he was talking on his wrist radio. 'Hotdog surveillance bandage on thirteen at oh-seven-five, if you ask me,' he said rapidly. 'We've got chummy here sweating antifreeze, over,' he said proudly, casting a flickering glance at an upstairs window of the hotel and baring his teeth, which he tapped intently with his thumbnail, listening to whoever was on the other end of his radio. There was another policeman in the car, in the passenger seat, staring expressionlessly straight through the windscreen.

Hussein waited politely. Suddenly the inspector

barked, 'Don't give me any aggravation, Lychgate! Looks like a rubber light-bulb job, repeat rubber light-bulb, and if Special Branch don't like it they know what they can do with their bath cubes. Out.' Brusquely he jabbed the miniature cut-off switch with the tip of his little finger.

'Sir?' said Hussein. He got the papers out of his pocket.

Instead of speaking to him, the inspector leaned down into the car. 'Bloody bath cubes,' he said disparagingly to his subordinate.

'Sir,' agreed the subordinate, unmoving.

'Hand me that bloody horn, Wallis,' demanded the inspector.

'Sir,' said the subordinate, and passed him a gleaming white loud hailer.

Switching it on, the inspector pointed it up towards the hotel window and bellowed into it, 'THROW THE GUN OUT, ATKINSON! GIVE YOURSELF UP!' He glared at the window, and so did one or two of the other officers, in a manner that was curious rather than hopeful. There was no visible result.

'Chummy's not bloody budging, Wallis,' said the inspector to his subordinate.

'Sir,' Wallis affirmed.

'WE'RE NOT GOING ANYWHERE, ATKINSON,' threatened the inspector through the loud hailer, then switched it off and threw it contemptuously back into the car.

At that moment he noticed Hussein, standing two feet away from him, trying to wriggle his jacket to lie straight across his shoulders.

'How did you get in here, Ali Baba?' demanded the inspector. 'What do you want?' Then, focusing on Hussein's suit, on the sheaf of forms he was holding out towards him, he groaned. 'The bloody Freak Show, Wallis,' he said. 'That's all we need.'

20

Wallis's eyes flickered sideways at Hussein. 'Sir,' he concurred.

The inspector took Hussein's forms without looking at them and threw them inside the car. 'What can you do, then, sonny, walk up walls?'

'No, sir, I —' began Hussein; but the inspector didn't wait for his answer.

'I'll tell you what you can do, sunshine, you can stay out of my bloody hair.' He advanced on Hussein quickly, in a threatening gesture that turned into a paternalistic squeeze of the shoulders. He spoke very softly. 'Leave it to the professionals, okay?' He looked at his hands, grimaced.

Hussein was not sure that Mr Cartwright would be very pleased if he returned to the Regional Office and said the officer in charge had sent him away. He thought perhaps he should assert himself a little, on behalf of the Department. He pointed into the car. 'My papers,' he said.

'I'll sign your papers,' said the inspector aggressively. 'Fucking bob-a-job, here.' He dug unproductively in his trouser pocket. 'You got any change, Wallis?'

'Sir,' said Wallis, and passed him some coins from the glove compartment of the car.

The inspector held the coins out to Hussein. 'Here,' he said, and gestured back in the direction of Oxford Street. 'Two teas,' he said. 'Two sugars in mine. Sugar, Wallis?'

'Sir,' said Wallis.

The inspector leaned his elbow on the car roof again and started talking aggressively into his wrist radio. 'Random turkey Senegal luncheon voucher in a baby's bottle, Lychgate,' he snarled, 'and I want it YESTER-DAY, OVER!'

Hussein walked away. He did not go in the direction of Oxford Street. He walked around the back of the Covington Hotel, where the tourists didn't go. There was

21

a filthy young couple sitting in a doorway beside a mound of torn and overflowing rubbish bags and sodden cardboard boxes. Their legs were wrapped in a tattered sleeping bag. 'Spare some change, please,' chanted the girl, not even looking up as Hussein passed. She was shivering.

Hussein stopped. As he reached down to give them the policeman's money, his jacket slipped suddenly sideways and slid down his arm. The collar flipped up and knocked his glasses off.

The couple looked at the glasses as if they didn't know what they were. Hussein bent down and picked them up. He checked that they weren't broken. Then he pulled off the jacket and gave it to the girl. 'Here,' he said. 'Are you medium? I don't think I am.'

Leaving the couple staring at the jacket as if it had just materialized out of thin air, Hussein put his glasses back on and walked round to the back door of the Covington Hotel.

There was another police car there, and an armed policeman on the steps. He looked bored. His radio was squawking but he was paying no attention to it. Hussein walked right up to him.

'You can't go in,' said the policeman stolidly.

'I was sent,' said Hussein. 'They've given me a job.'

The policeman nodded, dully. 'Kitchens, is it? Or cleaning?' Seeing a thousand illegal immigrants skivvying for rich Japanese tourists, he stared hard at Hussein, who had been born in Swindon. Then, turning away, he looked at his watch and sighed.

Hussein slipped into the hotel. Everything was quiet. He walked along a tiled passage and found himself in a room full of shelves of toilet rolls. There were overall coats there, hanging on a rack. He put one on, and pulled on a pair of rubber gloves. Then he took a dustpan and brush from a hook, and went upstairs.

There was a security cordon at the fourth floor: more armed men, more orange tape. Carrying his dustpan, Hussein went past them totally unnoticed.

Along the corridor, one door was surrounded by trays full of dirty teacups. Stepping carefully over them, Hussein knocked on the door. 'Mr Chummy?' he said.

The door flew open.

Inside stood a wild-eyed man wearing a brown suit and two days' stubble. He looked nothing at all like the Duke of Edinburgh. He was clutching an automatic pistol, which he pointed eagerly at Hussein. Hussein raised his hands, dustpan in one, brush in the other.

'What are you,' said the man, 'the cleaner?' He was clearly disappointed, and seemed to have been expecting more illustrious company.

'They sent me, sir,' Hussein said.

A crafty smile flickered across the man's gaunt features. 'You'd better come in, then,' he said, holding the door wide.

Hussein went in. Like the corridor outside, the room was littered with empty teapots and full ashtrays. There was a large brown envelope on top of the television. It had printed boxes with names written in them, one after the other, and all crossed out. It was held together with a piece of string wound round and round two little metal clips.

The man with the gun shut the door with a bang and locked it, then walked energetically across to the window. 'I keep shouting, but they don't take any notice,' he said. He strained at the window, trying to push it open. 'Here,' he said, 'maybe you can get this open, it's stuck.' He stood back, dusting his hands, the gun in his pocket.

Hussein examined the window. 'I'm afraid it's not meant to be opened, sir,' he said. 'It's screwed shut.' He pointed to the screwheads in the frame. 'I could go and get a screwdriver, sir, and try to open it for you, if you like.'

'Oh, no,' said the man, shaking his head with gleeful malice. 'You're not going anywhere.' Then he squashed his long nose against the window, standing with his head at an exaggerated angle to squint down at the police behind the barrier below. 'I've got a hostage here!' he bellowed. 'If you don't get me Alastair Burnett, I'll shoot him!'

He reached for Hussein, as if to pull him to the window, but failed to complete the motion. Instead he looked Hussein over vaguely, his previous expression of disappointment returning. 'They could have sent someone a bit more glamorous,' he said. 'What is it, Equal Opportunities? I thought they had women cleaners, hotels. I don't suppose there are any children around anywhere, are there? Double your ratings, if you can get children. Even one child.' He seemed to be talking to himself.

Muffled through the glass, the loud hailer interrupted him. 'YOU HAVEN'T GOT A CHANCE, ATKINSON! THROW DOWN THE GUN AND COME OUT NOW!'

At once the man threw himself at the window and started to wrestle with it again, as if he still hadn't understood that it was screwed shut. 'ADDISON!' he bawled. 'It's ADDISON, for Christ's sake! Trust the bloody British copper to get everything arse-backwards. What's it going to look like on the captions if they can't even get my bloody name right?'

In a fury, he lashed out at the litter with his foot. There was a clang, and an aluminium teapot flew through the air and splashed messily all over the Constable print. 'Damn,' said Addison, annoyed. 'There was still some in that one.' Dispirited, he started crawling about the room with the gun under his chin, opening teapots at random and peering into them hopefully.

Forgotten, Hussein stepped over him, picked up the brown envelope from the top of the television and put it in his dustpan. He unlocked the door, opened it quietly, and slipped out, closing it behind him.

Going down the back stairs, he put down his brush, unwound the string from the envelope, and looked inside. There was a single sheet of paper. He took it out. It was a photocopy of the minutes of a meeting — a meeting of the British Cabinet. Hussein read a bit of it. They were discussing the privatization of the DPR. He put the paper back in the envelope, wound the string around the clips until there was no more to wind, then went the rest of the way downstairs. He hung the overall coat back on its peg and walked through to the front of the building in his shirtsleeves.

Avoiding the receptionist and the police sitting watching television in the lobby, he came out of the front door of the hotel. The sky was quite dark now, and it was growing chilly. Hussein walked over to the police inspector's car.

The inspector was sitting in the driver's seat, with his subordinate next to him, still staring straight ahead as though he hadn't moved. The window on the driver's side was up, but the one on the passenger's side was down. Hussein walked around to the passenger's side and handed the envelope in at the window.

'Here you are,' he said.

The policeman looked at it as if he didn't know what it was. Then he turned to the inspector. 'Sir,' he said.

The inspector turned from contemplating the street ahead and looked at what his subordinate held in his hands.

'Bloody hell, Wallis,' he said, and snatched the envelope from him.

'Sir,' said Wallis.

25

'He's dropped the bloody documents, Wallis!' said the inspector intently. He held the envelope and rapped its edge enthusiastically against the steering wheel.

'Sir,' said Wallis.

'He's only bloody dropped them!' said the inspector, baring his teeth in a ferocious grin. 'That's all he's bloody done!' He shot his cuff and started jabbing the tiny buttons on his wrist radio.

Wallis was looking around, through the windows of the car, as if something out there in the street had caught his eye, something moving; nothing special, just something he had seen out of the corner of his eye, and only for a moment, so he wasn't sure what it was or where it had come from.

But the Invisible Boy was walking away, back towards the city.

Mrs Sandra Beeney
6, The Cuttings,
Sedlescombe,
Herts.

Dear Mrs Sandra Beeney,

Has it ever occurred to you that you might be special? Because that's what we're looking for: VERY SPECIAL PEOPLE.

If you have a TALENT, no matter how small, the Department of Paranormal Resources needs YOU. Now you may think, secure in your home at **6, The Cuttings, Sedlescombe**, that there's nothing you can give to your country.

But paranormal TALENTS are a resource – like coal, or gas, or water. And if, after testing, you, **Mrs Sandra Beeney**, prove to have a TALENT, YOU TOO CAN BE ONE OF YOUR COUNTRY'S RESOURCES.

Some Common Questions Answered

1 *How do I know if I have a Talent?*

Good question. For some people, it's obvious. (And remember, it can be an offence to be in known possession of a paranormal Talent without reporting it to your local branch of the DPR.) Many people, however, have Talents they don't recognize: either way, a trip down to the **Sedlescombe** department of the DPR won't be wasted.

2   *If I do have a Talent, what does this mean for me?*

Probably nothing. You'll be put on the DPR register, and
you'll receive a small income supplement. If the Department
actually needs you for an assignment, you will be
remunerated for days of work lost. It's a bit like jury duty –
and every bit as necessary. Your normal employer cannot
legally object to time spent working for the DPR.

3   *What if I don't want to?*

There are a number of circumstances in which people of
Talent are exempt from temporary secondment to the DPR,
Mrs Sandra Beeney. Expectant or nursing mothers, the ill,
the insane, and ministers of the church are all DPR-exempt.
(However, many ministers of all denominations work for
the DPR on a voluntary basis.) Otherwise the DPR has the
power to 'draft you' – for work that's fun, exciting, and a
break from your day to day routine!

4   *What benefits are there to working for the DPR?*

Now you're talking, **Mrs Sandra Beeney**. Well, first, the
financial reward – as I said, simply registering for the DPR
Talent list ensures you get a modest weekly income
supplement, and while on active duty you will receive
additional remuneration. You will also receive clothing, and
training. (Trial training schemes are underway in a number
of areas; your local DPR will know whether one is ongoing
in an area near you.) But none of these benefits can compare
to the real benefit – that of knowing you're helping others,
and helping your country.

5   *What do I do now?*

Get tested. Get your family tested. You know it makes
sense.

If you're special, **Mrs Sandra Beeney** – we need you!

T. D. Sharpe
Recruiting Officer
Department of Paranormal Resources

LEAKS

David Langford

———————

It had been a definite mistake to spend so many hours last night practising. Making his way up the street, Ken struggled not to think of that obscene grey bladder in the local baker's window, which inflated and deflated in a miraculously unconvincing simulation of dough being kneaded. His own brain seemed to be doing much the same. Small wobbling flaws, perhaps UFOs or fragments of detached retina, floated through his field of vision, and that solitary spoonful of cornflakes lay in his stomach like a cluster of leaden dumplings.

What a wonderful thing it was to be Talented. He could sympathize two hundred per cent with that bloke in the Bible who hid his Talent in a napkin rather than stick out his neck.

Even the green double-decker buses exuded an alcoholic dread as they ground slowly past. Crisp packets leered mockingly from the gutter, sharing some terrible knowledge with the passers-by who so very pointedly ignored the moral leprosy stumbling in their midst. And how had he managed to get beer in his *hair*? Did it just ooze through one's pores from the foetid jellies inside? In every way it was a typical morning.

Behind the offices' grimy Victorian façade, a lift which doubled as a municipal convenience heaved Ken up through Social Services, Housing and Consumer Advice, Traffic Planning ... This Department of Paranormal

Resources' branch shared the fifth floor with the town council's nerve centre for coordination of cemeteries and crematoria. Ken thought longingly about a nice coordinated coffin as he steered himself past death's door.

It had been many unpaid months since he'd last been called for Temp work at the DPR office; going by appearances, their cleaners followed roughly the same schedule. In a familiar display of method acting, the receptionist behind the desk managed to convey that Ken's own paranormal resources included uncanny powers of invisibility and inaudibility. Air molecules of superior importance had passed through her door, Marcia's posture made it clear, and likewise bluebottles with greater social charm. She continued to apply nail varnish.

Ken peered at notices sellotaped to the dingy cream walls — THE SECTION PRINCIPAL WARNS THAT DISCIPLINARY ACTION WILL FOLLOW IF THERE IS ANY FURTHER REPETITION OF THE UNAUTHORIZED RAIN OF FROGS IN CONFERENCE ROOM 2 — and wondered about his chances of drawing on Departmental resources in the shape of paracetamol. Time passed.

'Mr Vanrey? You're *late*,' said Marcia severely and without prior warning. Her nails glowed iridescent purple.

'That's Varney.'

'Oh. It says here ... Mr Vanrey, the Department's time is very valuable. I have a travel warrant for you, and a briefing sheet, and you're to start at once.' She sniffed. 'And the Senior says he hopes you remember something from your college work about enortpy.'

Kenneth Varney, B.Sc. (Physics) (3rd), stared. 'About what?'

'Enortpy.' She pushed a slim, puke-coloured folder at him. The typed label said: CONFIDENTIAL *ENORTPY RAY.

'... Entropy, maybe?'

'I *spell-checked* it, Mr Clever. Now, you're to be a Departmental observer at the nuclear place, whatsisname, at Robinson Heath. Special investigation. I suppose the physics made them think of you.' She sniffed again. 'It's only an S-H job. Don't go getting above yourself.'

His head gave a particularly vicious twinge. Stalking horse. You heard about these things in a theoretical kind of way. When the DPR had only half a mind to intervene, they'd try stirring up the situation by sending half a Talent. Just knowing a 'specialist' was on the case could be enough to make your criminal or enemy agent show a detectable break in behaviour patterns. Such as, for example, staying late at the lab and dropping Ken Varney into a convenient swimming-pool reactor.

He asked the question uppermost in his mind.

'No,' said Marcia, 'but I can do you a Fisherman's Friend if that's any help.'

With a groan Ken tucked the folder under his arm and turned away ... then back again. 'One thing. Um, your word-processor, you use one of those spell-checkers where you can, you know, add new words ...?'

'To the built-in luxigon? Yes, that's right.'

Leaving, he felt ever so slightly cheered. Clearly he had some talent for investigative work after all.

Somewhere out west of Paddington his spirits made the significant leap from whirling dread to mere powerful unease. Could he really be sitting legitimately in First Class No Smoking? Ken Varney with his second-class denims and designer stubble? The ticket inspector had also had obvious difficulties with this concept, but in the end had stalked away baffled.

Feeling a return of the eerie power to tackle words of more than two syllables, he studied the file on entropy (or enortpy) rays. They were hypothetical, and statistical, and saved from nonentity only by a communication

written on a sheet of headed A4 (classified) with a worn
HB (classified), intercepted by (classified) at location
(need-to-know status insufficient), and reading:

> MIKHAIL. ENTROPY BEAM DEFINITELY EFFECTIVE ON
> TRANSPORT HERE. CONTINUE TRIALS SAME LOW LEVEL.
> TROJAN.

As he hacked his way through the surrounding
layers of soft, clinging, wet-strength officialese, Ken
gathered that this note would have been dismissed as
a rollicking jape if it weren't for the transport pool of
the Nuclear Utilization Technology Centre on Robinson
Heath which, when examined with a keen statistical
eye, had detectably (classified). Only a little bit – LOW
LEVEL, he thought, feeling momentarily clever – but
most definitely (classified).

Stalking horse. Marcia had wanted him to feel
humbled, but actually his usual assignments for the Department were humbler still and consisted of helping
move office, rearrange filing cabinets, fill out the numbers
for manpower inspections ... any little job where payment at his sub-competent Talent level was cheaper than
contract labour. As paranorms went, he rated as the
kind of small change it was easier to stuff in the charity
box than count. Everyone remembered the *Monty Python*
sketch where Ken's grade was rated just below penguins,
though just above BBC programme planners.

And now he was roaring towards NUTC, a place so
high-powered and high-security that paranorms weren't
normally allowed within a mile of it, just in case of
(classified), or even of (need-to-know). It was a famous
quirk of the civil service that, like the Home Office forensic unit, the Department's research lab was attached to
NUTC – presumably meaning that they could conduct
research on anything but paranorms.

'dS,' he mumbled painfully, 'equals dQ over T.' There, he still knew the definition of instantaneous entropy change. A few more hours' recovery time and the information might even start making sense.

Gasometers bulged like fungi outside the carriage window, succeeded by plastic-faced office blocks in contrasting shades of liver, lights and spam, and then a grimy expanse of station. Ken shouldered his bag and was soon shuffling down the platform, cautiously swivelling his head in slow motion and wondering whether a quick hair of the dog would be advisable just for the sake of practice. This gambit was blocked by a small placard saying MR K. VANREY, held up by a uniformed driver of few words and one implacably pointing finger. Score another first for Talent Grade Z: he'd never before been chauffeured in an official car, even one that banged and wheezed through Reading and the countryside like this.

'Ducts!' was his first thought when the heart of Britain's defence industry lurched into view, as though with incidental music from *Brazil*. Huge silvery ducts ran inside the miles of high wire-link fence, rearing up in triumphal arches to allow traffic at each gate. Smaller, black-clad ducts linked the square buildings, whose inner walls and ceilings were threaded by narrow pipes painted in Civil Service cream: they circled the security office where he was photographed holding a prison-style number; they paced him and his escort along endless two-tone corridors; they clumped companionably in the bare room where briefing was supposed to happen. The Robinson Heath installations had clearly been designed by some perverse lover of spaghetti.

The briefing group . . .

Dr Fortmayne from Weapons Physics had thick grey

hair, a glittering eye, and bounding excitement. It seemed he must be strapped in place, otherwise he'd vibrate off his chair. 'Let me make one thing clear: I want this gadget. I want it very much. I disagree with our whole approach. We shouldn't be piddling around, we should be going through the site and surrounds with a tooth-comb.' He frowned. 'Whatever a tooth-comb is.'

Sergeant Rossiter of MOD Police/Security mumbled something and was understood to be saying that tooth-combs came expensive these days. His raggled moustache and furtive manner evoked memories of the least reputable of Ken's occasional employers, Greasy Mal from High-bury, the man of a thousand fiddles.

Someone called Brownjohn, large, bland and moist, represented Transport. 'Run of bad luck. Could happen any time. Obvious hoax by one of our bright lads. And when we catch him —'

There was a wrangle between Theoretical Physics ('An entropy projector is a plain and simple impossibility.'), the DPR Lab Principal ('So is he,' with a nod towards Ken: 'Six impossible things before breakfast.') and NATO Liaison ('I don't care whether it's impossible or not: if it's available it'll make a nice bargaining point to squeeze some more counterforce goodies out of the bloody Americans. Since we can't seem to develop our own.'). At this, Fortmayne leapt upright in sputtering outrage, and the decibel count rose sharply.

Theoretical Physics turned out to be the sort of man who could in cold blood say words like appertaining, tantamount and even predicated.

Ken's head had reverted to full throb-level, but he gleaned that the entire NUTC transport pool was suffering mysteriously accelerated decay. Vehicles wore out naturally but too fast, as though spending all their nights in loud clubs burning the carburettor at both ends. It might have passed unnoticed, but then the message to 'Mikhail' had turned up in a routine check of outgoing site mail, addressed to an empty house in the nearby village of Bogley . . .

'If I had a contraption like that,' said Brownjohn, 'know what I'd do? Get rich beaming the thing at whisky. Twelve years aged in cask, only take a few months. Why waste it on our vans? Why not Trident?'

Fortmayne pointed out with heavy irony that NUTC transport was serviced every other week, that economics did not permit Trident warheads to be detonated quite so frequently, especially in the Home Counties, and that it was entirely credible that the same insidious influence was indeed being directed against the British deterrent. 'And what do they send us? This person Mr Vanrey.' (Marcia's spelling was now immortalized within the sealed plastic of his new security pass.) 'Possibly he'd like to tell the committee in a few words what special talent he brings to this critical situation? An unnatural gift, perhaps, for turning his face pale green?'

'Touch of flu,' Ken lied.

'I have Mr Varney's dossier and can vouch for him,' said Dr Croll, the DPR Lab Principal. 'I think the details of our operation should remain on a need-to-know basis. Our watchword is security.' Ken gazed at him admiringly. What a wonderful human being.

'I don't agree with what you're saying,' Fortmayne said reflexively, but people were looking pointedly at their watches and Rossiter rubbed his beer gut with slow significance. Lunch was declared and Ken found himself annexed by Croll.

'We call it the Mushroom Cloud,' said the DPR researcher, in the tones of one apologizing for a tedious family joke. Ken agreed that once you'd regarded the local pub's sign in that light, it became impossible ever again to see it as the Wheatsheaf. They entered.

This Croll seemed a cheerful fellow, rotund and bouncingly bald, and deeply untroubled by entropy rays. Ken felt distinctly less lichen-coloured as he contemplated an imminent hair of the chihuahua, if not of a full-scale St Bernard. Pints and curly sandwiches arrived at the table.

'To your success,' Croll said with mock formality. 'Had we but world enough and time ... but I have to talk a little business. It is really very simple. You will wear this and move around NUTC, observing and sometimes taking sinister notes, and we shall see what is stirred up.'

This was a conspicuous lapel badge in Day-Glo lime, about three inches across, carrying a single bold character. Drawing on the Dead Sea Scroll remnants of his physics, Ken said, 'Greek. A capital psi, right?'

'Very good. Yes, like a pink triangle or a yellow star. You will be noticed. Good. But I must admit that I brought you here for another reason, because I am professionally interested in your abilities.'

'Ability. With a very, very small A.'

'No modesty, now. You can't imagine how much, as a researcher, I truly envy any genuine paranorm. The gulf between us is narrow but it is deep.'

Ken was embarrassed. 'Honest, it's nothing, like being able to wiggle your ears. I used to send off to the small ads in *Knave* and *Private Eye*, you know, Dr Farrell's Famous Cerebral Enhancer Tonic, a guaranteed 44-inch talent within two months. Wore my fingers out, rubbing the damn stuff on my temples every night before retiring. I think it was oil of wintergreen actually.'

It wasn't something he cared to talk about, especially in a pub. But Croll quizzed him further with the unblinking earnestness of a Scientology interviewer closing for the kill, and at last said, 'Perhaps, you know, we can help. Measure your mind's height by the shade it casts. First, though: show me.'

Ken had gulped half his pint and Croll was lagging, so it was straightforward enough. He concentrated on the beer mugs and thought parched thoughts. For some reason it always helped to clench his teeth askew and close one eye. Potentials shifted and his mental thumb pushed down hard on the balance of Nature. Quite rapidly, though without any fuss, his own beer level rose two inches.

'That's it. I mean, that's all there is to it. It has to be alcoholic and it has to be my glass, I don't know why.'

'What about conservation of mass? No, don't tell me, I think I see.' Croll slid the two mugs together for comparison. 'Beer finds its own level. My loss is your gain. But, hmm, what about range? Could you perhaps tap that whisky bottle up behind the bar?'

'Well, I have to want it, and I don't much like whisky in beer. And I'd have to stand up and look all conspicuous: otherwise, there's a 3-foot drop from the Teachers' optic to this table here, and the potential energy gets a bit frisky. You know, fountains, waterspouts. Whisky and splash.'

Croll clicked his tongue. 'It is not exactly "that one talent which is death to hide". From the dossier I had imagined that, with training . . . Just imagine the scenario. A hostile spyplane flies low over Robinson Heath; you glance upwards, narrow your eyes, and vital hydraulic fluid leaks disastrously away!'

'Gallons of it, into my beer mug, with a horizontal velocity vector of seven hundred miles an hour? I hate getting barred from pubs.'

'With training, much is possible. You seem to have made room in your glass already. Do please show me again. There, the owner of *that* one is in the lavatory.'

Ken clenched his teeth askew and closed one eye. This time Croll kept his attention on the unattended drink twelve feet away. 'Excellent. The glass is falling hour by hour, the glass will fall forever . . .'

'But if you break the bloody glass you won't hold up the weather,' Ken quoted.

'A man of culture, I see.'

'Oh, you meet a lot of big brains with degrees down at the job centre and Social Security. The word is "over-qualified". Which is why —' On second thoughts, this was no place to discuss hauling anonymous clinking boxes off the backs of lorries for Greasy Mal.

'Nevertheless, a Department spotter recruited you. "Nature's handmaid Art makes mighty things from small beginnings grow" — Dryden. I would like you to visit our laboratory later today. You have potential.'

'And I have a bloody drink problem. Every time I try to practise what I can do . . .' Ken tried not to remember his unwelcome reunion with last night's Chinese takeaway on this morning's pillow. He made a queasy toasting gesture, drank, and convulsed disastrously. '. . . oh *shit*, it's lager and lime.'

'Fortunately this is only an old suit,' said Croll a little coldly.

For the next couple of hours, Ken prowled within what he'd been told was ten full miles of wire-link fence around the Robinson Heath site. How much area was that? About eight square miles if it were a circle, which it wasn't, or six and a quarter for a square, which it wasn't either. Now the average size of a typical entropy-ray projector would be . . .

Much of the area seemed about as derelict and useless as this statistical line of thought: grass and gorse, decaying tarmac, rabbit droppings, marshy expanses harbour-

ing only a few far-flung ducts. It must be out of sheer
embarrassment that the MOD insisted on maps showing
the site as a blank white patch. Clearly, when you passed
at last through the secret door of the inner circle and
walked the throbbing corridors of power you'd envied all
your life, the most earth-shattering revelation was how
even more boring than the real world it could be.

The beer buzzed in him, and he hoped Croll's own
several pints would be interfering with the fellow's afternoon study of the dictionary of quotations. Meanwhile,
nobody started back from Ken with cries of guilty alarm.

Instead: 'Aagh!' he said in guilty alarm as a hand
clamped on his shoulder.

'Just a word in your ear, mate,' murmured Sergeant
Rossiter. 'Just one word. The word is . . . pathetic.'

'I'm doing my job.'

'No, you've already done that, so why arse around? . . .
Oh dear, all new to you, innit? We leaked it two days
back about this dead unusual visit from a DPR weirdo,
pardon my French, special talent. Anyone acts funny
here *today*, they must be small fry because every big-time
guilty conscience is already going to be off sick or taking
leave. They're the names we'll feed in for correlation.
And where does that leave you, sunshine? Having you
here at all's just the follow-through, not the job.'

Feeling shrewd and acute, Ken said, 'I suppose a really
bright villain wouldn't risk acting suspiciously like that,
and he'd come in today just as usual.'

'Maybe, squire, maybe. So you reckon we should keep
an extra close eye on all the ones who stay home suspiciously, *plus* all the ones who suspiciously don't, and that
narrows it right down to our entire workforce of . . .
lemme see . . . 11,676 suspicious characters.'

'All right, I get the general idea.'

'Less a few who went sick or was already off to

41

Benidorm before we let out the rumours. Of course they could be double-bluffing, couldn't they?'

'All *right*.'

'Lighten up, now. Enjoy the sights if you like. Nifty little badge you've got there with the wossname, Greek for "piss" – ask me nicely and I'll get you another with the Greek for "off".'

Pausing only to call him 'chummy', Rossiter drifted away and left Ken thinking dark, entropic thoughts. He prowled on.

At one stage he loitered as suspiciously as he could by the north gate and watched Ford Transit vans accelerate smoothly past security guards who seemed unconcerned about possible stacks of nuclear warheads being smuggled out in each. At another he found the fire-door of a concrete blockhouse flapping its EMERGENCY USE ONLY lettering in the wind, slid cautiously inside, and left in haste when threatened by a big wall sign lurid with trefoils and the interesting rubric PURPLE RADIATION ZONE.

This must be part of Fortmayne's plutonium-infested playground. If I were a great detective, Ken thought, I would see right through all that stuff about tooth-combs, and say 'Fortmayne doth protest too much' (no, that would be Dr Croll's line), and thrill the assembled suspects in the library by asking which of all these characters was most likely to be the proprietor of a fiendish entropy ray? The number-one weapons physicist, of course: Fortmayne. Gesturing grandly to the imaginary inspector closing in with the handcuffs, Ken snagged his finger against the rusty barbed-wire shroud of a passing duct. Ouch. All this, and tetanus too?

The huge ducts and pipes, he decided grumpily, represented the government cash-flow into this unpromising hole in Berkshire. Vast sums surged down the MOD arteries, while the DPR pipeline would be a hair-thin capillary, subject to continual leaks. Billions for defence and about 50p for Ken Varney.

Sucking his finger, he shadowed an ailing and consumptive minibus into what turned out to be the Transport yard. Here government vehicles were being subjected to artificial respiration, intensive life-support and major transplant surgery. The stench of petrol was too thick to cut with a knife, and would have required industrial lasers. Entropy lay around in almost visible pools, like the local lake system of sump oil. From an office window two floors up a fat white blur that might have been Brownjohn watched him narrowly.

Who could be a more logical choice for the inside job, playing the dreaded entropy ray across the NUTC service and garaging areas? On the other hand, wasn't Fortmayne the most plausible villain? And hadn't Rossiter more or less warned him off? At this rate of detection he'd soon have a strong circumstantial case against every single bloody member of the briefing committee. We are all guilty. All the world's a symphony orchestra, with some on woodwind and most of us on the fiddle.

Something clicked then in Ken's mind, as though a fruit machine were signalling *nudge nudge*. Hadn't someone in a smoky pub in Highbury once winked and mentioned what they called the car-pool fiddle? He thought again about the precepts and philosophy of his very occasional employer Greasy Mal, and quite suddenly laughed out loud. Then he wished he hadn't: jarred by the noise, the inspirational light-bulb flared out and left his skull a blackened, smoking socket. Never go boozing with a hangover *and* a parapsychologist. Which reminded him . . .

The DPR laboratory was an unassuming wooden shack, propped up by the more opulent Home Office Forensic

Unit. Both were liberally spattered with what might have been red-hot evidence in the form of semen stains, but after some thought Ken placed the burden of guilt on pigeons, especially the one which had dropped its burden on him.

'Welcome!' said Dr Croll, buttoning a white lab coat. 'The raven himself is hoarse that croaks your fatal entrance under my battlements, if I might put it like that.'

Ken flicked without success at the shoulder of his best denim jacket. 'It was a pigeon actually; it just looks like it must have been a horse.'

'Come in, come right in.'

Inside the sanctum, the old familiar laboratory smell attacked his nostrils with a wire brush. Dull green tiles covered the floor. High-tech things with screens and digital readouts jostled on the benches with archetypal brass instruments that might have been used in the early experiments of Faraday, or Newton, or Torquemada.

For a moment, Ken felt disoriented by the feeling that this place was more like a lab than any real lab could be. Something movie-like about it, perhaps, along the lines of exploding control panels or Dr No's art-deco reactor.

'If you could just sit here,' said Croll, indicating the electric chair. Yes, that was the subtle anomaly. University physics labs were always short-changed when it came to important equipment like electric chairs.

'Er . . .'

'Oh, yes, I suppose it must look a trifle intimidating. I am very interested in physiological readouts, in trying to map what the body *does* when paranormal abilities come into play. There's no art to find the mind's construction in the face. And so we need all these sensors.'

Somehow Ken found himself gently crowded into the chair. 'Trust me,' said Croll. 'I'm a doctor.'

What he had in his bulging scientific mind was both simple and deeply irritating. Not content with borrowing Ken as an experimental subject, Croll wanted to play social worker and do him a bit of good. He'd nipped out to the village grocer for test materials in the shape of countless Tetrabrik litre boxes: orange juice, grapefruit juice, pineapple juice, mango juice and, worst of all, tomato juice.

'I can't possibly. It only works with something boozy, I told you.'

'My snap diagnosis, Ken, is that you are too permanently fuddled ever to transcend your talent's limitations. What you do at present . . . It provokes the desire, but it takes away the performance. However, if this will console you in the slightest, we do first need one control reading.'

The last of the chilly disk electrodes, slimed with something like KY jelly, had been taped in place. Croll handed Ken a plastic cup, the sort guaranteed to translate coffee directly into scorched fingers, and took a hopeful-looking brown bottle from a cupboard.

'Would, ah, light ale provoke the desire sufficiently?'

'You bet.'

'Now good digestion wait on appetite,' said Croll in his special quotation voice, 'and health on both.' Recorders were whirring and displays dancing with a sinuous EEG jiggle.

Ken clenched his teeth askew and closed one eye. The universe duly moved for him, and he raised the suddenly full cup. There was an outraged pause. 'Fuck me, what's this?'

'Nothing but cold civil service tea, I'm afraid. My secretary always used to say they brewed it from old tights. Personally I would not know . . . So, Ken, it has to be alcoholic, does it?'

Croll had him there. It was the lager-and-lime effect all over again.

'Let me tell you an anecdote. There was once a fellow called Logan whose Talent seemed even more spectacularly useless than yours. He was able to incinerate individual dust motes, no more than one at a time. They filed him as a micropyrotic for want of a better word, and then wrote him completely off the useful list with a grade of – well, your grade. Years later he made the imaginative breakthrough all by himself and emigrated to glory in America, the land of vigilantes and handguns.'

'Oh yeah, I saw a "Day In The Life" of him in one of the colour supplements. Local clod makes good. Learned to focus it on gunpowder or something, didn't he? Mr Misfire, The Man Whose Adversaries Shoot Themselves In The Foot. He looked a right sight in those puce leotards.'

'Pre-cisely. I am convinced that I, here, could have developed his ability much sooner: but our beloved masters, after first building this laboratory at Robinson Heath to save money, had a security scare. They became paranoid about letting wild Talents anywhere near the nuclear work at NUTC ... unless they happen to be in Security or Intelligence, and by definition too lofty, too busy to spare me one miserable afternoon. You know that today is the first time in a year that I've been able even to calibrate the psychotronic readouts?' He added, with dreadful inevitability, 'We all know Security is mortals' chiefest enemy.'

Ken writhed in the hard seat, which at the seat of his jeans also felt oddly cold and damp. Being wired up was even more uncomfortable than it had looked, but being wired up *and* lectured at ...

'Ow!' he said. Croll had sneaked up behind him with a needle.

'This will help make you more suggestible. No, no, don't move now, it might affect the sensors. The instruments of darkness tell us truths, but not if you wiggle the wires. Let me just tighten this strap, and this one. Now I want you to try for some juice. Just one small change in your Talent. You know you can do it. Tip the tea out in this beaker ...'

Open wide. Rinse. Even the bloody dentist never strapped him in. Ken made his miracle-working face again, staring with concentrated loathing at the box of grapefruit juice; and, almost at once, nothing happened. Except that his head hurt even more.

'Look,' he said patiently, 'it's as though you convinced me to walk across this dark room, and then showed me that I'd been on a narrow plank over a sodding great crevasse a mile deep. And there you are saying "You can do it, just walk back again now." It's not the same.'

Croll beamed, and hunched himself over a small console to one side of the EEC soft-drinks mountain. 'I had not yet mentioned that we can provide a counter-stimulus.' His hand pounced.

What followed was a mixture of red-hot needles and severe cramps in each buttock, as though the dentist were mounting a surprise attack from the rear. Ken made loud appropriate noises, and added, 'Stop that!'

'You cannot imagine how irritated I am by the sheer waste when a potentially fine Talent is bestowed on someone like –' A sort of visual ugh passed over Croll's face. 'A giant's robe upon a dwarfish thief. What a cheap, sleazy use you make of your priceless gift. Now, if I were in your place ...'

Ken offered to change places (and even robes) immediately, but this cunning ploy got only the response it deserved: a second and hotter dose of National Grid. No wonder the blasted hot seat had been damp. Croll was going to do him good even if it killed him. The after-twitches felt like sitting in a bowl of small, muscular and hyperactive eels.

'Look. I can't concentrate when you do that. Just give me a minute. Did I tell you about what I worked out this afternoon? Only bloody solved the entropy ray business, that's what.' In just such a way, when in the dentist's chair, Ken always found himself able to deliver frighteningly voluble monologues, without hesitation, repetition or deviation, on subjects like drizzle or bus tickets. 'It's all a load of rubbish, it's just someone doing the old car-pool fiddle over in Transport. The only thing I don't understand is . . . oh.'

Oh no, he thought. What hadn't made sense was why, with a nice little con going, anyone should be so yoghurt-brained as to draw attention to it by sending open letters about entropy beams. Who in this business was several protons short of a nucleus? Well . . .

'That is doubtless very interesting and rewarding for you, but as an attempt at distraction it is childish. I ask you to focus your mind, Ken. Focus on that one small change. Present fears are less than horrible imaginings, and the voltage dial can be turned up a great deal further.'

Yes, it really stimulated the mind, this sitting in the seat of power. 'You sent that letter, didn't you? The one from TROJAN to MIKHAIL, and very funny too. I bet you sent dozens till they intercepted one. You'd spotted the con and you moved in.'

Croll's hand wavered over a particular red button, as though it were a fat beetle he didn't quite want to squash because of the mess. 'Why should I do a thing like that? What possible motive could I have?'

Dominoes were still falling with a painful *click click click* inside Ken's head. 'It got *me* down here, that's what. Your first bloody guinea pig in, what did you say, a whole year? Of course you suggested the stalking-horse game to that committee. Come clean, chummy.' Oops, that had slipped out.

By now Croll had whitened to the point where the dome of his baldness looked like a peeled hard-boiled egg, awaiting the descent of some teaspoon of the gods. He closed his eyes and said, apparently to himself, 'Screw your courage to the sticking-place.' Then, mostly though not perhaps wholly in Ken's direction, 'I will complete my experiment. What's done cannot be undone. Afterwards I think there will have to be an unfortunate accident. This high-voltage equipment does not receive nearly enough safety inspections. There may be an inquiry and even a sharp reprimand.'

Of course, Ken was brooding, after spending my life reading all those thrillers I should have thought that when you're strapped to an insidious torture machine in the arch-fiend's secret den, it is not the best time to gloat out loud that you've got the goods on him.

The red button went down. This time the shock to his tormented buttocks included overtones of jagged teeth, killer vindaloo and barbed wire.

'Just a reminder,' said Croll. 'I *will* see you prove my theories by overcoming your petty self-imposed limits. If even on pain of death you can't bring yourself to love fruit juice, then think of hating me. The labour we delight in physics pain. Look there on the shelf: concentrated sulphuric acid. If some of it were transferred to your cup, you could try to throw it over me. Think of that.'

Ken studied the flimsy cup and rather thought the stuff would burn instantly through to irrigate his groin. He pointed out with irrefutable logic that offing Ken Varney was bound to cause more embarrassment than explaining a mere ... um ... late April Fool letter. Croll

retorted even less refutably that the one was a temporary
inconvenience while the other would be Wasting MOD
Police Time, and therefore meant a security downcheck
for unreliability, leading by steady logical steps to the
dole queue. Unfortunately, this made sense.

It was time, Ken decided, to panic. If only this were a
sci-fi story he would, around now, discover an unheralded
new Talent for causing entire crates of whisky to materi-
alize in the air three feet above his tormentor's head.
Small delirious details loomed at him, like the particularly
important-looking bluebottle buzzing up the window. He
noticed for the first time that Croll was wearing a copper
bracelet bulging with magnets, the sort that small ads
claimed would help against rheumatism, warts and tele-
pathic intrusion. At any other moment this would have
brought him a cheering rush of superiority.

Then he looked at the bright new scab on his finger
where the wire had snagged it, and thought: ducts. There
were plenty running under the wall benches or slung
from the ceiling, but those weren't the ones. No, but if, if
you just concentrated in the right way, made that one
small change in emphasis . . .

With a shudder he clenched his teeth askew, and
closed one eye, and after a long moment drank. It was
every bit as horrible as he'd expected.

'Tomato juice?' said Croll, looking up and peering,
white with excitement. 'Excellent, my dear Ken, excellent!
By this move to abstinence you have significantly
extended your lifespan, by numerous minutes.' He scrib-
bled a note.

Ken's stomach was already making urgent distress
signals to him, but he ignored them. Spilling one damned
spot on the floor might give the game away. He drank, and
watched one-eyed as the cup refilled, and drank again,
and again. And again. How much more could he take?

'Excellent. I think we might have a few minutes . . . to examine some other aspect . . . before . . . time and the hour . . . terminate this experiment . . .' Croll was even whiter now, positively cream-faced in fact, but his brain still seemed to be working. 'Wait. Why have . . . none of the . . . tomato juice . . . boxes . . . collapsed? Liquid should . . . be gone . . .'

He turned, swayed, and to Ken's enormous disgust slumped over the console and its red button. Evidently the voltage had been turned up yet again, to the extent of simulating a gigantic fire-breathing dragon with teeth like Cleopatra's Needle that bit you in the bum. Ken lost control of his consciousness and stomach more or less simultaneously.

. . . Someone, somewhere, had for quite a long and drawn-out time been trying to wake him with their knocking.

'Are you all right?' A uniformed MOD policeman was shaking his shoulder. It had not previously occurred to Ken that this could be a beautiful sight. Another uniform was bending over something blobby on the floor beyond the control panel. 'I just came round to warn that it's site locking-up time, and . . . Are you all right?'

A pretty sodding silly question, Ken thought, considering the lumpy crimson outbreak that spread down his clothes and across the floor, making the green tiles one red. Who would have thought the old man . . .? Enough quotations already.

'It's not mine,' Ken articulated with great and spurious clarity. 'It's his.' Then he blacked out again.

'Do sit down,' said Fortmayne next day. It was the same committee room.

'No thanks,' Ken replied firmly. 'I have injuries of a delicate nature.' He had spent the night in a hospital bed on his stomach, and his jacket was blotchy and smelly beyond repair (all the perfumes of Araby were clearly not going to do a lot of good), but he looked forward to explaining everything to the remnants of the briefing group. His finest hour. 'The first point that struck me in my investigation was a tiny one, but . . .'

'No need to cover most of what happened,' Fortmayne said hastily. 'Dr Croll was a good enough scientist to record yesterday's lab session. We played the tape.'

'Lucky thing for you,' Rossiter put in. 'Otherwise you'd be nicked for assault by unknown means on the old loony. He's in intensive care, you know. But they couldn't find a mark on him.'

'Never mind that. How precisely did you conclude there's no entropy ray? Was it a valid logical process? I want a sound explanation,' said Fortmayne, poised for disbelief.

'Oh, good old Occam's razor, I suppose. I wandered round the site yesterday and sort of got the impression that, well, whenever I saw something driving out it purred along, and everything coming in was all clanking and wheezy. Greasy . . . that is, a DPR associate I'm not at liberty to name . . . once told me that for the car-pool fiddle you need a rich stupid firm that doesn't audit its inventory too carefully. You take the company cars round to a bent garage, and swap the engines and tyres and things for clapped-out ones, and pocket a nice fee every time. Then the company pays to overhaul them or replaces them, a good bit sooner than it would have, and after a while you can do it again. Works best with a big motor pool, like in a place with nearly twelve thousand on the strength. Very profitable business, entropy.'

There was an embarrassed little silence as everyone made a point of not looking at the chair where, today, Brownjohn was not sitting. Apparently he'd been psychic enough to detect something in the wind.

Theoretical Physics said, 'How extremely uninteresting, though very much as one might have predicted. I must confess that I myself am more curious about what happened pertaining to Dr Croll.'

'Ye-es,' said Rossiter. 'Security angles there too, mate. Not meaning any offence, we indented for a low-grade paranorm thick, not some kind of super voodoo killer.'

'The DPR has its secrets,' Ken said, preening a little and laying a finger alongside his nose. 'I can just inform you that – very nearly too damn late – I remembered Dr Croll had been sinking pints in the Mushroom Cloud at lunchtime, and therefore he'd still have alcoholic stuff trickling through his ducts. His veins. That left him at a disadvantage. There was a leak in his security.'

Something seemed to be dawning on Fortmayne, who now looked distinctly unwell. 'And you . . .?'

'Some people,' said Ken mysteriously, 'will swallow anything.'

He didn't feel it necessary to explain that all those shocks and horrors and suggestibility drugs had, overnight, jolted loose his Talent in just the sort of small change Croll had wished. Well, almost.

After that last bloody awful drink – a sort of ultimate hangover cure – his subconscious seemed to have sworn off and shifted its attention to more practical desires than beer refills. Maybe down there in the basement of his mind there was an unexpected stratum of good taste, and this was taking no risks that he might now decide to emigrate and ponce around New York night-life in tuxedo and scarlet-lined cape, under some stupid name like Bloodfeast.

Small change, indeed. As he left the duct-infested committee room, with teeth clenched askew and one eye unobtrusively shut, he could feel his pockets growing heavier with a steady leakage of 20p and 50p and £1 coins. They were all permanent civil servants. They could afford it.

So it wasn't too bad when Marcia haughtily red-pencilled all his most cherished expenses: replacement jacket, soothing Num-Tum indigestion salts, perfumes of Araby, etcetera. But he winced anyway, having failed to brace himself for her final, crushing remark, 'And what's more, you *still* can't spell entopry.'

LORIC, Deputy Secretary with General Responsibility, Dept. of Paranormal Resources since 1976; peerages disclaimed, 1962; *b* 1940;[1] *s* of Sir Massingham Cholmondeley-Fitz-Conybere and The Honourable Valentine Sissingham (both *d* 1940);[2] *m* 1st, 1965, Caroline Pennyfeather (marr. diss. 1967); no *c*; 2nd, 1967, Madeleleine St Christophe (*d* 1971); no *c*. *Educ*: Eton; Christ Church, Oxford. Entered Diplomatic Service 1964; Cultural Attache, Port-au-Prince, 1965–7; Cultural Attache, Prague, 1968; Cultural Attache, Warsaw, 1969; Cultural Attache, Washington, 1971–5. *Publications*: Pharmacology, Death and Social Control in Rural Environments, 1966; The Heritage of Rabbi Lowe, 1969; Three Students from Cracow: Polish Influences on Johannes of Wurtemburg, 1971; Essays in the Secret Learning,[3] 1978. *Recreation*: herb gardening, arachnology, superiority. *Clubs*: Athenaeum, Travellers'.

---

1   The editors cannot be responsible for the accuracy of this information; *Burke's* gives a date some twelve centuries earlier, while *Debrett's* gives 1938.
2   Genealogical authorities generally agree on Loric's parentage, which he has neither confirmed nor denied; in the 1950s, the Court of Chancery declared him to be the Conybere heir, but he took advantage of the changes in the law introduced by The Right Honourable Tony Benn to disclaim his peerages, stating he had no reason to believe this assumption to be correct. *Debrett's* follows the precedent of the Greystoke case, in regarding the inexpert opinions of the subject as irrelevant in matters of this kind.
3   Withdrawn 1980.

THIRD PERSON SINGULAR

Liz Holliday

She had hair like molten gold and eyes the colour of whisky, and the first time I saw her I knew she would burn me.

I pretended to wash glasses while I watched Ian Solomon play games with yet another of his women. She was dark, with shadowed eyes and red, red lips: and as brittle as all the rest, by the sound of her laughter. I should have been so lucky.

The door opened, and *she* came in like she had been blown on the winter wind. Just then, someone put some old jazz saxophone on the jukebox. So that's how I remember it: her all golden, with the dim lights and cool music, and rain fracturing the neon behind her.

She looked around and smiled, and it was as if the world held its breath and the sun had come out at midnight just for me.

I know it wasn't really like that. I know it. If I'm honest I'll admit I had fallen in love. Again.

Out of the corner of my eye I noticed the other barman, Steve, grinning at me.

She came over to the bar and asked me for a white wine. Her voice was husky; my hands shook as I poured the drink. I tried to hold her with my eyes, but she looked over my shoulder, as if I simply were not there.

Love me, love *me*, I thought at her, trying to make that tiny synaptic jolt at the back of the brain that means my

Talent has worked. Making people love each other is the only Talent I have, but it doesn't work for me. Neither does the natural method, come to that.

Her fingers brushed my hand as she took her money. I shivered with pleasure that was almost painful. Love me, I thought again, but of course she simply smiled and left. There was no third person to complete the arc my talent describes.

When she went over to Solomon's table, I realized I had been expecting it all along.

I watched. Of course I did. Watching Solomon was what I was being paid to do, after all. Like me, he was a freelance: he programmed computers; I programmed brains. The Department of Paranormal Resources thought he had put something a bit devious into a computer programme he had written for them. He had been siphoning data out of their North London office. They had found the leak, but let it go in hope of following it up the chain. Now it appeared that Solomon was going to sell it to the highest bidder.

They were paying me to do something even more devious back to him.

'Susannah,' Solomon said. He was as dark and sleek as any rat, and he did not sound at all surprised to see her. Susannah. Something clicked in from my briefing: this was the wife he cheated on.

His lady friend stood up. She picked up her jacket, her flowered umbrella. 'I'd better go, sweetheart,' she said. She bent to kiss him, on the cheek, but lovingly.

'Don't bother,' Susannah said. 'I wasn't stopping.' She put her wine on the table, turned and left.

'That bird you had your eye on is in again,' Steve said.

'Sorry I'm late,' I said, hoping he would not push for an explanation. I could hardly tell him that I had spent half the night sitting in a car outside the hotel Solomon had taken the dark-haired woman to.

'You want to clear the tables?' Steve asked.

I nodded. He grinned at me and winked, but we both knew he was a sheep in wolf's clothing. At least that was what Barry, the landlord, called him.

Susannah was sitting in a corner seat. A business report jostled for space on the table with an uneaten ploughman's lunch and a half-empty wine glass. Funny, I had forgotten they told me she was successful in her own right, a director of a medium-sized PR company.

She stared out of the window, ignoring the report and her food alike. She was wearing sunglasses despite the dull weather. They could not hide the shadows round her eyes, much less the bruise high up on her cheekbone.

I knew Solomon had gone home after he left his girl-friend. The Department had told me he was a womanizer, but this had not been in the briefing. I slapped the cloth down on the next table a little harder than I needed to, wishing very much that it was Solomon's face.

'You all right, love?' was all I said.

'Yes,' she answered. Then: 'No, not really.' A sad little laugh came out of her. 'Some days are just like that, you know.'

'I know,' I said. 'If you want someone to talk to, I'm allowed. First-class honours in listening to customer's troubles, University of Life, me.'

She laughed. It still sounded shaky, but better than before, and I was pleased.

'Seriously,' I went on, hoping I wasn't pushing my luck.

'Seriously it's a very old story, but not one I think I ought to . . .' she stopped, looking past me.

Steve tapped me on the shoulder. 'Phone call, Pete. Name of Marcia.'

I looked at Susannah. She was picking at her ploughman's.

'Sorry, mate,' Steve said. I walked away.

'Peter Morgan?' Marcia said. I was working directly with Head Office, to be sure there were no leaks. I'd never have guessed it from Marcia's voice, however. She sounded as dozy as the one from the Camden office. 'Message from God for you,' she giggled. 'Watch out for Louise Cranmere, she'll be visiting you soon.' The line went dead.

So that was that. Louise Cranmere would turn up and I would make Solomon fall in love with her. She was an exxer, someone who could negate any Talent that was used on her: so Solomon would be in love with her, but not the other way round. She would persuade Solomon to talk, or find the evidence we needed. The case would be closed.

Susannah would do whatever wives do when their husbands are in prison. And I would never see her again.

'Solomon should be here any minute,' I said. Louise Cranmere stared at me over the top of her glass. The orange juice looked as cool as she did, tall and slim and very icy. She sipped it. 'He won't be here long, just a quick one before he heads off for the evening. Usually brings whoever it is back here though.'

'You don't like our Mr Solomon, do you?' Louise asked me. She shifted slightly on her barstool.

'No. Not much,' I said. I knew better than to trust her. If the Department got so much as a hint of my feelings for Susannah, I'd be off the Temps register for good. Policy. As for Louise, I didn't even know if she was one of us, or whether the Department had brought her in from the Odd Squad or from MI something or other: so I had no idea what she would do if she found out.

Still, she seemed nice enough. 'Listen,' I said. 'Our boy Solomon seems to be a nastier piece of work than the Department thought: beats his wife as well as running around in front of her back, that sort of thing.'

'Thanks for the warning, Pete,' she answered, and took a long sip of orange. 'But you aren't the only Talented individual around, you know?'

I nodded. Just then, Solomon came in. Susannah was with him. She looked even paler than she had the day before, though the bruise had begun to fade.

I moved off down the bar: no point in letting him think Louise knew me. Besides, I was having difficulty trying to keep my composure. This wasn't something I had planned for.

I was about to break Susannah's heart.

Solomon came up to the bar. He headed straight for Louise, just as we had hoped he would. The man was as predictable as rain on a summer's day.

'Excuse me, miss,' he said to Louise. Susannah was hovering behind him. Her mouth tightened with anxiety. She was still the most beautiful woman in the bar.

It occurred to me that if I loved her — really *loved* her — all I had to do to make her happy was to make Solomon fall for her again. He would stay home then. And in the nature of things, she would never love me anyway.

I couldn't allow that to get in my way. The North London office had been conducting experiments in using telekinetics to calibrate orbital laser defences; it was information that could have industrial applications in space stations' technology. Half-a-dozen emerging nuclear powers would pay highly for that information, as would several multinational conglomerates; the implications for world peace, and the world economy, were staggering. We *had* to find out who his contacts were.

Solomon smiled at Louise. She turned towards him.

They hardly needed me at all. I went over to them, and placed my hands on the bar, one near each of them.

'What can I do for you?' I asked.

Between the question and the reply, I let my Talent work. Pleasure/pain jerked through me, and then I was in Louise, in Solomon. Images cascaded down, around me, through me, like a waterfall of light.

'What can you love, Solomon?' I demanded of the twisting braids of light.

A woman's hand came down, touched his face gently. It drew back, and by the time it reached the top of its arc, it belonged to his father. It was holding a belt; light glinted off the buckle and pain flashed through him as it came down on his back, and came down, and came down.

He looked up into his father's face, smiling. The world inverted. He looked down at a face, as androgynous as an angel's and not at all beautiful: his own, Susannah's, his mother's, Louise's, the young boy he had been, every woman he had ever made love to. His father's face, staring up at him. He put out his hand and I felt his desire, his hope that this one might love him, might let him love it.

The face coarsened. Make-up painted it in harlequin bright colours. It smiled. He tried to touch it, and it turned away. He hit it and . . .

The stranger he must learn to call daddy, with his arm around his mother, standing outside the seaside cottage that would become home.

. . . a bruise blossomed like a flower on the cheekbone of the face . . .

His mother, sitting crying at the kitchen table, elbows planted on the blue formica, hands wrapped around a coffee mug. The sweet sickly stink of gin.

. . . the top lip split . . .

His wedding day. Susannah radiant in ivory silk and

lace. His wedding ring as heavy as a length of chain. 'Forever' tightening around his heart.

. . . and the left eye puckered closed.

Susannah — all the women he has had — laughing at him, turning from him, making him small. Leaving him. Not listening to him. His life as a succession of doors closing, with him trapped on the inside of a small room. Silence and the sound of sobbing.

He takes the face in his hands, squeezes the cheek-bones, watches in delight as tears start in the eyes.

Lying in bed as the sounds of his new daddy beating his mother shatter the night.

Tears smearing the make-up and the face turning away from him, escaping his heavy hands.

A morning, with the smells of stale beer and vomit and old tobacco. Shouting. His father's upraised fist, and his mother's scared eyes. But he's older now. When it begins he attacks his father. He is strong, and he knows that bravery lies in overcoming fear. He punches the older man in the stomach, the face. Turns to his mother to comfort her, and she screams at him, runs to his father. Orders him out of the house.

A voice, a woman's voice, a boyish treble, begging him to stop.

Susannah weeping under him, begging him to stop as his hand comes down hard on her face. His Susannah. All his women.

His fist smashing down again and again until his body spasms in rhythm with it and pleasure jerks through him.

She lies there shaking, trembles at his touch. But it's over now, and he strokes her cheek with the side of one heavy thumb, and whispers 'I'm sorry, I'm sorry.'

I stood again in the torrent of images. I called upon Louise, and she showed me her life, her needs. There was a military childhood, her father a daunting, mostly absent, figure. Her mother, chasing valium with vodka and hiding affair after affair. Louise at thirteen, fifteen, eighteen, slowly piecing it together. Her first lover, and a secret private abortion she never told her parents about. There was the police career, where she never quite struck the balance between being the Ice Queen and one of the boys. The cold marriage to a civil service grey man, who couldn't hold on to her respect, let alone her love. The discovery of her Talent and the hard-won transfer to the Odd Squad. The too-civilized separation. The divorce, soon to be finalized . . .

I took up strands from her life and Solomon's, and braided them into a single thread. Solomon would see in Louise the distant, unjudgemental lover he thought he had been searching for all his life. Louise, if she let my work stand, would find Solomon the perfect father-figure, demanding but ultimately pleasable.

They might not find the answers they sought in each other. But they would think they did, and in the end there would be no difference.

All of that faded. I stared at my hands, flat on the bar in front of me. Light bronzed the reddish hairs on my forearms. I tried to imagine my hands smashing into a defenceless face. I failed, though I've been in plenty of fist fights in my time.

'— have a Grolsch, please,' Solomon said. He smiled at Louise. She whispered something, and touched his sleeve.

I banged the bottle down on the counter, with the upended glass over it. Solomon took it. He led Louise by the hand to a corner table.

Susannah came to the bar. I had thought she might leave, was glad for her when she didn't. She ordered a vodka, no ice, and downed it in two gulps. Then she ordered another.

The bar got busy enough then that I had to serve other people. I worried that she would leave without my having a chance to speak to her.

Eventually, though, I got my chance. Her face was a mask of tears. Behind her, Louise and Solomon laughed and smiled at each other, and ignored everything else.

I hated Solomon. I hated Louise. But not as much as I hated myself.

Susannah ordered another vodka. As I held the glass to the optic, Steve said, 'That's her fourth tonight. Much more and you'll be carrying her home. You should be so lucky!'

'You keep your filthy thoughts to yourself,' I answered, hoping it sounded like banter but meaning every word of it. 'She's having a bad time of it.'

I put the glass down in front of her. She picked it up and slid some coins across the counter. The liquid in the glass sloshed as her hands shook.

'No more, now, after this one,' I said.

'What the hell is it to do with you?' she asked me. Her eyes were the colour of whisky, and they burned.

I love you, I thought at her. *Love me.* But of course nothing happened. 'You'd be better off talking to me than your glass,' I said.

'All right,' she said. 'I'll tell you. My husband over there, he's gone off with some woman he only met tonight. He's never done anything like this to me before. Now do I have your permission to get drunk?'

'Never?' I asked. I could hardly believe she didn't know what Solomon was like.

Behind her, Solomon got up to go. Louise was a little way ahead of him. He put his hand on her waist, very solicitous.

'Not like this,' Susannah said. She gulped her drink, then made a funny little whimpering sound in the back of her throat. 'Not in front of me.'

Then she really was crying, her hands over her face, fingers knotted in the bright hair. Her shoulders shook. I took her hands in mine, wished I could hold her.

Solomon reached the door. He glanced over at us. As he saw what was happening, his look turned to one of hatred. Knowing what I knew of him, I understood that. I was taking what he thought he owned, and he would not forgive.

I took Susannah home that night. We walked the quiet midnight streets hardly talking, touching not at all. The house, when she brought me to it, was dark. I was glad of that; I had been afraid Solomon might have taken Louise there.

She went up the steps to the front door. The porch light caught her cheekbone, still smeared from all her crying. Hesitantly, I reached out and touched her face. It was a gesture that brought back a false memory: Solomon reaching down, touching the places of pain he had just created, full of instant, cheap regret. Realizing, I took my hand back, but she had already pulled away.

'Don't,' she said. 'I'm sorry. I can't.' Something like that, anyway.

And then the door opened and closed, and she was gone.

A couple of days went by before anything else happened. I phoned head office, but Marcia had no news of Louise. I suggested she put me through to someone higher up. You would think I had asked for a direct line to God, because she became as hysterical as a Mormon on the eve of Armageddon. In the end she put me through to Comfrey, the Chief Executive Officer in charge of Odd Squad liaison. All he would say was that I should stick to orders: no surveillance, nothing that might make Solomon suspicious of Louise; let her contact me or the office.

Then Susannah walked in, which was good for my heart if not for my nerves. It was just before afternoon closing. A little of her old spark seemed to have come back, and I was glad of that. She seemed nervous, though.

'Not at work?' I said, by way of an opening line.

'TRM Promotions won't fall apart if I take the afternoon off.' She grinned. 'It's called having a good PA.'

'All right for some,' I said, meaning the PA, though Susannah didn't realize it.

'I think I'd like a drink,' she said.

'Vodka?'

'Perrier. Although I must admit, a stiff drink might help.' She laughed nervously.

I opened the bottle and poured the water over ice, added a slice of lemon. Her eyes never left me, as if I was some kind of wild animal.

Condensation beaded the side of the glass as I handed it to her. My palms were sweaty.

'The other night . . .' she began, then stopped, as if she was deciding how to finish the sentence. '. . . I was thinking about what I said. I mean, if you still wanted to, maybe we could see each other? Or something?'

I smiled. I could think of nothing to say that would not scare her off. So I took her hand and, with mock formality, kissed it as gallantly as any eighteenth-century fop. Susannah giggled like a child, and suddenly we were holding hands and grinning at each other over the counter.

And that, of course, was when Louise walked in.

To do her credit, she went and sat up at the far end of the bar, away from us. Susannah went red. She pulled her hands from mine and left.

'Very nice,' Louise said. 'You want to explain that to the Department, or shall I?'

'I won't let it hurt the job, so what do you care about it?'

Louise laughed. 'I'm the one on the front line here, remember? I need to feel as safe as I can to do my job. That –' she cocked her head towards the door '– makes me feel bad. Stop it.'

'Things not as you expected, Louise? I tried to warn you.'

'Quite the opposite. Ian has been wonderful.' She seemed coldly radiant, like the moon. 'Quite wonderful.'

Too wonderful, I thought. 'You were supposed to undo what I did,' I said.

'I did,' she answered. She slid from the stool and straightened her skirt. 'But chemistry's chemistry, after all.'

I walked with her to the door. One more try. 'Be careful –'

'Oh I will,' she said. 'I won't let it hurt the job. Not in the end. And if you don't tell, I won't.'

That night I hardly slept. In the morning, I phoned the Department.

'Solomon is a bigger bastard than your briefing gave him credit for,' I said to Comfrey when Marcia finally put me through to him. 'He's a functional sadist, and Louise seems to be in love with him, whether you want to blame my Talent or not. That puts her in danger.'

'WDS Cranmere is a trained operative who knows her business. Have you told her of your suspicions?' he said in his plummy voice.

I admitted that I had. When he continued, he sounded as if he had just discovered the plums were stuffed with razorblades. 'Then if she wants help, she'll doubtless ask for it herself. Meanwhile, if you are still concerned, I'd suggest you write a report. In quadruplicate.'

The line went dead.

I thought about Louise, and what would happen to my Department retainer if she decided to stir it over me and Susannah, and did nothing more.

That aside, I floated through the next few weeks. I saw Susannah frequently. At first we were very cautious, perhaps me more so than her: lunch occasionally, always very far away from Camden Town, or perhaps an hour together in the evening. Gradually, though, I began to believe her when she said Solomon was scarcely ever at home, that when he was he took no interest in her. We grew bolder then. We went to the cinema, theatre, Ronnie Scott's. There were long walks in the park, and quiet nights in, talking about books, films, art.

There was the night we spent together.

In all that time, I hardly heard from Louise. She came into the bar once. She seemed distracted: I thought she might be in love, with my help or without it.

She wouldn't answer me when I asked. Cold as the moon, as always, and as distant.

Comfrey phoned me one day. They'd had intelligence reports that Paratech International was using techniques that could only have been developed using data filched from the DPR. It meant that Solomon had completed his auction, and passed on the information. All we could do now was try to get enough evidence to nail him and Paratech.

The DPR had decided, Comfrey said, to continue as before. Louise was to maintain cover, with all the backup we could provide, but nothing that would compromise her position. I offered to return to surveillance duties, and was glad when Comfrey turned the idea down as too risky.

All it really meant to me was that Solomon was busy, and my nights were free: free to dream of Susannah, if nothing else.

We went to Regent's Park one rainy day. We shared my umbrella and stood on the muddy grass by the Zoo railings, watching the wallabies huddle miserably under the bushes.

I promised her that when the weather got warmer I would take her to the Zoo. She liked that.

I walked her nearly all the way home, then left her. It was our usual routine in case Solomon was in, but it never failed to leave me feeling bereft.

Much later, when I was dozing on my bed at home, listening to cool blue jazz – Susannah music – and trying to imagine a happy ending for the two of us, there came a knock at the door.

It was Louise. Even as she came in, I could see there was something wrong. She moved stiffly, holding her head as if her neck hurt. She sat down on the edge of the bed without taking her coat off. When she looked up at me, I saw that her nose was swollen down one side, and that her other cheek was grazed, a bloody patch like a strawberry birthmark. There was a lump on her forehead half the size of my fist.

'Solomon did this,' I said.

She nodded without speaking. I turned down the music and put the kettle on. We sat in silence while it boiled slowly on the Baby-Belling stove.

I pushed a mug into her hands. They shook, and coffee slopped on to the nylon bedspread. I ignored it.

'I should have told someone,' she said at last. 'But it would have looked so bad on my record.' I must have looked a bit surprised, because when she continued, her voice held the faintest trace of contempt. 'Oh, I know it's different for you DPR people, but in the Odd Squad we value our Talents. They're our lives.'

'Yeah,' I said, forgetting for a second that I felt sorry for her. 'Well, we can't all be monomaniacs. You'd better tell me what happened. Just in case the Department needs to know.'

'First time out and I screw up, that's what,' she said. 'Ian — Solomon — didn't stop his womanizing. I mean, he did at first. In the beginning, it was wonderful, all the things you're taught to dream of, but never really expect to find — at least if you're a woman. Then he started breaking dates, or I wouldn't be able to get past his secretary.

'I thought maybe he was seeing his contact. Even that he was trying to spare his wife. One night, I followed him. I had to for my own satisfaction, never mind what I owed the job . . .' Her voice tailed off.

'Do you love him?' I asked her, after a moment.

She put the coffee mug down on the lino. 'Yes,' she said, so softly I could scarcely hear. She pushed her hands through her hair, which the rain had turned to rat's tails.

'You did undo my Talent, though, didn't you?' I was hoping she would say no: that would give us an easy way out.

'Oh yes.' She laughed shortly. 'I'm good at following instructions. Anyway, I was saying, I followed him. He was seeing women, lots of them. Some I recognized from your reports, others were new. When I challenged him, he said he loved me. And after that I didn't see him or hear from him for two weeks.

'Then today I went to his house. I'd promised not to do that, not to ring him there nor do anything to make his life difficult. Susannah wasn't there. I suppose I have you to thank for that.'

I nodded, remembering Susannah smiling at me through the rain.

'We argued. Oh, how we argued. And then he hit me. I couldn't believe it at first, but he made me. He hit me and hit me.' She stopped then. I thought she would cry, but she didn't. 'Afterwards – when he'd finished – he was more tender than ever. *He said he loved me.* We made love, you know, and it was as good as it's ever been. He kept telling me how sorry he was, how he hadn't meant it. I believed him. I would have done anything to have that moment of tenderness again.

'Only now I'm here, and I feel so dirty. So betrayed. Not by him. By me. I let him. I *let* him do this to me. I mean, I'm trained. I've taken on worse than him when I was in uniform, and some of them were armed, too.'

'Look, let me phone the Department. You needn't go back. Nobody would expect you to. If they'd known what he was like, they'd never have put you in there in the first place.'

'No!' she said. 'I can handle him. I won't leave without finishing what I've started.'

'You need counselling. For one thing, you ought to let them psi-che you out, just in case you didn't ex my Talent properly. You do realize that's the most likely explanation?'

'No it isn't. I just happen to have fallen in love with him regardless. He's a good man, Peter. Really, he's kind and gentle . . .'

'He just gets off on beating up his lovers.'

'I made him angry, spying on him.'

'Bullshit. Do you want to know how many times he's hit Susannah? Shall I tell you about the time he broke two of her ribs? The time he opened her head with a monkey wrench? I saw it all when I went into him. He hit you *because* he loves you. Because that's what his screwed-up little subconscious thinks love means. I tried to warn you, dammit.'

'Well then, he needs help. I can help him, at least until I get the contact's name.'

'His deprived childhood isn't your concern. He'll get help all right, when we put him inside. I'm calling the Department, whether you like it or not.'

'Oh do what you want!' Louise said.

She left, banging the door behind her.

When she had gone, I phoned the Department. There was no one there, but I left a message on the answering machine. I was pretty certain what the result would be.

I was right.

The next morning, Comfrey phoned. He had a message from God himself this time: Louise was a trained agent; she knew what she was up against; the Department's only concern was that she might let her feelings get in the way of her job.

That night, I started surveillance on Solomon again.

The tiger paced back and forth. The weak winter sunlight barred the floor of his cage with pale shadows. Susannah put her arm through mine.

'Do you think,' she asked me suddenly, 'do you think he knows he's a captive? I mean, I wonder if he remembers being free?'

'I doubt it,' I answered her. 'They don't have the same kind of recall that we do. Not unless something happens to trigger a memory.'

Somewhere, a taped guide droned monotonously about feeding and mating habits. The tiger paused in his pacing, and flicked an ear, showing off the white, the warning spot.

'What would you like to see next?' I asked.

'Something too small to know it's in a cage,' Susannah replied.

It should have been a good day. It had begun well, almost warm, a day to let you know that spring is on the way. I had woken fresh, despite having spent most of the night before trailing Solomon from one squalid assignation to the next.

Somewhere before I fell asleep I had come to a decision: it was quite obvious that Louise was never going to get the information we needed to put Solomon away. So I would have to do it, somehow. But when I woke up, the thought had drifted away, leaving behind it only a residue of the good humour that comes from decisiveness.

So when Susannah had come into the Rising Sun at lunch time, I had taken the afternoon off and persuaded her to do the same. As I said, it should have been a good day. Yet she seemed quiet, almost withdrawn. She would hardly look at me, and when she spoke it was at right angles to the conversation.

We stepped from sunlight into the half-dark of the Charles Clore Pavilion. Susannah stopped in front of a galago cage. The light from it gilded her face but left the rest of her in shadow. I thought for a moment she was smiling, but then the light caught her tears. The bush-baby stared back at us, unblinking.

'What's wrong?' I asked.

'I was thinking, even he knows he's in a cage and can't get out. It's sad, not to be able to escape.'

'He's probably better off. He's got food and warmth, and nothing trying to kill him.'

'Yes, but to have to stay when you want to go –' She put her hand flat on the glass.

'You don't have to stay, you know. With Ian.'

'Should I let you take me away from all this?'

'That's my line. But if you like, we can do that.'

'Yes,' she said. The word hung on the air between us. I held my breath, afraid it would burst like a bubble. Then she smiled, and we were both giggling like children, and holding on to each other.

I don't remember anything much of the journey back

to her house. Certainly we didn't plan anything. Mostly, I think, we were too excited and too scared that Solomon would come back before we got away. Also, I was full of the idea that she loved me. Not that she had ever, ever said as much, but it was obvious. If she was going to leave Solomon to come with me, if she could look at me the way she did, if she could sound the way she did when she spoke my name ... obvious. It was all the things I had ever dreamed of, but never really expected to find.

I thought that when I walked through the front door, and it brought Louise to mind. I wondered what the Department would make of it, but it didn't really bother me. Leaving Louise to Solomon's loving care was something else, though.

While Susannah went upstairs to pack, I took my chance. I went from room to room, looking for his contact list. Just as I was beginning to think I wouldn't find anything before I ran out of time, I found his study. It was tall, with thick-leaved plants stark against white walls, and black venetian blinds. His diary was out on the desk. There was nothing of use in it, as I had expected. Nothing in the drawers, nothing under the blotter, nothing under the computer or any of the executive toys on the desk. Susannah called my name. Her voice sent champagne bubbles through my blood, but I couldn't leave without finding something, anything. I began to understand why evidence sometimes gets fabricated.

I checked the desk one more time. And found it: not a notebook after all, but a computer disk, sellotaped to the underside of the top drawer. I slipped it into my jacket pocket and went upstairs.

I found Susannah in her room. She was staring out of the window. Behind her, the suitcase lay open on the bed. It was almost empty.

'What's the matter?' I asked her. But I knew. I knew.

'I can't come with you,' she replied. She would not face me.

'But you said –'

'I know. I thought I could do it, but I can't.' She turned to me. Her face was as hard and expressionless as a porcelain mask, as if she had gone past pain, past sorrow.

'Don't be stupid,' I said. I went to the wardrobe and pulled a couple of dresses off the rail. I threw them on to the case. 'Come on. Ian will be back soon. We can discuss this outside.'

'I said no, Peter.' She stared at me. Her eyes were the colour of whisky, and they burned me. 'Look at you. You're behaving just like he would.'

'I'm sorry,' I said, instantly contrite. Then, after a moment, I said the only thing that made any sense: 'Why?'

'I don't love you,' she said. 'I thought it wouldn't matter, as long as you were kind to me. But it does.'

'I see,' I said. Emptiness filled me, stretched out before me, made me part of itself. 'I ought to go.'

'You're a good man, Peter. I shouldn't have done this to you.'

I said nothing. My lack of understanding went beyond words.

'When I met you,' she said, 'I thought you would be my way out. I mean, I'm sitting here, in my little cage with Ian. I have food and shelter. Anything I want, and all I have to do is let him poke at me from time to time, like a little boy with a stick at the Zoo.'

'What are you telling me, Susannah?' I asked. 'That you need his money? You with that 35-thousand-a-year, high-profile, let's-do-lunch job of yours? Don't make me laugh.'

'No!' She rubbed the bridge of her nose. 'It isn't that. He gives me security. Status. Safety, I suppose.'

'Safety! He half kills you, and you think you're safe?'

'In a way. You see, I know what will make him angry, and I know how far he'll go. With anyone else I'd have to start learning the rules again.'

'So you'll stay with him because you're afraid of finding anything better.'

'I told you it's a cage, didn't I, Peter?' She laughed shortly. 'Now the cage door is open, and here I sit, frightened to go out in the big, wide world.'

'Don't be afraid,' I said. I knew I didn't quite understand, but I had to try.

'If I went with you I would be swapping one cage for another. Can you see that, Peter?'

'No,' I said. 'I can't.'

'I don't love you. I don't even know why not.' She smiled, sadly. 'You're kind, you're attractive. You even make me laugh. But it just doesn't work for me.'

I knew what it was: the legacy of my Talent. The psychs said it was something to do with hormonal balances, the way my body created pheromones. I didn't understand it, but I understood loneliness, that door that always seemed to be shutting in my face.

'So I'm a worse bet than a bastard like Solomon, am I?' I had no other answer to my pain than anger. A car pulled up outside. 'Maybe I should beat you up like he does. Maybe that's what you need!'

'Don't!' she said, and I knew I had gone too far. The gate banged. 'You see one thing. You see that he hits me, and you think that's all there is. But he's part of the fabric of my life. I learned to love him before I ever learned that he would hurt me.'

'And you still love him?' A key grated in a lock downstairs. A door slammed. All my anger and my hurt contracted into a small tight place at the centre of me. I knew I would have to look at it later, but not then. Not in front of Susannah. Or Solomon.

'I don't know. I know I'll leave him one day. But not to go with you, Peter. It wouldn't be fair.'

Heavy footsteps sounded on the stairs. 'Because you don't love me.' There was nothing else left to say.

The door opened behind me.

'Well, this is charming,' Solomon said. I turned to face him. 'A lovers' tryst. Or a lovers' quarrel?'

'Peter was just leaving, Ian,' Susannah said.

'And you're going with him?' He went over to the bed and pushed the dresses into the suitcase. 'How nice.'

For a moment I thought he had overplayed his hand. I thought I had won.

'No,' she said. 'I decided to stay.'

'Good,' Solomon said. 'Because you know I wouldn't have let you leave, don't you?'

'Why not, for God's sake, Solomon?' The complex undertow of their relationship was quite beyond me. All I could see was that it was dragging Susannah under. 'You have Louise. You have half-a-dozen other women. Why do you need Susannah?'

He crossed the room and grabbed her. 'Because she's mine, and I don't let go of what I own.' His hand shifted on her arm. His fingers left red stripes when he moved them.

'Let go of her, you bastard,' I shouted. 'She isn't staying.'

'I won't go with you, Peter,' Susannah said.

'Why not, for pity's sake? You know what he's going to do to you.'

'I don't want to leave him. All I want is for him to stop hurting me. I'm sorry if you don't understand.'

'I don't. I don't understand why you want him and not me. All I want is to love you, to make you happy.' My anger was suddenly a thing that burned at the centre of me. Its heat left no room for any more complex thought.

Suddenly, I believed everything I'd ever heard about women who like a bit of rough, women who ask for it. If she wanted it, she could have it. I would use my Talent to make sure of it. After all, she deserved all she got: her and Ian, locked in their little cage forever, tearing each other's heart out.

Then he said, 'Maybe she wants a man, not a snivelling ball-less do-gooder. You wouldn't be able to give her what she needs even if you had a mind to.'

I turned and left. Not because I stopped wanting to punish Susannah, but because to do that would mean giving Solomon what he wanted. And I wouldn't do it. There had to be another way.

I kept my anger under control until I got home. Then it exploded, and I beat one of my pillows until it burst. I couldn't be bothered to pick the feathers up, so I sat among them while I stared at the television and got very drunk.

At some point I remembered the disk I had lifted from Solomon. At another I wondered if Susannah had spotted my own tendency to violence, and rejected me because of it.

Neither seemed to matter by that time.

'It's up to you, Louise,' I said. I had woken with a hangover. Trying to deal with Louise over a greasy-spoon breakfast had done nothing to cure it. Even after three coffees, my mouth still felt as if it was stuffed with sand and glue. I signalled the waitress for a refill, and let it scald my mouth before I continued. 'Either you come with me when I take the disk in, or I go alone. Your choice.'

'I don't care what you think,' she said. Early morning sunlight, hardly dulled by the cafe's dirty window, picked out the half-healed grazes on her cheek. I wondered how

Susannah was. 'Everything's fine. All I need is a bit more time.'

My head throbbed with pain. I had woken up feeling like someone had taken a tyre iron to it, and nothing had improved it since. 'Prove it,' I said. 'Wear a spy-eye and let me track you.'

She trailed her finger through a bit of spilled sugar, making patterns on the formica tabletop. 'All right. If it's the only way to get you off my back.'

'And you'll try to force his hand, get him to admit whatever it is he's up to?'

'I said yes.' She swept the side of her hand through the sugar, scattering the pattern. 'But no disk, Peter. I won't have them thinking you're doing my job.'

'The Odd Squadder can't bear to be beaten by the Temp, hey?'

'You would have to put it like that.'

'I'd have thought you'd be glad of anything that would get you away from that bastard.'

'You know something? So would I.' She smiled a bitter smile. 'Until I'm with him.' She stood up. 'Promise me, you won't do anything with the disk, Peter.' She left before I could reply.

'No,' I said to her retreating back. 'No.' I don't suppose she heard me.

Later, I sat in the reception of the Department's head office in Whitehall, drinking instant coffee and trying not to stare at the portraits.

I handed the disk to Marcia. She gave me a drop-dead look when I got too close watching her label it and log it in. I'm not sure whether she thought I thought she was an airhead — which I did, since they're all much the same — or whether she could smell the remains of last night's binge.

She seemed really put out when I wouldn't just leave it

with her, too. What the hell. I paced the room like an expectant father. I must have looked as though my wife had just had quins when Comfrey gave me the news.

The disk was a fake. Blank. Dummy.

For all her promises, Louise did not see Solomon that night, or even that week. Instead, I trailed Solomon from work to one dreary assignation after another. The studio he kept for the purpose in Bayswater. A hotel in Shepherd's Bush. I used up roll after roll of film: Solomon with a brunette, Solomon with a redhead, Solomon leaving a seedy disco with one of them, Solomon getting roaring drunk with another. It might have been entertaining, if it hadn't been so pathetic. At least it kept my mind off Susannah, who seemed to be out of my life altogether.

I knew he wouldn't be able to stay away from Louise forever, though, and he wasn't. There came a night when I sat in a receiver van down the road from the flat, watching as tiny figures played out their drama on the TV screen in front of me.

Louise threw her coat casually across a chair in one corner of the room. The picture tilted, settled at forty-five degrees as the spy-eye hidden in its hem skewed round. The colours were garish, distorted by the optical enhancements that improved the dim light.

I watched as they made love. I had thought violence was an aphrodisiac he needed, but the semblance of it seemed to do as well. Laughing, he threw her on the bed. Smiling, he pulled her clothes away, without any gentleness at all. His hand cupped her breast. She gasped as he bit her nipple, but through it all she was very still. He pinioned her wrists above her head as he entered her. Red stripes marked her wrists where his fingers had been. I looked away, but I could not shut out the sounds. After a time I could not tell whether her cries were of pain or pleasure.

I thought about Susannah, wondered whether this was how he was with her. She had not been this passive the night we were together, and I had tried to be so gentle. I wondered if even then she had seen my anger. It was something I thought I kept under control, until she made me face it.

They settled down to sleep. He turned his back on her. She kissed him at that delicate place where the neck meets the shoulders. They were very still, their bodies turned to marble by the creeping moonlight.

I stared at the room. Unless I had missed something, he had to be keeping his contact list here. In a way it made more sense: there would be no prying Susannah to find the disks, only a succession of transient women: whores or lovers, whatever.

There was the bed. A desk, with a phone and portable electric typewriter, but no computer. A dining table. Up at the far end of the room I could just make out a couple of armchairs grouped in front of an electric fire built into the grate beneath the old mantelpiece. There was a clutter of objects on it, and a painting above it, half-empty book-shelves to either side. In all this, nothing suggested itself as an obvious hiding place.

Louise stroked Solomon's back. When he did not respond, she slid carefully out of bed. For an instant she stared directly at the camera. She seemed unembarrassed by her nudity. I wondered if she guessed that I was watching. She turned and pulled a dressing gown on, and I decided that she did.

She began by searching his jacket but found only the usual clutter of wallet and keys and driving licence. She examined each item, then put it back in exactly the place she had taken it from. The desk came next. She hunted across its surface with equal care and similar success, then opened the top drawer. I could not see into it, but evidently it held nothing of interest, for she slid it closed quietly, and went on to the one beneath it. It was locked. As she pulled it, Solomon's eyes flicked open. By the time she had turned, they were closed again. She went to his jacket. Her eyes scarcely left his face as she fished the keys quietly from his pocket. He did not move, did not even seem to be aware of her. I thought perhaps I had imagined what I had seen.

She padded back to the desk, her feet barely making a sound. She knelt and slid the key into the lock, with her other hand cupped around the bunch to muffle it. I found that I was holding my breath. The drawer trundled out, making the slightest clank as it reached the end of its runners.

Louise began to leaf through the files. She pulled a sheet from one. Solomon stood up. The tilted picture made him seem huge, a looming presence in the suddenly small space. I felt my heart thud in my chest, willed her to look round, which she did not do.

Solomon took a single long stride across the room. Louise turned at the last minute. She tried to dodge away too late. He hit her with the back of his hand. She cried out.

I started to get up, but I found that I was as transfixed by the bright scene unfolding before me as a rabbit is by car headlights.

Louise scrambled to her feet. She started to back away from him, but he followed her. He grabbed her wrist and punched her in the stomach, then again across her head with his fist.

Somehow, I had never imagined this reality. I had thought Susannah might deserve *this*. I was wrong.

On the screen, Solomon slapped Louise across the face again and again. I managed at last to pull myself away. I grabbed the portable audio link, and ran.

Outside the van, the night was cold and clear, the trees etched against the night sky with uncommon clarity by a sulphurous yellow moon. Only the crackling of the commlink and the pounding of my heart disturbed the peace.

It seemed to me I could have run a marathon faster than I covered the hundred yards from the van to the flat. I heard noises from the commlink and my mind filled in what my eyes could not see. I heard a heavy thud, a light skittering. Someone grunted; I could not tell who. My imagination replayed the scene I had just watched: Louise's head bouncing slightly on the floor as Solomon hit her; her mouth contorting around her scream.

I had thought she could deserve that. Anger flared within me: anger at Solomon, anger at myself. I let it drive my pistoning legs.

The steps up to the front door confronted me; the dark eyes of the topmost windows seemed as distant as the moon. I leaped up the stairs three at a time, and tried to crash open the door. It took me four attempts, and by the time I succeeded, I knew I would have blood bruises on my shoulder. It's never like that in the movies.

As I entered, Solomon said 'Bitch!' clearly into the darkness.

Someone's ragged panting counterpointed my own as I ran up the stairs. I could no longer work out what was happening. There were too many unidentified scuffling noises, too many thuds, too many half-audible curses.

Louise screamed.

I was only at the bottom of the third flight. I gulped air but refused to stop. A confusion of crashes, and then momentary silence. A sharp crack. One of them grunted.

I forced my legs to work faster. The world was reduced to red haze and the effort to find footing in the darkness.

Words floated out of the air at me in stereo: 'Fucking cunt, you'll pay for this.' I realized they were coming from behind the door ahead of me as well as over the link.

There was a meaty thump, followed by another, louder one.

Then silence.

I kicked open the door, trying to remember everything the Department had taught me about unarmed combat, which wasn't much.

Louise was leaning against the wall. Blood was pumping from her nose, and had half dried across her face, her swollen mouth. Solomon was sprawled at her feet. I thought at first he was dead, and was pleased by it. Then I noticed his chest moving, the flickering of his eyeballs beneath the lids.

Louise went and threw up in the bathroom while I phoned the police. Then I tied Solomon up with his own belt.

When Louise came out, cleaned up but still pale, she would not look at me. She picked up the heavy brass paperweight she had knocked Solomon out with, and polished it with one finger. There was nothing to show what she had used it for.

'All this, and I still didn't find out his contacts,' she said at last. And then, conversationally, 'I wanted to kill him, you know. I wish I had.'

'But you didn't. And you didn't just let him hurt you, either, Louise,' I said, and realized immediately how patronizing I sounded.

'No, I didn't. But in all of this, I'm not sure what I've gained and what I've lost.' She turned to me. In that instant, she seemed utterly vulnerable. There was something desperate in her voice when she continued: 'Whether there can ever be that tenderness again.

Whether it was worth the price I paid for it. And whether I would pay it again.'

The next moment the mask came down, and the old Louise was back, cold and distant as the stars. 'Pity we didn't get the list.'

'We still might,' I said.

'Or the Department will. And take the credit for it.'

'Oh, come on,' I said. 'You couldn't have looked everywhere.'

The desk was the obvious place to begin to search, but of course Louise had already looked there. While she finished going through his files, I began to poke among the objects on the mantelpiece. There was a chunk of sharp-edged rock that would have made a better murder weapon than the paperweight, and one of those irritating ball-bearing cradles. I set it working, then stopped it abruptly: next to it, half-hidden behind a vase, was a small photo. Something pricked at my memory as I looked at it. It was older than its frame, a slightly overexposed, black and white picture of a cottage on a headland facing the sea.

There were no people in the picture. That thought released my memory: a stranger called daddy, with his arm round Solomon's mother. The first of the things that had made him what he was. I called to Louise. When she came over I slipped back the catches that held the frame in place. The hardboard backing fell into my hand. Between it and the photo was a computer disk.

The next few days were devoted to the mopping up. I moved my stuff out of my room at the Rising Sun. Louise took a long leave before going back to the Odd Squad. There were statements to make, reports to write, debriefings to attend.

All in all it was a little while before I got a chance to

go round and see Susannah. I knew things could never be what I wanted, but I had to make sure she was all right.

She wasn't there. The house was empty. Even the police had gone, having decided they had found everything they were going to be able to use against Solomon.

It took a bit of string-pulling – more than a bit, every favour I had ever been owed – but I got permission to go inside. After all, it was the last of her I'd ever see.

It was a mess. Between the CID and the Odd Squad psychometrists, so much had been ripped up, thrown around or removed that it seemed incredible that the house had ever been either elegant or charming.

So I sat in her room, on her bed, and tried to remember how she had looked the day she had told me she would rather stay to be beaten up by Solomon than leave with me. I wondered where she was, whether she was staying with some relative or other.

I hoped she was happy. Perhaps, I thought, I could find her. I'd get her together with, say, Steve. Someone solid and kind, who would love away her pain, because I would make sure he did. It would be the last thing I did for her; seeing them together would be more than I could take.

I decided if I couldn't do that, maybe I could find something to remember her by. There was nothing obvious. The police had left a few bits and pieces belonging to Solomon, but nothing of hers. So that was how I came to be hunting among the debris on the floor, and that was how I found the note, crumpled up in the shadows in the corner under the dressing table.

I smoothed it out. It was from Susannah to Solomon, a farewell letter. At first I thought it was something she had written after she had learned of his arrest: something she had decided not to send, or perhaps a draft copy.

She asked him not to try to find her. I was glad of that, thinking that if nothing else, Louise and I had forced her out of her cage. Perhaps I'd get her address from the Department — who would track her down as a matter of course — and take Steve round to visit after all.

Then I realized that the note was dated the seventeenth. She had written it the day after our trip to the Zoo.

Nothing had forced her to leave. She had seen the cage door open, and she had slipped out through it. By herself. I realized then that I would not seek her out. The world is large, and can be frightening. But from what she said, I knew she wanted to learn to live in it alone. I would not force her to exchange one cage for another, however gentle.

I slipped the letter into my pocket, and went outside. If I could feel the door of my lonely cage beginning to close in my face, well, at least there was comfort in the thought that I had opened hers a little way.

The spring sunshine was as bright as molten gold. And my eyes were burning.

DEMONIC STRETCH

Bidermann/Wigmore Hall

If Paganini was popularly believed to have sold his soul to the Devil, and Liszt became an abbé, what are we to think of the young piano virtuoso, Franz Biedermann, who gave his British début last night? . . . In the Lizst/Paganini Études, his phenomenal reach is enhanced by the lack of any necessity for him actually to touch every key he needs to play . . . In the Schumann, this flashiness of technique betrays him into the shallow . . . Is it necessary for Biedermann to announce his paranormal status by adjusting the height of his piano stool from the other side of the stage? . . . The lighting effects during his performance of his own solo transcription of the Gershwin Rhapsody were an unnecessary addition to a fine and sensitive performance. (*Guardian*, October 1970)

The young conductor and pianist Franz Biedermann was released without charges after questioning at Bow Street Police Station last night after an incident during his Covent Garden conducting début (see Reviews page). After a minor riot in the front stalls, three people were treated at St. Thomas's Hospital; no one was kept over night. The police are looking for nine Valkyries whom they believe will be able to help them with their enquiries. (*Guardian*, March 1975)

Franz Biedermann stepped in at short notice last night at the Royal Festival Hall when conductor and soloist were both indisposed. In the Mozart K.491, he did not conduct from the keyboard, but none the less gave his usual polished performance of the solo part from the rostrum . . . (*Guardian*, October 1976)

In that tedious warhorse, the Tchaikovsky Overture, Biedermann dispensed with the taped resources of the Royal Artillery and the bell-ringers of St. Paul's, and instead treated us to his own usual fireworks . . . Is there no end to this man's virtuosity? Probably not, alas . . . (*Guardian*, January 1980)

BIEDERMANN TAKES THE MICKEY

The Walt Disney Organization last night filed suit against Franz Biedermann and the London Symphony Orchestra for plagiarism, after their lawyers studied film of a Biedermann concert in which he allegedly infringed copyright during a performance of *The Sorcerer's Apprentice* by Dukas.

'I guess it just slipped out,' said an ashen-faced Biedermann. 'Sometimes you improvise, you know.'

A special detachment from Rentokil have closed off the Barbican. The public are advised . . . (*Guardian*, March 1981)

FRANZIE GOES TO HOLLYWOOD

Franz Biedermann, sacked by the London Symphony Orchestra after an incident during *La Mer* by Debussy, has taken up the offer of a contract from Stephen Spielberg.

'I need a break from my musical career,' said Biedermann.

'We need a break from Biedermann,' said a delegation of London music critics, several of whom could not swim. (*Guardian*, June 1985)

FROG DAY AFTERNOON

Marcus L. Rowland

His sequinned trousers glittering dimly under the 60-watt light of Bernie Sabbith's seedy office, Elvis picked up the guitar and attacked his latest song.

'Madame Cassandra,
picks up the papers she spilled on the carpet last night,
holds them up to the light.
Pulls on her glasses,
tries to decipher the scribble she writes in her sleep;
decides it'll keep.
All the lonely Talents, where do they all come from . . .'

Bernie winced as he listened to Elvis Grady's latest attempt at music. It wasn't the total lack of originality or skill; he'd never represented a star who had any. Elvis, or Eric if you went by his birth certificate, thought he was musical, and that, plus hype, was usually enough to con a few thousand suckers into buying a record. This time, though, Grady should have realized that there were a few problems . . .

'I'm sorry, Elvis, I think that tune's just a little too derivative. The lyrics are a bit familiar too. The Performing Rights Society would have your guts for garters if you recorded it.'

'No one listens to the music, Bernie. It's just got to sound good.'

'That's an interesting argument, but I don't think the

91

Performing Rights boys would agree. Anyway, she'd sue.'

'What do you mean she'd sue – who would?'

I'm surrounded by cretins, thought Bernie, saying, 'Madame Cassandra would sue. I read the *Sunday Sport*, you know. London's Premier Psychic, they call her.'

'Damn. I thought I'd made it up. I must have been pissed on Sunday.'

'Well, everyone has too many drinks now and again.' For Elvis it was more or less a permanent condition, but Bernie wasn't going to risk losing his ten per cent by saying so. 'Look, it's been fun, but I've got an appointment with Captain Croak in a few minutes, so we'll have to leave it there. Why don't you go home and write something else. While you're at it do something about the acne, it's looking a bit nasty again. I'll pencil in another appointment in two weeks.'

'You're a hard man to please, Bernie.'

'Look, I'm an agent, not Doctor Miraculous. Give me something to sell and I'll sell it; give me rubbish and all I can do is bin it.'

Elvis slung his guitar on his back, pushed on his cycle clips, and trudged downstairs. Bernie sighed. Life just wasn't fair. American agents got to represent interesting people like Michael Jackson or Doctor Miraculous; Bernie was stuck with losers like Elvis Grady and Captain Croak, probably the world's most boring paranorm . . .

Matilda Richards (Madame Cassandra: Psychic By Appointment To The Stars) usually felt a tingle in her right ear when someone was talking about her. It wasn't much use, because she never knew what they were saying, but it was nice that someone was interested in her. Today a few hundred volts might have penetrated her hangover, but a faint tingle didn't stand a chance.

As usual she began the day by tidying up the mess her astral body had left while she was asleep. Astra (well, you had to call her something) didn't seem to be deliberately untidy, just extremely accident-prone. Matilda supposed it came from being made of ectoplasm, or maybe she needed glasses. Sometimes Astra tried to cook, and that could leave egg and flour smears all over the house. Today things weren't really too bad; she'd broken a couple of plates and a potted plant, and a quick run with the Hoover took care of that. Matilda's headache was much worse by the time she switched it off and started to search the flat.

Eventually Matilda found a crumpled piece of paper under the flour bin; Astra had never grasped the idea of leaving her notes in the same place every day. This morning the writing was even worse than usual, and the spelling and punctuation were at an all-time low; Matilda wasn't sure how three glasses of port could affect an astral body, but there was no denying that it did something. Come to think of it, maybe it had been four glasses.

YU LfT Thr Cr kYS iN frig bHNd eGs – SholdN drive wen u aR pissed. TinNkBell wins 1.45 at antree. thEy Gon tu KiL ken in CORNatiON StrEet next week. On saTdy a tAll drk frog wlL svE loNdOn. Yu'll geT 9 to 2 on TiNKrbell if yu try.

Matilda read the note through, translated the semi-literate scrawl into her neat italics, and tried to work out what the message meant. The car keys were easy to check; she found them in a bowl of peas on the shelf below the eggs. Maybe they'd slipped through the bars. Tinkerbell was running at Aintree, but the odds were only four to one. It might be worth a bet. Astra didn't understand photo-finishes and stewards' inquiries, so it wasn't quite a sure thing. Coronation Street? That story was in the Sun a week ago; everyone knew it was going to happen sooner or later.

On Saturday a tall dark frog will save London. A bit odd, that. Astra wasn't usually so cryptic, and Matilda couldn't think of anyone who met that description. General de Gaulle died years ago, and he'd certainly never turned up in any of her seances. One thing was certain; it meant that London was in some sort of danger.

Matilda scrutinized the note again, and picked up the telephone. There were still a few bookies that didn't know her name; she wasn't surprised to find that one was offering 9 to 2 on Tinkerbell. She called her sister in Birmingham, and arranged to stay for a few nights. Finally, she called the Department of Paranormal Resources. As usual the main office line was busy, so she left a message on an answering machine on another number. An hour later she was on the M1, heading north past Watford services.

His name was Arnold Spaulding, but he wanted to be called Captain Croak, Crimefighter. It really wasn't fair; America gave paranorms everything from fancy costumes to their own TV series, and called them superheroes. Britain gave paranorms the DPR, an organization that routinely took six months and ten memos to process a £5 expenses claim, and sent him an annoyed letter whenever he tried to use his 'heroic' identity instead of his real name. He'd given up trying to persuade them to make him a special costume, and settled for a pair of elasticated swimming trunks. Yes, there was no doubt about it; America was the place for a paranorm with ambition, and Arnold was determined to get there somehow. With the right contacts he could give up his career in local government, and join one of the US superhero groups.

Make it big like Doctor Miraculous or the Amazing Stugat-ski Brothers. It would happen one of these days . . .

As Arnold climbed off the bus outside his agent's office a greasy-looking lout in sequinned trousers rode his bicycle across the pavement, clipping Arnold with a handlebar and the neck of a battered guitar. 'Get out of the road, four-eyes!' shouted Elvis, and wobbled away. Arnold straightened his glasses, pushed the daydream to the back of his mind, summoned the tattered remnants of his dignity, and went in.

'It isn't as though your Talent isn't interesting,' Bernie lied, 'it's just not very exciting. Not when you look at some of the paranorms the Americans have got. My cousin Maynard lives out there; he's representing a girl who can spray superglue from her nostrils – she's been sticking muggers to lampposts all over Boston. Maynard reckons there are five TV networks bidding for a series, and she's got all the big hero teams lining up to sign her on. Now, you turn into a frog . . .'

'A man-sized frog.'

'All right, a giant frog. That's a good start, but there's something about your presentation that doesn't quite work. You don't leap about much . . .'

'I may be a frog, but I still weigh twelve stone. I can only leap a couple of feet.'

'You don't talk much when you're in frog form.'

'I have to burp if I want to say anything, and it usually comes out sounding like a croak.'

'Pity. It would be much better if you could make heroic speeches. We've got to give you a more positive image. Maybe we could change your name?'

'No. I've checked, comic book companies have trade-marked all the obvious frog names. You know what they're like – do you remember the fuss when they forced Doctor Miraculous to drop his old name?'

'Forget I asked. Now, can you do anything about the slimy skin?'

'No.'

'Well, there's no way they'll ever want you as a stand-in on the *Muppet Show*, is there? Look . . . um . . . Captain, I'm doing my best, but you've got to help. Have you done something interesting since we last met? Something you could talk about on TV? Solved some crimes, or broken up an international spy ring?'

'I caught some vandals.'

'Yes, I heard about that. Four teenagers with spray cans, two of them got away, and one is suing you for wrongful arrest. Not exactly the Mafia, is it?'

'Can I help it if the DPR never gives me any missions?'

'It doesn't make it easy to build up your image.'

'Mr Sabbith, I took the day off work to come and see you. Surely there's something you can do to help.'

'Well . . . as it happens, I have heard of something. It's not very much, but maybe you'll find it interesting. A friend of my brother-in-law Melvin is directing a short film for television this Saturday. I think we can get you a cameo role in that.'

'It sounds wonderful! What do I have to do?'

'Well, the film's about swimming and water safety, one of those public information things they show sometimes. You'd be the lifeguard, saving kids from drowning.' Bernie saw Arnold frown, and added, 'I know it's not much of a part, but it's a start. It'll get your face on the box.'

'It isn't that. It's just that I can't swim very well.'

'A frog that can't swim? What sort of paranorm are you?'

'I never learned properly. I was excused games at school.'

'Bloody hell . . . Hang on a mo, though, that might work

quite well. I'll call up Melvin right away, and ask him to see if they can change the script. They could make you one of the people having swimming lessons. Setting an example, showing that even paranorms have to learn. Then maybe when you've learned properly they could do another one, and show you saving someone's life because you learned to swim properly. With a little luck you could be as big as the Green Cross man.'

'Do you really think it'll work? I wouldn't want people to think I was just looking for cheap notoriety.'

'You are looking for cheap notoriety, Arnie; we just need to wrap it up a little, make it more acceptable. If we can just get you on TV people will start to notice you. Who knows where that could lead. The *Wogan* show? That might just be the start. Now pop out into the waiting room, get yourself a coffee. This'll take a while. Melvin always chats for hours when I phone him. And relax. Have I ever let you down . . . ?'

In the DPR's London office Marcia waved her fingers, and calculated that her nail varnish was probably dry enough to let her do some typing. She stirred three spoonfuls of sweetener into her coffee, thought about typing, and decided to call her alter ego in Newcastle instead. As she dialled, her finger slipped, and the end of the nail cracked. Marcia swore, and rummaged in her bag for an emery board. Her elbow hit the eject button on the answerphone, and a tape flipped across the desk and knocked her coffee to the floor. By the time she'd cleared up the mess a dozen expense claims were in the bin, along with the coffee-sodden cassette. Marcia never noticed it was missing.

> INCOMING CALL FROM AGENT CODENAMED 'COUGAR'
'Activate counter-systems, then connect.'
> ANTI-TRACE SYSTEM IS OPERATING

\> SCRAMBLE SYSTEM IS OPERATING
\> VOICE DISTORTION SYSTEM IS OPERATING
\> CONNECTING AGENT 'COUGAR'

'Hello? Are you there? The password is lemon meringue pasta.'

'Acknowledged. The countersign is chocolate chip sandwich.'

'Good. My men are poised and ready to act; do you want us to proceed with the operation?'

'Yes ... carry on. Conditions are perfect on Saturday, all weather forecasts are favourable.'

'Good. What about the diversions?'

'All diversions are proceeding as planned. Four major football matches and a tax protest march are scheduled in London on Saturday, they should keep the police out of the way. Acting on an anonymous tip, army and police units have commenced a major anti-terrorist operation at Heathrow airport, while other army units are on NATO exercises in Europe. There are minimal units in Central London. No British intelligence organization is aware of the plan. No foreign agency has been in contact with the British government.'

'What about paranorms, the DPR and so forth?'

'Don't worry about those incompetents – they're civil servants, their offices will close at five on Friday evening and won't open until Monday. In any case they have no idea of the plan. This isn't America, you won't get a dozen costumed idiots throwing cars at you.'

'You're sure that they know nothing.'

'Absolutely. You should be in and out before anyone knows you are there.'

'Right then. We'll destroy London on Saturday, if you're still sure that's what you want.'

'Very good. You'll receive the rest of your payment when the job is done. Unless there is something else ...?'

'No.'

\> AGENT 'COUGAR' HAS REPLACED RECEIVER

'Deactivate telephone link, then self destruct.'

\> TELEPHONE LINES DISCONNECTED AT EXCHANGE

\> ANTI-TRACE SYSTEM DEACTIVATED

\> SCRAMBLE SYSTEM DEACTIVATED

\> VOICE DISTORTION DEACTIVATED

\> SELF DESTRUCT SEQUENCE INITIA...DDDDDDDFTRY JRY5HRHTYJ

'Perfect.'

'... and patches of fog on high ground. In the morning expect gale-force winds on the east and south-east coast, with strong winds and scattered showers further inland. In most parts of London temperatures will be about 15 °C, approximately 60 °F.'

'Well, Bob, it sounds like the weather isn't going to be too good tomorrow. Do you think it will affect the matches?'

'It is hard to tell. All four pitches have good drainage, so none of the games should be cancelled, but it'll be hard going for the players if the ground gets really wet. We'll have to see what happens.'

'Any other sporting events in London tomorrow?'

'Nothing major. Greyhound racing at White City, the finals of the Carlsford Trophy, and amateur athletics at Olympia. Otherwise it's going to be a pretty quiet day.'

Laura Smythe looked at her Rolex, and glanced at the clipboard and the shooting script. She raised a small loud-hailer.

'OK, we'll try another shot. This time you kids try to look really happy and excited. You too, ah ... Captain. Quiet please ... Brian, love, would you stop that water splashing, the needle's going off the scale here. We'll

have to do all the sound in the studio if we aren't careful
... That's better, big smiles everyone ... right, action!'

The camera panned along the row of happy children
clutching polystyrene floats, then cut back to the giant
frog in green trunks in the middle of the row. Arnold
gripped his inflatable rubber life-ring and wondered if
any amount of publicity could be worth this humiliation.

'Sod it, cut! Captain, would you please stop it. That's
the third time we've tried to film this scene. Once the
camera's jammed, and twice you've had your tongue out.
None of the kids are doing it, which is a sodding miracle,
so you have to spoil the shot. Don't you want to be on
TV?'

One of the children shouted 'Ugh ... Miss, he's eating
flies!', and the rest happily pretended to vomit or catch
insects of their own. Arnold guiltily swallowed the bluebottle, and shook his head in apology. A moment's inat-
tention, and no one would let you hear the last of it.
Sometimes he wished that the metamorphosis wasn't so
thorough. At least there weren't any worms around, the
last time he'd tried to catch one his tongue had ended up
wrapped around his own ankle.

'This is all I need, a frog that can't control his sodding
appetite. My old dad said I should never work with
children or animals, and I should have listened to him.
Can we try again, and this time would everyone try to
concentrate PLEASE! ... Right, that's better. Quiet now,
and ... Action!'

The camera panned along the row of children again,
then cut back to Arnold and zoomed out to take in the
rest of the poolside. A lifeguard blew his whistle, and the
children happily leaped into the pool. Arnold teetered on
the edge, clutching his ring and dipping a green webbed
foot in the water. The chlorine stung his skin. The children started to shout:

'Come on, last one in's a tadpole.'

'Frog's afraid of the water!'

'What's green and can't swim?'

The lifeguard stepped forward to stand beside Arnold and was revealed as Kim Yeovil, one of the hosts from *Blue Peter*. He began to read his lines so naturally that it was almost impossible to spot his eyes following the autocue: 'A lot of people hate to admit that they can't swim, but it's nothing to be ashamed of, and it's never too late to learn. Our friend here is a paranorm, and with a body like this you'd think he'd be at home in the water. Unfortunately, you can't always judge . . .'

Laura shouted 'Cut' again. A bearded man in a dirty brown overall was walking into shot along the poolside, mopping the tiles and whistling tunelessly. 'Would you PLEASE get out of it, grandad, we're trying to film here!'

The old man ignored Laura, and swept on. Abruptly he pulled off his beard, opened the coat, and produced a huge red book. Arnold gaped, recognizing a famous chin, as a familiar voice said 'You thought you were here to make a film about water safety, but we had other plans. Tonight Kim Yeovil, journalist and star of children's tele- vision, *This is Your Life*!' He put his arm over the dazed Yeovil's shoulder, and led him out through an exit where another camera was waiting.

Laura picked up her megaphone and shouted, 'All right, Steve, cut for real now. The other crew will follow them to the studio. The rest of you, I'm sorry we couldn't warn you. We didn't want to risk tipping him off. You'll all be paid for a full day's filming, and we'll make the real film next Saturday.' As she spoke, there was a loud warbling beep from the pile of equipment by the pool. One of the crew picked up a cellphone, listened, and handed it to Laura.

'Yes? . . . Oh . . . Oh, I see. Where? . . . If we were much closer I could spit on them . . . Right, we'll be there in ten minutes.'

She dropped the phone, and shouted, 'OK, everyone, pack up. Get everything in the van, pronto. Marion, stay here and make sure that the parents pick up these little darlings, the rest of you get ready to move. We've got to get over to the Thames Barrier, some lunatics are trying to blow it up, and we're the only spare film crew in the area!'

'. . . was completely unsuspected until an anonymous caller reported masked gunmen in the control building car-park. The terrorists are armed with machine guns, and have already fired at the police, who have erected road blocks on both sides of the river. Several river police boats are waiting up- and downstream from the Barrier, and have also come under fire.

'A film crew was in the area when the news broke, and a courier has just brought the first tapes of the siege.'

The screen shows a momentary view of a swimming pool, with several children and a large frog, then abruptly jumps to a vista of the river, bridged by the domed ramparts of the Thames Barrier. Police are gathered around several cars in the surrounding streets. The camera zooms in on several black dots on the Barrier, revealing them as masked men carrying ominous-looking steel boxes and cable drums.

'Experts believe that the boxes are limpet mines filled with plastic explosive, powerful enough to smash the gates and the hydraulic motors that move them. The high tide and storms off the coast make flooding inevitable if the Barrier is breached. At least four personnel were manning the control centre, and are believed to be hostages.

FROG DAY AFTERNOON

'Underground stations in the danger area are closing, and houses and offices near the Barrier have been evacuated. There are unconfirmed reports that SAS units have left the security exercise at Heathrow and are on their way to the scene.

'We hope to have live coverage of the siege in our afternoon bulletin. Now back to Wembley . . .'

Arnold shivered in the back of the van. He was wrapped in a couple of towels and a pair of trunks that were four sizes too big for his human form, and saw the world as a vague blur that began a few feet from his nose. Steve Watkins put down the hand-held camera he was adjusting, and poured Arnold a cup of coffee. He gratefully drained it in a few gulps.

'Sorry about this, mate. I'm sure we'll find your clothes and glasses eventually, they've got to be in here somewhere. We just loaded so fast that they're buried under everything else.'

'I hope so. Nice coffee.'

'I'm surprised you aren't streaking into action. Using your super powers, like.'

'What could I do? There are about a dozen of them, and they're all carrying machine guns. I'm not Doctor Miraculous.'

'It's a pity, it'd be marvellous footage. Great publicity for the safety film. Another cup?'

Momentarily the van was flooded with the noise of a police helicopter, and more sirens from the main road. Arnold accepted another cup of coffee, and sipped it a little more slowly. It tasted very good, and was warming him nicely.

'Of course the DPR never did appreciate my talents. It'd serve them right if I did streak into action.'

'Well yes, I suppose so.'

'I've half a mind . . . Got any more of that coffee?'

'Just a drop. Look, you do know there's brandy in it, don't you?'

'I do now. Thanks. Do you think I'd get on the *Wogan* show if I sorted it out? Saved London, I mean.'

'Count on it. *Daytime Live* too.'

'Right, then, let's talk to the police . . .'

Chief Inspector Geoffrey Pargetter struggled to retain the frayed shards of his temper. It wasn't easy.

'What do you mean, the SAS are caught in a traffic jam?'

'Sorry, guv,' the voice on the other end of the radio apologized, 'there's a huge snarl on the M4, thousands of people panicking and trying to get out before the tidal wave.'

'There isn't going to be a bloody tidal wave. If the Barrier goes all that'll happen is that the Thames overflows a little. People will get their feet wet, and bits of central London will be flooded after a few hours, but that's hardly a tidal wave.'

'I know, guv, but try telling them that. There's also the tax demo in the way. They seem to have decided that it's a cunning trick to get them to give up the march. God knows what will happen when the SAS run into that lot.'

'Isn't anyone else available? What about the rest of the army?'

'Most of them still seem to be out at Heathrow. Someone in the Cabinet apparently decided this could be a diversion, cover for a main attack at the airport.'

'Wonderful. Where are Commander CID and the Assistant Commissioner?'

'The Commander's on leave, won't be back until Wednesday. The AC's on his way back from Wembley, we're trying to get a helicopter to pick him up, but it'll be at least twenty minutes.'

'Look, I need some backup fast, and some more men for crowd control. All the nutters will crawl out of the woodwork soon. I've already had one pillock turn up in swimming trunks, pretending to be a paranorm, and it's going to get much worse if we don't get something done quickly. Can't you get hold of anyone? The RAF? The Navy? What about the funny mobs, Intelligence and all that shower?'

'I'm trying, but you know what it's like getting anything done at the weekend . . .'

Brian Tiptree, alias Cougar, was seriously annoyed. It didn't seem fair; he'd spent years trying to build up a reputation as a mercenary, which isn't easy for someone born in Bognor, and now his first big contract had gone wrong. Whoever the client was, he wouldn't be pleased. He wiped the sweat from his eyes, then pulled down his ski mask and risked a quick look through the control centre window. He wondered what the police would try next. His plan had been good, perfect if some passing busybody hadn't noticed one of his men. One little slip, and before you know it you're in the middle of a siege. The charges were already in place and ready to detonate, and he didn't fancy staying around while they blew. He fingered the radio trigger nervously. His men were already restless; if they didn't get out soon they might start to give him real problems.

'You ought to surrender,' said one of the hostages. 'You'll never get away with this.'

'That's just the sort of unimaginative remark I expect from a bourgeois pig like you. A typical product of the class system,' said Brian, without much real feeling. It was always a good idea to pretend that you were politically motivated, he'd heard. Made people take you seriously. Brian's main motive was his bank balance, but he supposed that some people needed causes. At the moment getting out without getting shot or arrested would do very nicely for Brian.

'Look, Captain, the police wouldn't let you help. Don't you think that trying to have a go anyway is asking for trouble?'

'The police are just jealous. The sergeant said he didn't believe I was a paranorm, and wanted to see my DPR identity card. They weren't even interested in letting me change shape to prove it. They all said they'd never heard of me.'

'Well, you said it yourself, you aren't Doctor Miraculous. Mind you, I do think they went a bit far threatening to arrest you for indecent exposure and obstruction.' Steve clipped the side panel back on his camera, and started to check meter readings and switch settings. 'Maybe it's just as well. There are terrorists out there, you know, they'll shoot you if you try to stop them. Leave it to the police.'

'No way. They're just watching the Barrier and drinking tea, we'll be flooded if someone doesn't get their finger out. Just give me a few minutes to get started then tell your director what's happening. Don't say anything to the police, they'll only stop me.'

'Maybe someone should.'

'This is my big chance. Just pump up that ring for me, and let me get changed. It'll be all right.'

Arnold bent his back and knees slightly, spread his legs and waited patiently for the transformation. As usual it started in his toes, which slowly elongated and webbed. For some reason the toes always reminded him of his childhood visit to the Cumbrian coast and the pet frog

106

he'd caught near St Bees Head. There was a sudden twinge of pain as his leg muscles quivered and began to change shape. A tingle in his arms told him that his skin was starting to soften and secrete slime. By now there was a little pain, as his bones began to soften and distort, and his testicles and penis retracted into his groin. Maybe British Nuclear Fuels would like to use him in their advertising – after all, he'd found the frog just outside the Windscale reactor complex, and changed for the first time a week after it bit him – perhaps there was some connection. His tongue flicked out and back and his eyes swelled as the sockets moved to the top of his head, improving his sight considerably. His arms shrank, and his mouth widened as his teeth sank into his gums. For a few seconds he felt breathless and dizzy, then his altered metabolism stabilized. As he recovered he decided that he'd tell the frog story on the *Wogan* show; someone was sure to ask him how he got his power, and it would fill a few minutes nicely.

Arnold made sure that the trunks were on properly, not that it mattered much now, and took the rubber ring from the suddenly nervous engineer.

'Blimey, I've never seen anything like that up close before. Gave me a nasty turn. Hope you didn't mind me filming you.'

Arnold hadn't noticed. He tried to say, 'Let's hope I scare the terrorists too.' As usual, all that came out was a mumbling croak.

The Thames isn't particularly badly polluted for a river that passes through one of the world's largest cities and is fed by dozens of sewage outlets. With the ring under his arms Arnold's nostrils and eyes just protruded above the water. He tried to fend off floating cans, contraceptives, and other little souvenirs. He was starting to get the knack of swimming with webbed feet, though not particularly well, and making his first tentative efforts to steer towards one of the piers of the barrage, a hundred yards ahead. A strand of toilet paper got past his guard and plastered itself across one eye, and he ducked under for a moment to wash it off. As he came up again a puzzled seagull swooped in for a closer look, and seemed to be ready to land on his head and peck at an eye. Arnold decided to swim the rest of the way underwater; one advantage of being a frog, you could hold your breath for a while. He tried to dive, but the ring would only let him bob up and down. He cursed mentally, groped for the plug, and started to sink as it deflated, then carried on struggling towards the Barrier.

'Cougar,' said Colin Braddock. 'There's something moving underwater out there, about sixty yards out. See, it's leaving a trail of bubbles. I think it's heading for the second piling.'

'A diver, I suppose. Maybe they think they can disarm the charges without us noticing. Give him a warm welcome.'

'He won't know what hit him.' Braddock turned towards the door.

'Wait. Don't shoot him if you can avoid it. Try to take him alive, we could do with more hostages . . .' Braddock nodded. '. . . but don't let that stop you if things look dangerous. If you have to kill him, kill him.'

'I'll see to it personally.'

Arnold struggled on to one of the Barrier pilings, and coughed out the polluted water he'd swallowed when he swam into the concrete wall. As he finished, a mocking voice said 'I've heard of frogmen, but this is ridiculous. Put your hands up.'

There were two of them, both wearing fashionable terrorist's clothing: camouflage jacket and trousers, leather boots, bandoliers loaded with grenades and clips of ammunition, radios, and scarves covering most of their faces. Both held machine pistols. Arnold tried to sigh, croaked instead, and raised his hands.

'What do you mean, you've caught a frog? Do you mean a frogman, Colin? Over.'

'No, a giant frog. Over.'

'How big? Over.'

'Man-sized. It's wearing swimming trunks, must be a paranorm. Over.'

'What has it got to say for itself? Over.'

'Nothing. It just croaked a bit. Over.'

'Bring it to the control building, and be very careful. If it's a paranorm there's no telling what it can do. Over.'

'Don't worry, we'll tie its hands. It doesn't look very strong, shouldn't be a problem. Over and out.'

As the terrorists pushed him down a steep steel staircase inside the piling, Arnold cursed himself for a fool. All he'd done was give them another hostage, with nothing to show for it. He slipped on a damp grating, swaying as he tried to regain his balance. One of the gunmen pushed him in the back, and he staggered and slid down several steps to the next landing, leaving a trail of soft skin, slime, and blood behind him.

'Shit. That's a paranorm? My grandmother could put up more of a fight. It can't even walk downstairs without falling over. Get up, creep.'

This one sounded like he came from the Midlands. Arnold was surprised that they weren't Arabs or Irish. He struggled back on to his feet and started down again, the terrorists following. As the second man crossed the landing he slipped on some of Arnold's slime, stumbling forward and pushing the other.

'Watch it. You nearly had us both over. Stop there, frog.'

Arnold realized that he was at the bottom, in an echoing tunnel linking the piers deep below the Thames. He turned towards the gunmen, a sudden plan crossing his mind, and tried to look harmless.

'Get on with it, we haven't got all day.'

The chatty terrorist raised his gun and poked Arnold in the stomach. Arnold flicked his tongue out to one of the gunman's grenades, and frantically tried to pull the pin. It wouldn't budge. The terrorist punched Arnold in the jaw and knocked him to the floor.

'Bloody hell, be careful. He nearly had you then.'

'Shut up.'

Braddock kicked Arnold in the stomach, drew a knife, and grabbed the end of Arnold's tongue. He pulled sharply, then coughed and toppled to the floor. The other terrorist spun round, and fell clutching his chest. He landed on Arnold, slamming his head against the tunnel floor.

As Arnold's vision dimmed he saw blood oozing from Colin's forehead, and the blurred shapes of his rescuers. He just had time to feel surprised before he passed out.

'How are you feeling?' Steve Watkins poked his head around the door to Arnold's hospital room, following it with a body carrying a bunch of grapes and a bottle of Scotch.

'Not too bad, really.' Arnold squirmed in the bed not wanting to reveal that his wounds were embarrassingly superficial, mostly scraped skin and bruises.

'Those commandos certainly turned up in the nick of time. You were bloody lucky.' Watkins absent-mindedly took a couple of the largest grapes, and popped them into his mouth.

Arnold winced as he remembered. 'Someone told me they were on a scuba training exercise a couple of miles upstream. When they heard about the terrorists they just loaded up with real ammunition and set off downstream. Didn't even bother waiting for authorization.'

'Yes ... they're in a lot of trouble about that, or would be if the papers weren't calling them heroes.'

'They are heroes, they caught the rest of the terrorists without anyone else getting hurt.'

'Funny thing, that.'

'What?'

'Seems that the terrorists weren't up to much. The bloke who was leading them was some sort of Rambo fan. He read all the mercenary magazines. Seems he answered an advert and found himself talking to a computer that seemed to think he was a big-time terrorist. He played along, and it told him where to pick up the equipment. All the others were his friends and people who advertised in the magazine. Funny, that.'

'It wouldn't have been funny if they'd set off the explosives.'

'Didn't anyone tell you? They did. He pressed the button when the commandos broke in. Lots of smoke and noise, plenty of pyrotechnics, but it hardly damaged the paintwork on the Barrier. They surrendered pretty quickly after that. Their guns and grenades weren't up to much either: old military-surplus practice ammo with reduced charges. They could have killed you, but they would have had to work at it.'

'It's all very odd.'

'Well, I've got my own ideas about that, and there are some funny rumours going around at the Beeb. Do you remember a few years ago, what they called the Falklands' factor? They reckon the government was re-elected on the strength of that war, and the Iranian embassy siege before that didn't hurt either. Showed they were tough enough for the job.'

'So?' Arnold grabbed a few grapes from the rapidly-vanishing bunch.

'Well ... The government's bloody unpopular right now. The betting is that there'll be an election in a few months. If the commandos hadn't shown up there would have been a long siege, then everyone reckons the SAS would have taken the terrorists out without letting them detonate the charges. They've got the equipment and the paranorms to handle that sort of problem. If they'd gone in shooting there wouldn't have been any survivors, just dead terrorists and bags of publicity. The bomb-disposal people would have steamed off the explosives without finding out how feeble they were. The government shows that it's tough and waves all the old flags; land of hope and glory, the bulldog breed, and so forth. They would have walked it at the polls.'

'Would have?'

'Well, it's all looking a little silly now. A bunch of dangerous terrorists threatening to destroy London is one thing, a bunch of incompetent amateurs with fireworks is something else. It looks like their weapons were diverted from Army stores, so everyone has egg on their faces. If I'm right, my guess is that the government will try to play the whole thing down now. Pretend it never happened.'

'If you're right about what?'

'Someone must have pulled a lot of strings to organize that raid, and they never did find out who reported it to the police. Now suppose that someone high up in the government was behind it all . . .'

'That's paranoia. There's no evidence.'

'None. Never will be, if my guess is right.'

'Wouldn't the government have made sure that the commandos were out of the way?'

'They weren't supposed to be there until next week, but someone mixed up two sets of orders. If they'd got it right they would have been in Portsmouth on Saturday. I'm not sure what to make of that; it could just be a normal cock-up, or maybe someone decided to put a spoke in the government's wheel. There's no way of knowing.'

'Do you really believe all that?'

'Why not? I can't prove it, so what does it matter?'

'What about me?'

'What about you? Most of the papers seem to think you were one of the hostages, the rest reckon you just got in the way. We didn't get any footage, because the police moved the camera van back while you were swimming out to the Barrier. At the moment everyone in the media is keeping a very low profile. I doubt they'll have you on the *Wogan* show, someone might ask the wrong sort of questions.'

'Wonderful. You've really made my day.'

After Watkins left, Arnold glared at the ceiling and wondered about his future. He didn't really believe in a conspiracy, but there certainly hadn't been much of a rush to interview him in hospital. He was interrupted as the door swung open again.

'Arnold – I mean . . . um . . . Captain Croak – well done.'

'Hello, Mr Sabbith.'

'You're a genius, Captain. A bloody genius.'

'I don't understand.'

'That little film you made on Saturday.'

'What, at the swimming pool?' Arnold angrily remembered the fake documentary.

'No, afterwards, the film of you turning into a frog.'

Arnold thought for a moment, then remembered Steve Watkins holding a camera. 'I remember it. What about it?'

'The chap that filmed you showed it to some friends. One of them happens to work in the BBC special-effects department.'

'So?'

'So, do you know how much something like that would cost if you tried to fake it? I'll tell you: thousands of pounds. As soon as he saw it he got on to me, offering you a job. Of course you'll have to spend most of your time in frog form, and wear a lot of makeup, but it's a chance in a million. At least four episodes, maybe six if we're lucky.'

'Episodes of what?'

'Didn't I say? *Doctor Who*, what else! I think they're going to call it "The Toad-Devils of Xenopus", or something like that. Every kid in the country will watch it. You're going to be famous!'

'As a special effect?' Arnold said indignantly.

'Look at it this way. They'll pay you to do it, and its bound to give you a bit of publicity. Anything unusual gets attention. And that's not all . . .'

'What do you mean?'

'My nephew Reuben works for the Children's Film Foundation, and he's told me that they want to make their own monster movie. They're already working on the model city. They were going to use a bloke in a rubber suit, but if the *Doctor Who* deal goes through Reuben's practically guaranteed to give you a starring role. Keep your diary clear for the end of August, that's when you'll be destroying London!'

Arnold leaned back against the pillow, munched the last grape, and began to smile.

Kenneth Baker: *Best Short Fiction of the 1980s* (Roc, 1996, £4.95)

Little is known about Jack Yeovil (1956–89), the reclusive creator of Pitbull Brittan.

His fictional creation, however, is another matter, particularly following the successful BBC series, starring Timothy Dalton as the eponymous patriot-for-hire. (In films, however, Pitbull has fared less well: Sylvester Stallone was unconvincing as the dashing former soldier, his English accent described by one reviewer as 'making Dick Van Dyke in *Mary Poppins* sound like Prince Charles by comparison', and Jack Nicholson's grinning arch-enemy Scraggle stole the movie.)

The five short stories that comprise the first book, *Pitbull Brittan Stands Fast*, originally saw print in 1985, in *Union Jack's Magazine*, a pulp-fiction periodical edited by David Pringle, and were published under Jack Yeovil's pseudonym of 'Grenadier'.

Collected into book form in the spring of 1986, *Pitbull Brittan Stands Fast* was an instant best seller, and it was followed by the novel-length adventures *Pitbull Brittan's Finest Hour* (1987), *Pitbull Brittan Flies the Flag* (1988), *Pitbull Brittan Gives Them What For* (1989), and the posthumous *Hurrah! For Pitbull Brittan* (1990). (The children's cartoon series, *Pitbull Brittan and his British Brigade*, and the related line of toys, bears only a tangential resemblance to the Yeovil character, but should be mentioned here.)

After Jack Yeovil's death in 1989, following an unfortunate incident at the Bridgwater sheepdog trials, the series was continued by Yeovil's friend and colleague, Captain Kim Newman DSO, on whom it was said Yeovil had partially based the character of the adventurous hero. Newman's books, while solid stories, are undistinguished when compared with what had gone before, with the exception of *Pitbull's Women* (1992), in which Annabelle, Scraggle's maddened widow, plots vengeance on

Pitbull for killing her husband – with the aid of twelve para-normal seductresses, each from a different member nation of the European Community.

In addition to the Pitbull Brittan books, Jack Yeovil wrote several tales about paranormal sleuth Jonathan Bull and his comical sidekick, Winston, collected in *Jon Bull Sees It Through* (1987), and, as 'Herbert Herbert', one horror novel, *The Red Peril* (1983, republished in an expanded edition 1989).

Arguably Yeovil's finest short story, 'Pitbull Brittan' (reprinted here in its entirety) introduced our hero, the evil Scraggle, the beautiful Phyllida, and the first incarnation of The Black Hat Gang, Pitbull's faithful band. Read it and marvel.

PITBULL BRITTAN

Jack Yeovil

———————

To: Norman St John Stevas, Minister for Paranormal Resources
From: Department of Paranormal Resources
Date: 9 December 1982

ASSESSMENT OF SUITABILITY

Subject Name: Brittan, Richard Lionheart
Known Aliases: 'Pitbull'*
Date of Birth: 23 April 1947
Nationality: British, Caucasian
Status: Single
Current Occupation: Lieutenant, First Paratroop Regiment

Talent   Subject's musculature is composed entirely of erectile tissue. When aroused, physically or emotionally, his heart pumps blood at an increased rate, producing pronounced turgidity of the surface flesh, extraordinary muscular strength, limited invulnerability and psychological capacity for feats of selfless heroism. Among the side effects of the process are reddish flush over the entire body (most notable in the facial area), an expansion of size necessitating the wearing of loose clothing and an extreme, painful genital erection. When our boy gets a hard-on, he goes into action like a pitbull terrier, and doesn't stop until the job's done.

———————

*At school (Millfield), for obvious reasons, they called him 'Dickhead'.

119

Comments Subject has been getting a lot of column inches (*sic*) since the yellow press latched on to his exploits in the South Atlantic during the Late Unpleasantness with Argentina. Subsequent to the Sheepdip Heights Incident, which resulted in his receipt of the Victoria Cross, it has been generally assumed by leader writers of the *Mail* and the *Express* that he will be joining us (see attached press cuttings) as 'a true-blue British hero'. Given the fortuitous coincidence of his surname and his undoubted patriotic zeal, he is considered by the opinion formers to be exactly the type of high-profile talent the DPR should be fostering as opposed to 'the colourless spoon-benders' most identified with the department. The Army has not yet concluded their investigation into Sheepdip Heights, but details will be 'forthcoming as soon as they are available'.

Thoughts Subject is due soon to 'resign' his commission and be granted an 'honourable discharge' which should tell you something. Also, 34 is remarkably old for a lieutenant. Once it looked like he was going to get the VC, several of his files — most notably, the psychological evaluations — have mysteriously become unavailable to this department. My conclusion is that One Para want to pass Subject on to us, and I would tend to assume this is an oblatory equine situation, and we should employ the services of a veterinarian dentist before further considering recruitment.

Conclusion It's hard to know whether to class this one as Talented or disabled. In the short term, his prowess is doubtless remarkable — as that Argentine machine-gun nest on Sheepdip Heights found out — but my impression is that there is a severe downside. Bluntly put, Subject can induce his bodily metamorphosis in all manner of ways — anger, sexual interest, fear, excitement, embarrassment — but can only reverse the process in the normal manner, by achieving a sexual climax. Note the references in the press accounts of Sheepdip Heights to Subject disappearing for a few minutes with 'a grateful shepherdess'. It has been suggested, but obviously not confirmed, that were Subject *not* to have some kind of emission within half an hour or so of arousal, the process would become irreversible, and the ever-increasing rush of blood into his tissues would lead, in rapid succession, to the explosion of Subject's genitalia, major veins and heart. The upshot is that if you want to deploy subject as a field agent, you would have to partner him with a trained prostitute or expect him to have a very short, messy career.

Suitability F.

PS: I know the Suitability Rating might seem overly harsh considering the attached clippings (ref: PITBULL COMES THROUGH FOR BRITAIN, *Mail*; BIG DICK STICKS IT TO ARGIES, *Sun*; VC FOR VICTORY, *Express*), but I have a bad feeling about this one, and after thirty years around talents I've learned to trust my bad feelings. Subject is an unstable braggart, and, after our recent bad publicity, the DPR doesn't really need to be known as the employers of 'The Man Whose Dick Exploded'.

Signed,

Raymond Noone, B.Sc., D.Parapsych (Oxon), O.B.E.

cc: Loric.

I

'Hang it all from the old oak tree, Slobotham, I'm bored!'

Richard Lionheart Brittan, 'Pitbull' to his friends, ground his teeth together mightily, handsome-ugly face contorted with mock agony. He clenched and unclenched ham-sized fists, wishing for an Argie or two within thumping reach. His veined marble knuckles needed a work-out.

'Bored, bored, bored!'

'Yes, sir,' agreed Slobotham, the quiet-spoken, ineffably deferential family retainer, passing him a deftly mixed cocktail of saltpetre and Valium.

'Don't want that filth, Slobbo,' he sneered, hurling the offending liquid, in its seventeenth-century cut glass goblet, at the wall. The glass shattered, and the medicine splattered, dribbling down the portrait of Brittan's great-great-grandfather, Sir Rodney Dangerfield Brittan, hero of the Mboto Uprising. The red-faced old fool looked even more angry than usual, with smoky cordial dribbling across his mutton-chops.

'Ahem,' reminded Slobotham, 'your problem, sir.'

'Rot my problem. Dosing myself with downers doesn't do a gnat's fart for my problem. What I need is some *action!*'

'Indubitably, sir.'

'Hah, yes, right! In-bloody-dubit-bloody-ably!'

Slobotham left the withdrawing room, as silently as he had come, leaving Brittan alone with his frustrations.

Since that spot of bother in the Falklands, there had been nothing worth doing for these beloved old islands. Peace bored him beyond all reason. Whipped out of the Paras on dodgy medical grounds, he was now cooped up in the family home like a trussed pig in a larder. Sometimes, he thought the docs had been right: left alone, he might just explode.

He heard the blood thumping in his ears, and knew that was a danger signal.

Calming himself by thinking of potatoes, he strolled through the French windows, out on to the carefully manicured lawns of Brittan Hall, Hertfordshire. In the distance, on the croquet pitch, he could see two figures disconsolately knocking balls around, plainly as bored as he. At the sidelines, in a deckchair, a smaller man sat, his nose pressed into a large book.

This was not to be tolerated.

He surveyed his life. At thirty-six, he was at his physical and mental peak. He had a good private income, no close family ties, abilities above the average, and a heart that yearned for adventure, excitement, *action*.

Ideally, he would still be in the service of his country, only the army didn't want him any more, and the DPR didn't want him full stop. It seemed that lesser mortals found it hard to work alongside a Victoria Cross Man. The envious little oiks and spiteful desk jockeys had kept him out of his chosen profession.

He had his honour, but nothing else, apart from his VC. And his estates. And his friends.

'Jock,' he hollered, 'Basmo! Swell!'

The croquet players looked up, and saw him coming.

The tall Scot, bare knees between kilt and tartan socks thick with the black hairs that covered his entire body, bellowed with bagpipe lungs.

'Och, Dick lad, 'tis gurrand tae sae yae,' the giant cried, his arms outstretched, suggesting a reach wider than the average man is tall, 'gurrand, gurrand!'

Brittan embraced his comrade, Jock McLochness, late of the Fifth Highland Fusiliers. Playfully, they hugged with rib-cracking force, laughing in each other's faces. Brittan felt his friend's arms constricting, and saw the muscles cording in Jock's neck, shifting the swatches of hair that extended from his beard down into the hollows of his throat. He thrust out his craggy chin, and squeezed back, hearing the Scot's ribs grinding together.

'I say,' drawled the other croquet player, languidly leaning on his mallet, 'what are you two gorillas playin' at, what? Look like a couple of tarts dancin' the tango.'

Brittan broke the bear-hug, and turned to his old schoolfriend, Basil Mapledurham (pronounced Mumm). Basil adjusted the monocle in his right eye, and passed a hand over his patent-leather hair, his receding chin wobbling as he laughed.

'I could break you in two, Basmo!'

'Oh yes, but then who'd jolly well tell you left from right in the mornin'?'

Brittan laughed. 'Silly arse,' he said.

Basil took an elegant bow.

The reader took his prominent nose out of his book, and whined, 'Can't you apes keep quiet? It's hard to concentrate on higher mathematics with all this gibbering.'

Jock took hold of the reader's head, detaching the bottle-bottom glasses from it, and twisted the few remaining strands of hair on the egg-shaped dome.

'Knack, knack,' he said, 'anyone at hame?'

Sewell Head — Triple First in Romance Languages, Philosophy of Medicine and Particle Physics — writhed in the burly Scot's grasp, book dropping to the grass like a broken-backed bird.

'Leave old Swellhead alone,' Brittan said. 'He can't help being a brainbox freako.'

Jock dropped the genius, and Swellhead scrabbled for his glasses.

'Primate,' he sneered.

Brittan looked around at his friends, the three people closest to him in the world. Brawl and bicker they might, but these were men to take into the jungle. And each had a hidden side, a capability beyond the normal. Not a Talent in the sense that he was Talented, but certainly a lower-case Talent. Jock McLochness, the caber-tossing man mountain with arms as thick as a man's waist, was also — his deepest, darkest secret — Maude-Lynne Drevelle, pseudonymous author of over 100 romantic novels. Basil Mapledurham, who played so well the part of the gadabout without a neuron to his brain, was a talented amateur actor, renowned for his ability to assume any role, any disguise, any face with total conviction, often improvising make-up and costuming on the spot. And Sewell Head, multi-disciplinary genius, was, should he have cared to compete, an Olympic-level boxer whose myopia belied his devastating left hook and ferocious attack.

With friends like these, Brittan couldn't understand why everything bored him so.

'I say,' said Basil, 'why don't we take a spin into Harpenford in the old motor, and have some jollies. We could rag the bally constabulary, all come home with police helmets and truncheons. We could scrump groceries from Old Mr Shapoor's emporium, just for a lark.'

It sounded dull to Brittan. Trivial mischief. The local coppers and officious tradespeople like Shapoor might be a thorn in the backside of every true Briton, but they were dimwit opponents, not worth the effort. A man who has faced Argie machine-guns, felt bullets bouncing off his chest, can hardly be bothered with a bill-waving greengrocer or a parking-summons-issuing bobby.

'Purrhaps wae should gae tae London, oond vuzzit thae cullub, hae a wee dram or thurrety-eight, oond chase showgurrels araind thae West Aind.'

Brittan and his friends were all members of the Troy, London's oldest, most prestigious and least restrictive club for young gentlemen. They had spent many happy nights in the private rooms upstairs, feeding champagne and truffles to a succession of cockney chorus girls with funny names like Tracy, Sharon or Tina, then rogering the bints silly and sending them home in a minicab to somewhere horrible like Barnet. Now, even that didn't appeal.

Tracys and Sharons and Tinas were all very well in their place, but lately Brittan — still single at an age when all his contemporaries at school, apart from this group of reprobates, were on their fifth or sixth brat and thinking of trading in the wife for a newer model – had started to wonder about women. Maybe he was due to become an old uncle, invited to his nieces' and nephews' homes for shooting or at Christmas, but never to know the comforts of a real family, the feel of a babe on his knee, the nightly kiss-and-cocoa of a wife . . .

Brittan sadly shook his head.

'Don't despair, Dick,' said Swellhead, 'we could always drop in on the Royal Society. There's a potentially fascinating lecture on tonight, about the parallel functions of Inuit Shamen and television newsreaders. Prof Persimmons is bound to leave himself wide open to a thoroughgoing refutation in the subsequent debate.'

Jock picked Swellhead up, and dropped him again.

'Ouch,' Swellhead said, 'no need for that.'

'Och, yae melon-brained marauder, canna yae see that oor Dick lad needs muir than a lecture on I-Knew-It Semen tae perk oop his spurrits?'

Brittan turned away, and looked across at Brittan Hall, its sixteenth-century towers nestled among ancient oaks and set in rolling, green English countryside. Slobotham, perfectly dressed down to his spats, was walking briskly across the lawns, a silver salver held up in front of him, catching the sunlight.

'A tenner says I can bean the butler with a croquet ball, haggis-breath,' said Basil, holding up a crisp note.

'Yerr on,' Jock growled, counting out £10 in small change from his sporran. The money was passed to Swellhead.

Basil dropped a wooden ball on the ground in front of him, and took careful aim with his mallet, holding it like a golf club.

Slobotham was ambling up the stairs by the rockery, weaving through the puzzle gardens, towards the ornamental bridge.

'Fore,' Basil shouted, thumping the ball a hefty whack, gouging a double-size divot out of the lawn.

The ball arced into the air, and lifted high over the lawn.

'She's lookin' damn fine,' Basil said.

Slobotham turned right at the summerhouse, stepping on to the boule court.

The ball bopped the butler squarely between the eyes, and bounced.

'There,' Basil snorted, 'right on the old noggin.'

'Och, yae jummy sassenach, a lucky toss,' grumbled Jock as Swellhead gave Basil the money.

'Bring the ball back, would you, Slobbo,' shouted Basil.

Slobotham, who had wavered but not dropped the salver and its precious cargo, bowed, and picked up the ball. A red bump was growing on his high forehead.

'Haw haw haw,' Basil laughed. 'Bit of jolly, what?'

'Indubitably, Master Mapledurham,' Slobotham said.

The butler's salver bore a folded-over newspaper. *The Times*, of course. The *Telegraph* was for social climbers.

'It has gone in, sir,' Slobotham told Brittan.

He felt a surge of blood from his heart, and his chest expanded a little, stretching his vest.

'What's this?' Basil asked.

'I've placed an advertisement in the personals.'

'What? Lonely bachelor goat with lots of surplus cash and a Jag needs popsy to pork, that sort of thing?'

'No.'

Brittan sorted through the paper, skipping the boring news pages – full of miners on strike, paranorms on the rampage and johnny foreigners scrapping with each other – and found the small ads. His was in a black-edged box, taking up a three-inch square of the journal of national record.

II

Phyllida Whemple's delicate lips trembled as she re-read the boxed ad in *The Times*: '... Damsels in distress a speciality.'

At twenty-three, she supposed she counted as a damsel. And distress was certainly somewhere in the region of what she was in.

The telephone rang, jarringly loud, near her. Her heart palpitated, and, with dread, she put the paper down and reached out for the phone.

She knew what she would hear.

Trying to ignore the sudden temperature drop in her backbone, she picked up the receiver, and recited Daddy's town number.

'Hello,' she said, 'hello?'

The breathing was distant, as if beamed from a far-off planet of asthmatic inverts with nothing better to do than to frighten tender-hearted folks.

128

'Hello?'

The breathing was interrupted by something that could have been a cough or a spasm of mean-spirited laughter.

'Phyllida Whemple?' The voice, horribly familiar, croaked.

'Yes? Who is this?'

A pause. 'You know who this is. Scraggle, heh heh.'

'I warn you, this line is being tapped. The Metropolitan Police are tracing it even now. They have Talents with them, pinpointing your exact location through mental telepathy.'

The noise was definitely a chortle now.

'Nice girls shouldn't tell nasty lies, Phyllida. Not when they're dealing with Talented individuals.'

'Talented?'

'Very.'

It was what she had been afraid of, that Scraggle, the mystery caller who threatened Daddy, was a paranorm.

'Is your dear old Dad there?'

Daddy was in his study, going over business with the Chairman of the Coal Board and the Minister for Energy.

'No.'

'I've told you before about lying, heh heh. Don't make me tell you three times.'

'He can't be disturbed. He's in a meeting.'

'With the Chairman and the Minister, I know.'

Merciful Lord, they were watching the house! No one was safe.

'Just give him a message, pretty Phyllida. Tell him he knows what the consequences will be if he insists on holding the union to the agreement. The consequences for him and, I regret, the consequences for you.'

'You ...'

'Heh heh, you shouldn't think such language. Not a well-brought-up young lady like you. By the way, don't you think the blue-patterned hose is a little ... um, provoca-tive?'

The line went dead, but the whispered words hung in the air, sinking like little grapples into Phyllida's heart.

Involuntarily, she looked down. She was wearing blue tights, £79.99 a pair from Le Hose of Paris. Somehow, Scraggle had seen her.

It was what she had always feared, that someone would try to get to Daddy through her.

She replaced the telephone, carefully.

Last night, coming out of the Covent Garden bistro with Geraldine and Annabelle, she had been sure a black car, creeping down the street, was following them towards the taxi rank. And the calls had been going on for months. She had been getting them at home, at work, even at friends' houses. She knew she was being shadowed. Sometimes, she thought tramps in the street were dawdling after her. Sometimes, it was an unmarked grey van.

Two weeks ago, someone had sent her a dozen lilies and a condolence card. Two days ago, it had been a gift-wrapped dead duck, with her face sellotaped to its stiff bill. The worst of it was that her father knew, and she could see it was preying on his mind, even when he should be concentrating on more important matters.

Like the union negotiations. This miners' strike was such a nuisance. If only that Arthur Scargill and his horde of horrible, unwashed pick-pushers could see how they were making Daddy suffer — why, he had hardly touched the '58 Chateau de Dieudonné with his honey-glazed lobster and Long Island lettuce at breakfast — she was sure they would all go back to their jobs at once in shame.

The inner doors opened, and the Chairman of the Coal Board — a tall American with a stetson hat — strode out, the Minister for Energy jogging alongside to keep up with him, Daddy remaining in the doorway.

'It's decided then, pardners,' the Chairman said, 'no goddamn compromises with the NUM.'

'Oh, absolutely,' purred the Minister.

'Damn straight.'

A valet helped the dignitaries with their topcoats. The Chairman turned to Daddy, and stabbed the air with a lit cigar.

'Remember, Walt, no compromise at all. It's Main Street and High Noon. We've got the NUM by the balls, and we don't let go until they sing soprano. Right?'

Daddy nodded, less sure than the Chairman.

'Of course,' he said. He was looking greyish and hollow-eyed, Phyllida thought, and, for the first time, a little old.

'Walter,' the Minister said, 'if there was anything ... anything that might hinder you in the negotiations ... you would tell us, wouldn't you?'

'Of course,' Daddy repeated.

'And there's nothing?'

'No,' he said, face falling, a glance shot at Phyllida, 'nothing at all.'

'Ride 'em, cowboy.' The Chairman made a fist. 'Remember, squeeze 'em like lemons.'

The Chairman and the Minister made their goodbyes, bowed to Phyllida, and left.

The telephone rang. This time, Daddy got to it.

Phyllida could tell from his face what was being said. Daddy was sweating, and looking shiftily at her.

'Until tonight,' she heard the familiar voice conclude.

Daddy hung up. 'Wrong number,' he said.

'Oh, Daddy,' she cried, slipping her arms around him, and hugging hard.

He kissed her on the forehead, and returned to the

interior room, without saying anything. He shut the doors behind him.

Phyllida felt excluded, left out of her father's world. He was trying to protect her, she knew. But he was taking the weight all upon himself, not confiding in his friends or colleagues, not calling in the police or the temps.

If he asked, she was sure the Prime Minister would lend him Corporal Punishment, her personal paranorm.

She wanted to cry. She was only a slip of a girl, and what could she do against the vast and sinister forces arrayed against Daddy and all he stood for? Delicately chewing the knuckle of her right forefinger – a childhood habit she had hung on to – she looked for inspiration to the framed photographs on the hall table.

There was Daddy with Joe Gormley, shaking hands. Daddy with Edward Heath (rather at the back of the collection). Daddy climbing a Yorkshire slagheap in bright green wellies. Daddy at a charity ball, with Princess Margaret on one arm and Barbara Cartland on the other. Daddy closing down a pit in Kent, waving to an idle and miserable-looking lot of shifty layabouts. Daddy at the negotiation table, tearing up a list of demands. Daddy with the Prime Minister, their fists raised in triumph.

Phyllida let her reflection fall upon the last picture, which was bigger than the others, and measured herself against the PM. The PM had been just a girl once, and she hadn't cried, hadn't given in.

She tightened her tiny fists, and resolved not to crumple. Maybe Daddy was right. The police and the temps were too inefficient, too easy to infiltrate.

Perhaps there was another corner to which she could turn. She looked for the newspaper she had put down.

III

He had been answering the telephone all morning, and nothing promising had come up. Most of the callers were obvious crackpots, frustrated spinsters who thought their neighbours were white slavers with unspeakable intents, or train-spotting duffel coats who alleged their parents were cannibal space aliens. One Northern-accented man had outlined an entirely admirable but essentially impractical scheme to assassinate Colonel Gadaffi, another soft-spoken lunatic wanted to establish a corps of crack paranorm soldiers to take over the United Kingdom after the coming nuclear holocaust. A Pakistani 'entrepreneur' complained that Talented skinheads were mentally smashing the windows of his video shop in North London, and Brittan snarled 'No tradesmen,' at him. Several professional ladies got in touch, offering themselves as damsels capable of giving or receiving various forms of distress. A couple of bored journalists tried to pump him for his motives in placing the ad. A civil service milquetoast who purported to represent the Department of Paranormal Resources politely reminded him that, unlike heathen America, Great Britain had laws against vigilante activities.

'Hang it all by the bollocks from Nelson's Column,' Brittan swore.

The most promising inquiry before lunchtime came from Sandy Stewart, a Colchester schoolboy who complained that playground bullies habitually beat him up. Things were so desperate that Brittan was almost ready to persuade Jock, Swellhead and Basil – collectively, they had decided to call themselves the Black Hat Gang – to get in the XJ98 and head off to Colchestershire or wherever Sandy lived to use all their powers of persuasion on Gurt Git Gaiman and Nasty Roz Kaveney to get back for little A. Stewart, 2B, the three years' dinner money that had been extorted with violence from him.

Then, she called.

'Did you put an ad in *The Times*?' she breathed, her voice bell-like in its clarity, trembling slightly with obvious distress.

'Yes, 'fraid so,' Brittan replied.

'And did you mean it?'

'Of course. A gentleman always means what he says in *The Times*.'

'You don't mind danger?'

'Thrive on it, actually.'

'Ex-services? Decorated?'

'Brittan, Lieutenant Richard Lionheart, One Para, Victoria Cross, at your service.'

'Victoria Cross?'

'You can call me Dick.'

'Dick. That sounds so ... so strong, so firm, so thrusting.'

He could hear the relief in her voice, the incipient panic damped.

'Steady on, old girl. Whatever the trouble is, we've got it covered. Pitbull Brittan is on the job now.'

'Pitbull?'

'Just a nickname.'

'I see.'

'Might I ask what the problem is?'

It came in a rush, but Brittan could sort it out as she went along.

'I'm Phyllida Whemple. I work in publicity, for Porcupine Publications. Well, that's what I'm doing now. It's just something to do until I get ... um, well, married, or something ... not that there's anything going on. I was engaged to a nice boy from the Guards, but that's all off now. Best thing, really. He wasn't very interested, I don't

134

think. Anyway, my father is Walter Whemple. He's very high up in ACAS, you know, the industrial arbitration wallahs. He sorts out strikes and things, you know. The unions hate him. And he's been getting these telephone calls, and messages. Threats, Dick. I've been getting them too. There's this horrible man with a wheezy, whiny voice and a nasty laugh. He calls himself Scraggle. I think he's a Talent, you know. Anyway, I just heard him on the phone, really trying to frighten Daddy. He said something about seeing Daddy tonight, and I'm so worried this horrid creature plans to harm my father. He's a dear old thing, and tries to spare my feelings, but I know he's really worried. He's not looking well, at all . . .'

'Phyllida,' Brittan interrupted, 'just tell me your town address, and you'll have nothing to fear. The Black Hat Gang will be right there.'

'The Black Hat Gang?'

'That's us. It's just a name. Swellhead thought of it. He's the brainy one.'

'Swellhead?'

'I'll explain later, when we meet.'

'Dick?'

'Yes?'

'Somehow, I think I can trust you. Thank you so much. Thank you so, so much.'

The girl hung up, and Brittan sat back, a warm feeling spreading out from his stomach. Phyllida's voice was still in his ears, her breathless, hurried tones resonating. He tried to imagine a face, a form, to go with the girl, but shut his thoughts off. If he tried too hard, he'd conjure up an angel, and Phyllida would turn out to weigh 30 stones and have a face like a relief map of Afghanistan.

The phone rang again. Dreamily, he picked it up.

'Dick,' said the familiar voice, 'I forgot to give you my address.'

So she had. She told him, and he wrote it down on the white edge of *The Times* crossword page.

When she was gone again, he told Slobotham to bring the rest of the Black Hats to the drawing room, so he could brief them on their mission.

The phone rang again.

'Phyllida, what did you forget now?' he asked.

'Nothing,' rasped an unpleasant voice. 'Nothing at all.'

'You're not Phyllida.'

'No, you're very observant, Lieutenant Brittan, very cunning, a very potent adversary.'

'Who are you?'

'I have many names. Some call me Scraggle.'

'Scraggle?'

'That's right. I understand you've just had telephonic intercourse with a Ms Phyllida Whemple?'

'How could you know that?'

Jock and Swellhead were in the room now. Brittan motioned to them to keep quiet.

'I have my Talents, Lieutenant. As you'll find if you persist unwisely in interfering in my affairs.'

'What do you mean by that, you swine?'

'Swine, eh? Testy, this afternoon, aren't we?'

Basil was in the room too, alert, attentive.

'Lieutenant Brittan, I will advise you only once. Do not meddle with my business, do not associate with the Whemples, *père et fille*, and do not take an interest in industrial relations. Go help out poor little Sandy in Colchester. That's in Essex, by the way. Or maybe you should take a shy at Colonel Gadaffi. He's a personal friend, but he can take care of himself. At any rate, and by any means, cease and desist. The consequences, otherwise, could be extremely uncomfortable.'

The line went dead.

'Burn him up in blasted blazes,' blustered Brittan, his

face red and bloated, 'I like his nerve. I like his ruddy
nerve!'

IV

Phyllida had taken the morning off work, and decided to
do likewise with the afternoon. It wasn't like it was a *job*
or anything. Porcupine could get along quite well enough
without her for the day. She just went into the office for
her pocket money. Anyway, she was too worried to be
concerned with authors or books or horrid things like
that. She hadn't read a book that wasn't by Jeffrey Archer
since school, and didn't intend to start now.

While her father worked in his study, she fussed
around in the hall and the living room, occasionally looking in on Daddy to make sure he was all right.

She hoped this Dick Brittan would be the answer.

He had sounded so strong, so good-humoured, so confident. He had told her not to worry, and the situation
didn't seem too bad now. Dick would see off Scraggle.

Every time a car passed in the street, she hoped it
would be Dick and the Black Hat Gang, turning up to
take over and make everything all right.

Peering through the net curtains, and craning her head,
she could see to the end of the mews, and watch the
traffic passing. A grey van cruised by, too slowly. Then,
a few minutes later, it passed back the other way.

Phyllida felt a clutch of terror. They were out there.

The doorbell rang, and her spirits rose. It was Dick,
come to save them all.

Giddy, she opened the door, almost singing with
relief . . .

And was confronted with a disgusting old woman,
rattling a tin and shoving ratty heather at her. She was

dressed in little better than rags, and had deep seams of dirt in her face. Her evil eyes glittered in a mask of filth, curtains of stringy brown hair framing her coarse features.

''Eather fur the norphans, missy?'

Phyllida backed away, trembling.

''Eather?'

She tried to slam the door, but the woman was on the welcome mat, shaking her heather.

She tried to tell her to go away, but words wouldn't come out of her mouth.

The crone looked around.

'Lurveley place,' she said, grinning to show off her yellow National Health teeth, 'lurveley.'

'Go away,' Phyllida said, quietly, trying to stand firm.

'Wot's 'at? I'm deef, luvvy. Deef as a bat.'

The old woman stretched out a crooked finger, towards Phyllida's cheek. She was afraid the hag would *touch* her, pollute her ...

The intruder was laughing now, dropping all pretence of deference. Phyllida knew this was one of Scraggle's agents.

'Lurveley,' she gargled.

A huge hand fell on the woman's shoulder.

'Wot?'

She was lifted out of the way, and put into the street, a square boot on her backside. She landed on the pavement, with a sharp crack, and ran off, clutching a bloody nose.

Healthy laughter followed her to the end of the mews.

A huge man came into the hall, and strong arms went around Phyllida. She had been feeling woozy in the head and trembly in the knees.

'Dick?'

The man nodded, radiating warmth and comfort.

'Phyllida?'

She smiled, and kept the embrace a moment longer than form demanded. Dick Brittan was a rough-faced, good-featured man, with a once-broken nose and laughing blue eyes with steely grey flecks in them. He wasn't exactly a *Face* model, but he was undeniably attractive in an earthy, British-beef sort of way. His skin had a red-apple ripeness to it, tight and fleshy. Phyllida knew this was the kind of man she would have to be careful around.

'Don't worry,' he said. 'We're here.'

'We' must be the Black Hat Gang. There were three of them besides Dick, and none wore a black hat. One was a kilted bear of a man, bigger even than the fairly big Dick, the others a reedy fop with no chin and an eyeglass and a funny little gnome with a huge and mainly hairless dome of a head and almost opaque glasses.

'Jock McLochness, Basil Mapledurham, Swellhead,' Dick said, introducing them.

Doors opened, and Daddy emerged from his study, horn-rims up on his forehead. 'What is this?'

He looked bewildered and baffled.

'Daddy,' she explained, 'I've called these people to help us.'

'Help? We don't need help.'

Daddy looked disapprovingly at her.

'I don't mean any disrespect, but I think you do need help, sir,' said Dick, taking over. 'I know about Scraggle.'

'Scraggle?' Daddy's face lost all its colour, and he slumped into a chair.

'I'm Lieutenant Brittan, sir.'

'Pitbull,' said Jock.

'We understand you're expecting an unwelcome visitation tonight?'

Daddy slid his face into his cupped hands. His shoulders shook.

'It's true,' he sobbed. 'I didn't know who to call. If I'd told the Minister, I'd lose my position.'

Phyllida put an arm around Daddy, and consoled him.

'Oh, Daddy,' she said. 'Don't be a silly. You're the PM's favourite. She was ever so grateful when you made the railwaymen cave in and accept those massive cuts.'

Swellhead was poking around the hall, looking at little objects. He picked up a shred of tatty heather, and tutted over it.

'Very interesting,' he said, producing a little Cellophane packet and prodding the heather into it. 'I'll have to examine this in minute detail later.'

Dick was looking around too, checking windows and locks.

'It seems secure, defensible. I think we can surprise our visitors, Mr Whemple. They aren't expecting the Black Hat Gang.'

Daddy looked up, relief dawning in his face.

'Oh yes, we'll be ready for them. Jock, get the ordnance from the Range Rover. We can set up a few surprises in the hall.'

Dick seemed to expand as he took in a breath, filling out his marvellously cut £1,299.99, Bradstock & Whately of Savile Row, suit. She had felt hard, solid muscle under his £149.99, Triple Q of Kensington, handmade shirt when they embraced. He seemed almost like a bronze statue, standing in her hallway. With him there, nothing could frighten her. Nothing would ever change for the worse.

'Phyllida,' he said, 'is there anyone you can stay with?'

'What?'

'There's no sense you being here, getting into danger. We can't risk that. Besides, things might get pretty dicey, pretty hairy. No sense in you being exposed to blood and guts and ruptured spleens and stuff like that. We have to spare your feminine sensibilities.'

'Oh yes,' she said, 'you're so thoughtful. I can call up Annabelle Krantzen, and stay with her in Bishop's Walk.'

'Fine. Weight off my mind. Now, Mr Whemple, let's start thinking tactics . . .'

Jock came into the hall, a couple of large iron mantraps slung on his back.

'Surrprise, surrprise,' he said, 'these'll snupp thae swaine in twain.'

'Rather,' said Basil. 'Ripping.'

Dick laughed, and clapped his friends on their shoulders. One of Jock's traps was sprung, and clanged in the air, leaping off his back.

'Dashed close thing, what,' Basil said.

'Nae harrum done, Dick lad, nae harrum done.'

Dick took the trap, and with all the apparent effort of someone opening a ring-pull can, eased the pressure-spring trap wide open, and locked it in place, setting it down on the welcome mat.

'Let's see any gyppo get their heather through that,' he said.

V

With Phyllida safely installed in her chum's flat and out of the way, Brittan felt more secure. Whatever happened, the girl − an entrancingly slim brunette, more angelic than anything he could have imagined − wasn't going to get hurt. He was free to get rough with anyone who caused trouble.

They tried playing '20 Questions' to pass the time, but Swellhead always got it within three questions, and Jock or Basil always hit him when he did.

The telephone rang once, and Brittan had tensed, waiting for the threat, but it was only the Minister for Energy, with some last-minute pit closure demands to be worked into the agreement with the NUM.

Whemple was fidgety, expectant. Brittan felt sorry for him, and tried to keep him distracted by explaining how he had won the Victoria Cross.

'I could see the Argies levelling their guns at the column of civilian refugees, and there was only one thing to do. With all my men at my back, I ordered the charge. I felt bullets spanging off my chest as I went up that hill in bounds. There were thirty-one of us when we started off, and only I made it to the top.'

The others had heard this story too many times, and were snoozing, doing crosswords or reading.

'The gun nest was commanded by an officer they called the Green Gaucho, a paranorm who could spit venom. I went over the side, and laid about me, scattering Argies here and there. The Green Gaucho hissed, and I thumped my way towards him, squelching skulls . . .'

'Quiet,' said Swellhead, 'I heard something.'

Brittan shut up, and listened.

There were the usual small noises of the night. And the click of Jock priming his Thompson sub-machine-gun.

'Thinkin' too much, brain-bean,' Basil scoffed.

'No, he's right,' Brittan said.

There was a soft hiss, like a slow puncture.

'Look,' Swellhead said, pointing at the lower edge of the door.

A curl of odourless white smoke was creeping in, and spreading like a pool of heavy liquid.

'Gas?' Jock asked.

'I don't think so.'

Brittan's heart was pumping iron, and his clothes were getting tight. There was a throbbing heat in his groin, and his John Thomas uncurled in his jockey shorts as it always did when he sensed danger. He knew he was about to go into action. The bloodbeat in his ears was a steady pounding now. The shoulder seams of his jacket strained, and bit into his bulging muscle.

The smoke was rising a little, taking shape.

Jock sighted on the man-sized column, and unloosed a brief burst of fire.

The wood behind the smoky form splintered as the bullets punched through.

'It was worruth a try,' Jock said.

The smoke was thick now, most concentrated about four feet off the floor, with trailing tendrils reaching out like the legs of an octopus. Brittan swore he could see eyes in the thing.

'Quick,' he said, 'the extractor fan.'

Whemple, who had been staring in amazement, was slapped out of his daze, and stabbed a button. A refreshing breeze pulled through the room, towards a whirling circle in the wall.

The smoke octopus was tugged towards the fan, and struggled in the air. It was getting more solid by the second.

Brittan grabbed the smoke, and pulled a fistful of it free. It came away, trailing tubers behind it, and whisped in the air.

'Everyone,' he said, 'before it becomes real.'

They all leaped on the smoke thing, and began fanning it into pieces, tearing candyfloss lumps loose and stamping on them. It was thicker than smoke, but could still be dispersed. It left scummy smears where it had been.

Out in the hallway, there was a wrenching clang, and a cry of high-pitched agony. Someone had tripped one of Jock's traps. Hooray.

The smoke thing was just a mess on the carpet. Then, the bullet-holed doors bent inwards as something heavy thudded against them. The lock shot out of the wood, and bodies forced themselves into Whemple's study.

The first one through the door was a wide-shouldered man in dusty overalls, with a miner's helmet on, a face-covering black visor extending underneath his lamp.

Jock got him in the upper torso with a machine-gun burst, and blood spat out of his wounds. His faceplate cracked, and he went down. But there were others, too many to shoot, pouring in. Jock was pushed back by two of them intercepting him with a rugby tackle, and slammed against a bookshelf, going down with leather-bound government reports bouncing on his head, his gun wrenched out of his hands.

Brittan's John Thomas stood straight out like an iron dowsing rod, tenting the front of his trousers. His belt was now cinched too tight, and his jacket had torn under the arms. He burst out of his shoes, his socks splitting like Turkish-made condoms.

One of the helmeted devils swung a gauntleted fist at him, and he caught the hand, crushing it like a sparrow. His assailant yelped, and went down on his knees. Brittan slammed his knee into the man's face, cracking the visor. He picked him, fingers digging into flesh like vices, and tossed him at two more of the attack crew. They had yapping animals with them, dogs the size of pit ponies. Brittan saw Basil shoot one of these things, and heard it flop against the wall, a sack of shattered bones.

Brittan grabbed a helmeted head and twisted it on its neck, wrenching the faceplate around, relishing the grind and snap of vertebrae. Someone raised an automatic, and emptied a clip against his side, bullets flattening against his kidneys, bouncing off his rigid stomach muscles and slamming into another of the attackers, making him shudder and collapse. Brittan grabbed the automatic, and twisted it into a Plasticine lump. Then he tugged the gunman's arm off, and tossed it away, leaving the one-armed man writhing on the floor as frothy blood jetted from his wound. He kicked the man, and jabbed a crushing elbow into the throat of another. Basil was taking care of a helmethead who was trying to set up some kind of apparatus, slamming his visored face into the workings of the machine. It exploded with a belch of white smoke, and Brittan guessed that was where the octopus thing had come from.

One of the helmetheads fiddled with a battery pack attached to his lamp, and green light shot out, in a concentrated beam, painful to look at.

Jock waved at the light, trying to make it go away, and yelled out as the hair on his hand started to smoke. The smell of singeing flesh was heavy in the air.

Brittan ripped the remains of his jacket away, and took a deep breath, bursting all his shirt buttons, reducing the Triple Q to a few tatters of bandage around his chest and biceps, sleeveless cuffs like taut wristlets.

Jock screamed, as the green beam was shone in his face, and his skin began to pucker and boil.

Brittan stepped in the path of the light, and felt prickling pain in the centre of his chest. He looked down, and saw a circle of green between his round and reddening pectorals, focusing a painpoint on his sternum.

He set his teeth in a grimace and stepped forwards, ignoring the intensifying hurt.

The helmethead kept the beam steady, and held his ground.

Every inch was more agony. The light circle got smaller, more painful.

Behind him, Basil was shooting a dog thing in the head. Swellhead was sparring with a helmethead, punishing his body with scientific blows.

Brittan's fists were swelling, fingers curved tubes like overstuffed sausages. He was just meat and bone, despite his Talent. He could be hurt. Sweat was pouring out of his armpits, trickling down his sides. He yelled his defiance.

The helmethead with the beam weapon was laughing

behind his mask. For a moment, Brittan thought it was Scraggle, but then he realized the tone was higher-pitched, more rodentlike.

He was close enough now to reach out and hurt the man.

He laid a hand on the visor, and squeezed, crumpling the steel-tempered plastic as if it were crêpe paper, catching quite a bit of nose and skin with it.

The helmethead's laughter turned to screams.

The beam was irritating his arm as he ground the mask shards into the man's face. With his other hand, he wrenched the lamp off the helmet. It didn't go out.

He pushed the man away, and turned his own lamp on him. His overalls began to smoulder, and then burst into flames. He screeched for a while, and the vile stench of overcooked human flesh rose from him. Whemple was there with the fire extinguisher, splurging white foam on to the fiery corpse.

The cries died down, and the night sounds came back.

Between them, the Black Hat Gang had seen off nine helmethead attackers, and two dog mutants. The study was a wreck, crowded with bodies and pieces of body. In the hallway, there was one more of the vermin, neatly snipped in two by the trap.

Brittan bellowed his triumph, the air roaring through his lungs. He was getting red spots on his vision now, and his John Thomas was a full foot of white-hot poker, iron-turgid with excess blood. He could have bitten through a steel bar as if it were a stick of rock.

His arms were inflated like dirigibles, blue veins standing out like fire-hoses, and his neck was swollen until it was almost as large as his head. His face felt as if it were sculpted of fire.

'Well done, lads,' he said.

'It was nothin',' Basil drawled, 'just a spot of much-needed exercise. Not even very sportin' really.'

Whemple, shaken but unhurt, caught sight of Brittan.

'Lieutenant,' he blurted, 'your face . . .'

Brittan knew what he must look like. His face filled with blood became a snarling Japanese dragon mask, bulbous cheeks red, swollen forehead, lips pulled back in a terrifying snarl.

'Oh my lord, Pitbull,' Swellhead said, 'that was fast. Too fast. I'm afraid the process is accelerating.'

'What is it?' Whemple asked.

'Pitbull has a peculiar and unique metabolism, Mr Whemple,' Swellhead explained. 'In moments of need, it gives him strength, resilience and an unparalleled force of will. But, unless he achieves release, he could hurt himself permanently.'

'Permanently?'

Brittan's fly could stand no more, and his John Thomas knifed through the zip-stitching.

Whemple whistled.

Brittan's knob-end was the size of a velvety purple cooking apple, the connecting vein a pulsing, finger-thick tube, strained to capacity.

'Quickly,' Basil said, 'straws. You're in too, Whemple. It's your life he saved.'

'What's this?' the arbitrator mumbled.

Swellhead produced four straws, one shorter than the others, and held them in his fist.

'Choose,' he said to Whemple.

Brittan felt electric discharges of agony. The red spots on his vision were turning white, and the rapid pumping of his heart was up to ramming speed, assaulting his ears. The veins in his temples were near bursting point, and he could barely feel anything below the waist but agony.

Whemple's fingers fluttered over the straws.

'Nae, lads,' said Jock, staggering to his feet. His face

was soot-black, and red weals peeled in his skin. His
eyebrows were white ash, and his fresh burns glistened
as if vaselined. 'I owe Dick lad mae life, oond 'tis oop tae
mae.'

Swellhead dropped the straws.

'Let's gae upstairs, Dick lad,' said Jock, grimly.

VI

Annabelle was trying to keep her mind off Daddy, prat-
tling on about her new bloke, and how disgusting he was.
Annabelle specialized in disgusting boyfriends, always
choosing someone racially or physically grotesque just to
have material for her monologues. Her last but two had
been a Talent, fully registered with temps, and his code-
name had been Mould Man. He could make things rot
just by looking at them. *Uck!* Phyllida Whemple had
been at school with Annabelle Krantzen, and the old wind-
bag was her best pal, really, even if she did have a kraut
name and a succession of wastrel b.f.s.

Phyllida divided her attention between Annabelle's
meandering and the ITN news. The PM was making a
statement about the miners, and how she didn't intend to
give in to strike blackmail tactics. Good for her. Daddy's
photograph was flashed up when they mentioned the
arbitration talks, and the girls cheered him, raising their
chilled white wine to the TV screen. Phyllida was pleased
to hear that another 100,000 miners had gone cheerfully
back to work. Then, they were on to a report about a
Colchester schoolboy who had been beaten to death by
school bullies. 'If only Sandy had asked for help,' a head-
master said.

Annabelle turned the sound down, and poured herself
another fluted glass of Moselle, dropping in a cherry.

'Anyway,' she said, fluffing a hand in her red meringue of hair, 'he's got a funny back, and laughs a lot while we're ... you know ... doing it. And he drools, repulsively.'

Phyllida shivered. She didn't look forward to meeting this one. Although, actually, Annabelle's repulso beaux usually turned out to be disappointingly ordinary, their faults magnified by her chattering imagination.

The doorbell chimed, the first line of 'Girls Just Wanna Have Fun', and Phyllida, more tense than she thought, jumped a little, spilling wine on a copy of *The Lady* she had been riffling through.

'It's Him,' Annabelle screeched, with delight.

'Mr Drool?'

'Yurp, the very same. Don't breathe a word, and don't, on pain of unmarried pregnancy, giggle at his hump. He's very sensitive.'

She was on the entryphone, buzzing the boyfriend into the house.

'Watch his hands,' Annabelle advised, unlocking the flat door.

The light in the hallway went on, and Phyllida heard someone coming up.

'Coo-ee,' coo-eed Annabelle, and Phyllida heard squelchy kissing, as they met on the landing.

'Here,' said Annabelle, ushering her boyfriend in.

Phyllida was taken aback. Mr Drool really was a hunchback, albeit a very well-dressed one, with a malacca cane and an astrakhan-collared £999.99, Trubshaw & Colneyhurst, camel-hair coat. He was older than Annabelle's usual tastes, with shocks of white hair above his ears and eyes and standing out of his beaked nose. He smiled, and his head oscillated from side to side.

'This is Scraggle,' Annabelle said.

A sliver of ice slipped down the back of Phyllida's

dress, slithering down her spine, weaving in and out of the vertebrae, and melting in the crack of her buttocks.

'Hello, Phyllida,' Scraggle said, wheezing in an awfully familiar manner.

Phyllida opened her mouth to scream, but nothing came.

VII

Slobotham arrived within the hour, bearing a complete change of clothes, and Brittan, suitably dwindled and refreshed after a turn in Whemple's shower, was perfectly attired again, a fresh carnation in his dinner jacket, trouser seams perfectly aligned, purple cummerbund in place.

The crisis had passed.

'Thanks, Jock,' he said, patting his friend's shoulder as the doctor patched up his facial burns.

'Think nothing of it,' Jock said between clenched teeth. 'Yae'd hae dane the same furr mae.'

'Of course, my old Stone of Scone.'

The doctor, Whemple's own Harley Street man, was circumspect enough not to mention the state of the study as he worked on Jock.

Basil had a few scratches from one of the dog monsters, but otherwise the Black Hat Gang had come through unscathed.

Swellhead was in with the dead men, looking for clues.

Whemple was serving brandy snifters, fairly bubbling with relief.

The telephone rang, and Whemple picked it up, Brittan listening in on the hallway extension.

'Hello?'

'Whemple?'

'Scraggle?'

'Got it in one, heh heh.'

'You must be smarting, losing all those hired hooligans.'

'Not losing, sacrificing.'

There was a jostling at the other end of the line, and a feminine squeal, 'Daddy?'

'Phyllida,' Whemple and Brittan blurted out, together.

'Ah, Lieutenant Brittan, you are there,' wheezed Scraggle, 'I rather thought you might be.'

'Phyllida!'

'Yes, that's right. The attack on you was just a ... how shall I put it ... divertissement. My real purpose was the abduction of the lissom Ms Whemple, and very delightful she is too. A man in your condition would do well to have a Ms Whemple with you. So soft, so ... um ... pliant. And so much more congenial than some hairy haggis, wouldn't you say?'

'You foul-minded fiend, Scraggle!'

'Temper, temper.'

Jock appeared at the doorway, and delicately crossed the room on bow-legs, listening intently.

'What have you done to her?' Whemple demanded.

'Why, nothing ... yet. Heh heh.'

'If you ...'

'"Harm one hair on her head"? Lieutenant Brittan, you have an appallingly unimaginative grasp of metaphor, if I may say so. And you severely underestimate my own breadth of capabilities when it comes to harming Ms Whemple. Could you not think of a more apt expression, "If you pull one nail on her foot", "If you burst one eye in her head", "If you eat one vital organ in her innards", "If you ..."'

Brittan felt the blood hammering his skull, and his new underwear constricting.

'Getting it up, are we?' Scraggle chortled. 'Careful, don't get so excited. You might burst a blood vessel.'

'What do you want, Scraggle?' Whemple asked.

'It's not what I want, Mr Whemple, it's what the people want. Specifically, the miners. As you know, I represent the interests of the working men of this country, heh heh.'

Brittan felt as if he were about to sick up an undigested side of beef. To think that this piece of excrement in roughly human form claimed to be on the side of the working man, when all his kind ever did was pull down great industries, throwing millions on to the scrap heap of unemployment, undoing the work of great men who laboured long and hard to run the corporations Scraggle and his filthy Trotskyist like were so incapable of appreciating! It was an obscenity!

'You are familiar with the demands of the National Union of Mineworkers? No pit closures without consultation, increased safety precautions, shorter hours, longer wage packets, earlier retirement, a dismantling of all nuclear power stations, union representation on the board, free cocaine and whelks in the showers, that sort of thing.'

'You scum!'

'Come come, Mr Whemple. You're beginning to sound like Lieutenant Dickhead here, heh heh.'

A current coursed through Brittan's urethra, and his John Thomas twitched like a trod-on snake.

'At any rate, you will put up a spirited defence of the government position – we wouldn't want the PM getting suspicious and removing you, would we? – and then, at the last minute, you will emotionally cave in and grant all the concessions that nice Mr Scargill is demanding. And everyone will be happy, no?'

'And Phyllida?'

'I imagine she'll be happy too. Well, at least *happier*.'

Brittan heard Phyllida's distant squealing and sobbing again.

'No, no, Greasy Eric,' Scraggle said to someone at his end, 'that's not how you attach those live wires.'

Brittan's shirt seams began to pop, his cummerbund stretched uncomfortably over his granite stomach.

'I must go now. It seems I have to do everything around here. You just can't get hooligans like you used to, heh heh. Abyssinia.'

Scraggle hung up. And Brittan swore that the Talent would die by his hand.

Whemple was crying again.

VIII

Brittan thumped his bowling-ball-like fist down on the polished table, imagining Scraggle's skull pulping under the force of the blow. Then he imagined fishing the fiend's eyeballs out with his thumbs, and shoving them as far up his foul nostrils as they would go, then getting a good grip on his lying tongue and pulling it out like a tape measure before tying it in a noose around his scrawny proletarian neck and pulling it as tight as a cat's arsehole and watching the union agitator's ugly face turn all the colours of the rainbow as the life leaked messily out of his verminous body. Jolted out of his reverie, he realized he had absent-mindedly picked up a Sung Dynasty vase and ground it to dust in his fists.

'Sorry, Whemple,' he said.

'Don't think of it,' the arbitrator said, waving the damage away. 'Ugly bit of crockery anyway.'

'Dash it to blistering blazes, I hate just sitting around here waiting for that monster's next call! I wish there were something we could *do* to save poor Phyllida from his lecherous horde of unwashed slackers!'

'Yes,' agreed Basil, cleaning his monocle on his ascot, 'it is rather distressin' to think of that poor, slim, virginal girl, slowly stripped of her flimsy underthings by bucks with gorilla brows and brawny forearms. To think of the horrible indignities that are doubtless this very minute bein' inflicted upon her helpless form, the ice baths and electrodes, the red-hot tongs and whippings, the caged rats pressed to her soft, white belly and encouraged to tuck in ... I say, Whemple's off again. Never known such a man for blubbin'.'

The arbitrator was banging his head against the table, and bawling, his entire body racked with heartbreaking sobs.

'Anyway,' Basil continued, 'what about the lighted cigarettes pressed to her quiverin' ...'

Whemple howled.

'Shut up, Basmo,' Brittan growled, 'you're being a silly arse again.'

'Sorry. Just tryin' to be realistic, what.'

'"Tis turrible, turrible,' Jock agreed, gingerly squirming in his seat, trying to settle down comfortably on the three cushions he had piled under him, 'and tae think wae bae sae haelpless. If only wae ken wheere thae vullains haid taeken purr wee Phyllida. Thae must hae same kaind ae haide-oot, whaire thae kin plot oond scheeme thair turrible, turrible deeds.'

Brittan thumped the table again, shaking everyone.

'Jock's right. We should find out where they've gone, and moustache them in their lair.'

'I believe, Pitbull, that the proper expression is "beard them in their lair",' Swellhead put in, 'the word "beard", in this case, meaning "to oppose face to face".'

Impatient, Brittan fetched his friend a gentle thump

around the earhole, unloosing him from his chair and sending him sprawling across the floor. Jock and Basil laughed at this comical turn, but Brittan didn't feel any better.

Basil had been right. What Phyllida must be undergoing at this very moment was unthinkable, disgusting, infuriating . . .

In the space of the twenty minutes Brittan had spent in the company of Phyllida Whemple, he had realized that his bachelor days were over. If they both came out of this scrape alive and intact, he intended to marry the arbitrator's daughter, and keep her safe forever from the designs of those who would wish to do her harm. His manly heart beat louder as he thought of her pale skin, bee-stung lips, lithe limbs, luxurious brown hair and appealing cloche hat.

Swellhead stumbled back to the table, righted his chair, and sat down. Brittan affectionately rubbed his friend's bald bonce, and Swellhead grinned, knowing that he had been an utter prig and that such abuse was all in good, masculine, comradely fun.

'Incinerate it in the lowest pit of the fiery furnace of Hell,' Brittan swore, 'we can't let Scraggle and his rabble win! We can't let down the PM and allow the unions to goose-step all over the country! Next thing you know, they'll be letting miners with dirt on their faces eat pie and chips at the Savoy! They'll lower the speed limit and have constables spend all their time bothering Jaguars and Porsches while nasty little foreign cars crawl by and nab all the parking spots in the West End! They'll move into the Troy Club, and you won't be able to get near the bar or the billiards room for stinky louts in cloth caps with ferrets down their trousers and brown ale in their bellies!'

Together, they shook their heads sadly at the prospect of the end of civilization.

Swellhead took a small packet out of his pocket and turned it over. It contained some sort of dried leaf.

'This is no time to blow reefer, egghead,' Brittan said, sternly.

Swellhead emptied the packet out.

'Obviously, these leaves are quite a different genus from *Cannabis sativa*. As even an uneducated eye should note, these are from some peculiar subspecies of *Calluna vulgaris*, commonly known as heather.'

'Typical of bloody old Swellhead, what,' said Basil. 'Poor old Phyllida's bein' mauled by mobsters, and he's sniffin' weeds. Deuced disgrace.'

'Shut up, Basil,' said Brittan, thinking he was only a few laps behind Swellhead mentally, and catching up fast as he got his second wind. 'He's talking about the gyppo.'

'That's right, the heather-seller who bothered Miss Whemple earlier. She's in the study now, with most of her head missing. Good work, Pitbull. It must have been a very tricky bit of thumping to whack her so properly. The maxilla was driven square up into the cranial matter, quite breaching the medulla oblongata. My guess would be that bone shards were distributed into the brain tissue as far as the fissure of Rolando. Anyway, my primary deduction is that quite a few of the other deceased types strewn about the place are her friends and relations. I found the quite distinctive puce and lemon yellow scarves of the *Mazuke Grobbo* tribe of *tzigane*, noted for their interbreeding of rottweiler and pit pony, and who are found, as you know, in only three places in Europe. The shunned village of Ostragrob in the Carpathians, the accursed Gronzelle Forest in the Loire, and the unemployment blackspot of County Durham, England.'

'That narrows it down,' Brittan said, slamming a fist into his open palm. 'Jock, you go to Romania, I'll take France and Basmo can go to Durham.'

'I say, I'd much rather I went to France. Could drop in on that frightfully nice gel Monique Tour-du-Monde in Montmartre. Oh yes, like that, I would.'

Swellhead picked up the heather.

'Before you argue further, I have made some more deductions, with regards to this humble scrap of roadside vegetation. You'll note the yellow edging of the leaves, and the discoloration of the underside. This genus is common throughout the Midlands and the North of England, but I'd hazard a guess that this particular strain of heather-blight could only be found in one spot within these islands . . .' Swellhead paused dramatically, waiting to be asked. '. . . that spot, my friends, is the mining village of Thornley, in County Durham.'

At that moment, just as the Black Hat Gang were congratulating Swellhead for his braininess, Slobotham insinuated himself into the room.

'Sirs, if I might venture to add some information, I was just going through the pockets of those cadavers in the study and I happened to find that each and every one of them has in his or her possession a return ticket from Thornley, County Durham, to London King's Cross. Standard class.'

'And that, I think, proves my deductions beyond a doubt,' Swellhead declared.

IX

'Where am I,' Phyllida whimpered, 'where am I?'

She had come to in a dark place, and found her hands cuffed behind her, and her legs tied together. She was on a cot of some sort, strapped down.

There was a most nauseating smell nearby.

'Safe,' a familiar voice told her.

'Annabelle,' she cried, heart squeezing past her tonsils, 'so they got you too.'

'Not exactly.'

Phyllida's eyes fluttered, and she realized the room was dimly lit. She turned around, wriggling in her straps.

'Annabelle,' she gasped in horror, 'your clothes!'

Her best friend had, when Scraggle invaded the flat, been wearing a quite fetching burnt orange shot-silk blouse and £750 slacks from Moritz of Swiss Cottage, with heavy amber–jade earrings and calf-hide pumps. Now, she wore a greasy bandanna, crossed bandoliers of bullets, a £2.50 Ken Livingstone T-shirt and camouflage pants tucked at the bottom into army surplus size-eight combat boots. She had ditched the earrings, and her major accessory was a big ugly machine-gun, slung around her shoulder.

'How could you do your make-up like that?'

Annabelle had green and brown tiger-stripes on her cheeks and hands, very sloppily applied, and no lipstick.

'It's awful.'

Annabelle prodded her with the business end of the gun.

'No,' she said, 'it's quite nice, really. Scraggle has pulled me out of my old, useless, pointless life and shown me how to be a real woman, how to take charge of my destiny, how to realize my place in the revolutionary plan. You wouldn't believe it, but yesterday I actually washed up four used tea-mugs. Yes, me! I got my hands in soapy water, and managed to get those mugs clean. And I rinsed them! And dried! It was a mystical experience for me, to understand the nobility of labour, to feel yourself a part of the great proletarian mass which will sweep away like a tidal wave the artificial privilege of the pampered and pointless classes to which I used to belong.'

'Annie, you are talking such rot. If you could only hear yourself.'

'Capitalist bitch, pawn of the ruling classes, oppressor of the innocent, despoiler of babies . . .'

Annabelle was enthusiastically waving her gun. Phyllida hoped someone had explained about the safety catch. Her best friend always had been laughably inept with mechanical things.

'Babies,' Annabelle enthused, 'I want to have lots of them, for the Revolution! I want to make babies with miners, to have them grow inside me, one after another, popping out. I always want to have two babies for each tit, and two or three more inside my womb. I'm an earth mother of the masses, Phyl. Scraggle has shown me the way.'

Phyllida turned her face to the wall, and cried.

X

Brittan's custom-made four-seater Jaguar XJ98 roared like a he-lion as it tore out of London, heading for the northeast. At the wheel, Brittan's mouth was set in a grim straight line. He ignored the blast of wind on his face as his machine, the physical extension of his eighth-of-a-ton of muscle and meat and bone, thrust into the darkness, eating up the throw of his headlights, driving lesser automobiles from its path. His hands were firm on the wheel and the gearshift, and his seatbelt hung unused beside him.

Seatbelts were for middle-class snails who cared whether they lived or died!

Brittan drew up close behind a slowcoach of the highways, an articulated lorry crawling along at 75 mph, lazily clogging the road, and blocking his path to Phyllida.

He could read the legend on the back of the lorry:
B. D. SMEDLEY & SONS, FINE PORCELAIN TOILETS AND INJEC-
TION MOULDED PLASTIC SEATS, EST. 1978.

'Scorch and cinder it to the very bowels of Pluto's
dominion, toasting crumpets on a trident in the all-con-
suming brimstone burner of Abaddon and Phlegethon,'
he swore. No privies would prevent him from saving
Phyllida. 'Hold on tight, chums, this might be a touch
gamey.'

The XJ98 swung out into the hard shoulder, crushing
plastic cones under its grill, and nosed even with the
articulated lorry. There were works up ahead, but Brittan
knew he could ease back in front of B. D. SMEDLEY and
leave the bogseat-bearing bounder in the dust before
they hit the holes.

Swellhead had his pocket calculator out, and was meas-
uring wind velocities and rate of acceleration.

'Thirty-eight seconds, Pitbull,' he concluded.

'Tchah,' Brittan spat. 'Hours to spare!'

Brittan looked at the driver of the lorry – a porky moon-
calf with a bewildered grin – and slammed his foot to the
floor, sending more spurts of power into the perfectly
tuned engine of his majestic beast of the road.

As he brought the car around in front, Brittan playfully
nudged the front bumper of the lorry, counting coup in
this minor victory.

He roared his victory, feeling his powerful buttocks
expand under him as the blood inflated his gluteal
muscles.

The XJ98 left behind the honking horn of B. D.
SMEDLEY's finest, and Brittan roundly condemned all
toilets and seats to the abyss.

Jock laughed.

Behind them, the lorry skewed across the motorway a
couple of times, and flipped over.

'Can't take the speed,' Brittan said, 'shouldn't be on the road.'

There were explosions as cars piled into the whale-size lorry, and a fine rain of porcelain fell. Burning petrol spilled across the asphalt. Then, the lorry was lost behind them.

'Thornley, here we come,' Brittan said.

XI

Thornley was Hell on Earth.

They had parked the XJ98 a few miles away, concealed in the undergrowth, then sauntered into the village. Basil had brought along his make-up kit and costume box, and now the four Black Hats were perfectly disguised as miners, so unrecognizable that they would have been refused entrance to the Troy Club. They wore cloth caps, mucky boots, and moleskin trousers with belts and elas-ticated braces, and their faces and hands were liberally dirtied with authentic-looking coaldust and machine grime. Just so long as they kept their mouths shut, they were as scurvy a crew of working-class scum as Brittan could hope to scrape off his shoes.

As they approached the village, they heard the sounds of riotous revelry, clogs slapping concrete, conflicting brass bands playing 'On Ilkley Moor Bar Tat' and 'Danny Boy', darts thudding into boards, kegs emptying of beer, callused hands slapping wobbly bottoms, rifles being discharged in the air, glass breaking.

They kept close together, as they passed the WELCOME TO THORNLEY sign, which was daubed with NO SOUTHERN BASTARDS and a skull and crossbones. Beyond, were rows of back-to-back miners' cottages, and lesser streets of squat prefabs with allotments out the back.

Hanging by a noose from the first streetlamp was a burning mannequin, with the Queen's smiling photograph pasted to the face.

Brittan could hardly contain his patriotic wrath, and felt a surging inside his furry britches. He knew there would be some action soon.

The next burning mannequin had the PM's face, and had had holes shot through its plastic torso.

Also massacred in effigy were Corporal Punishment and Loric.

It was a horrifying spectacle.

Dancing around the lamppost from which the disembowelled effigy dangled, book-pages spilling out of its violated stomach, was a ring of barefoot ragamuffin children, dust on their cheeks, holes in their dresses. They occasionally took time out of the ring to inhale glue from plastic bags.

Brittan's braces were stretching, his fly buttons tugging at their holes.

The others were equally disgusted, and appalled. Brittan could see the honest shock and disbelief on their disguised faces as they wandered closer to the heart of darkness that was Thornley, County Durham.

In his mind, Brittan heard again the retching laugh of Scraggle.

'Look,' Swellhead said, 'look . . .'

In the village square, surrounded by the brass bands, was a medieval five-person stocks, and heads were poking through the holes. Burly young men with beer bellies and fat cackling hags in floral print dresses were hurling rotten fruit at the unfortunates.

'Scabs,' they chanted as they threw the splattering projectiles, 'bosses' lackeys, scabs . . .'

Brittan felt his fury expanding his chest. He sincerely admired the courage of those who stood up to the tyranny of the NUM, and stayed at work while the slackers, the scroungers and the slime skived off for their measly strike. These were the true Britons, the honest miners who knew their place, who didn't want to stuff their pay packets beyond all reason, who selflessly toiled in the dark to keep society on the rails. And Scraggle and his scum were making monkeys of them, subjecting them to awful humiliations.

He saluted the martyrs. But, in order to blend in with the crowd, the Black Hats picked up some fruit and took a couple of good shots. It set the disguise off perfectly.

The focus of all activity was a huge building in the square, with well-lit windows. The odour of gassy beer poured out of it in a poisonous cloud. Above the double-doors was a sign, THORNLEY WORKING MEN'S CLUB. A neon noticeboard flashed SPECIAL VARIETY NITE, ALL WEL-COME (EXCEPT SCABS).

Among the tin-helmeted miners, Brittan noticed others: swarthy Cubans in guerrilla gear with sub-machine-guns and berets, bearded Libyans in burnouses with scantily-dressed dancers on their arms, dour Russian plotters in ill-fitting suits with hammer-and-sickle tiepins, garlic-smelling French terrorists in stripy jerseys and waxed moustaches, painted African savages with necklaces of knucklebones and seven-foot spears.

'This is obviously a nest of villains,' he concluded.

A little old man, his tatty jacket heavy with medal ribbons, advanced on his Zimmer frame, and waved a gnarled fist at a smiling gold-toothed Cuban, shouting 'God bless the Queen!'

Bullets slammed into his bent body, and he was propel-led half-way across the street, where he collapsed, cough-ing bloody foam. A team of clog dancers, their ribboned sticks waving, gathered around him, and started kicking viciously while singing 'When the Boat Comes In'. The crowd egged them on, crying 'give him another one, just like the other one . . .'

'We've got to get inside that club,' Brittan said. The others nodded in agreement.

Whistling Dvořák's Hovis Bread jingle, they strolled, hands deep in pockets, across the square, past the stocks, past the clog-killing mob, towards the doors of the club.

A tall, wide man stood at the top of the stairs, laughing evilly. He had scratches on his face, and was slowly hitching his braces on to his shoulders. A badge pinned to his dirty shirt identified him as a shop steward.

'You strikers?' the steward asked.

'Oh aye,' said Basil, his Geordie accent exactly right. 'Way-hay.'

'Welcome to t'club,' said the shop steward, 'I'm Greasy Eric Braithwaite.'

He dug into his pockets and pulled out a fistful of £10 notes.

'Fresh from Tripoli,' said Greasy Eric, 'with Colonel Gadaffi's blessings, brother, feel free to take some.'

Brittan's fists were expanding, but Basil took the money, and managed to laugh like a genuine militant.

'Oh aye,' said Basil. 'Way-hay.'

'You'd best be in soon, brothers. T'comedian's nearly finished. It's Gladys and her balloon tying next, and then t'big draw for t'raffle. Don't want to miss that. You got your raffle tickets?'

'Oh . . . er, aye,' Basil said. 'Way-hay.'

Greasy Eric pumped with his arm, and licked his lips.

'Don't want to miss t'raffle,' he said. 'There hasn't been so much interest in t'raffle since t'flying pickets nabbed that policewoman.'

They were admitted into the club, and found themselves in a thronging bar, with sawdust on the floor and overflowing spittoons.

Jock whispered to him, 'If wae're tae bae convincing in these dessguises, wae'd baist drink gallons ae yon beerr.'

Brittan nodded, and they squeezed up to the bar. A woman with three enormous breasts barely held back by an abused halter contraption and a foot-tall pile of mauve hair was pulling quarts, and handing them over. There were buckets of pork scratchings on the drenched bar, and miners were stuffing handfuls into their mouths.

The Black Hat Gang got their drinks and sat by the stage.

A bowed old woman was making obscene shapes with balloons, while a young man sat at an organ playing 'Down at the Old Bull and Bush'.

The stench of beer and sweat and coal was overwhelming.

Brittan pulled the table closer, to cover the maypole straining the lap of his trousers.

'Not long now, Pitbull,' Swellhead said.

Gladys finished, burst her balloons, and left the stage.

Things quieted down a little, and the organist played an up-tempo introduction. A spotlight played on the curtains, and a man dressed in a gold-and-silver-striped tuxedo, with a whirling red spangled bow-tie, stepped out. He was a hunchback, with a wig of slicked-back hair and circles of rouge on his cheeks.

The miners went wild, cheering and clapping. A Cuban at the next table emptied his machine-gun into the ceiling, causing a cloud of plaster dust to settle over the whole front row.

A stray bullet ricocheted off a light fitting and stung against Brittan's arm. He brushed it away.

He was intent on the compère.

He had never seen the man, but he knew who it was.

'Evenin' all,' said Scraggle, making flourishes with his hands, 'all evenin'.'

The crowd cheered again, and some of the tribesmen started banging bongos at the back.

'Settle down now, heh heh,' Scraggle said, 'don't get your braces in a twist. As we all know, it's raffle time. These raffles support the strike fund, and keep your union going. Last week, Brother Arkroyd won enough heroin to keep him zonkered for a year, providing he lasts that long. And before that, we all remember how Foggo Clegwittering won a Walther PPK with a full clip, and the chance to squeeze off eighteen shots at the scab of his choice. Well, this week's star prize is better than all those. Let's take a look, shall we?'

The curtains parted, and the spotlights danced, focusing on a small figure strapped to a hospital cot.

'Lucky winner, this week's prize is yours to enjoy in any way you see fit,' Scraggle announced.

The miners were stamping their booted feet in unison now, their bitter drool pooling around them on the floor and the tables.

Brittan's braces snapped as his shoulders heaved.

'Phyllida,' he breathed.

He could see her pale, frightened face in the shine of the lights, raised bravely, tear tracks down her cheeks, hair out of place.

His belt burst, and his trousers split at the seams.

'Phyllida,' he bellowed, 'Phyllida!'

XII

The follow-spot swung over the audience, and shone in Brittan's face. He had upset the table, and was exploding completely out of his disguise. The cloth cap shot off his head, his clothes fell away in pieces from his rippling muscles.

'Good evening, Lieutenant Dickhead,' Scraggle said, 'we were expecting you sooner.'

The crowd didn't seem so drunk any more. Brittan heard the rasp of drawn swords, the clicking of automatic weapon safety-catches, the thump of clips being jammed into machine-guns, and the revving of chainsaws.

Phyllida was squirming feebly. A girl in terrorist drag stood by her bed, gun pointed at her head.

Brittan's neck swelled, bursting his collar, the last of his disguise.

'Eee,' said someone common, 'look at the stiffy on that.'

He saw the red spots.

The miners had cleared a circle around the Black Hats. Jock broke his glass against the stage, and held up the jagged remains as a weapon. Swellhead had his fists up. Basil was holding a miner's pick.

'Really, I'm disappointed in you. That clue about the heather was so *obvious*. I'd have suspected a trap. But then again, I'm devious. Heh heh.'

Three hefties with whizzing chainsaws were surrounding the Black Hats, jabbing at the air.

'You've all heard about Dick Brittan, brothers, hero of Sheepdip Heights,' Scraggle announced. 'He killed thirty-two Argies with his bare hands, remember. The *Sun* had that picture of him with the grateful shepherdess who relieved him of the enormous all-over boner that was going to blow him up.'

Brittan saw white flares over the red spots, and heard the popping of his expanded veins as they threaded along his muscles, pumping adrenalin throughout his massive body.

'Actually, heh heh, they had to matte the girl into the picture . . .'

Brittan began to roar.

'... because after the Sheepdip Heights incident, our True Blue British hero had to seek solace, not with a grateful shepherdess, but with a grateful *sheep!*'

The crowd began to laugh and make baaa-ing noises.

'Shut up,' Brittan shouted, a mighty gust of steamy anger escaping from his lungs. 'Shut up, you crookback fiend!'

'Time for a jolly old work-out, I think,' said Basil, embedding his pick in the head of the nearest Libyan, neatly pinning his sunglasses to the bridge of his nose, and squelching into a scheming, foreign brain.

With his rock-hard forearm, Brittan parried the first of the chainsaws. It ground uselessly against his steel-tough skin, teeth spinning off like shrapnel, oily smoke belching out of the engine.

The miners came forward, and the fight was on.

Brittan took away a couple of chainsaws, and whirled them around, parting tattooed limbs from shoulders, fetching fat heads off necks, scooping yellow guts out of beer bellies.

The organist segued from 'Tie a Yellow Ribbon Round the Old Oak Tree' to 'You Don't Get Me, I'm Part of the Union'.

Swellhead boxed with a wiry whippet of a man, repeatedly breaking his nose.

Jock had two tables in his hands, and was squashing strikers between them. Blood ran around his feet.

Brittan's disguise had completely fallen off, and he stood, naked and erect, covered from head to foot in gore, downing slackers by the second, heel-crushing their chests with a single stamp.

A Cuban threaded an ammo belt into a hand-held heavy machine-gun, and began to fire a burst at the Black Hats.

Brittan stepped in front of his comrades, and felt the

familiar mosquito pinpricks of bullets bouncing off his
iron muscles, spreading throughout the room.

It was just like Sheepdip Heights all over again, men
falling all around him as bullets found other targets.

The Cuban found the gun too heavy, and angled down,
pointing his weapon at Brittan's crotch. Bullets flattened
against his John Thomas, and tickled his balls.

Brittan screamed at the pain, and threw his chainsaws
like darts, one after the other.

Still buzzing, they cut through the air, and fell on the
Cuban, carving him into five or six pieces, tossing his
intestines high around him.

The triple-breasted barmaid vaulted the bar, and
levelled a flamethrower, coughing a jet of fire.

His chest hair burned, but he deflected the blast. Sucking air into his lungs, he held his breath for a beat, then
exhaled at speed.

The stream of fire broke against his breath and flowed
backwards towards the barmaid. Her tank of fluid
exploded, and she was cooked through instantly, tum-
bling down like a hissing, smoking ruin with an ugly
perm.

A sharp feedback whistle cut through the room, and
everyone turned to the stage.

'Lieutenant Dickhead,' Scraggle wheezed into his micro-
phone, 'before you do anything brave like fighting to the
death, might I point out that Ms Whemple here isn't
quite as bulletproof as some Talents we could mention.
Heh heh.'

The guerrilla girl still had her gun up, and it was
slipped into Phyllida's heart-shaped mouth.

Brittan lowered his tree-branch arms, and stood down.
He nodded to his friends, and they threw down their
weapons.

Greasy Eric Braithwaite sniggered.

'That's better,' Scraggle said.

The organist was playing the 'Floral Dance', fiendishly fast.

'Go on,' Brittan shouted, 'you're very good at threatening helpless women, aren't you? Shoot me in the head, why don't you? See what good that'll do you!'

Scraggle produced a Luger and aimed it point blank at Brittan's nose.

'I do believe I'll try,' he said, smiling.

The gun went off, and Brittan felt the bullet glance off the side of his nose, whizz along his cheek and spray off to the left somewhere.

'Gulp,' said Basil, a red hole appearing where his monocle had been, three pounds of grey gruel bursting out of the back of his skull, splattering against the framed picture on the wall behind him. It showed Gracie Fields simultaneously taking on George Formby and Ramsay MacDonald.

A manly surge of hatred hammered the insides of Brittan's ribs.

'You'll pay for that! Basmo was my fag at Millfield, you know!'

'I didn't bounce a bullet his way,' Scraggle said, innocently, 'you did.'

Brittan swallowed a sob. 'Poor, brainless Basmo, never hurt anyone, always wrote to his mother once a week, let the younger boys have the pick of his stamp collection, fine useful winger, good off-spin bowler, and the best damned Poor Little Buttercup I've ever seen in my life.'

'Well,' said Scraggle, 'I think we can agree on "brainless". Someone take a dishcloth to that picture. It's historic.'

Basil Mapledurham grinned up from the floor, shattered eyeglass over the empty red socket.

Thinking about it, Brittan wondered whether the

monocle and purple ascot quite went with the miner disguise.

'I wonder how many of your comrades at Sheepdip Heights bought the farm the same way, cut down by lead bouncing off you? You were the only one to make it to the top of the hill, weren't you?'

The floorboards were buckling under Brittan's huge feet, feeling the pressure of his curling toes.

'Still, I suppose those sixteen-year-old conscripts deserved what was coming to them, heh heh. It must have been easy for you to mistake that white flag they were waving for a death-ray aimed at the church school down below.'

Brittan snorted plumes of steam from his engorged nostrils. His brass balls beat like bulls' hearts, pumping into his pig-iron rod.

'Enough of this conversation, heh heh,' Scraggle said, 'let's take them to the Pit.'

XIII

Brittan strained mightily at the manacles that pinned him to the wall of the coalface.

'Don't even bother, Lieutenant Dickhead,' Scraggle said, 'those were custom-made for you by our comrades in the British Steelworkers' Union. The tensile strength is incredible. Even more incredible than yours, heh heh. You know, what with all that blood pumping around your body turning you into an upholstered Adonis, I still think that the hardest, heaviest muscle you have is the one between your ears.'

Brittan was getting near the end of it. His knob-end was pulsing and empurpled, sweating little drops of blood.

'A fascinating process. I'm surprised the DPR didn't scoop you in and dissect you to find out how you work. I'm sure there are industrial applications for your bizarre metabolism. Something for the lonely housewife.'

'Curse you, may you writhe in eternal torment with maggots squirming in and out of the pus-filled open sores on your lice-infested, leprous carcass as you scream forever in the Domdaniel pits of Erebus and Acheron!'

'Tut tut tut, that temper really will be the death of you.'

Brittan rattled his chains. They were embedded into the rough coalface by three-foot-long pins.

'I believe that if you had time, you could probably pull those out.'

Scraggle was smoking a cigar in a long holder. With him was Greasy Eric Braithwaite, who could hardly contain his foul mirth, and the mad-eyed guerrilla girl who turned out to be Annabelle Krantzen, Phyllida's treacherous friend. She should have known better than to trust a kraut, of course.

'Sadly, time is a commodity you don't have in abundance.'

The union leader consulted a gold pocketwatch.

Jock was unconscious in the corner, his head a mass of blood-filled lumps. Swellhead was by him, mummified with a coil of thick rope. And Phyllida was shackled only a few feet away, just out of his reach, slumped decorously in a dead faint.

'First, of course, you'll have to tell me Walter Whemple's private telephone number at the Arbitration and Conciliation Service. That way I can tell him to cave in immediately.'

'You'll never get it from me,' Brittan said, jaws clamped around his tongue.

'Not even if I play a few little games with your friends?'

Scraggle stubbed out his cigar on Swellhead's bald dome. The genius yelped.

'Don't tell him, Pitbull,' Swellhead screeched, 'don't tell.'

Scraggle took out his cigar clipper, and clipped off the tip of Swellhead's nose.

'Don't tell. Don't mind me, just don't tell him anything.'

Scraggle bit off one of Swellhead's ears, and spat it out, daintily wiping his mouth with a lace doily.

'Just keep quiet. I can take anything.'

'Greasy Eric,' Scraggle said, 'do you have that rock-drill about you?'

The shop steward chortled as he handed Scraggle the piece of heavy equipment. The union leader cradled it in his hands, and checked the connecting leads and the drill bit.

'I don't care what you do to me,' Swellhead shouted, 'I'd rather die than see your perfidious strike succeed! The forces of history are against you, you addle-pated socialist fool! The dark days of the early seventies when a miners' strike could bring down a democratically elected government are defunct and departed!'

Scraggle blew on the bit of the rock-drill, and shoved it against Swellhead's rope-bandaged back.

He looked at Brittan. 'The telephone number?'

Brittan looked at his friend, who was silently pleading. Knowing he was doing the right thing, he shook his head.

Scraggle smiled and shrugged, and the drill whined through the rope, cloth, bone, flesh, lungs, more bone, skin, more cloth, and more rope, poking out of Swellhead's chest, dripping red gobbets down his front.

'Don't tell,' Swellhead gurgled, coughing lumpy gore. 'Don't ever tell.'

The drill bit whirred, spraying bits of Swellhead's

insides about. The genius' bald dome bobbed, and lolled lifeless.

'He didn't mind dying to foil your plans, union scum! You still don't have that number! Ha!'

Scraggle let the drill die down, and left it where it was.

'I suppose I'll have to go through directory inquiries then, heh heh. I was never sure whether it was Westminster 689 0543 or Westminster 689 0534.'

Swellhead's corpse fell over, and Greasy Eric laughed at the dead man.

Brittan's balls were the size of honeydew melons now, taut as overinflated balloons. His John Thomas was a full four inches longer than it had ever been, his knob-end a toadstool-shaped cannonball.

'I wish we could stay around to see that schlong explode,' Scraggle said, consulting his watch, 'but we have to be off now. We've got to be at the negotiating table tomorrow morning, early. A pity. It would have been fascinating to watch the veins all over your body popping like bangers, and to see your eyeballs bug out on six-inch stalks and your heart go off like a hand-grenade wrapped in Semtex. Heh heh. My theory is that when you go boom, your bones will be turned into shrapnel, and we'll also get Ms Whemple and Mr McLochness here with the same blast. Bonus points, you might say. I could be wrong, of course. We'll be back sometime next week to check out the damage. By the way, watch out for the pit rats.'

Scraggle shut his watch, and, his vile cohorts with him, left. Greasy Eric was whistling 'Working in a Coal Mine'.

It was dim, but there was a single bare bulb hanging from the rock roof. Somewhere, water was dripping. They must be miles below ground.

Brittan looked down at himself. The veins on his John

Thomas were a patriotic bright red and blue, the skin stretched thin over them.

'Goodbye, old son,' he told his manhood, 'we've been through a lot together.'

There was nothing for it but to wait it out.

He looked at Phyllida, lovely in repose, chest rising and falling with faint breath, hair over her face.

'Goodbye, darling,' he said.

XIV

'Goodbye, darling . . .'

Phyllida was dreaming. She was on the Riviera with Dick, trying to decide between dresses in a couturier's. She liked the pink, but the mauve was appealing also. She nibbled the edge of her Amex Gold card, unable to make up her mind. She kept asking what Dick thought. And Dick kept saying 'Goodbye, darling . . .'

Slowly, she swam towards the surface of consciousness, her head aching politely. She was weighted down with chains.

Suddenly, she was awake, and shaking. Something furry had rubbed against her tights.

She had a ladder!

She hated having a ladder in her tights. It made her look so common. She couldn't stop shuddering at the thought.

'Phyllida?'

It was Dick, chained naked to the wall. She couldn't help staring. He was *enormous*.

She'd talked about her size preferences penis-wise with Annabelle and Geraldine, but never had she even considered something on this scale. Not even on her horses. It was almost *ridiculous*!

'My God, Dick, but you've got an absolutely *huge* . . .'

'Yes, yes,' he said impatiently.

She giggled. 'I mean, God, imagine . . .'

He looked up at the ceiling, his face bright red. The poor dear must be dreadfully embarrassed. It was most cruel of Scraggle to humiliate him like this.

'Tell me . . . um, er . . . doesn't it . . . um, er . . . *hurt* or anything?'

Dick groaned, the arteries in his neck pulsing away like bicycle pumps. Veins stood out all over his immensely muscled body.

'Oh, I see,' Phyllida said, 'it's your *Talent*. I wondered what it was. You turn into a Human Hunk, like that American fellow who's always in the Sunday supplements.'

'Ye dinnae understand, lassie,' groaned a voice from the dark. It was Jock McLochness.

Dick's head seemed to be swelling along with the rest of him, slabs of muscle under the skin blowing up like an inflatable cushion, mouth gaping open, eyes staring forwards like a fish's.

''Tis turrible, turrible. Puir wee Pitbull's done furr thus taime. After all wae bain throo.'

'What is it?'

She had shifted her position, sitting up and edging nearer to Dick. If she leaned over in her chains, she could almost reach him.

'Dick's going tae gae boom.'

'I don't understand.'

'It's . . . the Talent . . .' Dick gasped, '. . . unless I get some sort of . . . um, well, um . . . sexual relief . . . um, well, I'm . . . going . . . to explode . . . very messily.'

The enormous penis was right in front of her face, throbbing visibly, its veins stretched to breaking point.

Dick rattled his chains. It was obvious that, even if he

had been a foreigner and accustomed to practise the un-British sin of Onan, he could do nothing with his hands.

'Well,' she gulped, 'There's only one thing to do then. Mr McLochness, if you'd be so kind as to look the other way for a moment.'

'Phyllida ... darling ... you don't have to ... I didn't want ... it to be like this.'

'Nonsense, I want to.'

'Somehow ... I'd thought of flowers, and strawberries, and champagne, and silk sheets and things ...'

'Don't be silly.'

Geraldine Leighton-Critchley had shown her how with an ice-lolly when they were at school. She hoped her mouth could open wide enough.

'Remember,' he gasped, 'lots of spit ... lots of tongue ...'

XV

Nine o'clock sharp.

Greasy Eric Braithwaite, crammed into a brown off-the-peg suit, handed him a fountain pen.

Scraggle looked across the table at Walter Whemple. The arbitrator hadn't slept, and his tie was fifteen degrees off the mark. He had cut himself shaving, and his hands were still shaking.

'How is your daughter, Mr Whemple?' he asked. 'Philippa, wasn't it? Heh heh.'

Whemple's eyes burned fury at him.

The agreement lay unsigned on the table, granting the NUM everything they wished for. Scraggle felt exultation, this close to the achievement of his purpose. A selective telepath, he could see in Whemple's mind that he was about to give in, much good it would do him.

Greasy Eric stifled a snigger. He was expecting three months' holiday with pay from now on, and a session every shift with Mr Entwhistle's daughter Ethel, and a cut of every miner's union dues, and the chance to kill anyone in the Pit he didn't get on with, and tax relief on his mortgage.

Scraggle swallowed his impatience. The miners were fools to think he really wanted their strike to succeed. His aim was nothing less than the destruction of British industry, and the dragging-down of the elected government. That Consortium of South American dictators, Marxist ideologues, organized crime figures, Irish Republicans, hippie drug-fiends, Japanese big businessmen, KGB hard-liners, French pastry-chefs, Middle-Eastern mullahs, Nazi mad scientists, shapechanging vampire paranorms, Labour Party politicians and anarchist agitators who paid him so handsomely would be delighted at the accomplishment of this mission.

Even if this gambit had failed, he still had Plan B.

He looked forward to not having to mingle with brutish working-class morons any longer.

'Well,' he said, 'no sense waiting.'

With a flourish, he put his signature on three copies of the agreement, and then pushed them across the table to Whemple.

'Do you want to borrow my pen?'

Whemple had his own out, and was fiddling with it. Scraggle had put pencil x marks where the arbitrator was to sign.

Annabelle, in a plain black dress with seamed black stockings and a black leather shoulder holster, massaged his hunch and neck, soothing out the aches of the recent troubles.

Scraggle smiled, and waited for Whemple to sign. The arbitrator took the top off his pen.

178

Then, he shot a look at the gallery, sensing the minds beyond the mirrored window. The PM was up there, and the Chairman, and the Minister, and the media. Scraggle hoped Whemple could put on a proper show for them.

'Lovely girl, I remember, that Philippa. Heh heh.'

Swallowing hard, Whemple put pen to paper, squeezing a blot of ink from his nib.

Scraggle's chest tightened. Victory!

'Stop,' bellowed a voice, and there was the sound of breaking glass.

XVI

His body expanding inside his loose combat jacket, Brittan vaulted through the windows into the committee rooms.

Whemple looked around, startled. Scraggle screeched fury, and Annabelle pulled out a Colt Police Python and squeezed off a shot.

Brittan caught the bullet in his huge fist, and squeezed it cold, tossing it back at the guerrilla girl. It bounced off her and clanged against the glass table.

'How did you . . .?'

'Escape?' Brittan asked, grinning. 'It was easy. A little ministration from a healing angel, and I was small enough to slip those manacles of yours.'

'Curses,' Scraggle swore.

Jock and Phyllida were right behind him, Schmeisser machine-pistols primed and ready.

Three of Greasy Eric's miner goons, wearing those damned helmet deathrays, stepped forwards, hands going to their battery packs.

Phyllida and Jock sprayed them with hot lead, and they jitterbugged against the wall, spray-painting the radiators with blood.

Scraggle sat back in his chair, suddenly and sinisterly calm, and watched the fight.

'This one's mine,' Greasy Eric said, standing up. 'Come on, you Southeren bastid, let's see you try it on with a *real* man!'

Greasy Eric growled like a Bradford grizzly bear, and leaped at Brittan.

The two giants locked in a wrestling hold, Greasy Eric's hands trying to get a purchase on Brittan's steel-tense muscles. Brittan tossed the shop steward at the table, and it shattered in a thousand pieces under him.

Spitting blood and teeth, Greasy Eric got up again and made a grab for Brittan's John Thomas, grasping it firmly through the camouflage trousers.

'Let's see if t'pole comes off.'

Brittan breathed hot air into Greasy Eric's face.

'Nobody does that,' he shouted, grabbing a bone-powdering hold on the shop steward's wrist, and wrenching off his hand.

'Bloody Nora!'

Brittan dropped the still-writhing hand, and launched a straight piledriver right at Greasy Eric's blood pudding of a face.

The shop steward's neck snapped, and his head flopped down, the back of his head bumping against his spine, a split gaping in his throat.

'Die, capitalist exploiter of the proletariat!' shouted Annabelle, taking careful aim with her gun.

Phyllida stepped in, and pulled a fistful of her best friend's hair out, then went for her eyes with sharpened and polished nails.

Annabelle screeched, and Phyllida slapped her silly, pushing her down on to the floor and kicking her properly.

'Phyllida!' Whemple gasped, 'you're safe!'

'Daddy!'

'Very touching,' said Scraggle, looking at his watch.

Brittan suddenly had a bad feeling about this hard-won victory of free enterprise democracy.

'I just thought you'd all like to know that, in about twenty seconds, my associates will put Plan B into effect.'

'Plan B?'

'Yes, my comrades in the service unions have been pumping coal gas into the London sewers all night. When the word comes through that this agreement hasn't been ratified, they'll toss in a match, and it'll be the Great Fire of London all over again.'

'You dirty dog!'

Scraggle laughed, and stood up. He bowed to the gallery.

'Madame Prime Minister, it's been a load of laughs, but now's the time to go bye-bye.'

Brittan was in a state of full erection again, a mountain of iron-threaded bone and engorged muscle ready to do or die for his country, his prime minister, and his woman.

A trapdoor was lifting up in the floor behind Scraggle. He was applying a flame from his cigarette lighter to one of his cigars.

Coal gas was odourless, but Brittan could hear it seeping.

Scraggle turned, but Brittan moved with a speed that belied his massive size and weight.

Grasping Jock around the waist, Brittan hurled his friend like a caber, pitching him accurately at the man-hole.

Scraggle gasped in horror as the kilted tornado landed in the hole, plugging it up completely.

'Hah,' said Jock, 'yae cannae dae a thing aboot it.'

There was a rumble deep in the earth, and the floor was shaking.

'One stray spark, heh heh,' Scraggle said.

It was like an earthquake, building up slowly.

A look of horror and surprise crossed Jock's bearded face, and his eyes rolled upwards. Then, with a champagne-cork pop, Jock shot out of the manhole at the apex of a geyser of flame and slammed against the roof, flattening the top of his head like a breakfast egg.

There were distant explosions, and bursts of flame came from everywhere. Jock hit the floor, a broken puppet.

Brittan reached for Scraggle, and his fists closed where the archfiend's throat had been an instant earlier. He saw Scraggle gingerly lowering himself through the manhole, ignoring the flames swarming around him. It was as if the man were made of asbestos.

He stood over the manhole, looking down at Scraggle. Their eyes met, and they understood each other perfectly, with a white-hot purity. Hero and villain, linked by their struggle, they were the same, two sides of one coin. Scraggle's lips puckered in a kiss. He was having trouble getting his hunch through the manhole.

Brittan stamped on Scraggle's hands, and the union leader lost his grip. He looked up, panic on his ugly face, and was pulled down as if by a massive suction from below, disappearing into the inferno of the London sewers. Brittan thought there was a distant splash, and spat after Scraggle, hoping the world had heard the last of the monstrous mastermind. The echo of Scraggle's chesty laughter was in the flames.

Then, he was being bustled out of the committee rooms, Phyllida pulled close to his side. There were policemen and firemen everywhere. Scotland Yard men were dragging Annabelle away. He saw the PM and the Minister of

Energy being whisked off, surrounded by uniformed Talents. Brittan recognized Corporal Punishment, the PM's personal bodyguard and night-time avenger, in his distinctive black bodysuit, swinging his cane to clear the flames.

Phyllida was hugging him, arms not quite stretching around his chest.

'It's all over,' she said, as they got into the open air.

Parliament Square was lit up by the burning buildings on the other side of the Thames. The air was thick with the din of fire alarms and fire engines.

Brittan looked at the skyline of London, that ever-changing symbol of everything British and noble. Flames were sprouting everywhere. He thought he saw the Post Office Tower leaning like the one in Pisa. Helicopters buzzed over the city.

'Out of my way,' shouted a fireman, unrolling a length of hose.

Brittan tapped him on the chest.

'Ahem,' he said, 'courtesy costs nothing.'

'Out of my way, *please!*'

'That's better.'

He stepped aside, and the chastened public servant got on with the business of dousing the flames.

Brittan felt the warmth spreading from his groin.

'Phyllida,' he said, 'will you marry me?'

'Oh yes, Dick, yes, yes, yes.'

His John Thomas was aimed like one of the guns of Naverone.

Phyllida pressed herself against him, lifting her leg up and over his erection, kissing his chest, her hands in his hair.

'Let's find a quiet spot,' she said, 'before you explode.'

XVII

He wore his old uniform for the ceremony, feeling it stretched tight across his chest.

In the antechamber at Number 10, Corporal Punishment tried to keep him talking while the PM was busy with Loric, to soothe his obvious nerves. The Corporal was talking about the Victory Over the Miners, and the collapse of the discredited NUM. The fires were under control now, and the damage wasn't as bad as had been feared. One good thing was that, subsequent to this outrage, it looked as if Parliament would reinstate the death penalty. The Corporal whooshed his cane through the air at the thought.

Nothing had been heard of Scraggle, and he was presumed dead.

Finally, Loric emerged from the inner sanctum. The distinguished Talent raised an eyebrow at Brittan, and left without saying a word.

'The PM is ready to see you now,' Corporal Punishment said.

Brittan was admitted alone.

'Ahh, Lieutenant Brittan,' the PM exclaimed, rising and smiling, 'do come in . . .' and extended a limp hand to be held briefly.

Brittan felt awkward, but proud. Stiffly, uncomfortable in his starched trousers, he walked around the desk.

'You wore your Victoria Cross?'

Brittan nodded, and saluted.

The commendation lay on the desk, tied with a blue ribbon. There was a huge portrait of Churchill over the fireplace.

The PM looked out of the window, the orange of the last of the fires reflected on her face.

'So many sacrifices,' she said . . .

Brittan thought of the Black Hat Gang. Basil Maple-durham, grey matter dripping off Gracie Fields' face. Sewell Head, drill sticking out of his tit. Jock McLochness, skull pulped against the ceiling.

'. . . but all worthwhile. We can't give in, you know. We can't.' She was quite animated on the point. 'If it's not the miners, it's the railwaymen, the steelworkers, the TUC.' She made a fist in the air. 'We must not turn from our purpose, Lieutenant.'

Brittan agreed.

Of course, all the sacrifices were worth it. After all, though he had lost his three closest friends, he had gained someone far more important: Phyllida. Already, she had left her position with the Porcupine people and was planning a big society wedding, picking out curtains for Brittan Hall, wondering who to replace Slobotham with, thinking of names for children.

At the thought of Phyllida, his John Thomas began to come to attention.

The PM picked up the decoration, and handed it to him.

'You have our thanks, Lieutenant. You are a British hero.'

He swelled with pride, his knob-end displacing the zip-fastener, pushing it down and open.

'Lieutenant,' she gasped.

His muscles inflated, his heart pounded, his balls rumbled. Brittan felt the danger zone throbbing near, and he knew there was only one thing for it.

'Ma'am,' he said, lifting the PM up by the hips, 'I hope you'll excuse me . . .'

TV BUNNY MADE PIGS FLY
'Too drunk to stand,' Court told

Eastenders' star Martin Phagor, better known to millions as paranorm cabbie Bunny Warren in the top BBC soap, was fined £200 at Bow Street magistrate's court after pleading guilty to being drunk and disorderly and assaulting a police officer at a swanky showbiz party on Saturday night.

Hostess and fellow cast-member Sheila Destry was forced to call the police after a drunken rampage by the 32-year-old actor, during which he *swore* at catering staff, *shattered* crockery in an improvised Frisbee game, and *hit out* at security staff who asked him to leave.

When the police arrived Phagor *levitated* PC Graham Beaumont into the branches of a nearby tree, from which he had to be rescued by firemen.

'I've heard of pigs flying before,' quipped PC Beaumont, 'but I never expected to be the one to prove it.' (The *Sun*, 25 October 1987)

'One of Branagh's most controversial decisions was the casting of Martin Phagor as Fluwelln; after all, the lad's not even Welsh. But freed from the straitjacket of his soap persona, the young Phagor turns in a performance of astonishing range and power, delivered with the grim conviction of a man who has seen a once-in-a-lifetime opportunity floating past and grabbed it with both hands. No wonder the RSC just snapped him up . . .' (Barry Norman, *Film 89*, undated off-air recording)

(Advertisement, *Sunday Express* Colour Supplement, 15 July 1990)

THE STRING MAN

Graham Higgins

Mrs O'Friel trilled a happy purse-lipped selection from *Prince Igor* as she prepared the salad. Her nimble fingers plied the well-ground blade of a shrewd knife along the grain and contour of the fresh vegetables she insisted upon. Her face mirrored many varieties of contentment as she worked; the textures of the salad veg, explored by the darting blade, resonated on the chopping board; their scents rose coolly around her, almost drowning the haze of freshly mown grass drifting from the clinic's cricket pitch through the refectory's sunlit bay window. The same warm breeze brought the whisper of countless broad-leafed trees in gentle motion, the fluting of wood-pigeon, the desultory percussion of strike and applause from the Staff v. Guests cricket fixture.

She rolled and shelled a hard-boiled egg and popped it into the mandolin. Then, with the cheese-wire frame poised, she paused. Pity to spoil the presentation at this stage. You get no second chances with a hard-boiled slice. Mrs O'Friel tilted her head to survey her arrangement of lettuce, red cabbage, shallots, chestnut-mushrooms, radishes, tomato, and capsicums: red, yellow and green. She was interrupted by a sharp double-rap on the metal counter.

Still humming to herself, she turned with fingers steepled at her breast.

'"*Take my hand,*"' she crooned, 'Mr Beasle,' she added, '"*I'm a stranger in paradi-i-ise!*"'

On such a day it did indeed seem difficult to contemplate the dark echoing tunnels of the soul.

'I prefer Borodin's version,' Beasle replied, then immediately relented. 'Tcha! You will think me churlish, Mrs O'Friel. It's the cricket. White-flannelled fools. Could ever there be a more perfect game more perfectly spoiled by human intervention?'

His index finger tapped his lips. 'Religion excepted, of course,' he added.

'You're teasing, Mr Beasle. Now make yourself useful, if you would oblige.' Mrs O'Friel tilted the plate in Beasle's direction. He in turn beckoned her to approach and sauntered off to fetch a chair to raise his 4 foot 9 inch. frame more substantially above the counter's lip. Spreading his hands out on either side of the plate, he surveyed its composition magisterially for a full thirty seconds before pronouncing it 'Very satisfactory, Mrs O'Friel.'

'Thank y—'

'However, if I may make a few minor modifications?' He made them.

'Bravo, Mr Beasle. Now I'd like your advice on the disposition of the slices of hard-boiled egg.'

'Egg? *Egg?*' Beasle planted a wrist on his hip in theatrical exasperation and turned to gaze into the shadowed depths of the refectory. 'Mrs O'Friel, you mentioned nothing about an egg at the outset. This of course puts a completely different comp . . .'

Beasle paused and peered. He hopped from the chair and his rubber soles squeaked across the brown linoleum as he dodged purposefully between the tables. In the far corner he stopped and smacked his hand down on a table top as if to subdue it. The slap, and then his voice, resounded round the cavernous room.

'This chair! This table! May I ask WHY they have been BOLTED to the floor? Are our mealtimes to be graced by some neanderthal Category "A" mouth-breather with a talent for random havoc?' He paused, palms raised in mock surrender. 'I jest, Mrs O'Friel, I jest. Are we not gentlefolk? I'll have to review the entire layout, of course.' He waggled a finger at the offending furniture. 'The spatial reverberations will be felt as far as . . .' Beasle stirred the air with his palm, backing towards the window as a cheer went up from the cricket pitch '. . . oh, here at least.' A tone of anguish now coloured his pique. He returned to the counter, his arms spread out, inviting sympathy. 'It's bad enough that they simply leave the chairs any old how after meals as if it made no difference! I can remedy that with a little effort. But if Mr Lorrimer is responsible for this . . . this VANDALISM . . . and no doubt he authorized it, then it amounts to a DELIBERATE act of PROVOCATION!'

'I hardly think Mr Lorrimer would go to the trouble just to fluster you . . .' Mrs O'Friel demurred. She proffered a plate of freshly sliced egg garnished with a winsome smile.

'Do you think now you might . . .?'

Beasle was putting the final touches to the revised salad with egg motif, when the new guest arrived. Mrs O'Friel heralded his entrance with a tuneless between-the-teeth-whistle obbligato and the slightest tick of her index finger in the direction of the door. Beasle's eyes swivelled in the direction she indicated. His head followed with greater deliberation.

The newcomer entered the swing-doors of the refectory with extreme caution, sweeping the room with a glance as though he expected an ambush by the furniture. He approached the counter with a curious stork-like tread which gave a certain elegance to his otherwise unkempt appearance. He wore a flak-jacket affair bulging with zipped and buttoned pockets. On his wrist hung an assortment of string and rubber bands, and a roll of decorator's masking tape. His appearance made Beasle's sense of order bristle, but he hopped down again from his chair, replaced it fastidiously at a nearby table, and extended a hand to the visitor.

'Beasle,' he offered.

'. . .'

'Beasle,' he demanded. 'My name is Beasle. And yours . . .?'

'Mr McPhail,' chimed Mrs O'Friel, who had received the special diet sheet in his name. 'We've been expecting you. I expect you'd like something to eat? Have you had to travel far?'

'M-McPhail,' said McPhail, placing his hand around Beasle's.

The hand was limp and gave Beasle an uneasy sensation, reminding him dimly of a heavy cold he'd once had which had unsprung his sense of balance. He was glad to complete the formality, glad that Mrs O'Friel was there to carry on.

'I've prepared a summer salad for you,' – she gingerly tilted the plate towards him – 'and maybe you'd care for some ham? We have a small selection of, although I say so myself, fine cheeses to go with it?'

Beasle might in other circumstances have bridled at the thought of further additions to his arrangement (worse was to come) but he was taking advantage of the diversion to study the straggling figure who swayed slightly a little distance from the counter, seemingly reluctant to approach. McPhail, he observed, as his height enabled him to quite clearly, balanced on the very tips of his toes, constantly shifting his weight as though caught in some gentle but insistent current.

Mrs O'Friel took the spectacles which hung from a lanyard round her neck and peered through them at the diet sheet.

'Now, I have followed the instructions given to me but as it's your first day with us, may I just double-check? There is just one, leetle proviso I'd like you to confirm for me . . .'

McPhail's toes curled up in anticipation. Beasle felt a whimper in his throat which he crumpled into an 'ahem' of no fixed purpose. It was not a trick of the light. His mind contrived but did not respond to such tricks. For some endless moments there lay beneath McPhail's boots a thick carpet of solid air.

'It says here under Special Instructions: All with gravy. I've made a nice red wine gravy . . . but on salad?'

'Oh aye, on everything.' McPhail shrugged. 'It's what you get used to, eh? *Wine* gravy, did you say?'

'Gravy?' Beasle spluttered, rocked from his reverie. 'Oh COME, McPhail! Salad! It's a SALAD! A light vinaigrette, a hollandaise perhaps, or mayonnaise if you will. Even . . . even SALAD CREAM for God's sake!'

Mrs O'Friel, with gravy boat poised, raised a quizzical eyebrow; McPhail gave a resigned thumbs-down. The rich liquid mahogany seeped around the dish.

'And a tea please, love. White, two sugars. Cup with a lid, OK? Don't bother with a tray.'

'You go and sit down, Mr McPhail. I'll bring your meal over.'

As McPhail made his way to the far corner, chairs and tables skittered primly out of his path. Beasle's shoulders bunched: he shut his eyes.

McPhail sat at the table and tore strips from the masking tape on his wrist: four long, two short. He tabbed them along the edge of the table. When Mrs O'Friel arrived, he busied himself with taping first the polystyrene cup, and then the plate, to the laminate surface, as Mrs O'Friel settled herself opposite. She placed a rolled napkin containing knife and fork by his plate. Before he could stop it, the napkin flopped open as the cutlery in it stood on end, pirouetting slowly. McPhail snatched it up, smirking sheepishly.

'I, uh ... I have this problem with gravity, see.' He looked over her shoulder. Beasle's head bobbed among the tables as he checked sightlines with a steel tape-measure.

The room echoed to the sound of shifting furniture grunting on the lino as it was herded into precise formation.

'Don't give it a thought,' confided Mrs O'Friel, 'everyone's abnormal here. Mr Beasle, for instance, very successful designer he was. He could make a little bedsit look like a ballroom. You know, the right colours, right furniture, right arrangement. Like those places where things appear to roll uphill, or those rooms where people seem to change size? He got quite a name for it, so he did. Anyone who had the money wanted a Beasle room.' She cast a glance over her shoulder. Beasle was slowly working his way towards them.

'His experiments got a bit out of hand.'

'Yeah? Go on,' urged McPhail, searching with his tongue for a tomato seed trapped behind a tooth. He prised the lid from his tea; a blob of the liquid rose in a treacly orb hovering on a tapering neck. His eyes turned to Mrs O'Friel, who to his pleasant surprise showed only mild curiosity.

'You know,' she said, 'we can do something about this gravy business. If it's simply adhesion you're after there are many tasty alternatives.'

'When you travel about it saves a lot of questions. It's difficult enough to cover up when you have all the problems of mass without the advantages of weight. When it turns out you bugger up ... 'scuse my, uh ... you interfere with the gravity field around you ... well, it's not easy.'

'Very often they feel like that when they arrive here. You may come to find in time that it's as much of a problem to feel relatively normal. But look, I don't see the files but I can't help being inquisitive so if you have the time, could you . . . would you tell me the story?'

McPhail inched a zip aside and fished in a pocket before producing a coin.

'Heads or tails?'

'Oh, tales surely.'

He flipped the coin from between thumbnail and finger joint.

It arced up and up, tumbled briefly, then fell as though through glycerine, slower and slower, until it came to rest in another slow tumble a hand's span above his palm. Mrs O'Friel clasped her hands together and rocked with laughter.

Secretly, both thought, it's an old trick, but it rarely fails.

Beasle looked up and noted the parlour-effect. He was only curious about the nature and scope of the gift; he wanted to classify it, to mitigate the chaos.

McPhail worked the zip, then clasped the coin out of the air and into his pocket in a practised move. He leant over to drink his levitating tea sidewise, as if from a drinking-fountain. Yes. He would tell this woman the story. He nodded thoughtfully as he ate. She laced her fingers on the table top as the story began to rise and take shape in his mind, like tea in his teacup.

Something like this: A grey-wash coastal town. Stone and slate and salt-scoured clapboard, where the ocean gales blew so hard they would press the doorbells and run away down the cobbles. People with closed faces and narrowed eyes to keep out the wind and break the sun's glare. Women bore the children of men wedded to the sea and the silver-flanked shoals of mackerel: hard men who hauled their nets with cracked brine-hardened hands and words of love – 'Come up, my darlings. Come on then. To me, my lovers' – to the fish they called the Queen of the Sea, and whom they were subjects enough. The Fishing required sacrifice, a human tithe which they gave most every season, so regular they forgot to be bitter.

Superstitious men, they took new names at sea, and didn't give them voice too often, perhaps for fear that the salt lash would flay it from them, or carry their name to something unnameable that they might be claimed. They trusted that their wives and especially the priest would keep their names safe, for the nameless corpse is an empty shell indeed.

The String Man lived alone on the shore. His name was Calum, or at least that was what they called him to his face, for they liked him. But he was the String Man. He could mend a net quicker, splice a line sounder, lash more knots more securely than anyone, or anyone they could remember in story, which amounts to the same. He could hitch a cirrus to a steeple or tie an idea to an anvil. The String Man lived alone on shore, but he was in love.

A love-knot was drawn tight around his heart so that as his heart swelled with the joy of it, he choked on the pain, and hastened about his work with fierce distracting concentration.

He loved the Chandler's daughter.

This is how magic works, by analogue. He worked with hemp and sisal, and love transformed them into the stuff of the sacrament. As he worked at the nets, though the words didn't come into his mind, his heart chanted at each perfect knot 'I bind thee'. As he spliced a sheet he felt the strength of the cords coiling about one another, becoming one, and though his head didn't know it his soul invoked a spell that sang 'This Coil Be Never Broken'. His fingers swiftly fashioned knots that strong men struggled to unpick; too deeply for words, he knew that if he could once secure her heart, it would be like this.

Her name was Janet, Nettie to everyone, and she liked the String Man as everyone did. He was nearly ugly, seeming to be made from a stock of weathered knuckles, head to toe, but he had an easy way, a ready smile for her, and That Skill. He came in for supplies, or because he was passing. People did; there was time.

One evening, as autumn hove to, a stranger ducked through the door and handed the Chandler a gravure poster announcing a travelling fair, stalls and rides, come one, come all. The news of it burst upon the town like confetti. As important as the shows, there was a full week of dour anticipation to be enjoyed.

On the third day before the first lorry arrived to pitch camp, Calum called at the Chandler's four times, looking drawn and ill at ease. He browsed distractedly — just looking, aye, no trouble, fine thanks — until on the fifth occasion he found Janet alone, and hunching over the counter he produced from inside his jacket a heart of rope and twine and fine threads intricately knotted in dazzling detail. He'd worked on it without sleep for two days and nights. Would she, if she had no other plans, that is, come to the shows? With him. No strings attached, ha ha. He looked so furtive, as though he'd already done something unspeakable, that she almost laughed, and held his heart to her lips to guard him from hurt. Of course, she said, and he began to apologize before it reached him that she'd said yes.

It is hard in these riotous times to imagine the effect of a small and tawdry travelling show visited on senses tuned to the colours of shingle and the sounds of air and water.

The familiar reek of diesel powered the roar of the Waltzer, the Cyclone, the Dodgems where lads from the surrounding villages jousted. The generators whined, charging the rippling light from millions (it seemed millions) of electric bulbs whose colour burst again and again directly into the skull like tethered fireworks, as the boom of slack-bellied speakers hurled the feral beat of rock'n'roll back and forth, at a time when music was made to be heard amidst the dangerous jostle of a fast night. The dark surrounding countryside stirred to the rasp of sideshow barkers, and joyous howls rose from the rides under the spell of that 'Blue Moon of Kentucky'.

In this heavenly hell on earth Calum led Nettie into the spotlight glare, and he was glad to see the attention they attracted. She wore the little heart of string pinned to her coat. Not for him the boxing booth, though her company gave strength to his swing when he brought the sledgehammer down and rang the bell. He was captivated by her face bathed in flickering coloured light, and every song at every turn was about love, and it was true, all love. Ambrosia, he decided, must be scented with onion and candyfloss.

They shared a pink candyfloss (could mere sugar taste so extravagantly sweet?) as they mounted the Waltzer to Jerry Lee, impossibly loud and lascivious, and as the cars began to reel Calum felt his throat tighten as the acceleration forced their bodies together, and he felt rather than heard her laughter. A fairground roustabout with fistfuls of silver skulls and snakes, and blue dragons coiling along his forearms, leant over to yell something saucy in Nettie's ear as he gave the car a dizzying spin, and Calum laughed to see her flush. He would always remember her round-eyed grin against a dazzle of hurtling light.

Magic. It works.

*

The coast road was beaded with little pools of torchlight as the String Man walked the Chandler's daughter home. Their conversation was sparse. They were too full of private, guarded thoughts.

At her door he didn't know what to do with his hands, so he let them dangle heavy on his wrists. She told him he was sweet and kind and thanked him and said, well ... goodnight then. In the brief following silence she touched her lips to his cheek.

She had given him a kiss, and he didn't know what to give her in return. He'd already given her a coconut after all. And his heart.

She had stood in the porch light, waving him goodbye. He ran home, feeling the burden of the long night all around him now she was gone, preferring to feel stone walls. He felt he should be feeling happy, but as he sat on his bed easing off his Sunday-best boots in silence he felt emptiness gathering inside him.

As he leant forward to loosen his boot, the string heart dropped to the floor between his feet.

The floor beneath his feet. The floor of the Waltzer car beneath her feet. He had lifted the safety-bar and noticed the heart unpinned, resting against the scuffed steel brake-pedal. He had bent to pick it up, and had put it inside his jacket for safety, as the tattooed man helped Nettie from the car.

Now, away from the spangling lights, out of the cross-fire music, he bent to pick it up from the tiles and held it in his palm.

This was a different thing from the treasure he took to her that afternoon in the Chandlery; oily dust and the sticky residue of candyfloss clung to it, picking out knots and rosettes in grime. He turned it over.

A pin pierced the heart. He angled his palm up in the

light. Where the pin emerged from the twine at either end there were tufts of wine-red wool, plucked from Nettie's coat. Densely red at the centre, they spread out to pink thistledown as fibres spiralled away from one another; near to the points of entry some threads strained to hold the gleaming shaft, while others had sprung apart, splaying out crazily, their fibres uncoiling in tufts. The little heart was unravelling.

He could not tell how long he sat, while his tears fell; he could feel their sudden weight as the drops burst on the heart. Its cords swelled as capillaries drew in the sharp draught. The wine-dark filaments of the wool became beaded with tears, each lit by its crescent image of the lamp overhead.

The pierced heart of string lay like a tattoo across his palm. He could barely recognize it as the work of his hands any more. Too much had happened to it. Each woven knot had been a detail of intent. He understood intimately what he had done in its making, but now ... what intention might a thing like this signal?

Beware. Magic works.

Pocketing the heart he stooped and retied his laces blindly.

Minutes later he sat on the sea-wall beneath her window, tying knots in lengths bitten from a ball of twine he kept in his pocket for use during sermons. He tugged on the knots until his finger-joints bled. He was interrupted by the Chandler who appeared in his shirtsleeves and braces at the door, squinting past the light of a hurricane lamp and demanding to know where his daughter was.

For a normally taciturn man he found a surprising number of ways of asking this simple question in a very short time, and in the way of those who find eloquence in anger, he seemed less than eager to waste time listening to answers.

The String Man allowed the sound of the sea-swell to wash over him while he threaded and knotted, looped and tugged at the twine he could barely see in the moonlight; pulling threads together until he could feel a growing symmetry in the dark. He was so lost in the rush of his own thoughts that he failed to notice the Chandler waving the lamp near his head until a free hand reached out and cuffed the pattern of twine to the cobblestones. For a fragment of a moment a random tangle of knotted twine sprang into the lamplight, clear as clear, before the String Man snatched the hissing lamp and made off along the coast road till he came to the van where Nettie lay coiled about with blue dragons and silver snakes.

He waited in the dark, crouched on the steps of the Waltzer until she emerged to follow a little beam of torchlight back to town. Then the String Man went to work with a vengeance.

And with magic.

He never returned to the town.

In the morning the camp was awakened by the din of the tattooed man's agonized screaming and pounding on the walls of his van. It had been secured with ingeniously knotted steel hawsers. By the time they found the bolt cutters someone had pointed out the circle of fibres in the mud around the van. It looked as if someone had carefully unpicked the cords of a length of rope, uncoiling it down to its minutest shreds. But this source of speculation was soon abandoned when they finally managed to release the howling roustabout who toppled out into the mud clutching his groin and protesting he didn't know what he'd got but it wasn't the usual. When they fetched the doctor he didn't know either, but the pain passed off anyway after a couple of days.

Janet had the baby in the usual way. It was not the child that grew to be McPhail.

He was conceived not long after Janet's child with a little shove from the same father. And there were others after him.

Search back-issues of 'The Lancet' in vain for reports of infants who slip from their midwives' hands and float gracefully at the ends of their umbilical cords, but they are the String Man's doing.

In the centuries that passed that dark, burning night, he worked to unravel, to unpick the ties of his knotted heart. His mind was an empty roar of coloured light. His brain would not pause to comprehend what fine work he was about. But his heart drove his fingers on to unravel a knotted heart. His fingers worked all night until his heart felt a little give.

Maybe his heart knew what he'd unstrung, probably not. He only felt a little less pain, a little lighter. That was all.

Beasle gave his handiwork a final appraisal and positioned a chair beside the bolted table. He noticed that McPhail had so arranged his jacket that the backrest of his chair was inside it. No friction, of course, to keep him in place.

'Mr McPhail was just about to tell us how he came to join us,' Mrs O'Friel said.

Beasle said, 'I gather you are somewhat gravity-resistant? What fun. Is this hereditary, McPhail?'

'Mmm . . . genetic . . .' McPhail replied, circling his plate with a gravy-stained lettuce leaf, '. . . something adrift with my DNA, so they tell me. It . . . where should I begin?'

He laid his knife and fork down on his plate and leaned back, crossing his arms. The knife and fork rose expectantly.

'DNA,' he began, 'is a double helix. Think of it as . . . as a length of string . . .'

Profile from the *Guardian* Woman's page, 27 October 1990

Sue Brown: The Listener?

Sue Brown at 26 has a reputation for being the best of Britain's phone-in agony aunts. Her night spot on Capital Radio brings in record listening figures. Who is Sue Brown?

She is a small, sad-eyed woman, who blinks owl-like in the sun. When I arrived for our interview she was already ensconced in the West End café. Sitting beside her, ignoring customers, a black-skirted Asian waitress poured out a stream of impassioned *sotto voce* confidences. Several minutes elapsed before she would take our order for coffee.

'It happens all the time,' Sue Brown says. 'Women in shops. Old women at bus stops. You wouldn't expect that in London, would you? But they all talk to me. I never *start* a conversation with them.'

'How long was it,' I ask her, 'before you suspected you might be a paranorm?'

'That's it, you see. I'm still not registered. I had a DSS letter and I went along to the local office. Somehow the manager and I got talking . . . we never did get around to filling out forms. That's happened five times at different offices.'

She gestures as she speaks, her palms open, with the body language of a willing listener.

'The Department did actually contact me. Their secretary, Marcia, made me an appointment. She still rings me up two or three times a week just for a chat, you know.'

We pause for a moment as the coffee arrives, brought not by the waitress but by the manager. This young man eyes me as if I am intrusive, and begins a murmured conversation with Sue Brown of which the only distinguishable word is 'ligature'.

'I did see a DPR official,' Sue Brown confesses, a good twenty minutes later. 'I don't remember his name, but he was a very troubled man. I suppose I might still hear from them. I don't know, you see. People like to tell me their problems. Does that make me a paranorm?'

Close your eyes and the familiar voice is there: young, warm, secure. The voice that prompts anonymous over-the-air confidences between 2 and 3 a.m., three nights a week. Capital Radio have already made known their plans to move her to a peak-time spot. What does she think of this?

'I'm in this line of work because I like to help people. It makes me feel . . .' She pauses, searching for a word. '. . . wanted.'

Playing back several hours of interview tape, there is surprisingly little of Sue Brown on it. There is much more of my own voice, and the café manager's, and that of the American tourist at the next table. Her answers are brief, non-judgemental, sometimes no more than a questioning 'Mmm?'

Sometime towards the end of the afternoon I ask her, 'Who hears your confidences?' She smiles resiliently.

'Quis custodiet ipsos custodes?' she quotes, and wryly rephrases it. 'Who will listen to the listener?'

SOMEONE TO WATCH OVER ME

Alex Stewart

Darren Braithwaite wasn't very bright. Otherwise he'd never have hitched down to London, expecting to make a new life for himself in the city. If you'd asked him what he was hoping to find there, he couldn't have told you; just something better than what he'd had, which was bugger all.

Or so he'd thought at the time. These days his memories of the damp-ridden council flat and the moon-scape estate he'd grown up in were hazed with nostalgia. Even the peripheral figure of Barry, the newest of his mother's resident friends, couldn't spoil his happy dreams; he'd called Darren names, and shouted at him, but he hadn't dared try to hit him after the first time. Damon had sorted him out, no bother.

If it hadn't been for Damon, Darren would never have survived on the streets. OK, it had been Damon that got him thrown out of the hostel in the first place, but the bloke had been asking for it. And since then it was Damon who got him food when he was hungry, and money when the begging hadn't gone so well. Damon had even got him the sleeping bag he was huddled in, propped up in the doorway of a photographic shop in the Strand.

Damon had been looking after him for as long as Darren could remember.

*

'Poltergeists,' Marcus Conway said, through gritted teeth. He'd been saying it a lot lately, usually with an adjective attached. Of all the bloody stupid assignments that had come his way over the years, this one took the patisserie.

It wasn't even as if he needed the money any more. Back in his student days, struggling to finish his degree without falling down a bottomless overdraft, the monthly cheque from the DPR, small as it was, had kept him in food and cinema tickets. These days he shuffled sterling into ecus and back, reading the underlying mood of the market with unfailing accuracy, and ran a Lamborghini on the proceeds. He would have resigned years ago if his association with the Department hadn't given him some useful contacts in the Treasury.

'*Kleptomaniac* poltergeists. On the *Underground*, for God's sake. Did you ever hear anything so *stupid*?'

Joanna Trent couldn't hear a word he said with the Walkman clamped to her head, but, being a telepath, she didn't have to. She took her hands from the pockets of her worn leather jacket and started swinging them from side to side with each step she took down the escalator, snapping her fingers in time to the beat.

'"Somethin' *weird*. An' it don't look good. *Who* ya gonna call?"'

'That's not funny,' Conway said, straightening his tie. It was bad enough getting stuck with this Mickey Mouse assignment in the first place, let alone teamed up with an irresponsible scruff he was embarrassed to be seen with. He nodded at the pair of Transport Police stationed in the concourse as he stepped off the escalator, and they shrugged in reply. Nothing happening again.

Incompetent plods. If they'd accepted the offer of DPR assistance three months ago, when the incidents started, instead of dismissing the scattered reports of paranormal activity as hysterical overreactions to ordinary muggings, it would all have been sorted out quietly by now. But they kept on insisting they could deal with it themselves, until an affronted American tourist complained to the embassy, and suddenly it was headline news and somebody else's problem.

Conway had better things to do with his time than help exorcize a glorified train set.

'You're just pissed off at missing your judo,' Joanna said smugly, catching a fleeting mental image of white-clad figures bouncing off a mat.

'Aikido,' Conway corrected. He glanced at his watch. They'd be warming up by now, doing some floor techniques. Practising breathing, letting the energy flow. The twice-weekly training sessions were the cornerstone of his life. Without them, helping to sustain the inner calm he needed, walling off his own sense of identity, the endless battering of other people's emotions wore away like surf against the beaches of his mind.

Getting his assignment from Marcia hadn't helped. Being close to her was like standing next to one of the speakers of a far-flung PA system; the sort you got at village fêtes, with a constant hum of feedback, and distorted echoes. She'd been talking to herself on the phone when he arrived, and he'd had to wait, while the inevitable headache swelled. It was like that now; surrounded by the rush-hour crowds, he felt the tension and irritation spilling out of them like a dull, hot afternoon before a thunderstorm. Here and there lightning flashed, little firecrackers of anger or, more rarely, *joie de vivre*; he wondered what matching echoes Joanna was pulling out of her equivalent of the background noise. Mostly stuff about love affairs, he supposed.

'That, and office politics,' Joanna said. Like him, she was a medium-grade Talent, able to receive impressions from other minds, but not transmit. Under media pressure for quick results, the DPR had poured every psychic they could lay their hands on into the Underground in the last couple of days, in a desperate attempt to cover all the stations where incidents had been reported. Even the faith healers. Even the guy whose only Talent was lighting his cigarettes by pyrokinesis. Maybe they thought the poltergeist was sick, or made of tobacco.

'A dog-end elemental,' Joanna said, and giggled. 'Butt Thing.'

Nothing continued to happen.

Loric sighed, easing himself gratefully into his favourite armchair, his feet stretched out towards the fire. It had been a difficult week; the conference in Rome, the PPS to the Home Secretary getting possessed by a demon, those documents being leaked to the *Guardian*. He sniffed appreciatively at his armagnac, watching the reflected highlights from the dancing flames flicker in the glass.

He didn't relax enough. Everyone told him so. Even Marcia, whose self-absorption was legendary. He frowned, sipping the drink, feeling the warmth spreading, and tried to ignore the faint premonitory tingle at the base of his skull. Overwork, that was all. And even if it wasn't, surely, just this once, he could leave it to someone else to sort out.

The TV sprang to life. Loric smiled, loosened his tie, and took another sip of the brandy. After a moment he started humming along to the theme tune of his favourite soap.

Darren was cold, and feeling ill. Damon had got him some aspirins, but they hadn't helped; he was running a fever now, and shivering inside the sleeping bag. His reflection in the shop window was pale, and sweating slightly. His throat was swollen, and hurt when he swallowed. He drifted in and out of sleep, unable to distinguish between fragments of dream and the real world.

'Oi. I'm talking to you.' Someone kicked him in the ribs, hard enough to hurt, but not enough to damage. He forced his eyes open; they felt sticky and swollen. 'Why don't you get a job, eh?'

There were three of them, about his own age, identically dressed in neat, dark suits. They were all drunk; even through the flu haze Darren could tell that. Their voices were slurred, and they swayed on their feet.

He knew their type. The homeless were always being harassed by affluent hooligans from the city; for some reason, it seemed, they couldn't enjoy what they had unless they were hurting someone without it.

'Leave me alone,' he said. 'I'm not well.'

'Not well? Pissed more like it.' The man kicked him again. 'Or is it the drugs, eh? Fucking junkie. I hate fucking junkies.'

Damon picked him up and threw him across the pavement. He landed about five yards away, flat on his back, with an audible hiss of expelled breath.

'Bloody hell!' His companions began backing away. After a moment their leader staggered to his feet, breathing hard. He took an unsteady step towards Darren, his face dark with blood.

'I'm gonna kill the bastard!'

'Tarquin, wait.' One of the suits tugged ineffectually at his arm. 'He's a fucking spook. Look, he never even touched you . . .' Tarquin shrugged him off, and took another step towards Darren. Then he stopped dead, doubling over with an audible grunt. An instant later he straightened, his head snapping round with the liquescent smack of something hard against flesh. A bruise began to form on the side of his face.

The three of them turned and ran.

Out of the corner of his eye, Darren could see Damon take a couple of strides after them. Then he turned and came back. Although, like always, he stayed in his peripheral vision, Darren could tell he was worried.

'It's all right,' he said. 'I'm fine.' But it wasn't true, and Damon could tell. The streets were no place for the sick. A brief fever image of the cheap hotel room he'd occupied for a day or two when he first arrived in London, before the money ran out, flashed across Darren's mind.

There was a flicker of movement, and Damon was gone.

'Getting anything?' Joanna asked.

'No.' Conway shook his head. Now that the rush hour was dying, and the crowds thinning out, the oppressive weight of other people's emotions was beginning to lift. It cheered him, like the cool, clean taste of the air after summer rain. 'I mean, apart from the regular noise.'

'Me neither.' She shrugged, unplugging the Walkman from her ears. If Conway was going to lighten up, they might as well talk. 'I don't even know what we're scanning for.'

'Same here.' Conway led the way on to the eastbound Central-line platform, slipping between the waiting commuters with the ease of long practice. They'd taken to patrolling the station, in wide, slow sweeps, more to break the monotony than because either of them thought it would achieve anything. He had no idea what sort of emotional radiation a poltergeist was supposed to put out.

Joanna shrugged again.

'I guess we'll know it when we sense it,' she said. But it didn't take an empath to recognize the doubt in her voice.

*

Loric couldn't concentrate on the programme, even though he'd been addicted to *Neighbours* since it started. Something was happening outside in the night, something strange, and potentially dangerous. Whatever it was, it left his seventh sense screaming for attention.

He couldn't ignore it.

'Why me?' a cardboard Australian shouted. Loric knew how he felt. He sighed, and stood, starting the VCR with a passing thought, cutting the man off in mid-rant.

His attaché case was where he'd left it, on the hall stand beside the front door. He knew nothing had been disturbed since the last time he'd used it, but he checked the contents methodically nevertheless. He wouldn't get a second chance if something went wrong.

Garlic flowers, a packet of salt, and a small brush of hyssop twigs. A child's water pistol, made of garish yellow plastic, full of holy water blessed by a bishop. Photocopies of selected pages from the *Fulvarum Paginarum*, wrapped around the disassembled neon tubes of a small but effective electric pentacle.

He snapped the catches closed, and reached for his hat.

Outside the air was cold, smelling of Guy Fawkes and magic. Loric warmed himself reflexively, took a tighter grip on his silver-topped cane, and strode off in search of a taxi.

The waning of the rush hour had left the tube train packed nearly to capacity. Twenty minutes earlier its cargo of human sardines would have had to breathe in rotation; now it was only uncomfortable. Strap-hangers shuffled their feet, trying to keep their balance around an obstacle course of luggage and carrier bags. Those with seats stared past the shoulders of their neighbours, avoiding eye contact.

One of the strap-hangers staggered.

'Do you mind?' He turned, glaring at the man beside him, a mirror image of his own dark suit.

'I beg your pardon?' The second commuter raised puzzled eyes over his folded copy of the *Standard*.

'Someone bumped into me ...' The first man's voice trailed off, panicky realization dawning in his eyes. 'My wallet! Someone's picked my pocket!'

'What?' The other dug into his own jacket, then relaxed visibly. Little ripples of alarm and paranoia started to spread among the passengers. 'Mine's still ...' His voice trailed away, an expression of anger and fear mingling on his face. 'Something's got hold of my fingers!'

The wallet rose out of his pocket, with an audible tearing of cloth, and twitched itself out of his hand. After a moment it fell to the floor, leaving a comet tail of levitating banknotes, which wadded themselves around a tiny hovering ball of crumpled paper.

'Oh my God!' A young woman jumped out of the way of the floating cash, the change from her purse rising to join it. She tripped over a carrier bag, spilling groceries, and fell sprawling across the lap of a Rastafarian reading *The Brothers Karamazov*.

Hysteria ignited across the carriage.

Conway and Joanna had returned to the concourse at the bottom of the main bank of escalators. By this time they knew every corner of the station more intimately than anyone, except possibly the spiders. Conway checked his watch; another two hours, seventeen and a half minutes to go until they were relieved. Almost thirty seconds since the last time he'd checked.

'We could always split up,' Joanna suggested, in the voice of a B-movie actress. 'That way it's bound to get one of us.'

'Good idea,' Conway said. 'I feel like taking a walk on my own beside the old deserted graveyard.'

They'd discovered a taste in common for low-budget horror films; it wasn't much, but it gave them something to talk about. They'd even caught some of the same screenings at the Scala, although he couldn't remember a girl with purple hair in the audience.

'It might have been green then,' Joanna explained. More likely he'd still been on a high from the emotional feedback surrounding him, and in no condition to notice.

'It's all right for you,' Joanna said. 'I have to make sure I'm not stuck next to someone who knows how it ends.'

Suddenly, without warning, the subliminal hum of other minds exploded in rainbows of panic. Conway turned, pinpointing the disturbance; it was on one of the Piccadilly-line platforms, moving up the escalator towards them, leaving eddy currents of fear and confusion in its wake. There was something else too, harder to focus on: loneliness and need. People always registered as individuals, their emotions clustered around a hard core of personal identity, but this was diffuse, nebulous; for a moment he wondered if it was a ghost.

Joanna was picking up the commotion, but looked confused; before he had time to ask why, the entity was on them.

At first it was masked by the knot of commuters fleeing ahead of it; a few of the laggards stumbled and fell, brushed aside by something invisible that scooped banknotes from their pockets and handbags as it passed. As the crowd parted, all they could see was a large wad of money, floating through the air as though crushed in a fist. The vague knot of emotions Conway could sense were clustered around it, like an invisible cloud.

'There's nothing there!' Joanna shouted.

'There must be. I'm picking up a bigger emotional charge than a Mills and Boon novel!'

'Nothing! No thoughts at all!'

'Then what the hell is this?' They moved forward together, stepping cautiously, probing at it with their minds.

The entity lashed out, suddenly, without warning. Conway felt an invisible hand seize his shirt front, lifting him bodily from his feet, and fling him aside. He twisted into the breakfall instinctively, rolling to his feet, bringing his hands up into a defensive stance. He glanced round; the passengers were fleeing up the escalator, forming a milling, bleating crowd around it; people coming down were being sucked into the vortex, and a few had turned, trying to fight their way back up the packed, descending staircase. It was only a matter of moments before someone got hurt.

One of the Transport Policemen was shouting into his radio, while the other tried to control the crowd. Conway looked for Joanna, feeling a momentary flash of relief as he found her; she was standing to one side, apparently unhurt, her eyes unfocused as she reached out with her mind. For some reason the entity had it in for him, specifically; he could feel the warm pulse of hatred beating in his direction. He didn't know why, but it seemed to have something to do with his suit.

How the hell do you fight something you can't see? He relaxed, waiting, and the answer came, so simple it almost surprised him. He'd stopped actively probing the thing; now it just hovered in his awareness, part of the pattern of forces surrounding him. He felt its intention to strike and moved without thought, blending into the flow of energy and diverting it into a new direction, as easily as an exercise in the dojo.

Suddenly he was holding an arm, bending the wrist

into a lock, but the moment he started to think of it in concrete terms it became insubstantial and began to pull away. He relaxed again, clearing his mind, and the sensation solidified.

Terrific, he thought. I've got it, but only so long as I don't think about it. Now what the hell do I do?

He felt a flicker of reassurance, overlaid with the taste of Joanna's personality, and risked a quick glance in her direction.

The telepath was already moving, scanning the struggling commuters, homing in on something pulled from the babble of their minds. As Conway watched, she took a step towards a middle-aged man with poached-egg eyes, milling on the edge of the crowd. As well as the inevitable briefcase he was clutching a raffia shopping bag with a frayed handle and trying to prevent his groceries from spilling out.

'Ladies and gentlemen! There's no need for panic! Please form an orderly queue!' One of the policemen was shouting ineffectually, trying to calm them down. For a moment Conway was surprised by the confusion; surely it was over by now. Then he caught sight of the clock, and realized the whole incident had taken less than a minute.

'Trent, DPR.' Joanna flashed her ID card at the startled businessman, and grabbed the shopping bag. 'I need your groceries.'

'What?' The poached eggs blinked in surprise as she rummaged through the bag, turning out bacon, beans, and a couple of girlie magazines. 'This is absolutely . . .'

'Important. Thank you.' She grabbed a carton of salt, and let the bag fall on the remains of his discarded purchases.

'Hold on, Marcus!' She scattered a circle of white crystals around her kneeling colleague, making sure the ends joined. He saw what she was doing, and nodded, smiling. 'Step over it. Carefully!'

Conway stood, feeling the arm dissolve like smoke, and took a step backwards. He could feel the explosion of anger and fear as the entity realized it was trapped, and let his breath out in a long, controlled sigh.

'What's happening?' one of the policemen asked. Joanna jerked a thumb at the wad of money floating forlornly round the circumference of the circle.

'We've caught your poltergeist. It'll stay caught, as long as no one disturbs the barrier.' She indicated the crowd around the escalator, which was starting to go slack as it realized the danger was over. 'So I suggest you get these people out of here.'

'Right, miss.' The policeman saluted, and started to turn away. Conway called him back.

'One more thing. We need a phone.'

'That won't be necessary,' someone said behind him. 'I'll take it from here.'

Something was terribly wrong. Darren didn't know what, or how he knew, but something had happened to Damon.

It was almost unthinkable. Damon had been part of his life since he was a child, left alone every night while his mother went out with a series of Barrys. Damon was just someone to play with at first; it was only later he'd started looking after Darren, hitting back when he was bullied, getting him the toys and sweets his mother couldn't afford. The other children on the estate wouldn't play with him, afraid of the invisible companion their parents refused to believe in, but Damon was worth a thousand flesh-and-blood friends.

By the time Darren went to school, Damon had realized it was better for him not to be noticed. Nevertheless, the word got around that Braithwaite was strange. Darren was left alone, making few friends, none of them close; he'd never learned the knack, and when he left, with no qualifications, he drifted out of touch without thought or regret. After all, he had Damon.

Now Damon was the one in trouble. Darren could feel it. He struggled to his feet, shucking the sleeping bag like a denim-clad moth spreading its wings. Without even waiting to gather his meagre possessions, heedless of the aching in his joints, he stumbled away, following the screaming in his head.

'Remarkable. Quite remarkable.' The tall man in the expensive suit was standing just inside the makeshift barrier of trestles, peering into the circle of salt as if it were a toyshop window. The entity had dropped the bundle of money some time before, and Conway was the only one who had even the vaguest idea of where it was, but the newcomer acted as if he could see it as clearly as anything else in the station.

Maybe he could. Loric was ... well, he was Loric. He was taller than he looked on television, and friendly, and charming, and he scared Conway spitless.

'Me too,' Joanna said quietly. He was impossible for either of them to read, his shield perfect and impenetrable.

'What we have here,' Loric said, turning towards them at last, 'is a good old-fashioned familiar. At least, it looks like one. Or it would if you could see it.' He glanced back at the circle. 'You're familiar with familiars?'

'I thought they were cats,' Conway said.

'Sometimes. Of course they've gone out of fashion now, since the scientific method came in. But in the good old days no self-respecting sorcerer would be without one.'

'Sorcerer?' Conway said, unable to hide his disbelief.

'Sorcerer, Talent, whatever you like to call it. I thought you'd realized, using the trick with the salt.'

'It worked for Lyle Talbot in *The Vampire's Tomb*,' Joanna said. 'So it seemed worth a try.'

'I see.' Loric looked vaguely disappointed.

Darren was getting close, he could feel it. There was a tube station ahead, on the corner of High Holborn, and through the layer of cotton wool between him and the world he could make out a number of vehicles with blue flashing lights parked around it. He felt a flare of panic. If Damon was hurt ... But Damon was inside, he was sure of that.

He barely noticed the unusual number of uniforms in the booking hall; police serge was almost the same colour as London Transport, and soldiers weren't that rare in the capital. If more of the passengers than usual were wearing what looked like conference badges, with neat little photographs, and carrying things that hummed and flashed lights, that hardly registered either.

'Just a moment, sir.' A hand plucked at his sleeve as he passed through the ticket barrier. Darren brushed it aside like a troublesome insect. 'Can I see your ticket?' A few feet beyond, the escalator rattled and squeaked. 'Oi! Come back here!'

Darren stepped on the escalator, worn wooden treads beneath his feet. He swayed, tired and weak, leaning his weight against the rubber handrail. It was moving slightly slower than the stairway, tilting him back as he descended. Running feet clattered down the steps behind him, and someone grabbed hold of his arm.

'Gotcha!' The ticket collector hung on triumphantly all the way to the bottom. Darren tugged ineffectually a couple of times, but couldn't shake him.

'That's all right,' somebody said. 'Mr Braithwaite is one of ours.'

'Well, he should have said.'

Darren looked up, surprised, as the hand on his arm fell away.

'I suppose he should.' The speaker was tall, with greying hair, and he looked at Darren with evident concern. 'But considering the state of his health, I think we're lucky to have him here at all.'

'Where's Damon?' Darren didn't even think of trying to explain. Somehow he knew the tall man understood him. 'What happened?'

'It's a long story. Most of which I'm sure you'll be telling me.' The stranger glanced across the concourse, to where Damon was standing. 'Both of you.'

Darren nodded. Damon was safe, and he was ... he was ... The pounding in his head was worse than ever, and the stranger's voice buzzed like an insect. All of a sudden he forgot how to stand.

'So that's what a sorcerer looks like,' Conway said, as the stretcher went past. He felt the familiar go with it, hovering solicitously over Braithwaite. It had been an anxious moment when Loric kicked the salt away, but even unconscious the young derelict seemed to keep it under some sort of control.

'Some of them,' Loric said. 'Of course these days we'd call Master Braithwaite a class A, semi-autonomous, psychokinetic energy-field generator, but the old terminology sounds so much more romantic, don't you think?'

'Indubitably,' Joanna said.

'Well, must dash.' Loric tipped his hat to her, and nodded affably to Conway. 'Don't forget to put the cleaning bill for that suit on expenses.'

'Count on it,' Conway said. The right sleeve and back of his jacket had picked up a thick layer of grime from the breakfall he'd made on the floor of the concourse.

'You know ...' Joanna was looking thoughtful, turning

her head to watch Loric and the stretcher party rising towards the street. 'It must be nice, in a way. Having someone around you can always rely on.'

'Uh huh.' Conway glanced at his watch. It was still early, and the reports could wait. Indefinitely, if Marcia collated them. 'Feel like taking in a movie?'

'Why not?' Joanna shrugged. 'You never know when it might come in handy.'

'My thoughts exactly.'

'I know,' she said, and Conway laughed.

(*Private Eye*, 26 October 1990)

Even stranger things than usual (*Eye passim*) appear to be going on at the Department of the Preternaturally Ridiculous. Despite last year's budget allocation failing to keep pace with inflation for the third year running, a fortune is being lavished on Tintern House, one of the training centres for new recruits.

Like most of the DPR outstations, the Grade II listed tip was 'donated' by the PSA, eager to pass the buck before it collapsed altogether. Tenders were invited for remedial works, but for some reason the bid accepted, submitted by local firm Colbeauman's, was over £200,000 higher than those of its competitors.

Senior DPR official Peter Colbeauman explained that 'it was felt advantageous to establish good relations with the local community'. Presumably the relation he had in mind was his brother the brickie; now Inspector Knacker looks like making things a little warmer than either of them had anticipated.

Ironically, the refurbished centre features prominently in the new 'Public Information Campaign' being run by the COI, in a desperate and probably doomed attempt to make the DPR seem interesting and useful. Campaign figurehead Carrie Smith is already rumoured to be causing her Civil Service minders palpitations with her visibly Greek Island lifestyle, and the misdemeanours of the Brothers Colbeauman could just be enough to deep six the whole shabby enterprise.

THE OEDIPUS EFFECT

Brian Stableford

As Simon Sweetland locked the doors of his dilapidated
Mini he looked up, as was his habit, to survey the graffiti
sprayed on the windowless wall of concrete which was
the northern face of the Department of Paranormal
Resources, Coventry. It was, as ever, a disappointing
sight; the Midland school of street art was still in its
super-naïve phase.

Ignoring the obscenities and the Rorschach-blot squig-
gles, he squinted through his spectacles at the one item
which had seemed to hold a possibility of better things
to come. Originally it had read: YOU DON'T HAVE TO BE
WEIRD TO WORK HERE BUT IT HELPS — an unoriginal senti-
ment, remarkable in context only because the word
'weird' was correctly spelled. Then someone had crossed
out WEIRD and substituted TALENTED — a predictable defensive ploy only slightly dignified by the fact that the
words had been psychokinetically embossed, obviously
not by any of the local Temps but by some passing
hotshot from the Metropolis. Then the original artist had
crossed out TALENTED and substituted FREAKY. Simon
had been hoping to see a fourth move for three weeks,
now, but Talent and literary flair somehow never seemed
to go together.

He was not tempted to make any contribution of his
own; he was essentially one of the DPR's — and life's —
spectators. Not only was he devoid of psychokinetic

223

Talent but of any other noticeable power to impose his personality upon the environment. Weird and freaky he might be, but superhuman he was not; he was a mere theorist, one of the fortunate few dozen whom the scientific civil service felt it worthwhile to devote to the study of Talents, with a view to one day discovering an explanation for their existence.

He crossed the almost-empty car-park — he was, as was his habit, twenty minutes early — and entered the building. He passed through the empty lobby and went upstairs to his office, where he hung up his coat before taking up his station behind his desk. Then he unfolded his copy of the *Guardian* and began to read.

His telephone rang and he picked it up, despite the fact that it was not yet nine o'clock. 'Someone to see you — a Mr Fay,' said Marcia, in an aggrieved tone. Simon inferred that she had only just arrived, and he knew full well that she did not like to have work thrust at her even before the day had officially begun. He had never heard of any Mr Fay.

'Send him up,' he said, wearily, closing the *Guardian* but not bothering to hide it.

Two minutes later there was a knock at the door. A young man in a smart suit came in, a practised smile appearing upon his well-scrubbed features, as if at the flick of some mysterious internal switch.

'Dr Sweetland?' he said, with careful enthusiasm. 'I'm Lewis Fay, of Family Provident.'

Simon's heart sank. 'I'm quite well insured, thank you,' he said, reflexively. 'I don't need any financial advice whatsoever.'

The smile neither cracked nor quivered. 'I'm not a salesman, Dr Sweetland. I'm Senior Claims Adjustor, Midlands and West. I'd like to talk to you about your paper in the current issue of the *Journal of Paranormal Studies*, if I may.'

Simon's eyebrows lifted in astonishment. He had not realized that anyone outside the DPR and a few university departments ever read the *JPS*. He had been a regular contributor for more than ten years — promotion in the scientific civil service was heavily dependent on one's publication record — but no one had ever before shown the slightest interest in any of his papers. In fact, Simon rarely bothered to read the journal himself, though he dutifully placed the quarterly issues on the bookshelf behind his desk when they arrived (usually six to eight weeks late). He took it for granted that all the other papers, as well as his own, were produced under the spur of career-building necessity, and that they would either be routine exercises in number-crunching or flights of philosophical fancy devoid of any semblance of empirical support.

'You mean,' he said, warily wondering whether Mr Fay might have the wrong man, '"A New Interpretation of the Precognitive Paradox".'

'That's the one,' said Fay, breezily. 'Brilliant work, Dr Sweetland — I was very impressed. So impressed that I'd like to talk to you about some consultancy work. DPR scientists are allowed to take on outside consultancy work, aren't they?'

Simon's eyebrows were incapable of further elevation, and he was too self-conscious to allow his jaw to drop, so he simply nodded, dumbly. He had, of course, heard rumours of fat retainers paid to senior DPR scientists by companies in return for mysterious advice — usually, he supposed, for covert assistance in identifying and luring away the DPR's more useful Temps — but he had never expected to catch a glimpse of that kind of gravy train himself. He was a Head of Department, but he only had one assistant, and was only one step removed from being a mere tester. 'Please take a seat,' he said, cautiously.

While Lewis Fay lowered himself into the PVC-clad chair which was usually occupied by mothers of that rare but avid breed who would try desperately to convince him that their unprepossessing children had hitherto-unimagined paranormal potential, Simon leaned forward, covering his newspaper with his elbows, and said, 'How, exactly, may I help you, Mr Fay?'

'We would like to retain your services as a consultant,' Fay repeated. 'The work wouldn't be very time-consuming; it would consist of writing the occasional report, and perhaps appearing in court now and again as an expert witness. The details are negotiable, but I ought to warn you that the remuneration would be modest, at first. We envisage a fixed retainer in the region of a thousand a year, but there would be a bonus scheme, by which you would get a fee for every successfully aborted claim of one per cent of the averted payout. It doesn't sound much, I know, but you'll be surprised how it mounts up. In five years' time, if you can back up the claims made in your paper, you might be pulling in tens of thousands a year.'

Simon clung on to the last vestiges of his composure and managed to nod, as if he received such offers regularly.

'As you've undoubtedly noticed,' Fay added, serenely, 'recent circumstances have thrown up an excellent test case for your thesis. If you can persuade a jury that what you say in your paper is true, or even that it's possible, it will create such an important precedent that the rest of your career should be plain sailing.'

Simon tried valiantly to figure out what Fay was talking about, but he couldn't do it. He felt like a non-swimmer dropped in at the deep end; the circumstances were simply not conducive to orderly and patient mental procedure.

'I'm sorry,' he murmured, 'but I don't quite see . . .'

Fay beamed – not, this time, the practised smile of welcome and reassurance, but a shark-like grin of casual superiority. Simon had seen similar expressions on the faces of Talented people, and had never liked them. They were expressions which said: 'I'm better than you, and I know things you don't, and because of that I can make you do what I want you to.'

'I do apologize, Dr Sweetland,' said Lewis Fay, insincerely. 'I'm going too quickly, aren't I? One sometimes forgets that academics like yourself, preoccupied with matters of abstract theory, don't always see the practical applications of their work. Far be it from me to try to explain your own ideas to you, but perhaps you wouldn't mind if I run over them for my own benefit, so that I can make sure I'm not making a fool of myself. Then, perhaps, I can, ah, show you where I'm coming from.'

Supercilious bastard! thought Simon. But he said nothing, contenting himself with a nod.

'Your paper,' said Mr Fay, calmly, 'is about the so-called paradox of precognition, is it not? This arises from the fact that among paranorms there is a small sub-group who seem to be able, in various slightly different ways, to have foreknowledge of the future, and to be able to issue true prophecies. The paradox, if I understand the matter correctly, comes in when the prophecies are made, and arises because of the effect that the making of a prophecy has on the likelihood of the event in question occurring. I believe you call it the Oedipus effect.'

Simon nodded again, and – feeling that he had made enough of a fool of himself already – quickly took up the argument: 'That's right. It's so-called because the prophecy that Oedipus would one day kill his father caused his father to set in train the chain of cause-and-effect which later enabled the event to occur. It's not a very good name really, because it refers to a self-fulfilling prophecy, while the effect is usually the other way around; prophecies are more often self-negating than self-fulfilling. If a precog tells you that you're going to die in a plane crash you simply don't take the plane – the fact that the prophecy has been issued prevents it from coming true. That's the paradox.'

Fay was still beaming. 'And it casts doubt, therefore, on the status of so-called precognitive Talents. If the event which the precognitive foresees doesn't happen because the people forewarned take steps to avert it, how can we claim that he really is seeing the future? Now, as I understand it, the orthodox answer is that the future isn't fixed, and that precognitives can only see *possible* futures. But your paper proposes a different interpretation, doesn't it?'

'It points out that another interpretation is theoretically possible,' Simon said, warily. 'You see, there are a lot of Talents which aren't under conscious control – paranormal abilities which can't just be summoned up at will, but break out in moments of extreme stress. Talents of that kind are more like emotions than instruments of the will – they're not really things which the paranorms consciously *do*. That's one of the reasons why there are so few really powerful and effective paranorms, and so many who are ... well, unreliable. What my paper suggests is that some paranorms whose Talents are classified by testers as precognitive are really powerful but undisciplined psychokinetics. The events which they seem to foresee are, in fact, events which they subconsciously intend to *cause*. When they predict that a fly on the window will shortly drop dead in mid-flight they're really anticipating an action which their own psychokinetically talented, subconscious mind will carry out – their foreknowledge may be no more paranormal than my foreknowledge when I say that I'm going to get a rolled-up newspaper and swat the fly.'

'Precisely,' said Lewis Fay. 'A very clever idea, if I may say so.'

'It's only speculation,' said Simon, 'and I don't quite see . . .' Then he stopped, because all of a sudden he *did* see why Family Provident might be interested in his paper. He cursed himself for not having seen it before. After a moment's pause, while he and Mr Fay watched one another carefully, he said, 'You mentioned a test case.'

'That's right,' said Fay, cheerfully. 'Did you see the evening paper last night?'

'No,' Simon admitted. 'I usually pick one up on my way home, but it was raining, and I couldn't be bothered getting out of the car.'

'Of course,' said Lewis Fay, as though it were obvious. 'And I see that you take the *Guardian*, so you would also have missed the item in this morning's tabloids. There was a death on a building site in the city centre yesterday. A crane was moving a concrete pile. The chains broke and the pile fell. Nobody was underneath it, but the toppling pile smashed a stack of tiles and sent the shards hurtling in all directions. One of them struck the head of an architect named Thomas Hemdean. It fractured his skull and caused a haemorrhage. He was dead on arrival at the hospital.'

'And who predicted it?' asked Simon, his voice hardly above a whisper.

'Nicholas Hemdean — the man's eight-year-old son. He begged his father not to go to work, apparently having described exactly what would happen, in front of four witnesses: his mother, his twelve-year-old sister, a neighbour and the neighbour's twelve-year-old daughter. It was in the local paper last night, and some of the tabloids picked it up for this morning's editions. Apparently the boy had been tested by the DPR at his mother's request, but the evidence for his Talent was considered inadequate. One or two of the papers have suggested that the Department's failure to identify the Talent might have caused the father to disbelieve the prediction – and thus, indirectly, have contributed to his death, but I don't know how far they'll be prepared to take that line of argument. Anyway, you and I know how it really happened, don't we?'

Simon felt suddenly rather sick. 'Your company insured this man's life?' he said.

'That's correct,' agreed Mr Fay.

'And you stand to pay out a lot of money if the death was accidental – because of double indemnity?'

'Right.'

'But like all insurance companies, you have an exclusion clause in your policies which means that you don't have to pay out at all if someone dies as a result of assignable paranormal action – it then becomes the task of the beneficiary to sue the person responsible for the amount which the policy would have realized.'

'It's a necessary precaution, given the kind of world we live in,' said Fay, spreading his arms wide. 'And the matter of intention is, of course, irrelevant to the matter of responsibility.'

Simon could now see the whole pattern, in all its horrific detail. 'You want me to write a report,' he said, haltingly, 'and, if necessary, to give evidence in court, to say that this man's death was caused, unconsciously, by his own son.'

'You don't have to prove it,' said Fay, agreeably. 'You only have to establish that it's possible. We don't necessarily expect to get off scot-free – we'd be quite happy to settle for a compromise. And you'll get a percentage of any money you save us. At the moment we stand to pay out £120,000. We think there's a good chance you can at least save us from the double indemnity. You might also save your Department – perhaps yourself, if you were the one who tested the boy – from some bad publicity.'

One per cent of £60,000, Simon knew, was £600 – not much more than a fortnight's wages. But Fay had already pointed out that one case would create a vital precedent. The price that was being put on Simon's soul was by no means meagre. How many deaths, he wondered, were predicted by precogs? How many more were claimed to have been predicted by liars and lucky guessers? How many cases a year could Family Provident call into question? Hundreds? Thousands?

'But it's his *eight-year-old son*,' said Simon, weakly. 'You want me to put the blame for this man's death on his own child.'

'On the child's *unconscious desires*,' Fay was quick to stress. 'Well-documented desires, at that. Didn't Freud say that all boys are unconsciously jealous of their fathers, because they see them as rivals for their mothers' love? Didn't he call *that* effect after Oedipus, too? Quite appropriate really, don't you think?'

Simon simply stared at his visitor, rendered speechless by the nauseous enormity of it all. Lewis Fay stood up, and placed a business card on the desk. 'That's the number,' he said. 'Think it over and give me a ring. I understand your reservations, of course, and only you can decide where your own and your Department's interests lie. I'll be in all day should you wish to contact me. Please don't bother to get up – I can find my own way out.'

Even as Lewis Fay turned to go to the door, Simon's telephone began to ring. He picked it up. 'There's a call for you,' said Marcia, in a breathlessly respectful tone which he had never heard her use before, even when talking to the Division Head. 'It's a man from the *Sun.* Shall I put him through?' She could hardly have sounded more surprised had it been a man from the sun.

'No,' said Simon, quickly. 'I can't talk to reporters now. Tell him that I'm tied up. And that goes for Carol too. If they keep trying, tell them we'll be available for comment later.'

Considering that her remarkable propensity for saying no to callers was the nearest thing to a Talent Marcia had, she sounded surprisingly resentful when she said, 'Oh, very well then.'

Simon left the phone off the hook, just in case.

Simon tried to call up the record of Nicholas Hemdean's testing on the computer, but the system was down and he had to go instead to the huge filing cabinet where the scoring-cards were kept. Here he discovered that Nicholas Hemdean had been tested five months earlier by Carol Cloxeter, his one and only assistant.

That made him feel slightly better – not because it might enable him to pass the buck if the Department were to come under fire, but because it explained why he had no memory of the case.

The handwritten notes on the card registered Nicholas as an alleged Dreamer – not only the commonest kind of precog but also the easiest to misidentify – and observed that most of the supposed evidence for the child's Talent was not only anecdotal but retrospective; which was to say that the child had mostly claimed to have foreseen the relevant events after they had happened. Tests with Zener cards and dice had given scores no better than average, and the child had been unable to issue any sufficiently specific predictions to warrant further investigation. Simon knew that there must be several hundred more-or-less identical cards in the file.

He carried the card to Carol's office and showed it to her. 'Can you remember this boy?' he asked.

She looked at the card, furrowing her brow in concentration. Then she looked up and nodded. She had lovely grey eyes, perfectly set off by her large-lensed spectacles, and a very sweet smile. Simon had been half in love with her for two years; unfortunately, she was happily married to one Edward Cloxeter, Consultant Ergonomist.

'Vaguely,' she said. 'Very shy boy. Handsome mother, distinctly up-market – not the usual type at all.'

The mothers most ardently desirous of discovering Talent in their offspring tended to be dissatisfied members of the working class. Middle-class parents usually preferred their kids to be normal – by which they meant polite, articulate and high-achieving.

'Why did she bring him in at all?' asked Simon, guardedly.

Carol shrugged. 'If he'd had a toothache she'd have taken him to the dentist, and would have been equally relieved to be told that he didn't need a filling. She just wanted professional reassurance that there was nothing to worry about. Why? Has something happened?'

'You didn't see the evening paper?'

'No. We do take it but it's Eddie's really.'

Simon sighed. It didn't take a genius to work out what had happened. Mrs Hemdean had taken little Nicholas home and told her husband that there was nothing to worry about, and that the boy's dreams would go away in time if they ignored them – like an imaginary playmate or acne. The father had probably been glad to go to work after the child begged him not to, just to prove once and for all that the dreams were nothing to be afraid of. He told Carol what had happened to Thomas Hemdean, but left Lewis Fay out of it for the time being.

'We'd better get the papers and see how much of a

problem we have,' he said. 'Then we'd better go see Mrs Hemdean and find out what really happened.'

'Am I in trouble?' asked Carol, anxiously.

'Of course not,' said Simon, wishing that he sounded more convincing. 'You did everything right. The papers will probably drop it. They enjoy putting the boot into the DPR, but this isn't in the same league as a juicy story about some wacky temp fouling things up.'

'Yes, of course,' she said, though her anxiety was obviously unquieted. 'I'll get my coat.'

Simon drove to a local newsagent, where he managed to buy a copy of the previous evening's paper as well as the morning tabloids. The evening paper's coverage was headlined LOCAL ARCHITECT KILLED IN FREAK ACCIDENT, and it presented a relatively sober account of the facts beneath a photograph of the dead man; it only mentioned Nicholas's pleas in the last paragraph and his testing by the DPR as an afterthought. The reporter, who was probably some novice fresh out of college, had obviously thought the information irrelevant — as, indeed, it probably was.

The *Sun*, not untypically, had turned it all around, even though it had relegated the story to the desultory wilderness of page 6. 'NORMAL' BOY PREDICTS FATHER'S DEATH was the headline, and the photograph accompanying the piece was a snapshot of Nicholas, apparently two or three years out of date. Nicholas was blond, thin-faced and unsmiling, somehow rather furtive; he looked completely unlike his dark-haired, chubby and seemingly self-satisfied father.

While Simon drove on towards the suburb where the Hemdeans lived, Carol read the two articles.

'It'll be a storm in a teacup,' she predicted, with more hope than certainty. 'Everyone knows how many supposed Dreamers come forward for testing, and how few of them have a hit rate worth scoring.'

Simon noted how carefully she had phrased the claim. Like most scientists engaged in paranormal studies, Carol had a pet theory which she promoted in her published papers. Carol's theory was that everybody was Talented, and that intelligent life would be quite impossible without Talent; her solution of the age-old mind–body problem was that the mind was a paranormal phenomenon and that its conscious control of the body was a species of psychokinesis. In her view, classifiable Talent was only different in degree, not in kind, from everyday mental activity; anybody and everybody might therefore have the occasional precognitive insight, in a dream or any other way, and those who got to be certified paranormals were simply those who had exceptionally accurate insights with exceptional regularity.

'It might be a bigger storm than you think,' Simon told her, dolefully, and went on to tell her about Lewis Fay's proposition.

She was disgusted. *'Family Provident,'* she said, as though it were an off-colour phrase. 'What a ghoul! You're not thinking of doing it, are you?'

'I've already published the paper,' Simon pointed out, glumly. 'He was quite right – it simply had not occurred to me to think about possible practical implications. I suppose it could be given in evidence whether I agree to play ball or not. I might be summoned to testify even if I refuse the consultancy – and if I try to recant I'll look like a complete fool. And after all, it *is* conceivable that my interpretation of the precognitive paradox is the correct one.'

Given the nature of Carol Cloxeter's pet theories he could not expect her to agree with his speculations, but he appealed for moral support regardless. He was not overly surprised when she simply sniffed and said 'Anything's possible,' in a tone which suggested that one had to be very charitable to think so.

The Hemdeans lived in a large detached house surrounded by a 6 ft wall. It was a very nice house – as one might expect of the home of an architect – with big wrought-iron gates; these were guarded by a uniformed constable, who was exchanging desultory remarks with a small group of idle bystanders, some of whom carried cameras. Simon guessed that the bystanders were bored newspapermen, who knew perfectly well that they would not be allowed through the gate, but were obliged to hang about anyhow. He could not help wishing that he had a blanket to put over his head, but he took comfort from the fact that the reporters were few in number, and certainly did not have the air of men on a promising assignment. A shower of rain would probably send them hurrying off in search of something spicier, and the dour November sky was obligingly threatening.

When the Mini pulled in to the gateway the newspapermen became mildly curious and the flash bulbs began to pop. The annoyed policeman bent down to order Simon to go away, but he showed his identity card and said that it was imperative that he talk to Mrs Hemdean. The policeman – presumably a *Sun* reader – saw the logic of the situation instantly, and unfastened the gate to let the Mini through, closing it again very firmly afterwards. Simon parked the Mini behind the silver Volvo which stood outside the front door.

Mrs Hemdean answered the door herself. She looked at Simon with naked hostility, and perhaps a measure of distaste, but she recognized Carol and welcomed the revelation that they were not newshounds.

'Oh,' she said, 'it's you.' She grudgingly let them in, and took them into a sitting room. 'Nicholas is in bed,' she said. 'He's very disturbed. I honestly don't know *how* the papers got hold of that story about Nicholas being tested. One of the neighbours, I expect.'

Simon sat down gingerly on the sofa. Carol sat beside him and Mrs Hemdean lowered herself into an armchair. Mrs Hemdean looked distressed, but not in a grief-stricken way. She was, as Carol had said, a handsome woman, and though her handsomeness was mostly gloss and grooming it had not been significantly disturbed by tragedy; her hair and make-up were perfectly in place.

'Perhaps it was the neighbour who was with you yesterday morning?' Simon suggested. 'I understand that there was someone else present when Nicholas tried to prevent his father going to work.'

'Oh no,' said Mrs Hemdean. 'It couldn't have been *Alex*. He came to collect Debbie. She and Patricia — that's Alex's daughter — go to school together. Alex and Tom take it in turns dropping them off. It's quite a way, you see, and the girls daren't go past the comprehensive while they're wearing their uniforms. Alex wouldn't have spoken to the *press*.'

Simon had felt worried about the prospect of intruding upon a widow's grief, but Mrs Hemdean was obviously not the kind of woman to let her loss disturb her manners. He couldn't help wondering whether the widow's stern composure might be more severely dented when she found out that Mr Fay was trying to figure out a way of weaselling out of the insurance company's obligations to her.

'Can you tell us exactly what happened yesterday?' asked Simon, politely. 'I know it's a terrible time to bother you, and I really don't want to cause you any further distress, but there's a chance that those reporters outside might blow the matter up out of all proportion if the mood takes them. They've already asked for a statement from the Department, and I really do need to know the full facts.'

'I can't remember, exactly,' said Mrs Hemdean, unhelpfully. 'Nicholas can be so trying at times, and one gets quite used to ignoring him. It was just another piece of nonsense. He didn't say anything at breakfast, and he watched Tom get ready for work as usual. It wasn't until Alex rang the bell and Debbie answered that he began to get excited — just when everything was at its most hectic. Tom was talking to Alex in the hall — just hello, how are you, that sort of thing — and Nicholas was suddenly tugging at his trouser leg, telling him not to go.'

'Mrs Hemdean,' said Carol, gently. 'It's vital that we know exactly what Nicholas said ... what words he used. We have to know how detailed this so-called precognition was.'

Mrs Hemdean shook her head, impatiently. 'I told you,' she said, 'I didn't really listen. I was in the kitchen when it started, and when I went into the hall my main concern was to get Nicholas away so that Tom could go to work ...'

'The papers claim that he foresaw every detail of the accident,' Simon said, doggedly. 'Personally, I find that hard to believe, given that it was such an unusual occurrence. Please try to remember, Mrs Hemdean — did he use the word crane at all, or the word tile?'

Mrs Hemdean clucked her tongue, and shook her head again. 'He certainly said crane,' she said, eventually, 'but I don't think he said anything about tiles.'

Simon exchanged glances with Carol. They both knew that even if an eight-year-old boy had seen every detail of the accident in a dream, he might not quite understand what would have happened, and might not even know the word tile. The only things which would have impressed themselves strongly on his frightened mind would have been the crane dropping its load and the death of his father.

'Can we speak to Nicholas?' asked Carol.

'If he's not asleep,' said Mrs Hemdean, with a fatalistic shrug of the shoulders. 'But you won't get any sense out of *him*.'

As they went up the stairs, Simon said: 'Mrs Hemdean, it's obvious that neither you or your husband took this premonitory dream at all seriously — yet five months ago you brought Nicholas along to the DPR to be tested. Why did you do that, if you didn't believe he had a Talent?'

'I knew it was all nonsense,' retorted Mrs Hemdean. 'It was Debbie and Tom who thought there might be something in it — Debbie was the only one who'd heard any of these so-called predictions before the accidents happened, and Tom always listened to her. Tom insisted that I bring Nicholas to you, but you only confirmed what I thought all along.'

Simon frowned slightly. 'So, despite the fact that your husband once thought Nicholas might have a precognitive Talent, he was still prepared to discount this particular prediction.'

'I don't know about discounting it,' Mrs Hemdean said. 'I couldn't get Nicholas away from him until he'd promised that he wouldn't go under the crane, but he probably just said that to keep Nicholas quiet — and anyway, he didn't go under the crane, did he?'

Perhaps he did try to negate the prophecy, thought Simon. Perhaps he just didn't move away quite far enough!

Nicholas wasn't asleep, but he looked in far worse shape than his mother: tired, listless, utterly stricken by grief and horror. He too remembered Carol Cloxeter, but the look he gave her was so redolent with misery and pain that Simon felt mortally uncomfortable.

At Simon's request Mrs Hemdean left them alone, but Simon hung back while Carol sat on the bedside and took the child's hand in her own.

'I'm sorry, Nicholas,' she said, 'but I have to ask you some questions. Should I call you Nicholas, or Nicky?'

'My friends call me Nicky,' said the boy, lifelessly. Simon noted that his mother didn't.

'Can you tell us about the dream you had?'

'I saw the crane. It was lifting something. Then it fell. It killed my daddy.' As he spoke the last sentence tears welled up in the boy's eyes, but he didn't quite break down and cry.

Carol hesitated, and Simon knew that she couldn't yet bring herself to ask precisely *how* Nicky had seen his father killed. 'Why didn't you say anything before?' she asked, instead. 'Why did you wait until he was actually leaving the house?'

'I didn't remember until then,' said the boy, miserably. 'I don't always remember when I get up. Don't you remember — that's why you didn't believe me. I told you I sometimes didn't remember the dreams until after things happened. That's why mummy wouldn't believe me when she laddered her tights and when her dress got splashed. She just got mad at me, because I didn't remember the dreams till afterwards. This time, I remembered in time . . . but she wouldn't believe me anyway. Nobody believed me, except Debbie. You didn't.'

'It wasn't that I didn't believe you,' said Carol, forlornly. 'It's just that . . . we have to be very sure, you see. There are so many people who think they have a Talent, and so few who really can do anything extraordinary. It's not easy to tell, sometimes.' She turned uncomfortably to face Simon. 'I'll carry on here,' she said. 'Maybe you should ask Mrs Hemdean about . . . other possibilities.'

Simon nodded, and was ashamed to find himself rather

relieved as he descended the staircase and went in search of Nicholas's mother. The 'other possibilities' which he had to ask about were, of course, psychokinetic incidents. If his own theory were true, and Nicholas had unconsciously engineered the events which he had earlier 'dreamed', they were unlikely to have been the only evidences of his capricious Talent.

He tried to tackle the subject in a roundabout way, but Mrs Hemdean was no fool. She couldn't know why he was asking, but she knew what it was that he was fishing for. 'Of course things sometimes fall down,' she said, snappily. 'Of course they break. Accidents happen. But no matter how infuriating Nicholas can be, I'm not such a fool as to think he's responsible. It's annoying when he tells me that he knew something was going to happen, but he doesn't mean any harm. We're no more accident-prone than any other family, and we certainly don't have a *poltergeist* in the house. Look around you, Dr Sweetland – do you think I'd keep ornaments like these about the house if things were always getting hurled through the air?'

Simon surveyed the knick-knacks on the sideboard and the mantelpiece. They weren't antique Dresden, but they weren't cheap either. No specific evidence, however weak, of psychokinesis, he thought, making notes in anticipation of a possible cross-examination. No evidence whatsoever – I hope – that there was any antagonism between the boy and his father ... in fact, in his shoes, I'd have been more inclined to drop a concrete pile on his mother. He blushed at the last thought, but Mrs Hemdean didn't notice. He wondered whether he ought to tell her about Mr Fay, but decided against it, not knowing whether to call the decision diplomacy or cowardice.

Carol was a long time coming down, and when she did eventually come down she wasn't alone.

'This is Debbie,' said Carol, introducing her companion to Simon. Simon had already guessed – the young girl was stamped from exactly the same mould as her mother. Her school uniform was uncannily neat, despite the fact that she seemed so unhappy. Simon saw from the corner of his eye that Mrs Hemdean was only very slightly annoyed to see Carol and her daughter together: she obviously had no particular worries about anything that Debbie might have said.

'Debbie's the only person Nicky always tells when he has his dreams,' said Carol, more for the girl's benefit than Simon's. 'She says that when he tells her something's going to happen to her, she makes sure it doesn't. She says that he's never let her down.'

In other words, thought Simon, she knows he was right because what he said would happen didn't, although it might have if he hadn't warned her. It was the precognitive paradox in all its glory.

'I did tell Daddy to be careful,' said Debbie, mournfully. 'I thought that would be enough. I thought that if he knew about the crane, he wouldn't be in any danger. He did promise – he did.' She too was on the brink of tears. Only Mrs Hemdean was immune.

'The papers seem to have got it wrong,' said Carol. 'Debbie remembers quite clearly what Nicky said – he never said anything about shattered fragments flying about; he only said that the crane would drop something, and that his father would fall down. Mr Hemdean thought he would be safe, if only he was careful not to get underneath the crane ... which he probably wouldn't have done anyhow.'

'We'll have to make that clear,' said Simon, mechanically, for Mrs Hemdean's benefit.

'And we'll have to test Nicky again, when he's well enough to be tested,' said Carol, also speaking for

Mrs Hemdean's ears rather than his. 'Just to make sure.'

'Yes,' said Simon, hollowly. 'Just to make sure.' He had a feeling that Mrs Hemdean might not be too keen on that idea, when she found out what Mr Fay had up his sleeve. In fact, he had a feeling that Mrs Hemdean would be decidedly unready to speak to him – or anyone else from the DPR – ever again. He only hoped that she wouldn't decide that the idea of talking to the press wasn't so hideous after all; there was nothing more likely to keep a tabloid story running than a rich source of spiteful accusations.

But there was nothing he could do but wait and see what happened.

'What do you think?' asked Simon, unhappily, as he drove back to the DPR building.

'Neither of the kids said anything to lend support to the idea that he's a subconscious psychokinetic,' she said, bluntly. 'And we also have to bear in mind that he was seven miles away from the scene of the supposed subconscious crime. How many PKs do you know who could direct the flight of a fragment of a tile at that sort of distance?'

Simon sighed. 'One of the Gods could do it,' he said, 'but none of our Temps could, that's for sure.'

'At this point in time,' she said, mildly, 'I certainly wouldn't swap my pet theory for yours.'

'I don't blame you,' he said. 'Do you think he really is a precog?'

She looked at him as if she were Sherlock Holmes saying 'You know my methods, Watson, apply them!' What she actually said was: 'We all have precognitive flashes, Simon. It's just that most of us don't remember them, don't trust them or call them coincidences. The sort of evidence which convinced Debbie could be produced by almost anyone. If the boy does have an out-of-the-ordinary Talent he'll have to get far better control of it before we could take him on.'

'Maybe you'd better write the press release,' he said, bitterly.

'You're welcome to quote me,' she assured him, looking and sounding rather smug. Then, after a pause, she said, 'Don't worry about Fay. He won't dare to play his malicious games unless he has your active support – insurance companies have to be pretty sure of their ground before they put their public image at risk. Even if he does, you can always use the King James defence.'

'What the hell's that?' he asked.

She looked faintly surprised that he didn't know. 'James I wrote a book on witchcraft, arguing in favour of the case that witches did exist – but every time he got involved with an actual witch trial after he became king of England he had the charges dismissed, on the grounds that although witchcraft was real, it played no part in the particular cases in question. So, you can still stick to your theory if you want – all you have to say is that this isn't an instance of it.'

Simon knew that she was only trying to let him off the hook, but he also knew that it would still be going back on his argument. *Her* view was that precognition was real, but that this particular instance of it was no big deal; *he* had argued in print that the idea of precognition, given its paradoxical implications, was logically untenable, and that *all* the supposed examples of it might be explicable as mistaken psychokinesis. The 'might be' had certainly been cautious enough, but there was no way he could worm his way out of the 'logically untenable'. He had stuck his neck out, knowing at the time he was being slightly daring, but actually feeling rather pleased with himself. Now the axe was falling. If he now turned round

244

and said that perhaps there was real precognition after all, he was going to look very silly indeed. Lewis Fay had seen that clearly enough – and that was why Fay had thought it worth the trouble to offer him a consultancy.

When they got back to the DPR, keeping the lone waiting reporter at bay with promises of a statement to come, they found Marcia glued to the portable TV which she kept under her desk – which was, Simon supposed, marginally preferable to finding her glued to the telephone. She was watching the local news, on which a building contractor in an orange safety-helmet was explaining how extremely unfortunate poor Thomas Hemdean had been. 'It was a chance in a million,' he said. 'Never seen one like it before, and I don't expect ever to see one like it again. But accidents do happen. When you put up big buildings, you get falls and breakages – and the bigger the building is, the more likely it is that someone will get killed. A lot of the lads are superstitious – they get premonitions too, you know, and the company has a couple of Talented troubleshooters of its own – but in the end, you just can't cover all the angles. Least of all the million-to-one shots.'

Marcia looked up when Simon and Carol paused. 'Isn't it marvellous?' she said. 'That little boy knowing *exactly* what would happen to his father, even after you said that he was perfectly normal. It just goes to show that you never can tell.'

As Simon trudged upstairs to his office he felt as though his feet were lined with lead. He was not looking forward to writing a statement for the press, and he was *certainly* not looking forward to facing Mr Fay again.

It seemed like such a good idea at the time, he thought.

He worded the release with the utmost care, pointing out that Nicholas Hemdean's warning had in fact been rather vague, and reiterating that there had been and still was insufficient evidence to support the hypothesis that Nicholas had *any* kind of paranormal Talent, but it seemed feeble even to him, and he knew that it would not satisfy the press if they decided to follow up on the story.

It was not merely his and Carol's promotion prospects which were under threat, he knew, but also his own intellectual self-respect. But when he thought of Nicholas Hemdean's miserable face, he knew that he could not possibly follow the course which Lewis Fay had proposed. There was no way in the world that he could ever say, if asked, that Nicholas might actually have brought about the death of his father. Such a thing could not be said, and could not even be thought – not because it could not be true, but because it would be far too cruel.

Silently, Simon turned in his chair and plucked the latest issue of the *Journal of Paranormal Studies* from his bookshelf. He dropped it in the bin. Then he took his phone off the hook and got on with his work.

By the time five-thirty rolled around, mercifully without further incident, Simon was feeling a little better. It seemed that the storm in a teacup had already blown itself out, and he had convinced himself that the newspapers would drop the story. Then, just as he was about to leave, Carol Cloxeter came hurrying into the office, waving a fax.

She no longer looked smug. In fact, she looked somewhat shaken.

'Simon,' she said. 'Look at this!'

He scanned the piece of paper quickly. It was from a firm of solicitors, Montgomery & Clift, notifying Carol of the intention of Mrs Elizabeth Hemdean to file a suit against her and the DPR for compensatory damages in respect of the death of her husband – which, alleged the fax, could have been prevented if Carol had not been negligent in failing to establish the precognitive abilities of Nicholas Hemdean. A second copy had been sent to the Division Head, but had presumably arrived too late to be seen by him – yet.

'They're crazy!' said Simon. 'There's no way in the world they can make it stick.'

'Maybe not,' said Carol. 'But the fact that they intend to try will be enough to promote the story from page 6 to the front page, and we're going to look very bad indeed.'

Simon frowned. 'But it doesn't make any sense,' he said. 'When we saw Mrs Hemdean this morning she didn't show the slightest sign of thinking that we might be to blame, and she seemed determined to hold on to the belief that Nicholas *isn't* a precog. What changed her mind?'

'Mr Fay?' suggested Carol, in a tone which was nakedly accusative. Clearly she thought that Simon's heretical opinions had now rebounded upon her. He winced at the thought that she might be right.

'You think he's told her that there might be a problem with her insurance claim, and that she's decided to get her retaliation in first?'

'What else?'

Simon found the card with the record of Nicholas's tests, and checked the telephone number recorded there. When he got an engaged tone he guessed immediately that he was not the only one who had thought it politic to be unreachable.

'Get your coat,' he said, with unusual decisiveness. 'We'll go round there again.'

'Is that wise?' she asked.

'Probably not,' he admitted. 'But there's just a chance we can get this cleared up if I tell her that I haven't the slightest intention of backing up Fay's gambit. If she knows the insurance claim will be met, perhaps she'll be prepared to abandon this nonsense before she contrives to ruin the pair of us.'

It had finally begun to rain, and the sky was so heavy with cloud that it was nearly dark. The raindrops drumming on the roof of the Mini as it ploughed its weary way through the last vestiges of the rush hour sounded dreadfully ominous, but Simon's weak attempts to start a conversation were stonewalled by his anxious companion. Although he knew that he was not really to blame for the deepening mess that they were in, Simon could not help but feel horribly guilty. There was nothing in the world he hated more than to have Carol's displeasure aimed in his direction.

The rain had, as he had earlier hoped, driven off the reporters and the cameramen, and the dutiful policeman was looking distinctly bedraggled as he tried to make the most of the inadequate shelter offered by a sullen sycamore. When he recognized them he simply waved them on, clearly in no mood to question their right of access. The parking space in the driveway was severely constricted by a black BMW which had joined the still-ungaraged Volvo, but Simon managed to squeeze the Mini in.

When he rang the doorbell Simon had awful visions of the door being promptly slammed in their faces by an angry widow, but in fact it was Debbie Hemdean who answered the door, in the company of another girl of similar age, dressed in a similar school uniform.

'Please come in,' said Debbie, scrupulously. 'This is my friend Patricia Clift.' She waited until Simon had wiped his feet on the mat, then shouted, 'Mummy, it's the lady and gentleman who came to see us this morning.'

By the time that Elizabeth Hemdean had arrived at the sitting-room door, Simon was practically through it. The widow did indeed look wrathful, and it was evident that they might indeed have had trouble obtaining admittance had she come to the door in person, but the reflexes of polite hospitality made her stand back now that the unwelcome guests were actually inside. She was not alone; there was a man sitting on the sofa on which Simon and Carol had earlier perched – a tall, slim man with piercing blue eyes.

'Alex,' said the flustered Mrs Hemdean. 'These are the people I told you about . . .'

'The people you rather suddenly decided to sue,' said Simon, surprised at his own acidity. He quickly put two and two together and extended his hand to the stranger. 'Mr Clift, I assume,' he said. 'Of Montgomery & Clift, no doubt.'

While Mrs Hemdean ushered the two schoolgirls from the room, shepherding them towards the staircase, the tall man accepted the proffered hand and shook it disdainfully. 'My firm represents Mrs Hemdean,' he agreed. 'In the circumstances, Mr . . . er . . . I am rather surprised to see you here.'

'Sweetland,' said Simon, unabashed. '*Doctor* Sweetland. This is Dr Cloxeter, against whom you seem to intend issuing some kind of writ. And we're here because we don't quite understand what the circumstances are. Was it *your* idea to proceed with this action?'

'I have advised Mrs Hemdean of her rights, of course,' said Clift, smoothly, glancing towards the lady as she returned to the room and shut the door behind her. 'I shall not be handling the case personally, of course, because I may be required to appear as a witness.'

'A witness?' repeated Simon, with a distinct edge in his voice. 'And I suppose that you – unlike Mrs Hemdean – have a perfect recollection of what Nicholas said to his father in the hall.'

'I have,' agreed Clift, serenely. 'I heard the prophecy uttered, and I saw its fulfilment. I can testify to its accuracy in every particular, and can say without hesitation that if only Tom Hemdean had not been assured that his son had no precognitive ability, he would never have taken the risk of going on site that day – he would have been a beneficiary of what I believe you call the Oedipus effect.'

Simon was slightly flustered by this further revelation.

'You saw the accident, too?' he queried.

'Certainly. I was meeting Tom for lunch – partly social, partly business. I had just driven on to the site to pick him up when I saw the pile begin to fall. I could see Tom quite clearly, and I saw him fall when the fragment of tile struck him.'

'But Nicholas didn't say anything about a fragment of tile, did he?' said Simon. 'He *didn't* foresee what happened – not exactly.'

'I'm afraid,' said Clift, icily, 'that it would be most irregular for me to discuss with you and Dr Cloxeter the nature of the evidence which I may be required to give in court. And I must say that I see no point whatsoever in your continued presence here.'

The expression on Alex Clift's face was by no means a smile, but it had in it that same superciliousness that Simon had earlier seen in Lewis Fay's face. 'I'm a lawyer,' it said, 'and you're only some dumb scientific civil servant. I can run rings around you.' Simon guessed that he and Carol had jumped to the wrong conclusion about what had brought this on. This was simply one more clever bastard with an eye to the main chance – and that, he realized, might give him an opportunity to dispel that look from Alex Clift's face.

While his resolve was hardening into anger, Simon turned to look at Mrs Hemdean, who was still hovering

near the door. 'You know that Nicholas didn't say anything about a tile, Mrs Hemdean,' he said, levelly. 'Neither
Nicholas nor Debbie remembered him saying any such
thing when we talked to them this morning.'

Mrs Hemdean wouldn't meet his eye. 'I'm sure Alex
remembers far better than the children what was said,'
she told him. 'I was distracted, but he is perfectly reliable
in such matters.'

Simon turned back to Clift. 'Do you know a man named
Lewis Fay?' he asked, bluntly.

Clift was obviously surprised to be asked, and Simon
was glad to see it. 'Slightly,' said Clift. 'He's a member at
my golf club, but not a friend.'

'Do you know what he does for a living?' Simon asked.

'Not really,' said Clift, warily. 'I think he's with Family
Provident.'

'He's a claims assessor with Family Provident,' Simon
amplified. 'He came to see me this morning, about Mr
Hemdean's life insurance.'

Simon took considerable satisfaction from the sight of
Clift's guarded surprise changing to open astonishment.
He glanced sideways at Carol, but she simply looked
worried. She didn't believe the ploy would work, and she
was scared of storing up even more trouble.

'What about Tom's life insurance?' said Mrs Hemdean,
suddenly coming forward to stand beside Clift, facing
Simon and Carol. The hostility of the four stares seemed
almost tangible.

'You're not the only ones who had a bright idea about
using this case to establish a precedent,' said Simon,
with a humourless smile. 'Would you care to sit down,
while I tell you what he said to me?'

They all sat down. It seemed to take a little of the
tension out of the air, but not one of them sat comfortably.
Briefly, Simon told them the substance of his article, and

the opportunity which Lewis Fay had read between its lines. While he did so, he watched Alex Clift's expression become even frostier.

'You'll never get away with it,' he told Simon, when the substance of the argument had been made clear. 'You could never prove it.'

'Mr Fay seems to think that strict proof isn't necessary,' Simon countered. 'He seems to think that it might be enough simply to create a doubt in people's minds. You should be able to sympathize — after all, you can't possibly hope to prove that Carol was negligent in testing Nicholas; you could only succeed in sowing enough seeds of doubt to encourage the Department to settle out of court rather than risk a jury's decision.'

Clift stared at him for half a minute, then said, 'Are you trying to make a deal, Dr Sweetland? Are you offering to refrain from alleging that Nicholas may have subconsciously caused the death of his father in return for our dropping the suit against your colleague?'

Simon looked sideways at Carol again, but she was almost expressionless, waiting to see what would happen. He looked back at Clift, meeting the bright blue eyes squarely.

'No,' he said, 'I'm not. I don't think you'd accept the offer, and I think you might try to use the fact that I'd made it against us.'

Clift grinned, sure of himself now whether he had been sure before or not. 'You're right, Dr Sweetland,' he said. 'We would have fought you to the death — and we'd have won. Not only because your case is lousy at the logical level but because you wouldn't stand a chance with a jury if you tried to nail an eight-year-old boy for causing his father's death. Tom loved that boy, and the boy loved Tom. We would have made you look very sick, Dr Sweetland. Very sick.'

Then he smiled, in sharklike fashion.

Carol was staring unhappily at the floor.

'On the other hand,' said Simon, without a trace of emotion in his voice, 'I'd still like your assurance that you won't proceed with this fatuous suit against Dr Cloxeter.'

'I'm afraid that I can't give you any such assurance,' said Clift. He was obviously not a man to refrain from seizing and retaining any and all initiatives. 'It is still our intention to proceed. And now, I think, we have no more to say to one another.' He came to his feet as he spoke.

'You're wrong,' said Simon, flatly. 'If I leave here without your guarantee, I shall go straight to Lewis Fay.'

'But you just said . . .' Clift began.

Simon stood up so that he could look the man as nearly in the eye as the disparity in their heights would permit. 'I just agreed that I had no intention of going into a witness box in order to claim that Nicholas might have killed his father. All the evidence says that he not only didn't do it, but couldn't have. But it so happens, Mr Clift, that I really do believe what I wrote in my article. I believe that precognition is logically untenable, and that what we think are cases of successful precognition are actually cases of subconscious psychokinesis. I know that Nicholas didn't cause Thomas Hemdean's death, Mr Clift – but I don't know that you didn't.'

The colour drained from Alex Clift's features. Mrs Hemdean sprang to her feet, and Carol belatedly stood up too.

'You're mad!' said Clift, loudly.

'Am I?' Simon retorted, wishing that he was as calm as he was trying to sound. 'If I were in the witness box, Mr Clift – and I'm sorry if it's irregular to give you advance notice of my testimony – I would have to point out several things. Firstly, Nicholas only became agitated about the danger to his father when you and your daughter came to pick Debbie up in order to take her to school. He *thought* that he was remembering a dream he'd had, but perhaps he wasn't. He isn't, so far as we can tell, a precog – but we haven't tested him for telepathy. Secondly, you were present at the scene of the accident; you've just told me that you saw the pile fall, and that you saw Thomas Hemdean struck down. No PK I know could have affected the flight of that piece of tile from several miles away, but I know three or four right here in Coventry who could have done it from where you were sitting.'

'I didn't have any reason for wanting Tom Hemdean dead,' said Clift, uneasily.

'Maybe not *consciously*,' said Simon. 'But I don't have to prove anything, remember? I only have to sow the seeds of doubt. Of course, you'd have every opportunity to demonstrate your lack of motive. You'd undoubtedly be able to prove beyond a shadow of a doubt that all your business dealings with Thomas Hemdean were above board – after all, you're a friend of the family, aren't you? – and I'm just as certain as you are that genetic fingerprinting would prove that, in spite of superficial appearances, Nicholas really is Thomas Hemdean's son, and not yours.'

Clift's pallor had become almost ghastly. 'You say that in court and I'll crucify you!' he said.

'I won't have to say it in court, will I, Mr Clift?' said Simon, drily. 'I won't even have to confide it, off the record, to the man from the *Sun* – because in the morning, this will all have died down, won't it? No writs, no fuss, no story. *Now*, I think, we have nothing further to say to one another.'

Without another word, Simon turned and marched to the door. He held it open while Carol passed through, and looked back at Alex Clift and Elizabeth Hemdean, who were staring after him.

'Don't bother to show us out,' he said. 'We know the way.'

Not until he was at the front door did he glance back again. Neither Clift nor Mrs Hemdean had come out into the hall, but at the top of the staircase, just visible above the rail of the banister as it curved around the corner, were three faces in a line. The one in the middle was Nicholas Hemdean, who was watching him with mournful eyes. There was, of course, no way that the three children could have overheard what was said, but Simon shivered anyhow as he closed the door behind him.

He could not put away the memory of those mournful eyes while he drove Carol Cloxeter home through the driving rain. He dropped her outside the gate of her neat semi, and watched her as she hurried up the path. He saw the glass-fronted door open to welcome her even before she reached it. Then he went on to the empty flat which awaited him.

Simon was to remember that face, and those eyes, three days later when he stopped on his way home to pick up an evening paper, and read a minor headline which said: LOCAL SOLICITOR KILLED IN FREAK ACCIDENT.

According to the story, Alexander Clift had been on a shopping trip to the city centre. He had driven his BMW to the top floor of a multi-storey car park, stopping briefly near the lifts to let out his passengers: a friend and her two children, and his own daughter. Then he had driven on a little way, and had begun to manoeuvre the big car rear-first into a narrow parking space. Somehow — perhaps by hitting the accelerator instead of the brake — he had overshot. The reinforced concrete parapet which should have stopped the car had crumbled away, despite the low impact speed, and the car had somehow gone over the edge.

A spokesman for NCP, which owned and operated the car park, said that the failure of the parapet to stop the car was quite inexplicable. 'Our car parks are perfectly safe,' he was quoted as saying. 'This was a million-to-one shot. No one could have possibly anticipated it. We will make certain that it can never happen again.'

The names of the other passengers were not given. Nor, for that matter, was the name of the architect who had designed the car park. Presumably the reporter, who was probably a novice not long out of college, considered such details irrelevant – as, indeed, they probably were.

(The Sun, 12 April 1991)

20 THINGS YOU NEVER KNEW ABOUT THE TEMPS

1 They get a regular **weekly wage** from the DSS.

2 Every new recruit gets a free Savile Row suit at the taxpayers' expense; even the women!

3 They are trained in unarmed combat by the SAS.

4 The top civil servants at the DPR are in the same Masonic Lodge as **Prince Philip**.

5 The Tintern House training centre was recently refurbished at a cost of over £2m!

6 No one knows Loric's real name.

7 Even the catering staff at the DPR have to sign the Official Secrets Act!

8 Every **US airbase** in the country has a Paranormal Operations Liaison Officer on permanent standby.

9 Temps on active duty are authorized to carry **guns**.

10 Empaths have a higher percentage of emotional problems than any other Talent.

11 The DPR has Talent scouts in every universtity.

12 Only about 10 per cent of the paranorms in the country bother to register with the DPR.

13 If you don't declare a Talent when you apply for Unemployment or Supplementary benefit, you can lose your entitlement.

14 All the really powerful Talents work for private industry or the Civil Service.

15 A big name on the American superhero circuit can earn over **2 million** dollars a year from product endorsement alone.

16 The entire Civil Service is run by a **secret society** of paranorms who call themselves 'The Gods'.

17 The DPR is so underfunded it has had to close eight regional offices in the last two years.

18 Professional footballers have to volunteer for testing by the DPR before the FA will allow them to play in case they use hidden Talents on the pitch.

19 A hard-hitting documentary taking an *exclusive* look at the secretive world of the temps is on Sky TV this evening. **Don't miss it!**

20 You can always tell someone with paranormal powers by the hair on the palms of their hands.

THE COLLEGE SPIRIT

Storm Constantine

Julianne Farr did not want to be paranormal. She wanted to be a competent secretary and, perhaps later, somebody's wife. Her ambitions were small, on a cosmic scale.

Her powers had simmered quietly away inside her until she reached puberty, when they had rudely come to a boil. Only a strong instinct for self-preservation and a good deal of common sense prevented an early exposure of her condition. It had begun with a tingling in the fingers, nothing more, which she attributed to having gone to the library without her gloves – it had been an especially chill day. Later, she had become aware of an unpleasant metallic taste in her mouth, and her toes had gone numb, so her mother wisely bundled her off to bed and consequently turned out the bathroom cabinet in search of cold remedies.

Lying beneath the duvet, in a ginger murk of orange-flowered curtains drawn against the drab afternoon, Julianne listened, with mounting unease, to the inner rhythm of her juices. She now regretted having gone round to a friend's house the previous evening to watch a horror film. It had been a particularly lurid movie, which had portrayed, in gleeful detail, the possession of a teenaged girl by devils. Julianne was normally far too sensible a creature to believe anything like that could happen in real life, but couldn't help wondering, given the puissant pressure of the sensations she was experiencing, whether the sub-aural groaning in her fibres presaged the imminence of something supernaturally nasty. She had a fever; her mother dosed her with remedies. That night, tossing and turning in a bed too hot for comfort, she directed her rage at the enveloping quilt. When it then flew off the bed and landed, in a clatter of deodorant and cleansing cream bottles, on the dressing table, she assumed she'd physically thrown it. That was the first manifestation of her Talent, but she did not recognize it as such.

Steven Rider quite liked the idea of being paranormal. His Talent had emerged in the crib, as it were, although *from* the crib might be a more accurate description. Luckily, (or unluckily, depending on viewpoint), his mother attributed the first vision she received in the baby's room, that of the walls covered in huge, softly furred breasts, to something other than paranormal origins. She thought it was a side-effect of the two tranquillizer pills she had recently taken, coupled with a furtive slug from the vodka bottle she kept hidden among the cereal packets in the pantry. The illusion cured the woman's tendency for drug abuse, although, as further manifestations presented themselves, she had to revise their cause. Baby Steven had Dream Fingers. He could waggle his fat little fists and fill the room with illusions of whatever took his fancy. During the weaning period, some of these illusions were quite alarming. Nannies came and went from the Rider house with the frequency of trainees on government training programmes. Steven's father came and went, usurped by the miracle child in his wife's affections. Some people thought Steven was bewitched. Mother eventually took matters into her own hands, dismissed the hired help and, steeling herself to the unsavoury task, administered corporal punishment whenever Steven became ectoplasmic. By the time he was old enough to attend a nursery school, the boy had been imprinted with several mother-fixated behaviour patterns for good. He had also learned the survival lesson of concealing his Talent from others. For quite a long time, he thought he had a lot to thank his mother for.

Leslie Carter simply accepted without argument that she was paranormal, being a prime specimen of the Archetypal Victim persona. Her tendency to shrink from more assertive children developed gradually into the ability to fade – with romantic grace, if only anyone had noticed – into a mere wisp of a phantom. She discovered her Talent while witnessing a particularly aggressive classroom brawl. As other children shrieked and goaded the opponents into greater depredations upon each other, Leslie, overcome by nausea and a desire to flee the horrid sight of bloody noses, poured herself away through the floor. Nobody noticed. Finding herself in the school basement, she sat for a moment or two, quite disorientated. Always an imaginative child, and possessed of a parentally-repressed visionary personality, she calmly experimented, amid the gruntings of the school boiler, with her new-found Talent. Leslie knew from the moment of its manifestation that her Talent made her very different. She, like Steven and Julianne, also managed to hide it exceptionally well. Its secret was a strength that sustained her through many a childhood humiliation. In private, she was a ghost and had visited the deepest caves of the earth. In public, she was a nonentity and, as such people generally are, was often on the receiving end of cruel taunts. She had no friends, but saw things of immense wonder that compensated for that lack.

Julianne's power grew from modest beginnings. She could

not remember when she actually became aware of it as a distinctly unusual part of herself, but knew that the absolute confirmation of her Talent had been the time when Zoe Bradley flounced past her in the artroom at school, aglow with the smugness of having recently claimed Julianne's boyfriend for herself. Blind with humiliation and, she regretted to admit, jealousy, Julianne had quite unconsciously directed the beam of her thoughts at a precarious bronze sculpture — the pride of the art teacher, though lacking in aesthetic merit of any sort. Everyone had been astounded by the way it had flown through the air like a burnt-out, crash-landing satellite. Julianne had known, with no doubt whatsoever, that she had been responsible for its flight, although, luckily, nobody else had the wit to realize it. She had not been proud of that victory. It had been the voiceless and anguished cry of a female deeply hurt. She had not meant to hit an artery.

Julianne could move objects, seemingly any object, by the power of her will alone. For a while, she had nurtured this secret power, considering herself possessed of an innately female Talent. Her mother had a bookcase full of distinctly suspect New Age literature, which seemed to confirm Julianne's beliefs. She knew she must not divulge her secret to anyone. Like everyone else, she was aware that a subspecies of humanity lurked within society's midst — the paranormals, people possessed of unusual powers.

For a long time, Julianne deluded herself that she was not one of these people. She was not a freak. Later, as womanhood led to a developing insight into her life, she realized the truth. Then, the Talent she had loved, and which had given her secret pleasure, became a thing to deny, to purge from her being. No more making cups of tea from the other side of the room so that her viewing of the portable kitchen TV didn't have to be interrupted. No more putting her feet up while her mother was out, and directing the Hoover and duster to clean the house themselves. No more watering the hanging baskets without having to balance on the rickety stool. If she wanted to be normal, she must hang on to it fiercely. If she denied the power, then it could not exist. It was still useful when cutting her toenails in the privacy of her room, however.

Steven Rider and Leslie Carter were also faced with this dilemma, when they realized they were not (as they had believed themselves to be) unique, but part of something rather more common. Paranormals were not as abundant as the media liked to make out, of course, and neither Steven or Leslie ever came across someone else who had a Talent.

Steven's mother actually discussed it with her son at the time the news broke. 'It was the tranquillizers,' she said. 'When I was carrying you. It must have *affected* you, in some way. You are definitely not one of *those* people.' Steven knew she was wrong, but did not contradict her. All paranormals were expected, as a courtesy, to make themselves known to the Department of Paranormal Resources and donate their Talents to the good of society. Steven's mother would not allow him to do any such thing and, as he himself considered there had to be sinister implications in registering himself anywhere, he was happy to concur with her decree. He and his mother spent many a happy hour as he entertained her with the delights he could spin from his fingers. Sometimes, he was forced to use his Talent to protect himself from assailants; his fey delicacy had inflamed many a bully's attack circuit. One night, after school, he had systematically driven a fat bully insane, and had watched the dismantling of his enemy's mind with the cool detachment of a scientist. He had the ability to discern exactly what would scare a person witless, and could provide an illusion to fulfil their worst nightmares with ease.

Leslie, of course, had no aggressive slant to her Talent. Privacy was important to her, which was the only reason why she never presented herself to the DPR. Everyone knew that paranormals were expected to want to work for the government. Leslie knew her nerves would never be able to cope with that. Anything that smelled even faintly official sent her into a dumb trance of fear, and the thought she might be forced to use her Talent for something dangerous, like spying, was intolerable. The sight of blood had her in a dead faint even before the first drop hit the ground, and spies had to shoot people, didn't they? Leslie considered that paranormals could not provide any service other than those connected with espionage. She imagined that most Talents would be very similar to her own. Her other secret was a shameless adoration of an American paranormal named Kid Spectrum. Americans, naturally, were not discreet in any way concerning paranormality, and to most people's eyes, the States were infested with posturing superheroes who had little regard for decorum and absolutely no good taste in dress. Leslie, however, had been entranced by the scrubbed, youthful exuberance of Kid Spectrum when he'd been interviewed on TV during an exchange visit. In her dreams, she evanesced into his affections like a winsome film star. It was a worship quite at odds with the rest of her personality, although devoutly pure.

As Julianne's life progressed and school was left behind, she prided herself on her self-discipline. She enjoyed her course at the local secretarial college and, because using word processor keyboards required so little physical effort, she had no real use for her Talent there, anyway. It shamed her that the occasional lapse was almost always generated by negative feelings towards her fellow students. She was careful, but it was noted by her peers that those who fell foul of Julianne often suffered accidents and mishaps of one form or another. She endured terrible guilt about this and went out of her way to make it up to the injured parties. Her friends joked that she must have an exceedingly efficient guardian angel, or something. Or something. In every other respect, Julianne Farr was an unsurpassably typical girl and this, more than all her precautions, probably preserved her secret.

Steven's mother told him he was artistic and packed him off to art college as soon as he left school. Steven would rather have become a psychiatrist, or something similar, as he was very interested in conditions such as schizophrenia, but his mother wouldn't hear of it. He managed to amuse himself through college by spinning the odd illusion at the expense of various tutors he especially disliked, or other students whom he felt deserved shaking up a little. Once, after he was supposed to have produced an analytical drawing of a chrysanthemum and hadn't, he conjured the illusion of a beautiful piece of work, which he presented to his tutor, only to snatch it back, fake an artistic frenzy, weep, tear it up and cry, 'It's not good enough! Not good enough!' The tutor concerned, a woman who strained for empathy with her students, comforted him for an hour and then awarded him a high mark for his work. It was a shame he couldn't use that trick more than once. Romantically, he tortured women, for he was an exquisitely attractive creature. Even after he discovered, (with no surprise, given his upbringing), that his romantic interests lay in a decidedly alternative direction, he did not abandon his adoring females. He needed them for developing his Talent; it took practice to create the illusion of a phone ringing from considerable distance away. After leaving college, he coolly abandoned his mother, (who had since descended into such an alcoholic oblivion his departure registered only slightly in her consciousness), and moved to a new town. The unsurpassable brilliance of his portfolio – he only had to implement his Talent a small amount in this respect – secured him a position with the first design company he applied to. Thereafter, he dedicated himself to shattering any female hearts he found himself sitting near to, and seducing happily married men. His job was attended to, with deft panache, in his spare time.

Leslie Carter graduated from shunned child to wallflower till-girl, drooping behind one of many conveyor belts and electronic pricing scanners in a cavernous hypermarket. She was a pale little waif, not ugly by any standard, but deliberately plain. Her mouth turned down at the corners and was too thin. In the staff-room, she drank her tea from a special mug she'd brought from home, and became quite agitated if her refreshment-break rituals were ever disrupted by newcomers insensitive to her requirements. She was affably tolerated by other members of the staff and, to some degree, protected. Leslie was a person who brought out the mother instinct in others, although people with the best intentions usually tired of trying to help her live what they considered to be a normal life, after all their efforts to improve her appearance and social graces were ignored. Leslie never, under any circumstances, used her Talent in the presence of others. She was not an unhappy person, for she had her own flat, with plenty of small rooms so she could drift between the walls to her heart's content. She was fulfilled by simple pleasures, such as an orderly walk on Sundays and a supply of good books. If ever anyone at work was crass enough to mention boyfriends to her, she never even blushed or simpered, but said, with firmness, 'None of that for me. I like my life the way it is, with just me in it.' It was the simple truth. She never craved company. Every night, before she drifted off to sleep, she spent a pleasant half hour conducting an imaginary affair with Kid Spectrum. This consummated her romantic inclinations to capacity, even though they had still not ventured beyond the meaningful-glances stage of the relationship.

Julianne never really developed any relationships with men either, although she did sometimes wonder whether using her powers somehow drained her in that respect. Well, there'd be plenty of time for that later. She had decided that the age of twenty-six would be a good time to get married. If difficulties presented themselves when the time came, maybe she could used her ability to nudge events along in her favour. Saving someone's life, for example, might well sway their affections, and it would be no problem organizing a convenient accident. After that, she promised herself she would stop using the power for good, devote herself to a fulfilling relationship, and raise children. She would not even use it to help her with the housework. She would not use it at all. Well, not unless her husband was unfaithful, or something.

Steven Rider's powers were unmasked when he was only twenty-one. He killed a man, but only by accident. How was he to know the illusion of a slavering Doberman would drive the fool into the path of a speeding car? Stupid. Steven had no regrets about this – the man had been an unfaithful lover after all – but was furious with himself that the shock of seeing the accident caused him first to evaporate the dog in front of over a dozen on-lookers and then, quite visibly, to spray out a selection of quasi-illusions as a reflex action. He had been bundled into a police car even before the ambulance arrived.

Knowing he had been discovered evoked a dark god from Steven's soul. The police, through violent experience, were well aware when something was beyond their ability to cope with, and when confronted with what appeared to be a paranormal criminal, always contacted the DPR immediately. Their caution with Steven Rider was entirely justified; his police cell resembled the seventh circle of hell by the time the man from the DPR arrived to interview him. Dark illusions thronged the air, mouthing obscenities and vomiting lurid venom.

'I think you need some help,' said the man from the DPR, apparently not discomposed. Steven merely sneered in response, in a distinctly Mephistophelean way. 'You can't frighten me,' said the man, unperturbed. 'Maybe you should put away the horns and fangs now.'

'You can't kill me,' Steven said, restored to angelic beauty.

The man sighed. 'My dear boy, I have no desire to. You are far more useful to us alive. My name is Mr Sharpe. Now, if you would be so kind as to answer a few questions...'

'It was an accident!'

'I'm sure.' Mr Sharpe leaned forward confidentially. 'However, you must be aware the police will tend to take a dim view of what has occurred, never mind the unfortunate victim's relatives...'

Steven shrugged moodily. 'There's little I can do about that.'

Mr Sharpe nodded. 'Absolutely. That's where I come in.' He leaned down to rummage in the briefcase by his feet. 'The DPR can help you, Steven. If you consent to join our register and undergo training, I can arrange to have any charges dropped.' He smiled. 'They will be quite amenable to that. After all, should you decide to use your Talent to make things difficult for the legal authorities – which, given your personality profile, I'm convinced you will – they will be dealing with something that demands rather more resources than their time or budget allows. Regrettably, no matter how much you inconvenience them, the outcome will be the same – imprisonment. I'm sure you don't need me to point out the advantages of cooperating with the DPR. In your position, there really is no alternative.'

'I dislike organizations,' Steven said, but his posture had relaxed. 'I dislike bureaucracy.'

'And you also dislike captivity and humiliation just as much, I'm sure. Now, if you would just take a look at these DPR leaflets . . .'

Leslie Carter presented herself to a local DPR office when she was twenty-five. She quite surprised herself by doing so. One night, she'd been sitting in her flat, drinking a mug of cocoa, her cat on her knee, while watching the late news on TV. Bad news followed bad news. The world was in such a mess: killings here, deceptions there, depredations to the fair planet everywhere. She had turned off the TV and sat in deep thought for several hours. Like everyone else, she always felt so powerless in the face of global destruction and yet, perhaps she was mistaken to feel that way. For too long, she had hidden herself from the world, concealed her unique Talent. Perhaps she had been put here for a purpose. Perhaps she could actually *do* something. Leslie, what's come over you, girl? she said to herself, although her heart had begun to flutter with the enormity of her decision. She knew that she was going to offer herself to the world, she was going to stand up and be counted; tomorrow, she was going to make herself known to the DPR! It was as if the path of her life had suddenly divided before her and, from somewhere, she had found the strength to take the more difficult road. Deliriously, she spun through the rooms of her flat, a shining phantom of random particles. In her peak moments, Leslie was an awesome sight.

Perhaps a certain overconfidence was responsible for the eventual unveiling of Julianne's Talent. She had worked her way up the bureaucratic ladder, her path eased by discreet administration of her powers. She was acclaimed for her efficiency. Eventually, she secured a position as personal assistant to a high-flying executive, for a company that manufactured metal tubes. It was here the truth of her condition came to light. As if the victim of monstrous bad luck, Julianne was caught out on one or two occasions by her colleagues. Once, a clerk had walked into her office to find her gliding round the room, watering plants, while speaking into the telephone, which floated alongside her ear. When her door opened unexpectedly, Julianne had turned round quickly and, but for a startled moment of mutual staring, managed to hunch up her shoulder against the phone, and smile brightly. The clerk looked confused, but made no comment. Julianne wondered whether she should cover her tracks in some way, in some permanent way, but decided against it. The girl concerned was considered stupid by the majority of the staff, so her word would be doubted anyway.

Then came the time when, up to her ears in paperwork, she had again been caught on the phone, but this time with a document hovering in mid-air before her nose. It had prompted an alarmed exclamation from her colleague, at which Julianne yelped and shouted, 'Shut the door, will you! Look what you've done!' The paper floated innocently to the desk, but Julianne suspected her excuse would not be believed. It was unfortunate that there'd been considerable coverage in the news recently concerning the activities of the DPR, and also an embarrassed documentary on a TV late slot. Suddenly, everyone was exposing their friends and neighbours as being paranormal, although it was almost certain the majority of these identifications were erroneous. Still, it was causing a lot of trouble. Failure to register a Talent with the DPR tended to invoke suspicion among neighbours about the way the individual concerned might be using their Talent. There had been one or two outrageous crimes where paranormals, who were undoubtedly psychotic, had donned ridiculous costumes, in the manner of Americans, and used their powers in a reprehensible fashion. The public feared for their safety and immense pressure was placed on the DPR to control these freaks of humanity, before they held all decent, normal people to ransom.

Julianne's colleagues had begun to talk. Rumours were exchanged, conclusions reached. The company did happen to have a contract with the Ministry of Defence, albeit a minor one involving the production of plumbing pipes, but having a paranormal on the premises might constitute a security hazard in the eyes of the government.

One morning, Julianne had a visitor, who was nervously shown in to her office by her secretary. From the way her stomach instinctively churned, Julianne knew instantly just what the arrival of this suave, black-suited stranger presaged.

She stood up, held out her hand. 'How can I help you?' She was impeccably groomed, her perfume expensively tart, her manner cool and confident. Inside, she was boiling jelly, but she steeled her exterior to conceal this.

The man shook her hand briefly and she gestured for him to sit, raising her brows in inquiry.

'My name is Mr Sharpe,' said the man. He held out a laminated card. 'I'm with the Department of Paranormal Resources.'

'Of course you are,' Julianne responded coolly, idly twisting a gold pen in her fingers. 'And what can I do for you?'

Sharpe smiled in a pained manner. 'I think you know the answer to that, Ms Farr.' He bent down and opened his briefcase, withdrawing a folder, thinly new and unthumbed. 'Could I have a few minutes of your time? I would like to ask a few questions.'

'If you must,' Julianne replied.

'How long have you been aware of your Talent?' Sharpe asked, a ballpoint pen poised above a form.

Julianne threw back her head and uttered an unconvincing laugh. This gave her the briefest time to consider her answer. Should she try and deny it or should she be honest? As she lowered her head, she appraised the unflinching, metallic stare of Mr Sharpe. He was, of course, Talented himself.

'How long have you been a telepath, Mr Sharpe?'

He grinned fiercely. 'Please answer my question.'

'I feel there's little point.'

He shrugged. 'This is a formality, you understand.'

Julianne sighed. 'Very well, but before we begin I want to know how this is going to affect my . . . well, my life.'

'That is really up to you, Ms Farr.'

It was a poignant moment. Julianne felt as if a comfortable cocoon of fluffy cotton had suddenly fallen away from her body. Within it, as it drifted into oblivion, were the seeds of her hopes and dreams: husband, home, child. Years later, she would recognize this wistful feeling as being one of relief, but at the time she felt only a weary resignation. Zoe Bradley's face flashed across her inner eye, grinning horribly.

'I suppose I have been aware since my early teens of my . . . difference,' she said.

'And the description of your Talent?'

She shrugged. 'It must have a name, of course, but I just look upon it as being able to move things with my mind.'

Sharpe ticked a box on the form. 'Telekinesis,' he said. 'Anything else?'

Julianne frowned. 'No, just that.'

'Hmm. And you are in the habit of using your Talent regularly?'

Julianne paused, feeling cornered by the question.

Sharpe's expression softened. 'We are all in this together, Ms Farr. Please don't be afraid to answer my questions. No one is judging you. If anything, I am here to help. It is not easy to live a normal life possessed of an unusual ability. Now, if you would tell me . . .'

'Yes, of course I use it!' Julianne said. 'There's nothing shameful about it. I've only used it to help me with my work! Where's the harm in that?'

Sharpe laid down his pen and slowly raised his hands, palms towards her. 'Please, Ms Farr, there is no need for defensiveness. I only want the facts. For the record, you understand. As you must be aware, your company might well feel compromised should you decline to cooperate.'

Julianne nodded irritably. 'All right. It's just rather a . . . shock to be . . . discovered, so to speak.'

'An inevitability, Ms Farr. I can't help feeling it's a great pity you didn't contact the DPR a long time ago, but I appreciate your reluctance.'

'I just wanted to be normal,' Julianne said.

Sharpe smiled, but not harshly. 'Really! And yet you still used your Talent.'

Julianne blushed. 'I just want to live my own life.'

'Naturally, and I'm not condemning you for your actions. Your Talent should be used, but for the good of society. You are a gifted young woman, Ms Farr, and you must accept that you have responsibilities. Now, if you could tell me, in your own words, the exact history of your Talent.'

Numbly, Julianne related the facts, although she attempted to skirt the issue of the unwanted vengeful face of her power. Sharpe made no comment, but she knew, given his own ability, he must have seen the guilty thoughts emblazoned across her mind. She felt exhausted by the time she'd finished speaking and, although her throat was dry, she could not face summoning the secretary to provide coffee.

'You need a drink,' Sharpe said, placing his folder back in his briefcase. 'Might I ask your assistant in the next room to furnish us with refreshment?'

Julianne nodded weakly. Her whole body was shaking. What would happen to her now? For a few moments, she sat blinking at the windows, her mind utterly empty. Sharpe came back into the room and sat down.

'I am sorry to have distressed you,' he said.

'What happens next?' Julianne asked. 'Will I lose my job?'

'Your personnel record suggests you are an exemplary employee, Ms Farr. If your employers feel that such a radical step is necessary, then it will be to their detriment. The Talented are generally well thought of by corporate bodies. You never know, my visit may even presage promotion.'

Julianne laughed bleakly. 'Somehow, I can't believe that. If I was so well thought of, then surely my boss would have spoken to me first, before running to the DPR. That *is* what happened, isn't it?'

'You must understand that the un-Talented are often nervous of our kind, Ms Farr. Do not judge them too harshly. I'm sure my presence will quell their fears.'

'Is that it then? I just become a statistic on your files? You go away and leave me alone?'

Sharpe blinked, but did not avert his eyes from her demanding stare. 'Ostensibly, yes. Although there is the problem of security, as far as your employers go.'

Julianne could not help laughing. 'There is? I would be delighted to discover how!'

'I agree, it *does* sound ridiculous, but I'm sure your employers will feel totally reassured, should you opt to join our register. I must confess that part of my job is to encourage you to join the ranks of the DPR, Ms Farr. There will be benefits if you decide to do so.'

'And if I don't?'

'I'm sure that will not be the case,' Sharpe answered smoothly. 'You strike me as a responsible young woman. As you are no doubt aware, once you have made this decision, you will be required, at the very least, to attend a brief training course at one of our establishments.' He burrowed once again in his briefcase and produced a handful of brochures. 'Employers are required to allow paid leave for this, so it will be no hardship. The DPR feels this is necessary — having a Talent can mean you need help in how to control it because, sometimes, it can cause untold psychological problems. Our training establishments can ease all this.'

'It sounds like a sentence to me,' Julianne said, picking up one of the brochures. There were high-colour photographs of an imposing country house, and several pictures of smiling groups of people dressed in track suits, running through the grounds, using a gymnasium, eating in the restaurant. It reminded her of a health farm.

'Should you decide to sign on to our register, you will

have several options. If you wish to continue in your present occupation, you need only work for us as and when a suitable contract presents itself, on a temporary basis. Again, your employers are required to give you leave for this, but the financial arrangements are something you must discuss with them yourself. Naturally, the DPR will pay you a small honorarium during the time you are in their employment.'

'And what sort of work will I be expected to undertake?' Julianne asked.

Sharpe shrugged. 'Well, it could be anything, but certainly nothing beyond the scope of your abilities.'

'You are very vague on this point, Mr Sharpe.'

'It is something that can be decided only after you have completed a training course, I'm afraid. I'm not trying to deceive you, Ms Farr. Dispersal of contracts is not my department. I'm only recruitment.'

On a crisp autumn morning, Julianne drove to the DPR training establishment, Tintern House. She had chosen a facility some distance away from her home town and had had to start out very early in the morning in order to reach the place by nine o'clock. Her hands were slippery on the wheel as she pulled up outside the gates and presented her introductory documents, provided by Mr Sharpe, to the security officer on duty. She had been prepared for military formality, but the uniformed, middle-aged man smiled at her benignly, made a joke about the weather, which she forgot instantly because of its utter inanity, and then patted her car's roof and opened the gates. Giving him a tight smile and a wave, Julianne accelerated up the drive.

Tintern House was a beautiful Elizabethan manor, set in a rolling estate of wide lawns, gravelled paths and stately, elderly trees. Julianne could see people taking leisurely morning strolls, some in groups, the occasional loner, obviously walking off a recent breakfast. It all seemed very relaxed, and some of her inner tension eased. She parked her car in front of the main steps and briskly marched through the open front doors, carrying only a small case. Inside, she found a magnificently appointed hall where a young, female receptionist sat behind a highly polished table.

'Good morning, Julianne,' said the receptionist. 'I'm so glad your journey was pleasant.'

Another telepath, obviously, Julianne thought, extending a hand.

'Now, if you could just sign in, someone will show you to the morning room. There are three newcomers today, and you're the first to arrive. I'll have someone bring your coffee into you.'

'I'd prefer tea,' Julianne said, perversely.

The receptionist frowned prettily. 'Oh ... well, of course.' She brightened. 'Ah, Roger's coming!'

Julianne nearly dropped her case as a man floated into the hall and hovered in front of her.

'Roger!' the receptionist admonished. He landed nimbly and shook Julianne's hand.

'Roger Mint,' he said, winking at her roguishly. 'I like to sweep a woman off her feet!'

'Julianne Farr,' she replied drily. 'I move heavy objects.'

Steven Rider was the last to arrive. Shown into a pleasant drawing room where the morning sunlight fell flatteringly on to the smart, young brunette sitting by the window, he rid himself of the invertebrate presence of Roger Mint with a timely illusion of having fangs. One smile was enough to send the corpulent Mint bobbing from the room. Steven advanced to assess his peers. The prim spinster was dismissed almost instantly from his attention; thin as a stick with a personality, no doubt, resembling weak tea. The other appeared more interesting. She thought herself to be a cool customer and her trappings oozed the perfume of money. He wondered what her Talent could be and found himself thinking of black widow spiders.

Julianne had afforded Steven one glance, so covert he didn't even notice it. 'He looks like a serial killer,' she thought and resumed her inspection of the magazine on her knee. She and Leslie had exchanged tight smiles and brief hellos. Julianne, scorning the whole concept of *training*, imagined all other paranormals to be freakish in personality. So far, given the evidence before her, she assumed this belief to be correct.

Shortly after Steven's arrival, a grim, towering, middle-aged woman presented herself as their Counsellor. Her name was Emily Band. She explained, without embarrassment, what her own Talent consisted of, and then demonstrated it. Emily had the ability to appear any age: crone or child or anywhere in between. At first, all three newcomers were puzzled as to why she chose late middle-age as her habitual form. Only when they saw an example of Emily in the full flower of youth did they understand. Not a beauty at any age, she was certainly a creature whose looks improved with maturity. Once the demonstration was over, Emily settled herself into a chair and said, 'Now, perhaps you can introduce yourselves to each other, and give examples of your own Talents.'

All three exchanged shy glances, although Steven's glance was perhaps less shy than those of the women. Both Leslie and Julianne confessed to feeling inhibited about giving a public display. 'It is always something I've done in private,' Leslie said, her face crimson.

'You're not being asked to take your clothes off,' Steven said in an airy voice, 'or, forgive me, is that part of your show?'

'Steven,' Emily Band said patiently, 'I think we'll all get along much better with a little team spirit, don't you?' She grinned, showing a lot of teeth, at the cringing Leslie. 'Don't worry, my dear, there's a first time for everyone. You'll soon get over your shyness.'

'Want me to go first?' Steven asked.

Julianne sighed noisily. 'Seeing as you're the one with the least problems about this, I don't think so. I'll go first.' Without further preamble, her magazine flew off her lap, flapped across the room like an origami bat, and hit Steven in the face. Julianne smiled sweetly and shrugged. 'Sorry. Nerves.'

Steven treated her to a wicked smile and transformed himself, in the eyes of all present, to something horribly wet and undead. Julianne blanched and gagged; he'd even managed to mimic the smell. Leslie uttered a dismal cry of terror and sank into the floor. Emily smartly clapped her hands together.

'Team! Team!' she said sternly. Steven evaporated the illusion and shrugged, looking sheepish. 'Come back, Leslie,' Emily said, 'it's all over.' She glowered at Steven. 'Can we please be professional about this? Time is the DPR's money; we have little to waste.'

At dinner that evening, the newcomers met all the other trainees in residence, and the rest of the staff. For the remainder of the morning, there had been a kind of group counselling session, where Emily Band had encouraged them to talk about themselves. Julianne and Steven had enjoyed cat-fighting their way through that, although, to Emily's chagrin, Leslie had refused to join in, sitting with arms folded and disapproving, lipless mouth. During the afternoon, they had been shown videos which educated them about the enormous scope of paranormal Talents. Some of the examples they saw paled their own Talents into comparative insignificance, while other abilities seemed unremarkable in the extreme, even laughable, in some instances. How, for example, could the ability of being able to detach all of your teeth from your mouth ever be put to practical use? Steven immediately dubbed the wielder of this Talent the Tooth Fairy and consequently suggested one way, at least, in which he would use the ability should he be fortunate enough to possess it. Julianne glanced at him sharply and he grinned back quite openly.

There were roughly two dozen individuals currently undergoing Department training at Tintern House, with a staff of nine to supervise them. The proprietor of the establishment, a Mr Derek Valiant, made a late entrance to dinner, which Julianne suspected was in order to impress the newcomers. She whispered to Steven, 'And what is his Talent, do you think?' No mention of this had been made, although it seemed likely that the person in charge should have one.

Steven shrugged. 'Imitating human life, perhaps?' It was obvious he hadn't liked what he'd seen in Mr Valiant.

'It must be pretty . . . well . . . *big*, though, mustn't it?'

Derek Valiant was tall and well-built with an almost American glamour.

'I would have changed my name, if I were him,' Steven said.

As Julianne ate, she inspected the people sitting round the table. They seemed utterly normal, the sort of people who worked in supermarkets, petrol stations or insurance offices. One or two of them self-consciously used their Talents during the meal, with self-effacing grins, flicking glances at the statuesque Derek Valiant to see whether he'd noticed and approved. Consequently, condiments sets whizzed up and down the table, wine poured itself, entertainments were provided. The Tooth Fairy carefully removed all her teeth after the meat course and cleaned them individually with a napkin before replacing them.

'Yuch!' Julianne said. She herself felt no desire to exhibit her own ability, and certainly not to court the favour of Mr Valiant.

Another person, whom Steven dubbed Present Arms!, grew an extra limb from his armpit, fringed by tentacles, and proceeded to tickle a coy, flouncy sort of woman further up the table, who cried black tears of joy in response.

The newcomers were all given individual rooms, although, after dinner, the three of them congregated in Julianne's room. None of them felt like joining the community downstairs to watch TV for the evening. All three confessed to feeling uneasy in the presence of the other paranormals. Perhaps this would pass.

Julianne reflected what an odd group they were. In everyday life, their paths would never have crossed. Even if they had met, they would never have been compelled to forge friendships.

'This is a bit like being in hospital, isn't it?' Steven said. He produced a large bottle of wine from his luggage and, in the manner of hotel guests consuming illicit liquor, they drank it from tooth glasses.

Leslie, who had never been in hospital, shrugged.

'A psychiatric hospital,' Julianne agreed. 'Surrounded by loonies. God, I just thought of something! Is it going to affect our own minds being cooped up with these creeps? It happens that way in mental homes, doesn't it?'

Steven grinned. 'We shall just have to make sure, my dear, that it doesn't.'

Next morning, after breakfast, Emily Band escorted her charges to an orientation lecture, to be delivered by none other than Derek Valiant himself. The newcomers had been required to dress in the House uniform of track suit and training shoes, and Julianne felt quite ridiculous sitting there in the spacious auditorium, appearing as if she was about to go to an aerobics class. It was all unpleasantly institutional.

Valiant wore his track-suit top open to mid-chest to reveal a bush of manly hair, which Julianne thought lacked only a large medallion to complete his image. She cringed as this larger-than-life individual bounced around the podium, trying to instil them with a sense of team spirit. She had never been a person to visit holiday camps. Valiant clasped his hands and stared above their heads with moist eyes as he extolled the virtues of their country, ending his sentimental speech with the entreaty that they grasp their Talents in their hands and offer them up to the welfare of their fellow men and women.

Julianne caught Steven's eye; he was smiling tightly, and the smile was edged with distaste. 'Do you suppose they have a bar in this place?' she whispered.

Valiant noticed her speaking. 'You have a question, Ms Farr?' he asked.

She shook her head, withering beneath the lambent stare.

'You are all possessed of a mighty destiny,' Valiant said. 'And it is vital you live up to it.'

Emily Band nodded vigorously at the end of the row.

'God, I hope so,' Steven whispered back to Julianne, in response to her question.

*

After the lecture, it was time for fitness classes. Julianne's heart sank; she had expected as much. 'I hate exercise,' she told Steven.

On the way to the gym, they were intercepted by an individual who, Emily explained, was practising his charisma. It was considered good manners to assist one's colleagues at all times, so the four of them had to stand there while the man, dressed in a black cloak, postured before them.

'Hello,' Steven said, introducing himself. 'Who are you?'

'I . . .' said the man, flashing his eyes and raising his hands, 'am *Darkness!*' Whereupon, he enveloped the surprised spectators in a net of utter blackness. Julianne winced. She could smell fly killer.

'And I,' came a voice beside her – Steven's, 'am Hallucinato, the Master of Pernicious Deceptions!' Steven manifested light from his fingertips, and Darkness retreated with a harrowing hiss.

'Kevin has yet to tone down the more flamboyant tendencies associated with his Talent,' Emily Band explained, dryly. 'Come along, straighten yourself up, Steven. Fun's over.'

The physical fitness instructor was disappointed by the newcomers. A few aerobic exercises caused virtual collapse. 'You haven't looked after yourselves, have you?' the instructor said, in a hurt voice.

'He's taking it so *personally*,' Steven whispered to Julianne. 'Does he have a Talent, do you think? What Talent would a physical fitness teacher require? Hmm. I know! An ability to deceive the world; he does, in fact, have a brain rather more advanced than that of a walnut. It works too, doesn't it? I mean, there's real intelligence in those eyes!'

Julianne smothered a laugh.

'Being fit can save your life in times of crisis,' the instructor said, directing an owlish glance at Steven. 'Are you feeling all right now, Leslie? Perhaps we can get on with ten minutes of jogging on the spot. We can't stand around. I have another class in an hour.'

Julianne groaned and Leslie looked as if she was about to descend into hysterical sobbing. An hour? They would be dead before then!

'Relax, girls,' Steven said, slinging a casual, reptilian arm around each female shoulder. 'Just relax. Sit back and enjoy the show.'

Both Emily Band and the instructor paid attention to the illusion Steven had constructed in front of them: that of three newcomers diligently being put through their paces. In reality, they had sat down at the back of the gym to do as Steven suggested: relax and watch the show.

'Hey, I'm really glad you came here at the same time as me,' Julianne said to him.

He winked. 'Early days yet, my love.'

Steven was summoned to the office of Derek Valiant later that day. It had to be because of something important, as he was plucked from one of Emily Band's proficiency sessions, where she encouraged the fledgling paranormals to stretch their powers.

Valiant had a thick, pale cream jumper slung around his neck, the arms tied insouciantly over his chest. He paced the room, while Steven sat demurely in front of his desk. Steven examined the walls, which were covered in framed photographs of Valiant smiling at the camera with wilting paranormals in track suits clutched under his arms.

'You've had ... problems, haven't you?' Valiant said.

'No more than anyone else,' Steven lied.

'I've read the report.'

'Oh.'

Valiant nodded. 'Yes. I am aware of how your Talent came to light.'

'Well, I had expected that.'

'And, as such, realize you might need *special treatment*, gentle handling. I do sympathize with your condition, Steven.'

'Do you?'

'Of course. That is why I'm in charge of this establishment. I'm here to help. But I do expect cooperation. It will cause *difficulties* if you play up, Steven. High spirits are all very well, and there'll be plenty of time for those, but you must put a curb on them during your classes.'

'I'm afraid I don't know what you mean.'

Derek Valiant sighed, sauntered behind his desk and flicked a switch. Monitor screens were unveiled as sections of the wall glided aside. On one screen, Steven could see a class in the gym, all on their backs, riding imaginary bicycles; on another, he could see Julianne and Leslie with Emily Band, Leslie just in the middle of dematerializing. He raised his eyebrows and gave Derek Valiant a look of inquiry.

'So?'

Derek Valiant blinked slowly. 'My Talent, Mr Rider, is that no other paranormal's ability has an effect on me. Now, do you see why I am the ideal candidate for the position I hold?'

Steven nodded, his expression thoughtful. He felt embarrassed, and Steven Rider hated feeling embarrassed. 'It seems you've caught me out.'

'Completely. You have a powerful Talent, Steven. Wise up, grow up and don't abuse it. OK?'

Steven raised his hands. 'Your worries may rest, Mr Valiant.'

'I'm glad. Now, run along to your class. Oh, and one more thing. Now you've settled in, I think you and the girls should socialize with the rest of us tonight, don't you?'

'See you later then.'

Steven was so furious that, on the way back to Emily Band's class, he could not contain the illusion he'd turned into a roaring, blood-soaked werewolf. It projected exactly how he was feeling. Other trainees and unfortunate members of the domestic staff who came across him cringed from his path. How dare that pompous, coiffured imbecile humiliate him! He would have to pay!

Both Julianne and Leslie could tell Steven was seriously upset when he returned to the class, but there was no opportunity to speak to him about it in private until the end of the day. Steven went to Julianne's room as she was getting changed for dinner and began to tell her what had happened.

'Shut up!' she said.

He looked surprised. 'What? Well, thanks a lot for the support!'

'Be sensible, Rider, this place is crawling with telepaths!'

'I see your point ...' For a moment, he looked utterly defeated. 'This is a prison, isn't it? I don't care who hears, it's true. We're prisoners.'

'It's only for eight weeks, Steven!'

'Yeah, and what will we be at the end of that time? Have you thought of that? What will walk out of here? Zombies? Robots?'

'I think you're overdramatizing the situation. You just hate authority. We'll simply have to play it their way, I'm afraid.'

'You've thought about this, haven't you?'

'Yes,' Julianne replied, busying herself with the application of lipstick in her mirror and trying to ignore the reflection of the dejected figure sitting on the bed behind her. 'Emily gave Leslie and me a dressing down over the gym episode. I realized then we were wasting our time trying to be anarchic. There are too many paranorms here. Even our thoughts aren't our own.'

Julianne hated having to speak to Steven like this, but in the light of what Emily had told her that afternoon, realized the DPR were paying special attention to him. She would not be doing him a favour by encouraging him to misbehave. She had also realized her first impression of him had been almost correct. He had devilish charm, of course, but she knew now his fooling around concealed something rather more dangerous. Emily hadn't wanted to tell her and Leslie about it, the information was highly confidential, but it was the bond of womanhood that had forced her to speak. Steven Rider destroyed women. He hated them. He was not to be trusted.

'You look really nice,' he said.

She steeled herself and held out a hand. 'Well, escort me to dinner then.'

Steven was surprised to find he was quite hurt by the way Julianne distanced herself from him that evening, dragging the malleable Leslie with her. He had thought they were on the same wavelength. True, Leslie had directed a couple of mournful glances at him, but had bonelessly allowed Julianne to lead her into a boisterous group of paranorms in the TV room. Steven followed them, somewhat wistfully, although it was clear his company was not required. So Ms Farr wanted to be a good girl, did she? He couldn't summon the energy to be angry about it. It was all too pointless. His vague depression was made more tangible when a furtive Kevin Darkness had sidled up to him and brayed in a soft voice how impressed he had been with the earlier defeat he had suffered at Steven's hands. 'Go away,' Steven answered in a toneless voice. 'You are physically repellent and conversationally coma-inducing.' Darkness had drifted away as a mortified black cloud. It momentarily extinguished the light in every soul in the room. Steven noticed this, for he was an observant person and had long been able to see into the core of people's hearts. For the rest of the evening, he essayed one or two covert experiments. It lifted his spirits considerably.

Julianne herself felt a little guilty about shunning Steven, but Emily had been quite emphatic about him. 'Between you and me, girls, he doesn't really belong here. He's trouble. Mr Valiant tried to argue against his placement at Tintern House, but was overruled. He knew there'd be difficulties.' Still mulling these words over in her mind as she readied herself for sleep, Julianne thought to herself, Well, here I am. This is it. Make the most of it. Head down. No trouble. Get home. She climbed into bed and turned off the light. Goodnight, Steven.

She was woken into darkness by two cold hands on her wrists. Instinctively, she directed her Talent at her assailant, but it was like fighting a mist. 'Leslie!' she said. 'Leslie! What are you doing?' The room filled with a dull blue glow and there was Leslie hovering above her, phantom face inches from her own. She was a nightmare succubus, all floating, sparkling hair and funeral nightgown. Her incorporeal fingers bit like the kiss of frost into Julianne's crawling skin. She shook her ghost's head and the hair floated on the air like ferny weed beneath water. She did not, or could not, speak. Just shook her head. And lifted. Julianne let out a feeble cry, as she was drawn, bodily from the bed. Her flesh tingled as if a thousand minute sparks dusted her skin. Then her whole body went numb. Her lips were frozen shut; she could make no sound at all. Leslie's phantom robe swirled around her like a ragged cloud. She was enveloped by the presence of Leslie; at one with presence of Leslie. And then air was midnight cold against her flesh. She shivered inside her thin nightclothes. Where am I? Far below, the dark roof of Tintern House surveyed the thin beams of light thrown out on to the gravel drive from long windows. Julianne could see her own car, spot-lighted. Leslie?

'The only way,' Leslie replied. 'The only way. They cannot hear us up here.'

'Why?' Julianne asked, breaking into a hysterical giggle. She was floating effortlessly in Leslie's Talented embrace. It was exhilarating, and deliciously scary too. Leslie manifested a chill, spectral wind. It signified displeasure. 'They lied,' she said. 'They lied to us.'

'What do you mean?'

'About Steven. It was lies. I know.'

'Don't be silly. Why would they do that?'

Leslie hissed meaningfully. 'Because they are afraid of him.'

'Then maybe we should be too.'

'No,' Leslie sighed. 'No.'

'Look, I really think we should go back. I don't care about Steven Rider . . . Leslie, *I want to go back.*'

'You are back!' Leslie replied. 'You never left.'

Julianne wiggled her toes experimentally. They felt real enough. 'You are more Talented than they think, aren't you?' she said.

'Steven showed me how,' Leslie replied.

On her way to breakfast, Julianne marched into Steven's

room without knocking. She pulled back the covers from his bed and hit him across the head with her open hand. He screamed and covered his head with his arms.

'You bastard!' Julianne said. 'What have you done!' She hit him again. 'Come on, tell me!'

Steven cowered away from her female rage. He knew how devastating that could be and also the pointlessness of illusion-spinning when faced with such a creature. Normally, the only action he took with furious women was swift retreat. He scrabbled into a sitting position.

'Come on, Steven, out with it. What did you do to Leslie?'

'Nothing!' Julianne raised her hand menacingly. 'Honestly! I just — well — fulfilled a little dream she has, that's all. I didn't touch her.'

'She told you what Emily Band said, of course.'

He shrugged. 'Yes.'

'I'd really like to hear you deny that accusation, Steven. I really would.'

'It's exaggerated. These people are paranoid.'

Julianne narrowed her eyes. 'I'm beginning to learn something here. There is more to you than illusions. Much more.'

Steven scratched the back of his neck. 'Well, there's something I've only recently discovered, as it happens. Perhaps all that group therapy brought it out, I don't know.' He smiled tentatively. 'I was going to tell you about it today.'

'In unforgettable fashion, I suppose.'

'Don't be a bitch. I've been thinking. About this set-up. It's not the right way to train paranormals.'

'No?'

'No. Want to know what is? Want to know the future, Ms Farr?'

Julianne sighed and sat down on the bed, intrigued in spite of herself. 'Astound me,' she said. 'Please.'

'Some people say that reality is an illusion,' he began. Julianne shrugged and folded her arms. 'Illusion is my Talent, therefore, I alter reality. Perhaps even *create* reality.'

'I don't think so,' Julianne replied. 'For example, if you made people think you had a gun in your hand, and shot them, no bullet would actually enter their skin. It could not kill them.'

Steven shook his head. 'Don't be naïve. If they believed they had been shot, they might well manifest an injury. It's the power of the mind.'

'You've tried it then.'

'Not exactly. But I discovered something by accident.' He leaned towards Julianne earnestly. 'Tell me, how much do you want to go back to your metal tube executive, how much *really*?'

Julianne didn't like the sound of that question. 'Very much so. I love my job; I have a great amount of responsibility.'

'Where everyone now knows you're paranormal . . .'

'What are you trying to say, Steven?'

He leaned back among his pillows, arms behind his head. 'What I'm saying is, all those organizational skills you have, your excellent business head — wouldn't they be just as useful in another bureaucratic set-up?'

'That goes without saying, I suppose . . .'

'Like *here*?'

Leslie Carter had become a glittering mist which filled her whole room. She could not regain corporeality, and did not even want to. Her joy dictated she must expand to her limits. Flesh would only make her ache. She had kissed Kid Spectrum. He had held her in his arms, and it had transcended all her desperate imaginings. Oh, she knew it had really been Steven, but for a few moments, she had lived her dream. And he had given her such strength, such strength. Coalescing into a kind of solidity, she regarded herself in the mirror for a few moments. Now, even in flesh, she appeared transparent. Her eyes were virgin's eyes, but the containment had become power. She had become prophet, angel, saint, all from a short embrace. She had come alive. Steven, Steven, you waited at the end of my difficult path. You were there with open arms. Oh, yes, and she had taken the outstretched hand willingly. Soon, everything would be different.

'Your lessons are really quite instructive, Mr Valiant,' Steven said.

'I don't remember you having an appointment.' Derek Valiant was perturbed to find this nuisance in his office at such an early hour. After the previous interview with Steven Rider, he had immediately contacted the DPR and repeated his misgivings about having such a potentially destructive presence under his roof. His complaints were being sent to committee. As if that did any good! The whole place could be in chaos before anything was done, and Derek Valiant was quite sure that something would have to be done. Weevil, he thought, looking at the smug smile opposite.

'Actually, I don't have an appointment,' Steven said, affably. 'I assumed yours was an open door.'

'What do you want? Please be brief. I'm very busy today.'

'Well, I have a small problem.'

Valiant grunted. 'You should go to Emily Band with problems. That's what she's here for. I'm very busy.'

'Well, I would have, but as the problem I have is you, I thought I'd better be more discreet.'

'What?'

'Well, I wouldn't want to embarrass you.'

'I think you'd better explain, Mr Rider.'

Steven leaned back in his chair. 'My Talent is more ... *interesting* than I thought. But then, I suppose, given you know everything, you're already aware of that.'

'Don't try to play with me. Say what you have to say.'

Steven stood up and sauntered, hands in pockets, round the desk. He relished the moment as Derek Valiant flinched. 'Well, your Talent enables you to run this establishment without mishap, without fear of deceit or cunning. Am I right? Now, tell me, if you discovered a paranorm who could somehow, through manipulating your mind, *emphasize* that Talent, what would happen?'

Valiant laughed, scudding backwards a few inches on his wheeled executive chair. 'You tell me.'

'Well, to be honest, I'm not quite sure. I do know that for a person who can turn themselves into a phantom, it means they magically find the confidence to extend that ability, to be able to turn other people into phantoms too, or at least draw the essence out of their bodies. How it would affect a person with an already impressive Talent for telekinesis I've yet to find out, but ... well, it's just a hunch, but surely for a person whose Talent is the ability to be unaffected by other people's Talents, expanding that ability would mean they'd also be unaffected by their own Talent, too, wouldn't it?'

Derek Valiant made one or two flustered noises. 'Your idea is preposterous!'

'It sounds so, I agree, but it *is* possible. Be so kind as to activate the monitoring device you have in Leslie Carter's room.'

'We don't monitor the trainees in their rooms!' Valiant said.

Steven shook his head. 'Please, it will save us having to walk up there.'

Valiant activated the screen. Leslie's room had been transformed into a whirling maelstrom of coruscating light. 'She is happy,' Steven said, 'very happy, but I must point out that, until last night, her Talent was nowhere near as powerful as that.'

'This is one of your illusions, then.'

'No, all I did was give her a belief in herself. That is the beauty of my Talent, Mr Valiant I can change reality for people, and thus give them the confidence to reach out further than they ever have before. It is all a question of belief.'

Derek Valiant tapped his lips with his fingers. He looked thoughtful. 'I have to admit I'm impressed — *if* what you say is true.'

'It is. But this raises another issue. Your methods of training paranormals involve imposing disciplines, defining boundaries. I envisage a new training programme, where trainees are encouraged to strive beyond the limits they have imposed on themselves.'

Valiant laughed. 'Far too dangerous. Ambitious, yes, but ...'

'No, not dangerous at all. It depends on how you define danger, of course. Anyway, I intend to implement this programme myself.'

'Out of the question.'

Steven sighed. 'May I remind you of how my Talent could affect you, Mr Valiant?' He laughed. 'Your way is history, I assure you. The DPR are going to be very interested in my ideas. Now, would you be so kind as to make a telephone call for me?'

'We are living in strange and wonderful times,' said Mr Sharpe, snapping his briefcase shut. 'As yet, it is a time of discovery, one of daring and gambling, too.'

'The sky's the limit then,' Steven said, putting his feet

up on the desk that used to carry the nameplate of Derek Valiant.

'Oh, far beyond that, Mr Rider. Far beyond that.'

'You are greedy people,' Julianne Farr said. She sat on the window-sill, composed in killer business suit, each nail perfectly filed to a point. 'You are sucking from us, aren't you?'

Mr Sharpe directed a hurt glance at her, faultlessly performed. 'We need the best,' he said. 'That's all. As I said, we are constantly learning.' He smiled at Steven. 'You have been given a chance, Mr Rider, don't abuse it. We want the best from the Talented, the utmost, and you can help us achieve that. Don't let us down.' He stood up. 'Well, that's all for now. I'll leave you to it. The administration of Tintern House has been officially passed to you and Ms Farr.' He smiled benignly at Julianne. 'Your responsibility, I feel, is to keep this young man's enthusiasm under control, and to groom his ideas into workable programmes. I also leave the staffing of this establishment in your hands, Ms Farr.'

As Julianne escorted him to the door, they passed a pretty waif of a girl who nodded to them as she drifted into Steven's office. For a moment or two, her identity quite escaped Mr Sharpe, despite having recently been shown a video of her Talent by Steven and Julianne. Then he realized: ah yes, the prototype. Steven had also described how he intended to implement her Talent into his training courses; out-of-body-experience classes would be fitted into the curriculum alongside fitness training.

Leslie closed the door behind her. Her heart was aflutter with the enormity of her decision. 'Kid Spectrum,' she said. 'Show me your most serious colours. Show me.'

Somewhere outside, a phone began to ring.

(*Daily Telegraph*, 10 November 1992)

GENERAL SIR ROYSTON MORTIMER

Sir Royston, who died at the age of 101, was known to friends and the public alike simply as Roy Mortimer. He began his remarkable career as a professional soldier, having enlisted as a private in the King's Own Scottish Borderers in 1909 at the age of eighteen. He served with distinction in India and the Far East, being mentioned in dispatches three times for conspicuous gallantry, and received his commission in 1914, just prior to the outbreak of the First World War.

During the bloodbath of the Somme he was one of the few commanders to see the military potential of paranormal Talents, forming a special section of telekinetics to divert gas attacks from the allied positions. Wounded by sniper fire, he spent his convalescence in England composing an early draft of his now classic monograph 'On the Battlefield Deployment of Unorthodox Inherent Abilities', still a required text at Sandhurst.

Between the wars he served as a staff officer, rising to the rank of brigadier. It was during this period that he persuaded the War Office to make the testing of all new recruits for paranormal Talents part of the induction process, so that by 1939 the 'odd squads' were an integral part of the military machine. The farsighted wisdom of this policy was vividly demonstrated after the American entry into the war, when, in complete contrast to the disciplined British and German approach, paranormal volunteers in garish 'patriotic' costumes operated independently alongside the US forces, often creating more trouble for the Allies than for the Axis armies opposing them.

Promoted to general on the outbreak of hostilities, Mortimer was quickly appointed C.-in-C. UIA Operations, in which role he frequently liaised with the SOE and his opposite numbers in the Navy and Air Force. His imaginative deployment of the handful of paranorms at his disposal may well have affected the outcome of the war, and his knighthood in 1946 was generally held to be in recognition of this fact.

Retiring in 1951 at the age of sixty, Sir Royston promptly threw himself into the challenge of co-ordinating the events involving paranormal Talents for the Festival of Britain.

This led directly to his subsequent career as a writer and broadcaster. An early and popular panelist on *What's My Line*, he rapidly became a household name, remembered with affection long after his retirement in 1977. His final commentary for the BBC, on the occasion of the Silver Jubilee, was, as always, witty and eloquent, and the perfect end to his career.

The remainder of his life was spent in compiling his memoirs, which stand as a lasting testament to the charm of a man who will be greatly missed. Perhaps fittingly, the final volume, *100 not out!*, saw print earlier this week.

He leaves a widow, Winifred, and numerous decedants.

THE ROSE GARDEN

David V. Barrett

———————

He dreamt.

> Blue-black, the sky,
> deep dark blue-black,
> clear without stars or clouds.
> Midnight blue.
> Cold night, late night, but light.
> Light enough to see the woman standing,
> dressed in blue,
> lit in blue,
> long blue dress dark with lighter flowers,
> shading to dark on slightly lighter blue.
> The dress, cut low
> lifting the upper slopes of her breasts to the air,
> blue-lit like her ankles, down to her blue bare feet.
> Her face is chilled.
> And haloed around her head, a tangle of barbed
> wire.

He woke, feeling excited, disturbed, a little frightened; most of all he knew the woman needed help of some kind. The wire: was it rusty or shining? In the blue light it had seemed both.

And he was embarrassed with an erection, for the first time since Natalie had died. He felt guilty.

He had not made love in those five years, but had scarcely missed it. Natalie had been demanding, fiery in

299

bed – and out of it – far more than he. He had wondered, more than once, whether they would have stayed together if she hadn't been killed; they seemed to so many who knew them – even knowing nothing of their sex life – to be totally unsuited.

But he had loved her, devotedly; and she, he was sure, had loved him.

He breathed a prayer for the repose of her soul as he made for the bathroom, then dressed for Early Communion.

The rite, as it always did, calmed him. There were never more than two or three people there, but he almost preferred it when, as now, there was only himself in the Lady Chapel.

'Where two or three are gathered together, I am with them.' When he preached on the text he always made the point that it only needs one.

And I am with them. Who is I? Is it the Christ or his Father, or the mysterious Spirit which theologians have argued about for nearly two thousand years? Or is there an I at all? More than twenty years in the Church, and he was further from that answer than ever. When he, rarely, felt a personal presence, it was diffuse, unnamed; certainly no resurrected Christ. He had problems enough with the crucifixion, let alone the resurrection.

The Reverend Sam Cowper removed his stole, kissing the embroidered cross as always, finding comfort in familiar High Church ritual where faith failed; 'more Catholic than the Romans', he'd been called more than once. He crossed himself, bowed to the statue of the Virgin, and returned to the rectory for his breakfast.

Another communion, matins, maybe a christening or two – he must check his diary – then evensong and compline. Another Sunday.

His mind kept returning to the woman in his dream, distracting him from his duties. He was conscientious; his own confusion of belief did not stop him from following Christ's injunction to feed his sheep. They needed feeding, caring, looking after; and though he sometimes shared some of his doubts with his flock, he was always careful not to rock any faith they might have. He fulfilled the role they asked of him; for the most part this meant telling them what they wanted to know, occasionally challenging them — though not too severely.

The woman. The woman in blue. In midnight blue. She was still there in his thoughts days later, her image still clear in his mind. Challenging him, though he did not know what was expected of him.

There was a funeral on Saturday, and he had been asked to let someone know. Who was it? He pottered around the garden, unable to concentrate on his sermon, tweaking the dead heads from the roses. Natalie's roses. The rest of the garden had gone almost to waste; he mowed the lawn two or three times each summer, but the borders and the rockery at the end had reverted to nature. They were a mess, and he knew it, but they were a pausing place for bees and butterflies, a home for mice and shrews, and goodness knows what else besides.

But Natalie's roses he tended with care, with love, with remembrance. Red and white they were, in the main, though here, in front of him, he noticed with surprise a small bush of blue flowers. Three days later, and the woman in the dream still haunted him: the blue of the sky, the blue of her dress and her skin, her face, her hair — and tangled in her hair, a halo of barbed wire.

They had loved here, in the garden, amongst the roses. Natalie had loved to make love out of doors, open to the sky, in the fresh air. He had always felt awkward, exposed, even in the privacy of their walled garden; but as in so many things, he had followed her lead. When he'd decided to become a priest, all those years ago, he had thought he might some day marry a comfortable, matronly woman, to whom he could leave the flower arrangements and the Mothers' Union. Then Natalie had seduced him one day in this very garden, and he had married her. Even in the throes of lovemaking, he'd never been able to shake off a feeling of wrongness. Someone more placid, less demanding, he might have felt less sinful with, and could have made love from time to time in bed, in the dark. But Natalie . . .

He caressed a rose, stroking off the drops of dew, glittering in the morning sunlight.

The summer fair. Ms Simmonds, that was it. 'Father,' she'd said after choir practice a week or two ago, 'you will tell us if there's to be a funeral that Saturday, won't you? If it's going to rain, we'll want to set up in the hall, and you know it always rains at your funerals.'

Country lore for once was completely true: twenty years in the ministry, and it had rained at every one. And his weddings were always on glorious days.

There had been a time when the Department made use of his minor Talent, but not recently – not, in fact, since Natalie's death. They'd been there, of course; she had been one of their prime Talents. They'd met through the Department, when they were both working on the same project; sometimes he'd wondered if their meeting and whirlwind romance and marriage had actually been engineered by the Department. He wouldn't put it past them; their ways were often inscrutable, and often one did not know the real reasons for one's involvement in a project.

Heaven knows, he thought — and if there is a heaven, then maybe it does — it gave some sort of solution as to why a beautiful, vivacious, half-French, long-limbed, red-headed dancer and actress, and one of the most powerful telepaths he had known, should end up with a balding, tubby, retiring priest who, if he had ever had a prime, was now well beyond it.

No, the Department hadn't contacted him for five years now, not since the funeral; perhaps their main interest in him had always only been to act as a moderator on Natalie. There was not that much call for a weatherman.

He took one more look at the roses, and went in to call his organist. What was her first name? He could never remember. She'd suggested they go for a drink after the choir practice, to discuss the hymns for the next couple of weeks; but he'd seen a look in her eyes he remembered from Natalie, and said no. Young women terrified him. What did they see in him? She wasn't the first to try to fill Natalie's place; and some had been far more blatant. He shook his head, and picked up the phone.

Swathed in flowers,
clothed in flowers,
vines twine around her white body,
red roses and white almost conceal her charms.
    The flowers and vines hold her tightly
but she looks peaceful,
at one with herself and her surroundings.
    A quiet smile lights her face
in the warm rosy light of the sunset she watches.
    She looks younger, maybe still in her teens.

She was the same woman. He felt troubled when he woke; he knew there was a task for him to fulfil, but had no idea what it was, let alone how he should accomplish it. Again he felt aroused. Again he felt guilty.

That afternoon he visited his archdeacon, an old friend and – equally High Church – his confessor. First he dealt with the guilt he felt over both his sexual feelings and his sense of inadequacy. Absolved, he was able to step through the dreams again, with a clearer mind. They sat in deep burgundy leather armchairs in Archdeacon Faber's study, surrounded by polished bookshelves.

'There is one obvious thing you could do.' Archdeacon Faber sat back in his armchair and steepled his fingers. 'But I think you've got to suggest it yourself.'

Cowper said nothing.

'Tell me, Sam, what are you feeling right now?'

'Betrayal.' The word felt bitter, unpleasant.

'And who is it that has betrayed you?'

'No. I feel I'm betraying Natalie.'

The archdeacon leaned forward.

'And why is that?'

'I'm not sure.'

'Surely it's not for your sexual thoughts, now? Natalie wouldn't be minding those, at all.'

'I know, I know.' Cowper spoke wearily. 'It's not just that. I'm betraying this woman in my dreams as well. I don't know what to do to help her.'

'You're not betraying her. Until you learn how you can help her, you've no blame. If you knew, and then didn't do anything, that would be something else. So who else are you betraying?'

Cowper was silent for long minutes. He rose slowly, as if exhausted, and walked around the study, picking up and putting down a paperweight on the archdeacon's desk, running his fingers along the leather-bound theology texts on the shelves.

Faber refilled their glasses, took a sip of the 12-year-old whisky, and waited.

'I was thinking about the Department yesterday,' the priest said, turning from the French windows where he had been watching early-browned beech leaves swirling on the path outside. 'It's five years since we've been in touch. Not since Natalie's funeral.'

He picked up his recharged glass from the antique cocktail table between the armchairs, and stared into the golden liquid. The archdeacon waited.

'I suppose I feel I've let them down in some way.' A touch of anger came into his voice. 'But they've let me down. Not a word in five years. Five years; they take Natalie away from me, watch me bury her, then that's it, no more, nothing. Not even a card at Christmas, not even the odd "How're you doing, Sam?" They're bastards, Tomas; they don't care. Use you like they used up Natalie, and then throw you away. Why should I ever do anything for them again? If they asked me ...' His voice trailed off.

The archdeacon waited a few moments, then said softly, 'That's where your problem is, Sam. Anger and resentment against the Department. You blame them for Natalie's death; it's been festering inside you for five years. You've got to do something about it, deal with it.'

'Like what?'

'Your dreams. Have you decided what you're going to do?'

'Go to the Department for advice, of course.'

Faber raised an eyebrow. 'Of course.'

Cowper suddenly grinned at him. 'That's what I came here for, after all, for you to get me to tell myself the obvious.'

'Good. I'm glad I've been of use.'

Cowper frowned. 'It won't be easy, though; I hadn't realized how strongly I felt. They have deserted me, you know; cast me off.'

'I'm sure they haven't. They don't have the time to deal with disaffected Talents. You're no use to them like that. I think they've been waiting for you to come back to them. You've got a problem; they're the best people to help you solve it. And then you might find that you're of use to them as well.'

Too fast.
The cart's wheels slam into the platform.
Its steel frame begins to buckle,
but too late.
The cart flips up from its rails,
flinging the woman from her plastic seat
straight through the glass screen like a stone from a
*   ballista.*
She flies, still upright,
her arms beginning to spread to save herself,
shattered glass an aura around her;
then stops,
as suddenly as she took to the air.
Six feet behind the platform edge a jade-green
*   perimeter fence;*
spreadeagled on it,
forced half through its steel mesh,
her blood spattering outwards around her
her face turned partly back,
the woman hangs on the fence.
It has become a part of her; and she has become a part
*   of it. For ever.*

The priest woke; he felt unable to breathe, as if the air were too thick, green and poisonous, pressing down on his face and chest. His groin ached as if kicked. Acid tears streamed down his cheeks.

An hour later he was coaxing his battered and beloved Morris Minor Traveller towards London, and the Department.

He was no dreamwalker; he rarely even remembered his dreams. Natalie had tried to explain to him the various ways of interpreting dreams, of encouraging them, of entering them and changing them, of using them to foretell the future, and using them to affect the future.

She had explained Freudian symbolism and Jungian symbolism; she had digressed into mythic archetypes, and had talked at length about psychological and physiological and biochemical causes of altered states of consciousness.

To please her he had tried lucid dreaming twice, with a total lack of success. The first time he had slept soundly apparently without dreams all night; the second time, more determined, he had spent the night trying to dream — and frustratedly trying to sleep. Though Natalie was convinced he was a latent dreamwalker, he was sure he was not. He didn't even want to be. She was so good; and anyway, dreams made him uncomfortable — which made the three he had had disturb him all the more.

The anonymous brick building that was the Department of Paranormal Resources looked shabbier than he remembered; the net curtains to prevent telescopic snooping were faded, yellowed, dusty; the government-cream corridor walls scuffed and peeling. The few people he saw as he made his way through the building hurried, scurried, but not with any excitement; shoulders hunched, heads down, their activity seemed purposeless, their faces cheerless.

Minor civil servants; with no Talents of their own

they monitored and filed and administered those who had. It was a job, a safe career, with some chance of promotion by a grade or two between sixteen and sixty; but always with the prospect of walking the same dull cream corridors, sitting at the same two-decade-old desks, smelling the same air of stale sweat and unwashed clothes, of ingrained urine in the utilitarian carpets near the lavatories, and of old gravy from the staff cafeteria.

He knocked on one door among many in the corridor, and entered a small office.

'Sam. It's good to see you again.' A neat little man came from behind his desk: Peter Worthington, the priest's main contact in the Department in times past. He took Cowper's shoulders between his hands and held him for a few moments.

Worthington looked older, the priest thought; greyer in the skin as well as the hair. Five years can be a long time, he thought.

'It's good to be here,' he said. 'I think.'

'I'm glad you're back with us.'

They exchanged news for a few minutes, until a secretary brought in two plastic cups of weak tea. Something else that hasn't changed, thought Cowper.

'Tomas Faber told me something of why you're here, Sam. Could you go through it again? Try to remember every detail of the dreams, and how you felt about them.'

The priest tensed, then realized he had to do it; that was why he was here. He described the first two dreams, and Worthington listened carefully.

'There was another one, this morning.' He stopped, and the civil servant waited.

His voice catching, Cowper told the dream.

He finished, and the silence lengthened. Eventually

Worthington asked, 'How old was the woman in each of the dreams? You said she was younger in the second one.'

'I'd say mid-twenties in the first one: twenty-four to twenty-six. The second one, she was about seventeen.' He stopped.

'And the third?' Worthington prompted.

'Thirty-two, thirty-four.'

'It was the same woman each time?'

'Yes.'

'You're sure?'

'I wasn't at first. She was so much younger the second time, it took me a while to realize.'

'So we have three moments in her life. They're out of order, but that might not be important; it often happens with dreams. Or it might be.'

'They're present, past and future,' the priest said.

'Yes, three points in her life, up to her death.'

'No, I don't mean that. The first dream is now; it's her present state. The second was some years ago. The third hasn't happened yet. And you're wrong, it's not her death.'

Worthington looked confused. 'But you said she –'

'They're all continuing states. They're not isolated moments; they're as she is now, and as she was once, and as she will be. Not dead, but hanging on that fence, in that fence, a part of it, hanging there forever, her mouth open in a continuous scream. I couldn't hear her, but I could see, I could feel ...' His voice choked; self-conscious, he fumbled in his pocket for a hand-kerchief.

'I ... I've got to stop that happening. She can't become like that. She mustn't.'

Worthington let him wipe his eyes, let him compose himself.

'There's something you're not telling me, Sam,' he said gently. 'What is it?'

Tears streaming down his face, the priest turned pain-filled eyes to the man who had guided all his work for the Department, the man who had sent him out that last day with Natalie.

'Her face, Peter. Her scream. The look in her eyes, as she realizes ... It's exactly how Natalie looked, the moment before she died.'

He was not a dreamwalker, but he must walk his own dreams. In a few days Worthington, with two Talents, took the little priest through stages and techniques of training that would normally take weeks.

– See a picture in your mind, a painting in a frame.
– Let the people in the painting move about.
– The picture is a window.
– The window is a doorway. You can see through it.
– You can reach through it.

He felt a touch in his mind, a small push, and realized he was in the picture. He could feel rough ground beneath his feet, feel a fresh sea breeze against his skin, smell salt and fish.

He stepped out, stepped back in again, knowing now how to do it. Teaching by telepathy can be risky, but when there is a need, it can be effective.

Now change something.

Cowper learnt to step through his dreams, to view them from different angles, to consider the possible different depths of meaning within them. Dream interpretation is an inexact art, certainly not a science, despite the learned treatises he immersed himself in, which seemed to offer hard and fast rules. It was only when he realized that every rule was only a premise within a model, and that every model was only one person's attempt to fashion a framework around conjecture, that he began began to make some sense of the texts.

They still weren't much help; his own intuition was more use – once he learnt to trust it.

Present, past and future; the present was now, and he had been shown it first because this was the turning point, the crux for this woman, the only point at which he could intervene and influence the flow of her life, to answer her call.

The past, couched in mythological imagery: the woman in flowers, the woman of flowers, in a state of oneness with nature. Everything is in balance, but the balance is not static, stultified, mordant; rather it is growing, in touch with the elements. The woman might be an elemental; he couldn't rule it out.

The future, artificial, mechanical, lifeless – as it might be, as it would be if he did not intervene. But it need not be; the future can be changed. She need not hang bleeding upon the fence for the eternity of her life.

He had been given dreams of her life; he had to change the dreams, change her life.

There had been no further dreams, but there would be one more, written, produced and directed by the priest himself. He knew what it must achieve, and how it should go; he knew what effect it must have to save the woman.

Who was she? She was not Natalie, though Worthington had tried to convince him that she might be.

'Look, I don't even know if she's real.'

'Do you mean in the sense that you and I are?' A typical civil servant's question, thought Cowper.

'No, I mean ... She could be a psychic projection from some other world. She could be from some parallel world, if they exist. Or she could be, I don't know, she could be from the realms of the dead, or the half-dead.'

This somehow seemed the most likely, even though his personal theology had never managed to make any sense of the afterlife. He wasn't comfortable with the traditional Christian heaven and hell, and other cultures' afterlives were little better. But nor could he believe in reincarnation. The idea of circling around again was attractive, but he had never come across any evidence strong enough to convince him.

But oblivion, complete cessation of consciousness with the end of life, struck him as aesthetically unpleasing as well as wasteful. And surely no god, of whatever name, would allow it.

Still, he felt that a link with another plane of existence, be it parallel spirituality or some post-death experience, was the most likely explanation.

The woman was not Natalie, but Natalie was linked with these dreams in some way. And Natalie was dead.

She stands, clothed in a riot of flowers of all colours and varieties. He makes the flowers all roses, red and white, wild roses twining around her arms, her shoulders, down over her breasts. The flowers grow from her, their thorns causing her no discomfort, pointing outwards for her protection. Red and white, blood and water, blood and semen, blood and body, wine and bread, life-giving. From her own flowers the priest gives her the sacraments of salvation and freedom, and she accepts them.

Priest and communicant, they recognize each other without creeds.

Wherever she was, Natalie was in the same world, and this knowledge gave him the strength and courage to summon up the three dreams.

Present, past and future surround him. He sees all three, side by side, overlaid at their edges and circling slowly together around the dream he is creating. Red and green clash: life blood and vitriol. White and green: purity and evil. There is no life, no beauty of nature, in this green.

The woman still hangs in the wire-mesh fence, but its tainted green turns slowly to brown as the half-rusting wire of the fence becomes branches, stems; her dripping blood becoming petals. The first dream, the now-time dream, is merging with the second; blue-lit still, in midnight-blue light, her barbed-wire halo becoming first a tangle of briars, and then a crown of roses. Blue and red become a deep, beautiful purple; blue and white, a summer's sky.

He was nearly there; the three dreams were almost one. He had brought her back from the despair of technology, from the deadness of metal and glass and plastic, to the state of life in nature which had been hers years before.

As the metal cart and the metal rails and the wire-mesh fence fade, she grows more solid in his dream, her flowers brighter red, purer white, the beauty of their wildness blent with the sharpness of the protective thorns and the hardness and roughness of the wood of her trunk. He can see the outline of her hips, her thighs, her groin, her legs, as a shaping, a suggestion in the wood of the rose tree from which, of which, she grows.

Daphne came to his mind: the Greek river nymph become a laurel tree. But no; that was desperation, escape from pursuit. This was fulfilment, living, growing, the sap her blood, the wood her natural body.

He looks at her face and sees the innocence and freshness and lightness she wore in his second dream, when she was younger; but now there is a maturity, a serenity in her eyes, her mouth, the set of her face. The coldness of the blue dream, the agony of the fence, both gone, at last, and she is what she should be, a natural woman in her own setting, for the eternity of her life growing within the rose tree.

The priest asks if he might visit her from time to time, in his dreams. Her smile contains welcome, and thanks, gladness, and love.

He woke, pleasantly tired, but rested within himself. In his dreams; and in the rose garden.

He found he could think about Natalie without pain or anger or bitterness. Yes, she had died in a moment of absolute agony, physical and mental and spiritual; yes, she had died on a task for the Department; yes, she had died. She was dead, and nothing would change that. But now he knew that she was at peace, in whatever afterlife she might be; it was enough to know that he would join her when his time came. Like the woman in the rose tree, she would always be with him now, as her strength had been with him in his dreams.

And the woman in his dreams: was she real, in whatever way? Or could his subconscious mind, the dream-creator, have created her, using mythic imagery to give shape to his fears, his desires, extending the momentary dying agony of his wife into a perpetual moment for the woman, to force him into action?

He had been crippled since Natalie's death, unwhole. It had taken the dreams, and his intervention in them, to heal him.

Was this the sole purpose of it all? And if that were so, perhaps the dreams had not come from his inner self at all; perhaps they had been given to him, to force the change, the healing in him.

For years, until now, he'd had only an uncommon

Talent, and that very weakly: he could affect the weather. Tornadoes and hurricanes were beyond his abilities; but weddings should be sunny, so his weddings were always sunny. Funerals should be grey, dismal, overcast, maybe raining, so that was how his funerals invariably were.

But now he was a dreamwalker, not quite so rare, but infinitely more valuable – and that much more useful to the Department.

Had they given him the dreams, engendered them in his subconscious to awaken a Talent they suspected was there, but that he had always suppressed? Was the whole thing simply yet another DPR machination?

He waited for his blood to rise, for the old antagonistic reaction to occur. But if this was how it was, then he had the choice to accept it or not, to be angry, or not. To be a useful member of the Department; or not.

But it didn't matter, not really. He laughed aloud. It didn't matter at all.

Whatever her origin, for him the woman was real, and he would see her again. He was at peace over Natalie. There was an afterlife, and she was in it. It might not have much to do with his Church – but did that matter either?

Father, crucified Christ and the Spirit: they were familiar terms, and they would do as well as any other. He had seen life grow from one outstretched in agony; call it resurrection, why not? And the Spirit? She would always have the face of the woman of his dreams, growing, living for ever. He had never known her name. She was the Blessed Virgin in his first dream, clothed as always in blue. In the third she had been the Christ. And in the dream he had created, she had returned to the naturalness of her younger self in his second dream: eternal youth: innocence with wisdom. If she needed a name in his thoughts, she could be Sophia.

Suddenly he remembered the name of his organist: Katie Simmonds. Katie. He thought of her eyes, hazel, half-hidden behind her long brown hair; and her hair, warm and softly curving as her body promised. There was a choir practice tonight, and she would be there. He felt desire flooding through him, and no guilt.

He would take her a rose from the garden.

Book review from the November issue of *History Today*.

Famous Paranorms in History, 600 BC to AD 1900, C. Tadminster, Roc Books 1990, 403pp, £19.95.

The implicit problem with a book of this nature is, of course, the lack of the eponymous subject. Can the average person name five famous paranorms of history? Unlikely. And on this showing, such interest is simply not justifiable. What pretext for an investigation, one wonders, are the Talents of, say, a Guy de Horvendile, or a Jenny Dyer?

Guy de Horvendile (pp. 156–88) was a twelfth-century Knight Templar whose Talent, it appears from the primary sources, must have been an ability to retard or prevent the surface oxidization of metal. The 'brite-shyning' knight de Horvendile may figure famously in the *chansons de geste*, and his 'spotless coat of mail' have passed into the language as a metaphor for morality, but neither of these facts seems greatly to have aided de Horvendile at the battle of the Horns of Hattin where, like so many others, he found himself in receipt of a well-aimed Saracen arrow. He would have benefited more, one feels, from a Talent pertaining to matters aerodynamic.

Similarly, one regards with little satisfaction the career of a Jenny Dyer (pp. 230–55). Simultaneously mistress to the rumbustious King Charles II, the scurrilous poet Rochester, and possibly Louise de Kérouaille (spy-in-ordinary to the court of Louis XIV), the Talent of young 'actress' Jenny Dyer manifested itself as the ability to render spoken doggerel verse pleasing to the ear of an audience. It is to Jenny Dyer that English literature owes the popularity of such turgid dramas as *The Fair Sophonisba, or, Love Beneath the Gallows*; *King Lear, or, Cordelia Restor'd*; and *Nine Nights of Bawdy* – to the confusion and distaste of succeeding generations of critics and theatre audiences.

317

The author is on even more uncertain ground when he posits paranormal reasons for the circumstances surrounding the Viking discovery of 'Vinland', as America was first named. Tadminster postulates from circumstance – the initial colonization, and then the apparent vanishing of the Newfoundland colony – that Leif Ericsson inadvertently carried a man in his crew whose Talent was for concealment from hazard. Nowadays, of course, technology would pierce through a psychic screen of this nature, but at that time it would prove effective against marauding enemies, wild beasts and, of course, succeeding colony ships. It is possible, Tadminster avers, that this historical accident may have robbed us of several centuries of New World settlement. However, this is mere supposition pandering to popularism, and will not hold up under sophisticated analysis.

Famous paranorms in history? If one is to seek the archetypal paranorm of the past, that is perhaps best illustrated by the subject of Tadminster's last chapter.

It is not widely known that the last alchemist did not operate, as is often assumed, during the seventeenth century. The last practising alchemist worthy of the name, Charles Claudius Martin, was a colleague and contemporary of Marie Curie. In 1899 he succeeded, by operation of a paranormal Talent, in turning two and a half ounces of other material into 22-carat gold. Unfortunately, the only substance upon which his Talent would operate was not lead, but Curie's radium, and Charles Claudius Martin perished at the age of twenty-three, one of the earliest victims of radiation sickness.

Such, one may suggest, is the career of the paranormal person; no more equipped, at least on the evidence of this study, to deal with the vicissitudes of life than we, the non-Gifted.

A LONELY IMPULSE

Roz Kaveney

When Hatchet-face asked her what she thought had triggered it, Carrie thought of blaming the chilli. It was the way Viola made it – heavy and full of yoghurt and with a choice of brown basmati or some sort of whole-grain crackers; it was very nice, but it took a lot of washing down. And you felt weighed down by it; maybe that had something to do with it.

At least no one said very much over dinner: Veronica and Spike had probably intended to walk out all along, at least once they realized Carrie was there, but there are separatist ethics on the one hand, and there is having to walk home and then get your own supper on the other.

'Well,' said Viola, 'I think we've got at least some common ground. I mean, the important thing is that women should be safe.'

'No woman can be safe,' said Spike, summoning sepulchral tones from somewhere inside her shedding mohair sweater.

'Not while there are men on the streets,' said Veronica, her bright bird-like eagerness making it unclear whether she was finishing her lover's sentence or making a ritual response.

'Well,' said Carrie, stretching back into her armchair so that her head rested on the leather jacket she had folded up and put on top of the cushion, 'perhaps unfortunately, imposing a curfew on all males is not, in fact, an option.'

'Of course, you'd side with rapists,' said Spike. 'I don't know why Viola asked you into the discussion.'

'I don't see that Carrie was siding with rapists,' said Viola.

'You wouldn't,' said Veronica. 'After all, you still sleep with them.'

'No I don't,' said Viola.

'What they mean,' said Carrie, 'is that you sleep with men. All men are rapists. You sleep with rapists. QED. It's like all their other little formulas. I wear eye make-up, so I'm not a real lesbian. Gay men oppress women by looking at pictures of each other. Paranorms have special powers, so they're élitist and oppress everybody.'

'That's a really simplistic falsification –' Spike started.

'Right,' Carrie continued, 'I forgot, it's all right to be heterosexual or paranormal as long as you don't actually do it. How that differs from the way Christians talk about dykes, I fail to understand.'

'It is typical,' said Veronica, 'that you insist on bringing it down to sexual acts.'

'And,' said Spike, 'that someone who goes around dressed in fascist leather gear will jump to the defence of people who think they're superior.'

'What's any of this got to do with trying to set up an anti-rape patrol?' said Viola.

'Nothing,' said Carrie. 'Sorry. I let them annoy me.'

'We,' said Spike, 'see little point in continuing all this.'

'We just wanted to expose the hypocrisy involved in people like you two even discussing the issue,' said Veronica.

They nodded to each other, got up, and left the room. Spike stumbled on the short staircase down from the living room to the corridor which led to the main stairs, and they slammed the front door as they left.

'I told you that was going to be a waste of time,' said Carrie.

'Well, Carrie,' said Viola, stretching out along her sofa in a cat-like way that Carrie did not particularly enjoy watching – does this ever-so-straight woman not know that she is cute enough to die for? – 'at least we tried.'

'But it's all so pointless,' said Carrie. 'I want there to be real discussion about making the streets round here safe for women, not some sort of stage-managed psychodrama in which those two refugees from the Royal Hospital for the Terminally Correct make impossibilist demands that every man in the neighbourhood have their willies padlocked or that there be some sort of Amazon warrior on every street corner.'

They did the washing up, and Carrie finished the Czech lager; then Viola poured herself a brandy, and Carrie a Scotch. And after that, Carrie felt a bit like lying down, and not at all like being sensible, cutting her losses and walking to the other end of the estate.

Trouble was, she knew perfectly well that Viola was uptight. Carrie had never made a pass as such, never would; but Viola knew Carrie was a dyke, and that sort of thus-far-straight woman is usually paranoid enough to misinterpret a perfectly ordinary request to droop across her crazy quilt.

So Carrie let herself drift a bit in her larger chair, as Viola played one of those Vaughan Williams symphonies that always sound as if they have a brass band playing on a village green somewhere in the distance.

'Carrie,' Viola said, after a bit. 'Shall I ring you a cab? Or walk you home? Or would you like to crash where you are?'

'Whichever you'd prefer,' Carrie said, *toujours butch galante.*

'Well,' she said, 'as long as you're content with a chair

... I mean, I know you're quite capable of looking after yourself. But no woman is ever wholly safe, is she?'

Carrie tried to look confidently hard and at the same time sufficiently vulnerable so that Viola would not turf her out like a stray cat that has scrounged once too often.

Viola wandered, not especially steady herself, down the carpeted steps from her living room to the passage and up again to the other half of the flat where her kitchen and bedroom were, clearly not expecting to get rid of Carrie, but not conveying huge pleasure either. But sod it, Carrie thought, she was genuinely a bit wobbly: she didn't usually get that drunk, but everyone slips up once in a while.

Viola came back and slung her a blanket, and Carrie smiled as devastatingly wistful a smile as she could manage; she was not going to humiliate herself by asking her way into Viola's bed, but there was no point in positively ruling out a request from her.

'Goodnight, Carrie,' Viola said firmly, turned out the main light and went to her room. Well, fair enough, though she did not need to be that firm over just a smile, Carrie thought; she pulled her top sweater off, undid the belt of her jeans and stuck her glasses on top of her head for safe keeping.

There was some mineral water left, and she drank it; it was that Italian sort whose label goes on about your liver. Later on, she remembered to mention this only because they always ask you for very precise details about what you consumed just before, and that was positively the last thing. Viola's housekeeping was not perfect, but there were no radioactive spiders floating in it, or anything; lots of people in Hackney had eaten her chilli, come to that.

Carrie scrunched round in the chair and pulled the

blanket round her and, after a few trial positions that ended up with cramp in her knees, managed to find one that would let her get to sleep. And that was it, until the morning.

That started with a vague headache and a sense that she might regret opening her eyes; light was streaming in from above — Carrie had always known that there was something obscene about skylights — and somewhere not very far away she could smell coffee.

'I'm up here,' Viola shouted, unnecessarily cheerfully.

Now, you, reading this, will know where Carrie's glasses were, but it rarely occurs to you when you wake in a strange flat with even a mild hangover that you did even one thing sensible last night. She felt around on the arm of the chair and dangled her hand over the side to the bits of the floor she could reach from where she was folded up; even by stretching her fingers like spider legs, she couldn't find them.

So she opened her eyes. It was not like any hangover she'd ever had; it was a bit like migraines sometimes are, only not quite the same. There were a lot of rods and cones like you see when a microscope reflects your eye; she had never had that before. She could see the room as well as she would normally have been able to without glasses; it just had all this crud in front of it.

'Coffee's ready,' Viola yelled from the kitchen.

Carrie reached for her belt; that may have been where she made her mistake, because she was concentrating on threading it through her jeans and doing it up tight all the way to the kitchen. She couldn't see all that well, but followed the smell of coffee right across the room.

'Careful where you step,' Viola said, 'I didn't pick up yet.'

Carrie knew this, in an abstract way, but her brain was working differently this morning; she could not quite see what she was picking her way past, but there were obstacles she was avoiding, she sort of knew that – and the floor felt sort of springy – as she tried to work out which hole on her belt would be most expedient the morning after a heavy meal.

'Oh,' Viola said, her kimonoed back to Carrie, 'and mind the steps.'

'What steps?' Carrie said, walking into the kitchen, but Viola was too busy pouring coffee into beakers through some sort of strainer to notice.

Carrie reached past her, avoiding brushing her arm, took a mug and started to sip. It surprised her that she was looking down at the back of Viola's head.

'It can't be very good for your feet?' Carrie said tentatively. 'I mean, I knew you wore heels, but I thought you were taller than me anyway.' She took a step back as Viola turned.

'But I am taller than you, sweetheart,' Viola said and then looked up at her.

'Can you see where I put my glasses?' Carrie asked her.

'They're on top of your head, Carrie; um ... could you go and sit down – you're making me nervous doing that.'

'Doing what?' Carrie said, and turned and headed back to the living room, slipping her glasses forward as she went. The rods and cones and webs and stuff did not go away; they became slightly clearer, and Carrie realized that she had been walking on them. That was what was different about things. She was also a couple of inches above the floor.

She made an effort of will and stepped down from the air on to the carpet; it was hard and unpleasant by comparison. It wasn't like putting your foot into a bath that is too hot or too cold; it was just that she'd already got used to that feeling of its being springy under foot.

324

Viola was getting quite upset; she started talking in that tone of impatience you use when there is a joke you are not quite in on.

'Carrie,' she said, 'I don't want to be a bore, but just what do you think you are doing?'

'I don't know,' said Carrie. 'I mean, I've never done anything like this before, but it seems really easy. Why don't I . . .?'

She reached down and took Viola's hand and tried to pull her up to where she was standing. Viola just stumbled forwards, and started to fall down the steps into the hall; Carrie threw her weight into supporting her, and discovered that in the process she had wandered distinctly from the vertical, without exhibiting any tendency to fall to the ground. She let go of Viola and used a sort of backwards swing of her arms and a twist of her shoulders to push herself back up into the perpendicular. She was standing straight up again, still about a foot and a half off the ground.

She had also managed to drop her coffee, and it had spilled dramatically everywhere.

Viola's left foot had got splashed.

'Do you always go around getting drunk in people's flats,' she said, 'and making a vulgar exhibition of yourself in the morning? It's bad enough when people are sick, but at least you know what you're cleaning up after.'

Carrie was embarrassed; she also had the distinct feeling of having uncovered a hitherto untapped vein of bigotry in someone she quite liked, and respected, and fancied. She turned on her heel, walked across to the chair, picked up and put on the the rest of her clothes, and headed for the door.

'And do at least try to use the stairs,' said Viola, in the sort of cutting tone that can really make you go off someone.

Carrie made her way downstairs, and by concentrating very hard was touching them by the time she reached the bottom.

She went home, and cleaned up and changed, and spent the day snoozing. That evening, Brett, one of her nicer straight male friends, came round, and she ended up going to the pub with him. The crud was still in front of her vision, but was getting to be how the world looks, like having eyelashes is.

'I saw Viola today,' he eventually got round to saying, 'and she seemed a little upset. You didn't . . .?'

'Of course not,' said Carrie, 'that would be hopelessly uncool. No, I was just a bit headachy and hungover and clumsy this morning, and I broke her cup. And she flew off the handle.'

'Fair enough,' said Brett, 'she gets a bit out of order sometimes, does Viola. Not like you, Carrie; you've got your feet firmly planted on the ground.'

'Oh, right,' said Carrie, and hid her blushes in her pint.

She was moderate in her drinking that night, but had had enough so that, when she walked home, she was feeling uninhibited. And, by the time she got to the monumental masons, on the corner by the church, her feet were hurting a little; she could not help remembering how nice they had felt that morning.

There was an angel in the mason's yard, and its wings were spread and it was pointing an admonitory finger upwards. The rods and cones and patterns, that had been floating across her sight, and tempting her feet, all day, came together as a long clear gradient ahead of her leading in a slow spiral to the top of the church tower, and then on, endlessly branching, like the ones in airline ads.

'Oh, why not,' she said to herself, 'go for it, gal.'

So she took a run at it, and soon she was walking

round the church tower, which was really in a shocking state once you got close to it; then she started running along one of the lines and it was like running had never been, a sort of soaring.

She thought to herself that she might as well go on, because if it *was* a dream, and she stopped and went home now, she'd hate herself in the morning.

Somehow she seemed to move faster like this, and running seemed like a sensible way to go on, but then her foot clipped something and she stumbled.

'Oh shit,' she thought, 'wake up time. It had better be.'

She was going straight over forwards on to her face and she struck her arms out to try and stop herself, like you would on the pavement, except that she was a hundred feet above the pavement. Sticking her arms out changed her balance, and she found herself briefly diving towards the ground, and then turning upwards again. It wasn't like soaring any more; it *was* soaring.

'Oh wow,' she said, looking down at the street lights, and the Thames beyond them, 'up, up and away. Or what?'

She dipped and dived and rose and fell, and the more she did it, the less she had to think about doing it. It was easy, that was what was wonderful, and scary, about it; it was like sex. You find out what you like to do, and the finding out is the hard part, and then you just get on and do it, and it never seems to be that much of a problem any more.

The nice thing about having short hair was that the rush of air through it was not too ferocious; if it had been really long, and streaming behind her, it would be just too much like having a web of intense sensation wrapping your skull when you were trying to think and steer and enjoy what you were doing. She had always wondered why cats sauntered so much when they were indoors, but imagine being a cat and running around and constantly twanging your whiskers on things. Whereas, as things were, it was a rush like cold showers and fresh orange juice and the sheer wild adrenalin zing of riding the powers of the air.

The force of the air against her face seemed to be keeping her glasses in place; presumably there were aspects of all this that had nothing to do with aerodynamics.

An hour or so later, she started to yawn, and she had to think a little about how to get home. She hadn't got her A-to-Z with her, and she didn't feel like going close enough to the ground to read street signs – there were still people about, and she had an uneasy feeling about all of this – but after a bit, she worked out that railway lines and churches and open spaces, and a general sense of where North is, will sort it out for you. It took only twenty minutes, which was quicker than a cab, and cheaper. She had left her bedroom window open, which meant she did not even have to go down to street level; this was the first time she had ever felt good about living on the tenth floor.

The next few nights were fun; she took to sleeping in – there was no point in not doing except on days when she had to sign on – and going out once it was dark. At first, she just got off on the aerobatics side of things – going high and fast and looking down at the city as if it were a carpet she was examining for a lost contact – but after a while it made more sense to practise at lower levels as well.

If she went too high, there was always the risk of air traffic, and she had been very lucky so far, and sooner or later she was going to have to get used to being nearer the ground. After all, sensing the currents and riding them was a bit easy when there were not things in the way that you had to get round or over – she was just going to have to get better – and paying attention to roof-tops and high-rises and fly-overs was probably the best way to get there.

She was still worried about passers-by, but she reckoned that if she only went out at night, and wore black, which she'd be wearing most of the time anyway, the chances of her being spotted were minimal. And she needed her leather jacket anyway; she did not have much trouble keeping on course when there were cross-winds – they did not stop her doing whatever it was she did – but they could still make her unpleasantly cold.

Then there was the night when she had nearly not gone out at all because it was pouring with rain. It is bad enough keeping rain off your glasses at street level, let alone when you are up near the clouds it is dropping from. But it did mean she could get some practice with low-level work, with less likelihood of anyone turning their faces upwards into the rain long enough to catch sight of her.

She was crossing London Fields, reflecting that there was a time when she would have had more sense than ever to go near the dingy common at night, when she spotted a woman walking down one of the paths. Carrie slowed down, one of the things she had learned, but somehow found easier to do when she travelled at high speed than if she went at a fast walk; hovering always left her dripping with sweat. It was worrying in retro-spect that she had slowed down in advance, because it meant that she was well-placed when two youths, who had not even been bothering to hide, rushed up to the woman, knocked her down and started to run off with her bag.

The awful thing was that it was so easy; Carrie did not even have to think about what she was doing – she dived down almost to ground level, and buzzed the pair of them, banging her fist down on their heads as she passed, turning rapidly and grabbing the bag on her second pass. She had not done more than daze them, but they were confused; she did not care to think what she might have had to do if they had come back for more, instead of pulling themselves together and running off as if bolts from the blue were a normal hazard.

As it was, she went back to the woman, letting herself down on to the ground so that she was ready to help her get up from where they had pushed her.

'I got your bag,' Carrie said. 'And they've run off.'

'Are you sure?' said the woman, brushing herself off, and pulling a face at the amount of mud on her hands. 'They might come back.'

'I don't think so,' said Carrie, 'and if they do, we'll be ready for them. They only got you because you were unprepared.'

'Maybe,' said the woman, 'but they'll get someone else tomorrow night, or the night after. People are unprepared, even people like them; that's what being people is. They don't expect people to come along out of nowhere, playing God.'

Carrie tried to act as if she did not know what the woman was hinting at; after all, she might have been just walking past – it was dark and gloomy enough that people might not have noticed her.

'You were flying, weren't you?' said the woman.

'I don't know what you mean,' said Carrie.

The woman stared at her with a degree of hostility altogether unexpected in someone you have just saved.

'I suppose I'm expected to be grateful,' she said, 'but what I can't stand is the way people like you think you're so much better than the rest of us.'

'What do you mean?' said Carrie. 'I don't think I'm

better than any other woman. I know there are dykes
who look down on straights, not that I know you're
straight, but I've never been one of them.'

'Oh, are you a bloody dyke as well?' said the woman.
'But that's not what I meant at all. Is it, *temp*?'

She spat the last word with a degree of venom that
Carrie found altogether unexpected.

'Fuck off then,' said Carrie. 'I'm almost sorry I got your
bag back for you.'

'Fuck off yourself,' said the woman, 'back where you
came from.'

Carrie found herself wondering where this stupid bitch
thought she had come from, then shrugged, and vanished
upwards silently into the dark and stormy night, as
silently as she had come. It is always important to feel
yourself part of a community.

She had never let herself, over these past few weeks,
think about her legal position, but somehow it did not
surprise her when there was a letter from the DSS next
morning, which called her in for interview, and included
a statutory notice of inquiry into any Extraordinary Abilities she might possess.

She wandered into the office late – there was no point
in being on time, and she wanted to make a point of
sorts. She even went on foot, as a sort of dumb insolence.
She went to get her number from the reception desk, and
the woman sitting there sent her straight upstairs to an
Executive Officer, Forbes, whom she had last seen when
they tried to send her on a training course.

This time, though, he was not behind his desk, but
standing uncomfortably to one side. A hatchet-faced
young man had the chair.

He turned to Forbes and said, 'I told you she was
going to be late.'

Forbes said, 'But she always is anyway.'

'Yes,' said Hatchet-face, flashing an ID at her. 'But the fact that she was going to be late was one of the first things I knew about her, that and the colour of her underwear.'

Ah, thought Carrie, this is the bit where they try to lull you into a false sense of security by being pleasant.

'Why have you never registered?' he said.

'What do you mean?' said Carrie.

'You've been signing on for the last two and a half years,' said Forbes. 'And you've never once mentioned in any of your interviews that you had ... well ... powers.'

'We don't want to be difficult,' said Hatchet-face, 'but it is technically a fraud to claim benefits without registering.'

'Oh,' said Carrie, 'I see.'

'We've had several reports,' said Hatchet-face, 'and it took us a while to narrow it down. It was only a couple of days ago that I knew for certain when I'd be meeting you. But you really should have been more careful if you were really serious about not registering. I mean, the odd precog or pyrotic can sneak past for a while, but let's face it, my dear girl, you have been being a bit blatant. What I can't understand is why – having been reasonably discreet for the past, what, twenty-five years? – you suddenly start zooming round the skies and putting out a level of psychokinetic energy that can be picked up as far away as Penge and Slough.'

'Oh, do I?' said Carrie.

'Believe me,' said Hatchet-face. 'You're not even doing anything right now. And it is a little painful for me to be in the same room.'

Carrie decided there was no point in keeping stum.

'The thing is,' she said, 'that it only happened about six weeks ago. I haven't been being discreet in the past; I didn't have anything to be discreet about before.'

'That,' said Hatchet-face, 'explains it. Well, come on; I'm going to have to take you to the Department and we haven't got all day. Ahm, Forbes, you can go on paying her benefits for the moment; we'll let you know when she starts earning EP allowances.'

Carrie had really not thought of herself as a para-normal; it was something she had not bothered to consider. A lot of her friends had a bad conscience about paranorms; of course they were an oppressed minority, but most of them ended up working for the State, or being the sort of tycoons of the psychic that the Gods were mostly supposed to be. She supposed she had never met a paranorm knowingly in her life, and because flying was not something that any paranormal she had heard of ever actually did, she had sort of thought of it as something entirely different. She explained much of this to Hatchet-face, whose name was actually Hackforth-Fford, just to confuse the issue, who looked amused. He had insisted on taking her to the Department in his car.

'Oh,' he said, 'and how would you know if one of your friends was a precog, even if they were registered?'

'I suppose I don't know,' said Carrie.

'The thing about us, dear girl,' he said, 'is that unlike some other minorities' — he cast a significant glance at her leather jacket and spiky bleached hair — 'we do not all consider it expedient to go around advertising wildly. I suppose it was inevitable that when a power as showy and perfectly useless as yours comes along, it would manifest in an exhibitionistic deviant. I trust you don't mind my speaking frankly.'

He said this in a tone of voice that managed to convey the fact that he knew perfectly well that she did mind. She had never appreciated the fact that one of the major temptations of telepathy is constantly rubbing people's faces in the fact that you know precisely what they are thinking.

'Just so,' he said, with a smirk. 'I am right in thinking that you have no abilities except this flying thing.'

She tried to keep her mind entirely blank.

'Ah,' he said, 'not even a mind shield. I suppose that when someone comes to full power as what I may as well, for the sake of politeness, call an adult, it would be too much to expect that they not be hopelessly specialized. I mean, it's very spectacular, but you're not going to be as much use as a fairly common-or-garden single-ability psychic.'

Without having to be able to read minds, Carrie suddenly realized why this over-chinned upper-class bastard was being so utterly offensive to her. If he wasn't one of the Gods, he was something quite close – she knew enough to know that someone who was a precog and a telepath and a psycho-sensitive all at once was quite rare, particularly if they had held themselves together enough to get to be some sort of mandarin – and he must have enough power himself to light up a skyscraper, and he was jealous of her. Stinking jealous.

'Yes,' he said, 'but I knew that I could spend a few minutes giving you a hard time before you'd realize it. If I'm going to have to put up with watching you zoom around uselessly, the least I can do is remind you of how ordinary mortals feel. And in this one respect, as you have realized, ordinary mortals include even most of the Gods.'

He looked out of the car window; she could not read his mind, but she could read even that poker face.

'I mean,' he went on, 'there are those who could fly. There are those who can do just about anything, if they want to. Loric, say, though he'd have to find a spell that will convince his credulous subconscious that it can do it. But what they can't do, is do everything they might want to easily or gracefully. Do you know – but of course

334

you don't; you don't know anything except your favourite brand of lager, the "in" way of rolling up your socks and some sort of half-baked bog-standard feminism – do you know how much power you control to be able to do the sort of fine-control flying you take for granted?'

'Lots, I suppose,' said Carrie, starting to feel more in control of the situation.

'I showed the police film of you to Zeus, in Washington. And he wept. A grown man who can throw mountains, and he wept. He moves through the sky like a bulldozer on ice, he doesn't fly.'

'Well,' said Carrie, 'if it's perfectly useless, there's not going to be much call for it, is there? So why not drop me at the next tube station?'

'You are confusing the fact of utter uselessness, with the potential of being, none the less, used,' he said, and the smirk on his face was as readable as his plans were inscrutable.

'How did you catch me?' she said. 'Police cameras aren't that good, surely.'

'You light up the sky, if you know how to look.'

'But I thought psycho-sensitives just sort of knew if someone near them was paranormal.'

'There are,' he said, 'quite a few paranorms with a knack for finding others; and then there are proper psycho-sensitives. It's like empathy and telepathy; an empath would know you were annoyed, and a telepath knows which sort of oil you want to boil me in and what – ah, scrambled eggs – you had for breakfast.'

When they got to the DPR, he proceeded to leave her sitting in a waiting-room for half an hour; a secretary, who said her name was Marcia, brought her the Official Secrets Act to sign, filed her nails while Carrie explained why she thought this a real imposition, and took it away when she had signed it. Carrie followed her down the corridor to her office; Marcia told her where it was and even gave her some of the office supply of paper – you don't need telepathy for everything.

Carrie wandered back in; she was bored. 'Anything I need to know about working here?'

'Well,' said Marcia, keener to moan than to ignore someone. 'Don't ever eat the fish pie in the canteen, for starters. And there's this flash Harry who comes in, advertising man; don't ever listen to a word he says. But anyway, you'll start off at the College; people usually do.'

'Not Ms Smith,' said Hatchet-face, coming into the room. 'She's going to be much too busy.'

Later on, as she sat in the pub with Brett, whom she had rung up because he moonlighted at the local Law Centre, she asked him whether they could really make her do it.

'Well,' he said, 'the trouble is that they can put the onus of proof on you. You say you've only been able to do this for a few weeks, but even then, technically, you should have gone and registered within a fortnight.'

'So they can send me to jail if I don't do what they say.'

'If they really wanted to,' said Brett. 'But they can send anyone to jail if they really want to: particularly claimants.'

'And I think I'd go nuts now, if I couldn't go into the sky.'

'Sounds to me dangerously like an addiction, Carrie,' said Brett. She was not wholly sure whether or not he was joking.

'Yes, Brett,' she said, 'but it's better for you to be clean and sober, and there is nothing better for you than flying.'

'I wouldn't know,' he said. 'So you'll let them use you to sanitize the whole Temps policy by being a PR front for it?'

'If that's the choice,' said Carrie, 'but it's not as simple as that, anyway. I mean, being everyone's dream of flying, well, it's got to be good for all the paranorms with boring powers. People in the street, they hate paranormals – there was this woman the other night. And besides, there is one thing they can't do, and that's make me go back into the closet.'

'Yes,' said Veronica, who had loomed into the back room where Brett and Carrie were drinking. 'But what decent woman would ever let herself be touched by you? I always knew that you were riddled with patriarchal crap, Carrie Smith – leather and cosmetics and Goddess knows what else – but this latest manifestation ... Well, Viola came and told us all about it; her politics stink, but she is at least a woman, and not some sort of monster.'

'I'm sorry, Veronica,' said Carrie, 'but I don't see precisely how my ability to fly is anything on which you could claim to have a feminist position.'

'Of course you can't,' said Veronica, 'and that just proves it. You're just an élitist, Carrie, looking down on other women.'

She turned on her heel and left. Brett looked slightly stunned.

'You see,' he said, 'that's what it's going to be like. People don't like it when old acquaintances go new and strange on them; I mean, I did wonder why you never came out for a drink any more, until Viola started making a bit more sense and I spotted you one night through my bedroom window, silhouetted against the moon.'

'And most of the temps I met round the office don't seem to like me very much either,' said Carrie. 'It's enough to put you right off the human race. And then there's Hatchet-face.'

'Where does he fit in?' said Brett. 'I didn't think they had paranorms that senior in the DPR, except for whatsis-name – Loric – like they don't have ex-teachers in DES.'

'Oh,' said Carrie, 'he's some sort of hot-shot from the Central Office of Information, on secondment. DPR sharpening its image, with me as the penknife.'

'Not much fun,' said Brett. 'Want another drink?'

'Might as well,' said Carrie. 'And then there's all this bloody public-school nonsense about Gods.'

'They're just high-powered paranorms,' said Brett.

'Well,' said Carrie, 'I know it started as slang — but you know how people are. Call someone a God and he'll start believing it — chance to despise people. I've not met this Loric guy, but he sounds like Hatchet-face times ten. Why are people so dreadful, Brett, why do they enjoy hating each other?'

'It's easier,' said Brett, 'than being miserable, which, I've found, is how liking people, or caring about them, or being nice, usually ends up.'

The next few weeks were indeed less than entire fun. On the one hand, Carrie quite liked being in the open and being able to fly by daytime, but on the other hand, there were all the attempts they made to clean up her image. They couldn't make her wear a skirt, that was one relief, because she pointed out, not entirely truthfully, that it would make her aerodynamically unsound, and constantly flash her knickers at the world; and the leotard-and-cape idea did not survive a couple of Immelman turns when she managed to send the whole thing flying. Hatchet-face tried to make her wear a wig, but it got into such a mess so fast they had to accept the haircut as it stood. The odd thing was that she seemed not to need her glasses as much any more.

When they put her through the press call, Hatchet-face butted in before she could say anything to avoid the issue of her sexuality by merely saying she wasn't seeing anyone at present, and letting the punters assume what they would. She wore her Act-Up T-shirt, and pink and black triangles on the lapels of her jacket, but that never got mentioned in the press stories.

And she grew to loathe shopping centres. All of a sudden, she was a celebrity, and she was always having to drag banners round the sky, advertising special deals on cat litter and canned tomatoes, in small towns in the Midlands. She quite liked children, but she got to hate going to schools and telling them a lot of half-truths about the Temps policy; it was a cleft stick she was in, because the policy was sort of working, for the first time in years. Bernard Manning was not telling nearly as many temps jokes, for one thing; and temps-bashing went into some sort of a slump, or so Hatchet-face told her.

On the other hand, though she had tried to be as bland as possible, the Great British Public did not like her very much. They wouldn't let her talk about being a dyke, but that did not stop the Sun dropping prurient hints about it. She was a stroppy cow, like Princess Anne or Edwina Currie, just not as much use, and hardly, when on the ground, even that much of an ornament. She found herself getting depressed a lot of the time, and she did not dare let herself eat or drink very much, because she knew how much they love you to become a lush or a fatty.

But the actual flying, that was a different matter. She rarely let them send a car for her, because she could go there faster by herself, and even the other end of the country never made her tired; she would have tried to go abroad, except that Hatchet-face said her contract forbade it, until the EEC agreed a unified Temps policy. And she was not sure that she could cope with crossing the Atlantic, not yet anyway.

She got to know the skies of Britain like the streets of Hackney; the thermals around Skiddaw were just a feature like the complicated zebra-crossings where Well

Street crosses Mare Street. There was one place where they could not touch the core of her, and it was a mile above their heads.

She stayed in Leeds one weekend; she had to sleep sometimes and one of the good things about all this was that at least they'd pay for a hotel for her. Marcia had booked her in at a hotel neither central nor pleasingly countrified, but it was Hatchet-face who got swollen feet from the under-floor heating.

Carrie rarely let her feet actually touch the floor these days. They had made her curtsy to the Queen, but they had not been able to make her land. The bed in the hotel was not very comfortable, but increasingly she used beds as a way to drape herself with a duvet to keep herself from drifting – the air was softer than springs.

That night she couldn't sleep, and so sneaked out by a back window, just to fly until she wasn't insomniac any more. She headed up to the city centre, and then there were police sirens going and fire engines. She followed them, and then overtook them once it was clear where they were going. There was a house half-way up the Chapeltown Road, one of those red-brick houses set back from the road, that used to be vaguely grand and now are run-down flats. It was ablaze, and there was a man on the roof, waving a crossbow; there were two children on the roof with him.

Carrie slowed up and let herself gently down behind him.

'The Beast is upon us,' he shouted through the smoke. An unpromising start to any dialogue, she thought. The children were crying.

'Don't cry,' he yelled at one of them, and brought the stock of the crossbow down on the girl's head, clubbing her to the ground. 'Time for crying when the seas give up their dead, and your whore of a mother descends from the sky.'

Smoke got into Carrie's nostrils, and she coughed. He turned.

'Look who's come to see you die,' he said to the children, 'but you'll die first, unnatural whore.'

Carrie had rarely done a vertical take-off that fast, let alone come straight back down kicking, but she was better at flying than she had been, and, though she hadn't been to the gym for weeks, she seemed to be stronger than when she used to work out. The bolt whistled yards below her, and she kicked the bow out of his hands.

What she had not calculated was how much it still hurt to stub her toe, and she lost a precious second or so reacting to the pain. In that time, he had seized the child still standing and hurled him from the roof.

Carrie grabbed the girl, clutched her to her chest with one arm, and dived past the father's furious punch. She had never carried anything before except a rucksack with a change of clothes in it; it had never before seemed something she needed to be able to do.

She was falling fast, and she let herself fall all the harder for the kid's weight, and forced herself to fall faster. They were almost at the pavement when she was able to reach out with her free arm and grab the second child, and thrust herself up as hard as she could. Even so, she came down hard, taking the fall into a crouch; she had not damaged anything, she guessed, but she was not going to be able to move without discomfort for a week.

There was a dull thump a few yards to her right, a thump that included the snap of bones; the father had overbalanced striking at her and had followed her off the roof.

'I suppose you couldn't have saved him, too,' said the fireman who helped her to her feet, and took the children from her. Both were crying, and she couldn't swear that

they were both entirely unhurt – she had wrenched at
the boy's arm in snatching him – but at least they weren't
hurt.

'Give me a break,' she said, 'I can't do everything.'

''Spose not,' said the fireman. 'They talk as if you can,
sometimes.'

'That's not me,' said Carrie. 'That's the Gods. But, yes,
it is a shame he had to die like that.'

The fireman turned away to hand the children to an
ambulance man; it was as if he wanted to keep them
away from the contamination of Carrie's gaze. So he did
not hear her mutter, 'It is a shame, because I would have
liked to see him burn.' In the firelight she had seen blood
on his hands, and she knew it was not his or the children's.

'Grandstanding?' said Hatchet-face, strolling slightly
gingerly out of the crowd that had gathered behind the
police cordon. Sick from the smoke and hurting in every
joint, Carrie let herself lean on him all the way to the car.

'Actually,' he said, as his chauffeur drove away, 'I am
impressed.'

'Oh,' said Carrie, 'and what is the "but" going to be?'

'Never,' he said, 'take risks like that again.'

'I wouldn't have got hurt.'

'That's not what I meant,' he said. 'As it is, fair enough,
you come out of this looking good. If they think you
could have saved the madman as well, well, half of them
would want him to hang for what he did to his wife and
her mother – yes, observant, you guessed right about
that – nailed to the wall with crossbow bolts, very nasty.
But imagine, you stupid little woman, imagine what
would have happened if you had missed the boy, or if
you hadn't managed to save either of them.'

'But they were both going to die,' said Carrie.

'Yes,' said Hackforth-Fford, 'but if you had tried and

failed, the punters would have blamed you. If it had been just the boy, it would have been worse; because then you'd have been a castrating man-hater who only saves females. I know you think I give you a hard time, but you should be grateful – there are people out there, there are people in Parliament, who would like to kill us all.'

'Well,' said Carrie, 'if they want to, why don't they?'

'They're frightened of the Gods, is why they don't; that and the fact that it is hard to be scared of most of the temps they know about. Captains Croak and Kipple may not be very much use in a crisis, but they deflect the hatred into contempt. But you and me . . .'

'You and me . . .?' Carrie said.

'Carrie Smith,' he said, 'despite appearances, you are not entirely stupid. You and me, we are two of a kind. We are, in our different ways, powers, but we are not Gods; I am smart, and you are brave, and that and the power we hold make us frightening. If they ever summon the nerve to kill any of us, it is you and I and our equals they will want to kill. No one wants to kill the jokes; no one could kill Zeus; but we can be hated, and we can be killed.'

Carrie thought for a bit.

'So I took a stupid risk,' she said, 'and it paid off, and no one is the worse for it, except that bastard, who wanted to be dead anyway. What I can't understand is why, if it was that stupid, you did not stop me before I was halfway out of the hotel window.'

'That,' said Hackforth-Fford, 'is something that worries me. You see, I didn't know any of it was going to happen until about twenty minutes ago, not properly. I knew something was in the air, and I got the car ready for a drive and cruised until I knew.' He looked at her speculatively and then leant down and kissed her on the mouth.

'No,' said Carrie, dragging the back of her hand across

her mouth, 'even if we share some things, there are others that we don't share. You may be able to con some of the punters that I'm straight, God knows how, but don't con yourself, sweetheart. Besides, you can read my mind, and I can't read yours, and that means that I have to assume that any move you make is part of some sort of unscrupulous scheme.'

The odd thing was, she didn't feel repulsed because he was a man, or because he was a prick, but because she just did not have much emotional energy for sex any more. This worried her, slightly.

'Besides,' she said, 'even if you were out of range of my mind, presumably you can track me with your other powers.'

'The future goes wavy round you,' he said, 'and you're this great burning blaze of energy. Over what street in Hackney or Leeds is the sun, Carrie Smith? And you can't look at it to find out.'

But he seemed nicer for a few weeks, and she stopped having to do supermarkets, and the school trips were less of a chore.

She went and visited the two kids in hospital, and the boy's dislocated shoulder was OK, and they were glad to see her, sort of, but there was fear in their eyes, and she did not feel like staying. She spoke to their psychologist, who said she didn't think it would be a very good idea for her to come again, but did ask her for her autograph. It was the first time an adult had.

The psychologist also asked her out for a drink; she was a nice woman with the sort of ponytail that reminds you how long horses' tails really are. They had cocktails, and went for a Chinese meal, and Carrie thought hard about whether to ask herself back.

She didn't, though. She went on Pride though, and flew up and down the march until she found a 'Gay

Temps' banner; she let herself down on the ground and walked with the small group, mostly men, until her feet started to give out, and even then, she just let herself a little off the ground.

'People told me you were out as a dyke,' said a man from Taunton who could make green sparks come out of his fingertips, in the beer-tent queue, 'but they say that about everybody.'

'I was a dyke before I was a temp,' said Carrie, 'but it never used to matter so much.'

'I got thrown out by my parents,' he said, 'but it was for both things at the same time. I don't know whether that's worse, or better. Still, the good thing about green sparks, is that no one expects anything of you; you can just be a silly old queen, who happens to have a party trick.'

Then Veronica and Spike turned up, and just stood there hissing at her, and she looked at the guy, and he made a green spark come out of his nose and his ears at the same time, and she lifted off, waving at him, and went to listen to the bands, from an acoustically advantageous position some twenty feet above the stage.

There was nothing in the papers about her being there, but there is precious little in the papers about Pride in any year. She asked Hatchet-face, and he said he had nothing to do with it, though he did not see why she had to make such a big deal out of her immature sexual preferences. Sometimes he seemed like a friend, and sometimes she hated him so much, and mostly she wished he was just not there.

Then one day, she was sitting in the office, cooling her heels like a good little girl, while Marcia concentrated on doing painful-looking things to her cuticles as a way of having an excuse for ignoring her, when the phone rang.

'Could you come to Trafalgar Square?' said Hatchet-face. 'Straight away.'

She dived out of the window, without even bothering to tell Marcia where she was going. It was not very far to Trafalgar Square, not as the crow flies.

There was a mobile crane parked between the lions, and a police cordon and an ambulance. Hatchet-face beckoned her down, and there was a shot, which came nowhere near her. He handed her a flak jacket, and drew her and his companion, a smooth-faced man in a sharp suit, to one side; she put it on, looking at him inquiringly.

'Well,' he said, 'you know how the IRA blew up Nelson's Column in Dublin.'

'Yes,' she said, 'pretty ace, wasn't it?'

'I might have known,' he said, 'that you would have the wrong sympathies on this one. None the less . . .'

'What are they doing?' she asked.

'They've planted a bomb up near the statue,' said the smooth-faced man, to whom Carrie found herself listening with oddly undivided attention, 'and stationed a sniper on top of Canada House; I don't know why he missed you, because he has winged two policemen already, and a WPC is critical.'

'They reckon,' said Hatchet-face, 'that, if you go up fast like you did in Leeds, and spray the bomb with foam, he'll give up.'

'And what is in this for me?' said Carrie.

'The gratitude of the nation,' said Hatchet-face, with a straight face. He really does mean that, she thought, poor sap.

'Well,' she said, 'the whole idea sounds really dumb to me.'

'What do you think she should do?' Hatchet-face asked his friend.

'Well,' Smooth-face said, 'you seem to know what's best.'

He turned to Carrie. 'I think you should do what he says.'

346

'Well,' said Carrie, her mind caressed by his voice and slightly cotton-woolly. 'I can't see how blowing up some statue is going to make Ireland free and one, and, while I can see the point in shooting coppers, I disapprove of men shooting women. Tell you what Hatchet-face, if I do this, you let me off the hook; if I'm a national heroine, I don't have to swan around being a role model, do I?'

He handed her a canister of something, and she went straight up like a rocket. There were several shots, but not one of them touched her; she went up high, so high. She wanted to swoop down on this like a stooping hawk; theatre never hurts when everyone is watching and she had to allow for the flak jacket.

Halfway through her dive, the bomb went off. She was still a hundred feet upwards of it, and it was a shaped charge that disintegrated the column while leaving the statue in several pieces to topple slowly rather than shoot up at her in shrapnel.

Even so, things whizzed past her on the wave front and something clipped the side of her head and left it bleeding; the front itself sent her spinning. The web of pattern that was usually so clear went jagged, and she pulled herself across the sky like a spider with a broken leg, sliding cancrizans and bouncing off loose ends as if they were the fragile branches of a falling tree. She managed to hang on to consciousness, long enough to drop the last six feet into one of the fountains. Luckily, there was some water in it.

An army captain rushed up to her.

'That was a damnfool useless stunt, Smith. What good did you think you were going to be able to do?'

Hatchet-face had a disappointed expression on his face; the smooth-faced man seemed to have gone away. She could not understand how they had managed to persuade her to be so stupid. She staggered over to them, wiping the blood from her torn forehead, her usual few inches above the ground. An ambulance man followed her.

'You're hurt,' he said. 'Where do you think you are going?'

'Second star to the right,' she answered, dreamily. 'And straight on till morning.' Then she passed out, waking several hours later in a hospital bed.

The odd thing was, she was almost more of a national heroine for failing, gallantly, than she would have been for succeeding. TERROR FIENDS IN CARRIE MURDER MISS, said the Sun; she preferred the Telegraph's more dignified MONUMENT DESTROYED: IRA CLAIM RESPONSIBILITY: TEMP SLIGHTLY HURT.

Oddly, there was no mention of any policewoman being hurt; Carrie came reluctantly to the conclusion that Hatchet-face and his anonymous friend had just known which buttons to push to get her to do something stupid.

When they let her out of hospital, she went back to the estate and rang Marcia to say she had got a sick note for several weeks; her flat was still there, even though she hadn't been using it very much. The horrid fascist old woman on the floor below insisted on bringing her up cups of tea every half-hour, which got tedious after a while, particularly because being someone that someone like that would regard as a national heroine was not Carrie's idea of a good time. Eventually she put on a pair of shades, and went down to the pub.

Brett was there, and was quietly sulky with her.

'I know you didn't have any choice but sell out; but did you have to become a hireling mercenary of the imperialist state?'

'I didn't know that there were mercenaries who weren't hirelings, Brett,' she said.

'I thought you used to go to Troops Out demos.'

'Well, yes, Brett, but there is a difference between how you feel when it is just politics and how you feel when someone shoots at you, at you personally. Besides, I was set up, I think. There was this guy...'

She told him the whole story; and her suspicion that Hatchet-face had decided that she was even more use to the Department, and to some sort of notional paranormal community, as a dead heroine than she would be as a PR bimbo, or as a fallible heroine who might always put her foot in it, or drop the baby, next time. Plus she had turned him down, and he probably wasn't used to that.

'What I don't understand,' said Brett, 'is how, if this guy is this total hotshot all-round psychic triple threat, he could fail to know what you were going to do next. I mean, it was your deciding to show off that saved your life, wasn't it? And that was something I could have predicted, let alone some ace precog.'

Carrie was still thinking about this, as she flew home afterwards. She decided to hang around London Fields, just in case; and after a while, two women wandered south along the path and the same two youths came out after them. This time, Carrie had stopped off at a building site and liberated a couple of poles; she dropped one of them, quivering, into the ground in front of the youths, and then hovered, with the other poised like the Louisville Slugger.

'I hate violence, boys. Don't you?' she said, though there was a side of her that was quite looking forward to a ruck. She had got fed up with being pushed around, and being conned into compromise. They disappointed her, and left.

It slightly spoiled things for her that the two women she had saved turned out to be Veronica and Spike.

'I suppose you think this is some way of scoring a political point,' said Veronica. 'Well, it isn't.'

'You're just participating in the same power structure that produces that kind of male violence, and perpetuates oppression,' said Spike.

'You haven't saved anyone,' said Veronica. 'Not really – because at a structural level you're helping destroy.'

'The nice thing about the problems I have these days,' said Carrie, 'is that I know you're talking nonsense. There are two children who are alive because of me, and would have been dead otherwise. That's a fact, and all your fancy talk won't cover that. Also, sweethearts, I don't have to stand around and listen to this crap.' And off she flew.

And since she had nothing particular to do with her evenings, that was how she spent them for a few weeks. Just hanging around in the sky, waiting for something to happen. Some of the women she helped were even grateful, not that she found herself caring very much. It is always good to be part of a community, but she was finding that all more theoretical; she didn't really feel that she loved, even in an abstract and sisterly way, any of the women she saved.

She ended up in casualty a couple of times; once she gave evidence in a couple of court cases, the youths she was hunting knew she was out there. Which meant some of them thought twice, and also meant that some of them thought of her as a target to be taken down. So she got a split lip one time, and another time a nasty gash across the palm of her hand. There is a limit, though, to what they can do when you can be a hundred feet above them in a second. There was a limit to how much anger she could feel with idiot bastards who were so vulnerable to her; those that she fought, she did not hate.

Viola came round to see her.

'Look,' she said, 'I'm sorry. I was out of order that morning and telling people about it. I don't know what came over me.'

'It's called bigotry,' said Carrie.

'Yes, I know,' said Viola, 'which is why I'm saying I'm wrong. Besides, I wanted to say how much I admire what you're doing.'

'Thanks,' said Carrie.

'You're actually doing something when all we did is talk about it.'

'I suppose so.'

'And I think it is really out of order for Veronica to go around talking about how she refused to let you rescue her.'

'Well,' said Carrie, 'it was nice of you to drop round. But I'm busy right now. I've got to go and look at some clouds.'

'Carrie,' Viola said, 'I've been thinking ... I know you used to fancy me; and ... well ... can we talk about it?'

Hero worship was not fun from any source.

'Nice of you,' said Carrie, 'but no thanks. It's like flying, you see, only it's not as good, and you have to have other people around. And I'm finding it harder to like people, much.'

She was flying a lot, for its own sake; she could enjoy it much more now no one was making her do it, and now her sense of duty was something she could take or leave alone. Where flight had once been a pure and virginal joy, now it was something that was battered and worn and true; there is a delight in doing something for the hundredth time that is different from the delight of the first, simply because the hundredth time the delight is plump with confidence, and the slight tang of boredom makes it rich. Patrolling was something she did to make her feel a solid citizen, but flying was the point, flying up as high as she could breathe, higher all the time, dodging the thunder and keeping an eye out for jets, and taking risks because that was what she wanted to be doing.

The Department was leaving her alone, except for the

small cheques, but eventually she came back to her flat in the morning to discover a car waiting for her. It went to Chelsea – the driver wouldn't tell her anything – but when she was shown into an elegant flat in Tite Street, she was not terribly surprised to see an elegant middle-aged man sitting in an old leather armchair. At a desk behind him, a gold-plated fountain pen was doing calligraphy exercises, without anyone holding it.

'We haven't met, of course,' he said.

'You're Loric, aren't you?' said Carrie.

'Why, yes,' he said. 'How gratifying to know one has some small recognition.'

'Well,' said Carrie, 'of course, I've never bothered to look at any photographs, but the press stories always make you sound like a posey prat. And there's a limit to how many posey prats the Universe can bear at one time.'

He ignored this. 'You've been a bit naughty, haven't you? You know we don't like vigilantes.'

'I don't regard the Department as having much claim on me any more,' said Carrie.

'When I say "we", I do not mean the Department.'

'Well,' she said, 'I'm just a concerned citizen, active in the community, I guess.'

'Stick to that line, and I suppose we can tolerate it,' Loric said.

'I intend to,' said Carrie. 'I used to be out on those streets, and no woman is safe.'

'And that's the other thing,' said Loric. 'No one is safe. Do you know what happened to me the other day?'

'Hackforth-Fford tried to kill you,' said Carrie.

'Are you just being perceptive,' said Loric, 'or are any little Talents creeping up on you that you haven't bothered to mention?'

'I don't know,' said Carrie. 'But I'm pretty certain he tried to kill me, though I don't quite understand . . .'

'I looked at the police camera video-tape,' said Loric. 'I suppose you'd never met the Persuader socially.'

'I think Marcia said something once.'

'Anyway,' said Loric, 'I thought I'd involve you in this; courtesy between colleagues and all that.'

He showed her into a large bare room, which did not seem to fit into the plan of the flat — but what did she know? — where, to her not especial surprise, sat Hatchet-face on a wooden chair, struggling with invisible chains.

'Young man,' said Loric, 'I really did not appreciate the device, you know. That sort of thing keeps one on one's toes, of course, but it ruined a perfectly good chess-playing automaton, and three erotic netsuke.'

'Good,' said Hatchet-face. 'At least it spoiled your day.'

'What *is* your problem?' said Carrie.

'You are,' he said. 'You don't understand, do you? When you do your aerobatics, you make patterns. The patterns are a music, but they play very loudly. I can't hear you think; I don't know what you are going to do.'

'Oh, ridiculous,' said Loric. 'Of course she makes a noise; but one can tune it out.'

'With respect, sir,' he said, 'there are some things I can do and see that even you can't.'

'Why don't you just stay away from me?' said Carrie. 'You don't have to look at the sun.'

'Oh, but I do,' said Hatchet-face, almost crooning. 'They are very pretty patterns, and once your brain is burned . . .'

'You see why I brought you round,' said Loric. 'He's making a bit more sense, now. Really, Carrie Smith, Gods do have to learn not to break people, you know.'

'"If there are gods,"' Hackforth-Fford interrupted, '"how could I bear not to be a God?"'

'Nietzsche,' Loric explained. 'Another maniac. I had hopes of the young man, you know. And now he is going to have to spend some considerable time in a comfortable clinic. Or somewhere. One might have wanted to retire one day.'

'Don't look at me,' said Carrie. 'It's not my fault. He never let me understand. Men, you're so stupid; you're all the same, you want to keep control. A woman would have been prepared to bend and change, when death and madness were the stakes.'

Loric said nothing, and ushered her from the room. He saw her to the door.

'I'll deal with this,' he said.

'You're his role model, after all,' said Carrie. 'Why else would he try to kill you too?'

'Suicide bid, perhaps,' said Loric.

There was one of those awkward silences that occurs when people have only one or two things in common, and nothing else.

'Nice suit,' Carrie hazarded.

'Oh,' said Loric, 'I have these little men.'

'In Savile Row?'

'These,' said Loric, 'are very little men indeed. I don't know that the Department will need you for PR now Hackforth-Fford has gone. What will you do?'

'Oh,' she said, 'human beings let me down, but that doesn't mean that I give up on women, or on men. Not entirely. You have to go on trying to be part of people, don't you? Even a God has to do that, or a Goddess.'

'Quite so,' said Loric. 'I'd appreciate it, my dear, if you walked at least part of the way down the street, and don't start flying until I've shut the front door.'

'Why?' said Carrie.

'When it comes to your particular powers,' said Loric, 'I fear that I too am a jealous God.'